DEBASE

AN ELITE BRATVA BROTHERHOOD NOVEL

by

RACHEL VAN DYKEN

Debase
Elite Bratva Brotherhood
Eagle Elite Book 11
by Rachel Van Dyken

DEBASE

ISBN-13: 978-1-946061-66-9
Cover Design by Jill Sava, Love Affair With Fiction
Formatting by Jill Sava, Love Affair With Fiction

To the readers,
this book, this series would not be possible
without you guys.
I would have never imagined back in 2011 that I
would still be writing about these men or that in 2019,
they'd have a WHOLE lot more to say.
Buckle up, things are about to get intense.
Blood in, no out.

AUTHOR NOTE

Debase takes place in the Eagle Elite World. You do NOT need to read the series to follow and enjoy Debase.

If you're new to the Eagle Elite world, here are a few things you may want to know. Though Debase is part of a new series (Elite Bratva Brotherhood), I'm still calling it Book Eleven in the Eagle Elite series because it gives everyone closure and introduces you guys to the Russian mafia at the same time! The men of Eagle Elite are ruthless, protective, loyal, not afraid to get their hands "dirty" and they love hard. Never forget that they are mafia and Family always comes first. I'm including this "family tree" in here just in case you guys have questions on who belongs to each family and which couple belongs to each book.

Welcome to the Family. Blood in. No out.

Quick Catch Up Guide to the Eagle Elite World:

All right, say you've never entered this world, what do you really need to know about the stories since this is a new spin-off series. Well, that's easy. The De Lange Family (one of the poorer Five Families) is in disarray after the betrayal and death of Mil De Lange (once married to Chase Abandonato). Not only did she turn her back on her husband and the rest of the Families but she tried to partner with the Russians to do it. Thankfully, Andrei Petrov, boss to the Petrov Russian Crime Family, was also playing both sides and has been mentored by Luca Nicolasi (now a ghost), to not only be a feeder to the FBI but also have the law in his pocket. The Italians swore fealty to Andrei and now the Russians and Italians are working together against the De Langes. A kill order has been announced for any De Lange associate. Chase Abandonato is the right hand man to the Abandonato Family, a captain, and assassin, hell bent on killing every single person in the De Lange bloodline, all except his new wife whose blood has been spilled on behalf of the Italians and who is currently pregnant.

This book starts off with Andrei Petrov, you learn his story, what makes him tick, and the darkness that drives him. Enjoy!

The Families

The Petrov Family is the Russian dynasty out to destroy all five Sicilian families. They have now spread from Chicago, to New York, and even Seattle.

The Five Families of the Cosa Nostra: Abandonato, Alfero, Campisi, Nicolasi and De Lange (ex-communicated). These families are all based in Chicago. They are the most powerful Italian mafia families in the US.

The Italian Mafia Families still in Sicily: Sinacore, Vitela, Buratti, Rossa and Di Masis. They don't have a say in the Cosa Nostra but are closely aligned.

The Men

Alexander Petrov (deceased). Father to Andrei, Maya, Pike (deceased) and Andi (deceased). Was the head of the Petrov Family. He was ruthless and played very dirty, ran prostitution rings. (Russian Mafia)

Nixon Abandonato married to Trace Alfero (Granddaughter to Frank Alfero). Nixon is the boss to the Abandonato Family. (Elite/Elect)
Nixon and Trace are the parents of Serena.

Frank Alfero married to Joyce Alfero (deceased). Was the boss of the Alfero Family (Elite & Enchant)

Chase Abandonato married to Mil De Lange (Phoenix De Lange's sister, deceased, RAT). Mil was the new mob boss to the De Lange Family, one of the most hated in The Cosa Nostra. While grieving Mil, Chase meets his true soulmate Luciana De Lange and they are now married. (Entice, Eulogy) Chase and Luciana are the parents of Violet Emiliana.

Tex Campisi married to Mo Abandonato (Nixon's twin sister). Tex is the Capo dei Capi, which basically means he's their version of the godfather. (Elicit)

Luca Nicolasi. Never married but had a small affair with the love of his life Joyce Alfero, this produced two children. Dante and Valentina Nicolasi. Former head of the Nicolasi Family. (Enchant & Enrapture in the Hurt anthology)

Phoenix Nicolasi (formerly De Lange) married to Bee Campisi (Tex's sister). He is the new boss to the Nicolasi dynasty. He knows everyone's secrets and keeps black folders on every individual close to them, himself included. (Ember)
Phoenix and Bee are the parents of Phoenix Jr (Junior)

Sergio Abandonato married to Andi Petrov (Russian mafia, deceased). Sergio was forced to marry her for protection, and later marries his soul mate Valentina Nicolasi. (Elude, Empire)

Dante Nicolasi married to El De Lange. Dante is the new boss to the Alfero Family. (Enrage)

Ax Abandonato married to Amy De Lange. He's a made man for the Abandonato Family and works now for Andrei Petrov as well. (Bang, Bang)

Ax and Amy have two sons.

Nikolai Blazik married to Maya Petrov (both Russian Mafia). He makes a brief appearance in many EE books, and is known as The Doctor. (Rip)

Vic Corazon Abandanoto married Renee Cassani. Vic is a made man for the Abandonato Family. (Envy)

DEBASE

Verb: To reduce (something) in quality or value; degrade. To lower the moral character of someone. i.e.

I am war.
I am Andrei Petrov.
I am impure; Debased.

PROLOGUE

Andrei

With blood on my hands, I held her.

With death in my soul, I drank her.

With the devil in my heart, I coveted her.

My name is Andrei Petrov.

My last will and testament is as follows:

Let me finally die.

Let me bring down this empire of filth and destruction into the depths of a fiery Hell.

Let. Me. Go.

Protect Alice De Lange at all costs and tell her I'm sorry.

I'm sorry for referring to her as a number — it was too painful to say her name.

I'm sorry for all the times I shoved her, when I just wanted to shield her from the pain.

I'm sorry for taking her virginity and giving her mine in

the process.

I'm sorry that she's left to clean up a mess she's not ready for.

I'm not sorry for loving her.

I'm not sorry for doing what was best.

I'm not sorry for killing them all.

I'd do it again.

For her I'd do anything.

Sincerely, Andrei Petrov, last boss to the Petrov Dynasty.

PS. I will not rest in peace.

One month into the future…

Blood and dirt caked her face.

And still I grabbed the whip.

I clenched it between my bloodied hands while they watched.

It came down hard on her snowy white skin, it ripped into her flesh and pulled it from her body — and I could smell their arousal. Their need to see violence in order to live in those disgusting bodies, surrounded by the most expensive women in the world.

Women I gave them.

Women I sold.

Souls I stole.

Hell was waiting for me.

I knew it as much as I knew my next breath would be the hardest I would take in my short life.

Because her eyes begged me for life.

Even when she knew, even when I told her again and again — all I had to offer was death.

They needed it, lived for it.

And she'd committed the ultimate sin.

Trusting me.

I slammed the whip down on her right thigh.

She cried out my name.

And I remembered.

I remembered then.

There was once a time where my name fell from her lips in ecstasy, in wonder — in love.

But she didn't know — I wasn't capable of it.

This was my legacy.

This was my destiny.

A tear slid down her cheek falling onto the rivers of blood streaming down the concrete.

Soon the blood would be gone.

The concrete clean.

And her life would be sacrificed.

Not by my hand.

But hers.

Because that was the deal, wasn't it?

"Kill me," she'd whispered between kisses.

"Yes," I agreed as I tasted her sweet sin for the last time. "I will kill you."

Her thank you fell on deaf ears.

So, I raised the whip again while she smiled.

CHAPTER ONE

Andrei

Then

"You know what you have to do, son." Alexander Petrov was many things to many people.

What he wasn't, was a father.

I despised that the only time he ever referenced me as his son was when he needed me to do something dark, something that would alter me, something that would take the tiny, minuscule pieces of the soul that I had left, and damn them to Hell.

Son, son, son, son.

I ached to hear it more than I would ever admit.

Son.

I was of his blood.

I was damned.

Son.

"They are nothing, simply scared girls who need to be shown to their rooms. Can you do that, Andrei? Can you get them to their rooms?" He always made it sound so simple.

It never was.

Rooms.

I almost laughed. A room meant they had comfort, a room typically conjured up good feelings of rest, windows, bright colors, and teddy bears.

I wasn't escorting them to their rooms.

I was taking them to their deaths.

We didn't call the path Red Row for nothing.

Because they would paint the cement red with their blood, with their screams, before ever seeing death, calling it Red Row, we figured, would be a kindness.

"Son." There it was again. I squeezed the tears in. After all, I'd learned my lesson on my sixth birthday when I let myself shed them over my dead dog, when my father and stepmother made me shoot it in the face because I hadn't cleaned up my dinner plate… and then laughed when I burst into tears over the warm blood splatters of my best friend all over my skin. Blood splatters I still felt to this day, laughter that still echoed in my head.

Fourteen. Fourteen years old, and I was already a monster.

I felt it shift within me.

Yes, I would remember this day for the rest of my life. I just didn't know why. So, when I nodded my head to my father, when he gave me the approval he knew I would kill to gain.

I felt the monster smile.

I sighed in relief. "Yah, Dad, I got this."

"Good job, Son." He put his hand on my shoulder then. It was covered in the ever-present leather glove; no fingerprints, no skin on skin contact, not even for his own son.

I didn't blame him.

Skin made me flinch.

It was too personal.

Too warm.

Too soft, delicate.

I did better with death.

At fourteen, I was better off with corpses.

I moved down Red Row and stopped in front of the cage, I slid the key in the lock and pulled the metal door open.

There were three of them. They were my age, maybe younger. Dirt caked their faces, scratches marred their feet, and I couldn't tell if they would get to keep their hair since it was matted so close to their head. They were dirty. Ugly.

Not human.

They had one thing in their favor.

They were virgins. Dirty. Virgins. So, it didn't matter what they looked like, did it? They had something men would pay for, die for.

Something I would kill to keep.

"This way," I said in a hollow voice. "Now."

Nobody moved.

I glared at the three of them. Didn't they realize? If I didn't do this right I would get punished? They were being fucking selfish! My father called me son! Didn't they know? Didn't they see the desperation in my eyes?

I walked into the cage, to the first one, and kicked her in the feet, she let out a scream so piercing that I covered my ears.

When she was done, I pulled out my gun. "You either die here or you move."

Slowly, the girls held on to each other and stood. I grabbed the first by the elbow, the rest followed after, and down we went, cages lined the path, another dark pathway appeared to my right; it led to the rooms.

They were soundproof.

They were death.

They also had showers and food.

It was like leading a starved animal to the slaughter, we fattened them up, and then we gave them everything they'd been begging for, for days.

And then. They died.

"In there." I shoved the girls into the small windowless room, with its one shower and a bunk bed. The only table in the room had an array of fruits, vegetables, and meats.

They ran to the table and started eating. I turned away from the disgusting view of their knobby knees, and dirty fingers as they shoved food into their mouths.

They didn't realize the food was laced with drugs.

Or that in a few short hours they would wish for more.

Beg for it, actually.

The younger-looking one lowered a piece of beef jerky and turned to me. She had blond hair, and she reminded me of my sister, the one I barely knew, the one with the boy's name, the one who had died. Or at least Dad said she was dead; I had no way of knowing what was real or not.

She wasn't with us.

It was better that way.

Sometimes I imagined she was free.

Sometimes I hated her because of it.

"Thank you," the girl said in a small voice that made me want to commit violence toward her. It made no sense, but her thank you was worse than a scream or a threat. I would welcome her violence. I had no clue what to do with her thanks, maybe because I knew how misplaced it was. "For the food, and the beds."

My heart thumped against my chest, it thumped with anger and defiance all wrapped up in one.

"Thank me when you're finally dead," I said in a harsh whisper. "Only then will you be free. Only then." I slowly backed out of the room and locked the door with a resounding click. "Will any of us be free."

I held my head high as I walked back down the hall to my post, and when I sat at that metal desk, alone in the darkness as the cold from the dungeon-like surroundings seeped into my bones, I realized. I was in the same prison.

And I was playing the game wrong.

All wrong.

I was trapped just like them.

Drinking the poison, just like them.

The only way out wasn't playing into his hand.

It was making him think I was the one controlling it.

I pulled out the old revolver my dad had given me after my first kill and emptied all but one bullet. Then I did what any sane Russian would do.

I spun the cylinder, the sound slicing through the dark cave like a knife.

I squeezed the trigger.

And shed the last tear I would ever shed, over the fact that I was still breathing.

Now

I jerked awake the minute I felt the tear on my cheek and quickly slapped myself. I was lying in a pool of sweat. Then again, whenever I dreamed of that girl's blue eyes and blond hair, and the trigger going off, I sweated.

Something about my father calling me son.

Something about my desperation, tested my sanity.

I wasn't a man desperate.

I was, however, a man barely sane.

Because I gave into the madness and fed the darkness.

I wiped down my face, and then I reached for my revolver, it was a bit tarnished with age on the outside, just like I was on the inside. I gripped it tight and spun the barrel, then I did what I did every birthday, I stopped it and cursed my birth right along with my existence.

I emptied all but one bullet.

Spun.

And held the gun to my forehead.

And I prayed to a God who never heard.

For death.

I pulled.

Click.

With a scream I threw the gun across the room and collapsed onto my knees.

Twenty-two years old.

And sadly.

Still living.

CHAPTER TWO

Alice

I had no idea how long it had been, only that my family most likely thought I'd died. Then again, they didn't really care, did they?

That's what my brother said when he handed me over to the men with the tattoos after being raided, they were the same men my father told me to run from if they ever came close to our house.

"Killers," he'd said. "Monsters."

Most little girls grow up assuming that the monsters in their head are fake, that there aren't monsters in the closet waiting to scare you and steal your scream for energy; that would be silly.

But there were monsters outside my window.

I knew it because my father told me every single night.

And my brother told me if I screamed, they'd hear.

So, I never screamed when he came into my room.

I just closed my eyes and waited for it to be over.

I dreamed about one of the monsters seeing and saving me, because death it seemed would be a better option, wouldn't it? Better than sitting across from those who said they'd protect me with their lives while they chewed on pasta and drank wine I served them.

I exhaled and looked around the small room. It was draped in rich burgundys and had no windows that I could see. Then again, I was chained to a bed so it wasn't like I could actually roam anywhere.

Every hour someone would walk in, unchain me, allow me to use the small restroom attached to the bedroom, only to chain me back again.

At one point, my teeth were inspected, and I was told if I bit I would get my tongue chopped off.

They didn't know that threats fell on empty ears.

I almost asked if they'd take my eyes too, or my heart. I almost asked if they'd take every organ that made me Alice De Lange.

My family was on the run, being hunted down by the monsters outside my window.

And the worst part was that I hoped the monsters in this story.

Would win.

The guilt I carried with me was the very truth that I wished for it to be over. All of it. And yet the nightmare continued, until a few days ago, three? Maybe four?

I shook my head and stared at the metal door in front of me. It had several locks on it, and looked like it could survive a bomb going off.

Unfortunate.

I pulled my knees to my chest and squeezed my eyes shut, forcing myself to keep the tears in.

Tears had betrayed me after all.

My tears and screams are what got me in this place.

They're what made my father finally come. Though he had a gun pointed at his head, and one of the monsters was there, holding it with a smile on his face, the look of a fallen angel had me sucking in a shocked breath as he eyed first me, and then my brother.

I tried to cover up.

I wasn't fast enough.

My brother's hand landed on my cheek then. "You bitch! You sick bitch! Stop throwing yourself at me!"

I said nothing.

I stared straight ahead.

And then something was thrown over my head as I was pulled to my feet. I heard cursing in Italian, my brother was yelling at my father.

A gunshot rang out.

I closed my eyes and escaped.

And then I was being forced into a car, my brother's warning in my ear as I was ushered away.

Two more gunshots rang out.

And I'd smiled the first genuine smile since my fifth birthday.

I leaned back against the soft bed and stared up at the ceiling. At least they were feeding me.

At least my door was locked.

How sad, that I had to be captured to realize that I preferred captivity over my own home?

Whatever happened… I would be okay.

Because my door was locked.
And he was gone.

CHAPTER THREE

Andrei

"What the hell is that?" I pointed my pen at the pink cupcake with rainbow sprinkles sitting in the middle of my desk, looking so out of place I would have smiled had I wanted to waste the energy.

"We drew straws." Tex, the Capo dei Capi of the five families grinned a stupid ass grin and crossed his arms. "I drew the short one, just in case you were wondering." The guy was lethal and a giant pain in the ass. If he brought you a cupcake, you fucking said thank you and left it at that.

But I wasn't most people.

And I didn't answer to him.

I was Russian.

The last of my line.

A Petrov.

The last living heir.

He could shit a golden egg and call me Bitch the rest of

his life, and I'd still want to rip his face off for putting me in a position I loathed.

Playing both sides.

Claiming my birthright in order to keep up pretenses.

And betraying my own blood by working alongside the families that destroyed mine effortlessly.

God, I hated them all.

Probably as much as they hated me.

We barely tolerated each other.

A cupcake?

Really?

What was next? A Christmas sweater?

"It's not poisoned." Tex felt the need to point out. "Bro, I gotta be honest you're staring real hard at that pink cupcake. Been getting any action lately, or does the color just remind you that you lack the goods to get a woman—"

"Is there a reason you're here?" I interrupted, changing the subject. "I have twenty-five girls ready for transport. The weakest ones will die on the way, the other ones have been given weapons. One of my men has been given strict instructions to give them a head start. It's all I can do."

Tex whistled and pulled out one of the leather chairs. "Working on your twenty-second birthday?"

I sighed in irritation. "Was there anything else?"

"Shit, you're old." He said it more to himself than to me. "Just answer me one thing…"

"And then you'll leave and let me do my job?"

"You know how I live for our conversations, Drei." Great, his nickname for me. And then the mask he always wore slipped. Shit, he leaned forward his elbows on his thick thighs, both of his favorite Glocks were strapped to his chest, held there by an ever-present holster that wrapped around his whole body. I knew the guy had enough ammo to make it out of here alive, he was that good, and people didn't want an all-out war, so they let him be.

Because we'd somehow found a greater enemy than each other.

The one from within.

The De Lange crime family was hated by everyone, Italians, Russians, Irish mobsters, the cartels — they were sloppy, and they made us look bad. Ergo, we were eliminating them one by one.

They had giant red marks on their backs.

Women. Children.

I narrowed my eyes at Tex. "What?"

He jerked his chin toward the cupcake. "Laced it with some Xanax so you wouldn't yell."

"Truly?" I smirked. "You know that wouldn't do shit."

He eyed me up and down. "Yeah you're strung tight as a drum. Sexually repressed assholes are my favorite, just ask Chase. Makes it so much fun to spar, he coughed up two teeth last year."

"So, you came to gossip about Chase?"

"One of the girls," Tex said slowly. "The one Chase brought in a few days ago..."

Interesting. I leaned back in my chair suddenly enjoying the conversation a lot more. "You mean the dirty one that tried to bite his fingers off?"

Tex smirked. "Best day of my life." And then. "Holy shit, are you smiling?"

"She tried to bite off his thumb, if that doesn't deserve a smile."

"It's why you and I get along." Tex chuckled. "Look, Chase went in blind following a lead for a De Lange nest, didn't know how many men would be guarding the house. The brother got off, everyone else is dead, but her brother was abusing her, mentally, sexually. He needs her. He'll come for her."

My stomach sank as I tried to keep my expression indifferent. I tapped my pen on the desk, once, twice, three times. I focused on my breathing, on the blank expression on my face as I tilted my head to the side. "You're saying you want me to sell her… here."

"I'm saying we want you to auction her off to the highest bidder, get him to come out of the woodwork."

"We can't kill him in front of other customers," I pointed out.

Tex stood. "No… but she can."

I stood, leaning dangerously close to the pink sprinkles. "What are you saying?"

"How much do you think they'll pay to see her slit his throat? How distracted do you think those men will be for thirty or so minutes?" He shrugged. "Distracted enough to provide an escape plan for the remaining girls your father bought?"

A weight settled onto my shoulders. "Tex, it's too many women. It would be a fucking exodus of women who've been abused for years, who have no clothes, and most of them with no will to live. You let them run, they come right back to me, I've seen it a million times, it's why we do it this way."

Tex locked eyes with me. "Family dinner, this Saturday. Bring someone so Chase stops asking if you're a virgin."

At that I did laugh. "Chase can suck my dick."

"Saying things like that doesn't really help, Drei."

I pointed at the door, my ever-present black leather gloves covered my cold hands. "Go."

"Enjoy your cupcake, Cupcake!" He started whistling. "Oh, and it's at seven, and you're in charge of wine."

I cursed under my breath.

Italians and their wine.

The door slammed behind him.

And I knew, he hadn't given me a choice.

In typical Tex fashion, he was letting me know what they wanted to plan, and I could either side with them.

Or against.

I slammed my knuckles against the desk and then stomped over to the side room and shoved the heavy metal door open. "Out."

Four of my men stood and left.

I faced the wall of cameras.

I knew hers by heart.

I knew everything.

Because the minute they'd brought her in, I heard silence. They screamed, all of them screamed, they struggled, they cursed.

This girl, this woman, looked relieved.

And as my men passed me by in the hall, for two seconds she lifted her eyes to mine and I felt a fissure of tension erupt between us. She was looking at me like I was the hero in the story, not the villain.

It was a new feeling, having a woman look at me that way. It was also hateful, because they all used to look at me like that, and I'd done exactly what my father did. I'd followed in his footsteps, it didn't matter that I saved who I could.

Because I still damned the rest, didn't I?

That was three days ago.

Three days of watching her lay across her bed, arms spread out like she was on a damn vacation in the Caribbean. A small smile on her face as she fell asleep like she was finally at peace.

Like I, Andrei Petrov, seller of women.

Had saved her.

She couldn't be more wrong.

I watched as she lifted her arms to the ceiling and then let them drop back down at her sides, and then she yawned, her blanket of hair moving across the pillows as she rose up on her side.

She wasn't just beautiful. She was stunning, the kind of beauty that made a man forget himself. The kind that would bring a man to his knees.

My least favorite.

Because women, in my experience, didn't know how to handle the chore of that sort of beauty, so they either manipulated it or wasted it.

I watched another ten minutes as she smiled.

I expected more tears.

And then she laughed

I put my hand on the screen, I had this impossible need to hear it, to close my eyes and see if it would make me feel better about what I did. And I knew I was the sort of man, to steal that laugh.

And replace it with hate.

CHAPTER FOUR

Alice

The man with the tattoo on his left hand would come again and let me use the restroom. I'd been left alone close to an hour already.

I leaned up on my elbows and stared down at my tattered clothing.

Black leggings.

A ripped baseball shirt that I'd put on for bed, and no shoes, not even any socks.

I stared at the door and waited.

It was the only constant in my life now.

My bathroom breaks, and when they would bring me food.

One by one, the locks jerked back making a shrieking sound as the door moaned open.

It wasn't the same man.

It was a man.

But different.

With lighter features, icy blue eyes, and golden blond hair that made him look like he should be on the cover of a magazine not giving me a bathroom break.

His cheekbones were high, his jaw firm.

I gulped.

Because he didn't look happy.

No, he looked pissed.

And I'd been on the other end of that look my whole life.

I very quickly squeezed my eyes shut and whispered. "Can you please just make it fast, please?"

I didn't sense any movement. My heart was beating erratically as I wrapped my arms around my legs and tucked my head against my knees, if I fought it would only hurt more, if I just let it happen, it would be over soon, it was always over soon with Aldo. Half the time he couldn't even perform let alone do anything other than touch me and squeeze me until I had bruises marring my breasts.

"Slut. Whore," he'd whispered in my ear. Saliva ran down my chin onto my shaking hands. "You shake because you want your own brother. Say it! Say you want me!"

I never did.

And he hated me for it.

More than he hated himself, I think.

He was raised to dominate.

And I was raised to look the other way.

Any minute now, this blond man's hands would be on me, any second, I would smell his breath on my neck, and it would have liquor on it, because that's where foolish men gained courage, wasn't it? And he would be sloppy because he was drunk, and maybe he'd pass out.

Dear God, help him to pass out.

I was shaking so hard that the bed was moving.

I couldn't stop it. At least I knew what Aldo would try. This man, I didn't know. This man didn't look like he was capable of a smile.

I knew it, like I knew that Hell existed — this man was many things.

Good, was not one of them.

"Come," he said in a rich voice.

Slowly I lifted my head as two men walked past him and unlocked the chains wrapped around my ankles.

I didn't move when I was free.

He seemed disappointed.

It was three against one, it was survival.

I was on high alert; anything could be used as a weapon if you hit hard enough, right? If they tried something, if a weapon was pulled, I would need to fight my way through it, I would need to do something — anything.

I was a De Lange.

My name meant something to me. Once a proud family, now on the run, my father was one of the last made men still alive.

It meant something.

I meant something.

I was valuable alive.

I knew this.

Did they?

My stomach sank as the two men who helped free me walked in the opposite direction of the blond-haired man.

"This way." He sounded bored or maybe just indifferent as he led me down a richly lit hallway with sconces lining the walls, nude art that had me blushing to the roots of my hair, and the sound of people screaming in the background.

Whether it was from pleasure or pain, I wasn't sure.

And even then, I asked myself, did it even matter anymore?

He stopped at the end of the hall, slid a key card over something black and then looked up at the camera.

The door beeped open.

And I was hit with steamy hot air.

A spa? He was taking me to a spa?

I narrowed my eyes as women of all shapes and sizes stared me down, several of them were in a hot tub looking thing, completely nude sipping champagne, the other half were getting massages.

Everyone looked, happy.

And curious.

We kept walking through that room.

Nobody made eye contact with him.

I kept my head down in fear that it would trigger the beast because that's what he was, a magnificent lion moving through the rooms like it was his kingdom and everyone else, his subjects.

People didn't bow. Then again, they didn't have to.

It was like he knew without looking from left to right that people took a step back when he took a step forward.

I swallowed the dryness in my throat when we came to another dark hallway, he picked up his pace.

My legs ached, but I kept up with him.

Until finally he stopped at a large set of black doors, they were at least twelve feet tall and said Dante's Inferno across the top.

I forgot to breathe as he shoved them open and whispered under his breath, "Hell, sweet, Hell."

CHAPTER FIVE

Andrei

Every human has a tell, whether it be a flinch, tapping of their fingers, lip biting, wringing their hands, popping their knuckles, deflecting with too much cursing — I had hundreds of ways to study someone.

And it was so easy it annoyed me when others didn't catch on, when they didn't see the slight movement of someone's fingers, the rough exhale or the darting eyes.

This woman — this girl who I refused to call by name, had too many to count.

And for some reason, it made me want to study her more, to actually look into her haunted eyes and ask her why she hugged herself when it was apparent she wanted nobody to comfort her.

Why her eyes widened in wonder when she walked down the hall.

Why she blushed, when she saw all the nude paintings.

Fucking blushed like she hadn't been on the receiving end of absolute hell at her brother's hand.

It was tempting.

Too tempting.

I didn't like it, and I didn't know how to deal with it, how to compartmentalize my feelings and do my damn job like the rest of the grown-ups I had to work with.

Bastards.

They'd be entertained by my lack of finesse.

Shit, I was entertained, and I'd been in her presence all but five minutes.

The doors closed with finality behind me. My rooms might look safe, but they were built with the same sin. The same prison that kept her here, kept me here too.

I could feel her soft intake of breath.

"Don't speak," I interrupted.

She listened.

I squeezed my eyes shut and moved down the hall toward the kitchen. She would be hungry. The least I could do was feed her before I told her what I was going to do with her.

The leather of my gloves tightened around my knuckles as I held my fingers tight against my palm and measured my steps.

Numbers helped, they gave me something else to focus on. Yes, the thirty-two and a half steps to the kitchen cleared my mind in a way that would alarm any sane person.

It kept my mind off her dark hair.

Off the way she still smelled — clean, even though I knew she was dirty in more ways than one.

"Come," I barked when I didn't hear her soft footsteps behind me, and then the sound of feet slamming against the cement floor as she fought to catch up to me.

Fifteen, sixteen, seventeen—

"Where are you taking me?"

I stopped suddenly.

She slammed into my back.

She was very soft, wasn't she?

Shit.

This was why it never got personal.

Why I never learned their names.

As far as I was concerned, she was girl number six hundred and thirty-two.

And it would stay that way.

It had to.

Nobody in.

Ever.

Because the worst thing the monster could do was believe he could be anything but what he was born to be.

This is where the Italians and I had different beliefs.

They truly believed that loved saved.

But I knew the truth — it damned you more than any of the other deadly sins, because love was the only thing in this world that demanded everything and promised nothing.

Love was a lie.

"You need to eat," I finally said in a sharp voice.

"What's your na—"

"—no names." I said through clenched teeth. "This is where you say thank you."

"Th-thank you?" she repeated in disbelief.

"Yes," I glanced over my shoulder and gave her a grin I knew would make her want to run in the opposite direction, a grin that a girl like her was probably used to considering how pretty she was, it was a promising grin one that said I would act against her if that's what it took to get what I wanted, it was a grin of a man who had no need for a moral compass, a man who would stop at nothing, destroy everything, kill. "I'm waiting."

I could feel her body tense.

Her dirty right foot tapped against the cement floor. It was bleeding, her pink nail polish looked ridiculous against the darkness of the room, of the building itself.

Hell, it was almost as bad as the cupcake wasn't it?

"Thank you," she whispered.

"For?"

"Feeding me."

"Again."

"What?"

"I need you to say it again, and this time, I need you to mean it, six thirty-two."

"Six thirty-two? My name is—"

"The minute you were brought here, you lost your name. You're nothing but a fucking number. Now, mean it or I'm going to have to lock up your ankles again and I hate it when a product is bloody. Furthermore, so do they, since it's their only passion in life, marring perfect flesh…"

She let out a gasp.

Good. Hate me.

It's the only way she'll live.

If she hates more than she hopes.

"Thank you." Her voice was stronger now, irritated, angry. It was the first time in years that I wanted to look directly into her eyes and convey something other than darkness, despair, but I knew better than anyone, it would only end up killing her.

Torturing her more.

Hope was the cruelest word in the human language and giving her any was worse than death.

"That's better," I said in a clipped voice as I turned back in the direction of the kitchen.

Eighteen.

Nineteen.

The kitchen was in view.

It was the only thing in the entire apartment at the club that had anything personal in it, personal of mine at least.

Food was a decadence.

Extra.

I'd been starved so much when I was little, purposely, that I made a promise to myself that I would never be without the best of everything.

And I paid to get it shipped to me on a weekly basis.

No guilt.

No regrets.

My directions were always specific. Fruits were sliced and spread out every two hours to make sure they stayed fresh, cheeses were flown in from around the world depending on my mood, and different types of proteins and breads were added along with wine pairings and vodka.

Eating was my sex.

My lover.

My life.

Damn it, also probably why Tex knew they had me every time I was invited for family dinner.

Fucking Chase's pasta.

I almost groaned aloud, snapping myself out of what I was supposed to be doing.

Business.

Shit.

I nodded toward the large granite breakfast bar. "Grab a plate, make sure it's full, two handfuls of protein, three handfuls of fruit and vegetables, add some fat, and if you're drinking, drink everything straight. Wine will just fill you up, and you need to eat." I finally turned and got a really good look at her that wasn't from the other side of a security camera, and I did it.

The first time in a decade.

I showed my tell.

To a woman whose name I refused to know.

To a woman I would sell.

To a woman who was already dead.

She didn't see it, how could she?

But I felt it, spread like a cold dread throughout my body.

For one brief second, hardly noticeable to the human eye, I let the darkness fall.

And I, Andrei Petrov.

Hoped.

CHAPTER SIX

Alice

The room was extravagant. No, it was more than that, it was something out of a dream, with long flowing red curtains that hid what I assumed were the only windows in the place.

Large ornate furniture that looked like it had once been in a castle before getting shipped here, in colors of blacks and deep browns that somehow all fit. A large fur rug was in the middle of what looked like a living room, framed by two couches, a fireplace, and a table that was more artwork than glass.

I grew up around money.

This wasn't normal money.

It was beyond that, way beyond.

This was the stuff you see on TV and have a hard time believing is true. Then again, my entire situation felt that way, part dream that I was away from my brother, part nightmare that I was sold, not rescued.

At least his hands weren't on me.

At least I was safe from him.

Even if that meant I was getting chained to something else, anything would be better, right?

Unless they were feeding me to fatten me up before the virgin sacrifice. I knew I was getting hysterical when that thought actually made me laugh.

Joke's on them. I wasn't a virgin at least not technically, even though medically I was. To be a virgin meant you were pure, untouched, right?

I was dirty. Used.

If they were looking to find anything clean or pure in me, they would need to look somewhere else.

I felt that loss every time I looked in the mirror and saw the shadows beneath my eyes and the pain in the way I smiled.

He wasn't looking at me anymore.

Six thirty-two.

I wondered if he had a number too or if that was his way of putting me in my place. Regardless, he was going to have to try harder to scare me when feeding me like this.

I'd been starving for days, so even though I was terrified and felt my heart leap in my throat every time he spoke in that slightly accented voice, I couldn't find it within myself to run or fight, I just wanted food.

So I very carefully walked over to the breakfast bar, aware that my feet were dirty, that the smell of sweat and blood was me and not the cheese, and that the fallen angel was counting my footsteps out loud like a crazy person — I picked up a plate and did exactly as asked.

Two handfuls of veggies.

Fruits.

Another handful of protein.

Some nuts for fat.

And I reached for the shot glasses.

No wine for this girl.

Because if they were going to kill me, I'd like for it to be fast, and I'd think that vodka would help soothe the way down, and honestly if they weren't going to let me shower then the best I could do is let alcohol clean my mouth, what I'd always been told by my brother was the dirtiest part about me.

The only part he never touched.

My lips.

So, in a way, it was the only part that was both pure and sinful at the same time.

I pulled out a chair, ready to sit, when his hand came flying through the air jerking the chair from my grip.

Cold blue eyes rested on me in a fury that was so palpable I stepped back and immediately started searching for exits.

"Those aren't windows." His choice of words. "And leaving only makes you thinner. Food will be withheld along with clothes and a shower, and believe me, you need all of the above along with a haircut and enough makeup to cover the bruises left on your face."

I shuddered as shame washed over me, it wasn't my fault, I did nothing wrong except for being born into the wrong family at the wrong time.

Wartime.

And for that I would always hate my father for having a girl, me.

And hate my brother for trying to take what wasn't his to take.

And I'd dream of the monsters that freed me.

And pray to see them again, even in this hell.

I reached for the chair again.

He sighed like he was irritated with me but used no words.

I almost expected him to slap me, but he kept his grip firm on the chair and then in a low voice said. "This chair cost more than your life. I suggest you stand."

Stand on bloody feet.

Stand while he watched me eat.

Stand and feel humiliation that I was this gross ratty abused thing while he told me he valued a chair over my existence.

I didn't cry.

I was good at that now.

Of telling myself it wasn't worth the dehydration.

Of believing that it wouldn't do anything except for get me more attention I didn't want.

I nodded my head once, not trusting my voice not to shake, and set my plate on the table and ate in silence while he watched.

I washed down the broccoli and cheese with a shot of vodka, reached for bread and dipped it in the vegetable soup and let out a moan before realizing I still had an audience.

He didn't so much as flinch.

So, I kept eating.

I ate the rest of my cheese and soup.

I grabbed the nuts and took another shot of vodka relishing the burn as it cleansed my mouth.

My plate was nearly empty.

I was already full and wasn't sure how my body would react to finally getting nourishment, so I took a step back and then grabbed my plate, walked around the counter and started washing it.

"What the hell are you doing?" he asked in a lethal tone that nearly had me dropping the plate in the sink.

"Uh…" I blinked up at him, still stunned that he was so striking, so young. The guy should be studying in college or modeling or acting or doing anything but watching in disbelief as I washed my own plate. "I didn't want you washing the plate, and I figured it was some sort of test so I—"

He actually grinned at that. "I don't wash plates."

Of course he didn't. Men like him paid people to wash plates and buy expensive chairs, and food.

He probably paid someone to chew for him too.

"I wasn't suggesting you did, I just wanted to save whoever it was, the time."

"Tell me, six thirty-two," He rounded the bar. It was then that I realized how tall he was; at least five inches taller than me, obviously packed with muscle that made him look like he was prowling instead of stepping. "Is this the first plate you've ever washed?"

"No," I said quickly as he moved behind me with such grace that I had a hard time focusing on the plate, on the tension in the room. "I was always in charge of dishes."

"Hmm." He seemed to like that answer. "So, you don't mind working?"

What was he getting at?

"N-no." I needed to get a grip. "I like working. It's the sitting trapped in a room that drives me crazy."

He was quiet.

Too quiet.

"And spas, how do you feel about spas?"

"I've never been," I said honestly. My family didn't want to pay for me to get anything done that wouldn't be needed, especially if I was being saved as a last-ditch effort to toss at one of the other five families for peace. I was a bargaining chip, nothing more, nothing less.

And that's all I knew.

Other than the fact that they would find great joy in marrying me off to a monster already used.

I shoved the shame deep down, away from the present, away from the conversation.

"I can tell," he finally said, hitting what was left of my pride as I continued to wash a dish that was already clean, not knowing what else to do. "And laundry, how do you feel about laundry?"

Was this a job interview?

"I've done laundry, yes."

"Have you ever had a job outside your pathetic house in the suburbs?"

I froze.

He knew where I lived.

Which means he knew who I was.

He knew my name.

Not just six thirty-two.

He knew.

And that meant I was already dead, didn't it?

He wasn't Italian.

But they would find me.

The monsters would find me.

And it would finally end.

I had nothing left to lose, so I turned and said, "I'm a De Lange, which you already—"

He cupped a hand over my mouth and shook his head slowly. "Utter that name one more time, and I'm going to be given no choice, do you understand?"

I nodded my head slowly as tears filled my eyes. He was close, too close. My brother used to put his hand over my mouth when he — I squeezed my eyes shut and waited, waited for him to pull up what was left of my shirt, to roll down my dirty leggings, to tell me I was disgusting, to tell me to beg for my life.

And then he stepped back.

"I may be ruthless, I may be a killer, I may be a lot of things, six thirty-two, but what I am not, what I will never be, is a fucking rapist." His eyes were cold. "You'll be safe as long as you stay anonymous, do you understand?"

"Safe from what?"

"The enemy of my enemy is my friend." He shrugged like it made him sad. "Maybe if they like you enough as six thirty-two, they won't kill you for what you are."

"A D—"

"Stop."

I put the plate down on the counter and waited for the next words, for him to chain my ankles back up and march me back into the room where I would wait for the monsters to come, or worse, where he would come and talk to me, with his cold eyes and knowing stare.

With a sigh, he pointed down the hall. "Shower on the right, bedroom connected to that same bathroom. No escape, you're still in prison. There's only one difference now."

"What's that?"

He licked his lips and tilted his head, a predatory smile crossed his features as he whispered, "It's mine."

CHAPTER SEVEN

Andrei

She stared at me like I was speaking a foreign language. I wondered if it would be easier if I just communicated in nothing but Russian. Didn't she see that I was saving her ass?

I expected her to burst into tears any minute or at least say thank you. Instead, she just stood there on her bloody battered feet, her body swaying like she was seconds from passing out.

Wouldn't be the first time someone had done that in my presence. Then again, half was because of blood loss, I was sure of it.

The only sound in that room was her breathing and the squeak of my leather gloves as I tightened my hands into fists.

I hated repeating myself.

She blinked slowly.

"Well?" I was agitated. I couldn't read her as well as I could read other people, and that was saying something. I was forced at a young age to get good at reading the room, the men in it, my father especially. It was how I outsmarted him in the end, and how I stayed alive, by making him think he was in control when I pulled the strings.

It's why I lasted.

Because I knew pride got you killed.

"Sorry." She eyed me up and down then looked away. God, she was dirty. What did they do… roll her in a swamp before bringing her in here? I shook my head. No, I didn't even want to know. It wasn't my job to know what happened to her before she came here, even though I knew more than I'd care to admit to her.

She didn't know that I was planning on killing her brother.

She didn't know that I was going to go with Chase Abandonato and make it personal because I could.

She had no idea the monster I would become.

The one I would embrace.

"Speak." I waited, my patience thinning by the second. "Or you could return to your room, the one with the chains on the bed and blood running down the cement floors, if you prefer that…"

"No, I just don't know what you expect of me." She chewed her lower lip and put her hands on her hips. She was skinny, her leggings showed off nice legs, but other than that I was too distracted by the giant mop of hair on her dirt-caked face and the blue eyes peeking out from sooty long lashes to notice anything else. "You said to take a shower — or commanded it, actually — but after the shower, after the food, do I just sit and wait for you?"

"This entire conversation is ridiculous; you get that right?" I smirked, almost enjoying her obvious discomfort. "You don't get to ask questions. I said eat, you eat, I said shower, you march your ass down the hall and shower, and if you finish and I'm not here, you make yourself useful. You like washing dishes, wash the fucking dishes. You want to watch TV, find the remote, you want me to draw you a list of chores, that's not gonna happen. I'm sharing my prison with you, may as well find out a way to co-exist without losing your shit every time I speak to you or look at you for that matter. If I say you're safe, you're safe. Now, if we're done, I have a man to kill."

"Wh-what?"

I grinned, this time enjoying her face going pale. "Well, first I'll torture him, then I'll let you get in a few good hits. I may chop off his dick if it pleases you, and then he'll die, slowly, when I think he's ready. Sometimes I give them IVs and just enough drugs to keep them alive. It's amazing what people will do when they're desperate. I think you'd like to see him beg, I think I'd like it too. In fact, I look forward to it. Now, if you'll stop looking at me like I'm the devil, I have a De Lange to destroy."

"You can't just—" She stopped herself, as I took a lethal step toward her. Six thirty-two put up her hands like she wanted to stop me. "The Italians, he's a De Lange, you can't just kill a De Lange without—"

A knock sounded on the door.

"Come in." I said, again enjoying myself more than I should.

"Literally the most depressing decorations I've ever seen in my entire life and I know my shit," Chase said as he waltzed into my sanctum and whistled, and then his eyes fell to her.

If she knew what was good for her she'd look away.

She'd run her ass down the hall and shower.

They knew a De Lange was here.

They didn't know it was her.

I'd give them someone else.

I'd lie.

I still had no idea why I was putting myself on the line for someone like her, someone I would kill without blinking. Again, I had a fascination with her strength, with the fact that she didn't scream when they brought her in, that every time I looked at the monitors she wasn't crying.

But staring up at the ceiling like she was on a fucking vacation.

"Six thirty-two, meet Chase Abandonato, De Lange executioner and sometimes friend."

"Sometimes my ass," Chase muttered eyeing her up and down. "You look like complete shit." He looked to me. "One of your new ones?"

I shrugged. "Came in a few days ago."

He sighed. "I just killed seven people in cold blood and had brunch like it wasn't a big deal, but this—" He pointed to her like she didn't even exist; it pissed me off. "This is worse. I don't know how you keep doing this."

"I'm Russian." My answer.

He burst out laughing. It always sounded strange, the one that had the most pain laughing, but there he was, in my hell filling the room with its odd sound and making this life look easy as he strangled people with the same hands he used to make love to his wife.

Italians.

All of them were insane.

"You need me to wait outside?" He lowered his voice.

"No, she won't escape, will you, six thirty-two?" I taunted.

"No." She gulped. "No, I won't escape… um…"

"Petrov," Chase offered for her, his voice filled with disgust. "He's your new heaven, your new hell, your god, your devil, I'd learn his name and know not to forget it lest he get pissed off and ask you to spell it and kill you for doing it wrong."

"Thanks, Chase." I muttered a curse.

"No problem." He slapped me on the back. "You got your shit?"

"All my shit." I looked at her one last time and gave her my back. "You have zero tact."

"Compliments? Bro, it's only noon, I'm touched. Now let's go find some De Langes and see how much blood we can spill. I don't want to miss dinner."

"Italians, always thinking with your stomach."

"Russians always thinking with your tiny dicks, oh wait, you still have one, right? It hasn't withered away from all that vodka?"

"Sometimes I wish I didn't like you more than the others," I grumbled, locking the door behind me and walking with him down the hall.

"I like killing, you like killing, I have rage, you have rage. We're pretty much married by now." He seemed oddly happy about that, and then I realized he was in a better mood than I'd ever seen him in.

I stopped walking.

He sighed like he knew what was coming.

We were around the same height. I was leaner than he was, he'd packed on a lot of muscle since the loss of his wife eighteen months ago. Her betrayal was the reason we hated the De Lange Family in the first place. They tried to betray everyone by doing a deal with me. I was in on it, knew what was going on, and had always worked with Luca Nicolasi, the only mentor in this world I ever had, the only man I would die to protect.

The rest was history.

I, Andrei Petrov, was somehow more Italian than I was Russian, if anyone could believe it, though I refused to claim it.

And ever since I was given that second chance by a man who should have shot me on sight.

I'd been paying the price.

Playing both sides.

Helping my enemy.

Helping my friends.

It was almost too hard to keep everything straight and like Tex pointed out last year, I knew I was getting in too deep, allowing what I did to affect me in a way that would one day kill me if my gun didn't do the trick on my next birthday.

"Out with it." I waited.

Chase actually grinned. "Luc's pregnant again."

"You have sex more than anyone I know," I stated matter-of-factly. "I'm not surprised. The question is why are you smiling about it when we still have a line of De Langes in hiding, and worse, ones who like to hurt their own women?"

His smile fell. "What?"

"Ah, Tex didn't tell you."

"Tex was eating lunch. You know how he is when he's eating lunch…"

I frowned and then realization dawned. "With Mo, he was with Mo. Just say that next time, and he was already here, and we talked things through. I'll debrief everyone during family dinner."

Chase's eyebrows shot up. "You bringing a date?"

"I'm this close to punching you in the dick and making it

so you can't have any more kids. This close, Chase." I shoved him against the wall.

The guy enjoyed violence. He just shoved me back and tried to hit me. I ducked and slid my knife from the sheath at my ankle.

"Save it for the De Langes." Chase grinned. "And I want to hear all the details about six thirty-two in the car. I still don't understand how you name all of them with numbers; fucking awful way to live, man."

"It's easier when you don't know their names." We continued walking.

"Easier for them, or you?" Chase asked.

I didn't answer.

Because I knew the truth.

If I named them, I wanted to save them all.

And I knew, I would never be able to.

As long as a Russian ran this club, this demented club, I could save some of them, and that's all I wanted, to save who I could, until I could rain holy hell down on the people behind the scenes.

The only problem?

I still had no clue who was grabbing the girls and bringing them to me, only that they showed up every day at the same time, barely clothed, shivering, and half dead.

I had cameras.

They were careful.

And the payments were all offshore accounts.

My father, it seemed, had done one thing right in his life. He'd made it almost impossible for anyone to infiltrate his empire.

Even his own son.

CHAPTER EIGHT

Phoenix

"I miss war." I slid the black folder across the table and waited. Luca was supposed to be golfing. Hell, Luca was supposed to be dead, and yet there he was sitting across from me smoking a cigar and staring down at the black folder like it was diseased.

"War," he said as he clenched his teeth on the cigar, "is easier to plan for than peace, don't you think?"

I grunted. "It's all there, Luca."

"I see that."

"You haven't even opened it."

"I know what's inside." He drummed his fingertips along the table and then eyed me. "Two boys, one girl?"

I nodded.

"And they have no idea?"

"No, but they'll find out soon. I don't know how the De Langes got the information, information only you and I have access to other than Mil…" I grit my teeth. "Mil, may her soul fucking rot in Hell, gave it to them. She was the only other person who would dare. We don't have a rat that's living, we have a rat that's dead, festering in the ground, still ruining what peace we have left. They'll use whatever they can to gain the upper hand, you know this."

"Yes." Luca tapped his fingers along the black folder like it would suddenly open and read itself to him, like he was afraid of the truth inside of it.

The secrets I held as the head of the Nicolasi Family would one day kill me. Truth.

The secrets he refused to share with me, and would take to his gave, were already killing him. Truth.

"Who have you told?" he asked, his clear blue eyes locked in on me and I knew what he was really asking. He wanted me to keep it quiet for as long as I could.

"What's one more secret between friends?" I stood and grabbed the folder and slid it back toward my side of the table while he reached for his wine. "Andrei doesn't have any clue, does he?"

"What I kept from him, I did to protect him." Luca stared into his wine. "He was too young at the time, too angry."

I snorted out a laugh. "He's still young, still angry."

Luca shrugged. "Apparently, I like to pick young angry little miscreants, don't I?"

I grinned. "Touché."

"We'll keep it quiet for now, see if the De Langes strike first blood."

"And if they do?"

"We may lose one life, we may lose them all, but one thing I know for certain, is we will rain a holy hell on that bloodline, the one you asked me to cut from your very skin, the one that defies the rest of the four families by standing alone, I would rather take in the entire Petrov Family than let the De Langes win."

I sighed. "That's good, because you may have to."

"It's not that I'm disgusted with vodka, it's that wine is so much more… classy." He lifted the glass to his lips and with that, I knew our discussion was done.

He would disappear like he always did, until it was time for me to find him again.

And I would work like hell to make sure that I kept the secrets safe.

Kept the families safe.

Kept my wife and my son safe.

Blood stained my hands, blood the color as thick and red as the wine in his glass. I built my life on it; I would leave this world with it.

"Luca…" I shouldn't have spoken it. That's what I thought even as I said it. "We'll need to raise our children different. Junior will need to know pain in order to survive."

Luca's face was sad. "The next generation must know the difference between peace and war, pain and torture, they will need to respect the families in ways that will haunt them for the rest of their lives, and this will be your job, Phoenix. Your curse will be that your son will one day look at you with hatred and you will be thankful for it because as long as you hate, you survive. Yes, you will raise them different, because you will want them to live."

We sat in silence as we often did when he visited.

And I wondered if I was the sort of father that would rather kill my own son than expect him to become a monster like myself.

I loved him too much.

My love made it even more dangerous, because I knew it wasn't just me, but every other man in the four families, each of us would one day have to ask ourselves if it was worth it.

And we would each have to decide for ourselves.

I could have sworn in that moment I had a premonition of Serena and Junior sitting at this very table with black folders talking.

I shuddered at the thought.

And knew I had my answer.

I would raise him to love as much as he hated.

And I would not let it break him the way it did me.

CHAPTER NINE

Alice

He locked me in.

I wasn't sure if I was safe not with that man, not with any man, but at least he locked me in which meant he was keeping others out.

I wondered if that was my only future, being locked in rooms until the men around me decided what to do with my body, with my soul, I was worthless, a bargaining chip hardly worth using.

I was either dead by the Italians.

Or used by my own family.

No matter what, I didn't really have a life, did I?

And as pathetic as it was, I was happier in that prison than I had been in my old room, waiting for the inevitable, waiting for the smell of whiskey as his hands touched me.

I squeezed my eyes shut.

No tears.

Six thirty-two didn't cry.

At that I almost laughed.

My life had come down to this. A number.

A long ass number.

I walked down the dimly lit hall to the bathroom. I expected it to be the same as the rest of the house and was actually surprised when the entire thing was bathed in white marble. It was a walk-in rain shower bigger than most apartments, no doors, just a corner you walk around, there were jets sprouting out of each of the white tile walls.

I quickly turned on the hot water, pulled off my disgusting clothes, and walked into the shower.

The water hit my back so hard that I let out a gasp, and then I looked up and let it consume me as the dirt and blood ran down the drain, the color was so bright against the white, so telling.

I imagined I was washing away his hands too.

My brother.

I imagined him getting tortured, killed. And I wondered why it made me feel nothing but calm. I knew what the mafia did to people. I heard the whispers amongst my family about how much they hated the Abandonatos.

Most of all they hated the guy who was killing them all off.

Chase.

He had been married to Mil, our dead boss, the one that truly screwed us over in more ways than one. We were making money, doing fine, according to my father, but she wanted more, and her pride wouldn't let her take it from her rich husband, so she worked for the Russians. That, I knew.

Who they were.

What they did.

And how she worked for them.

I had no idea.

I just knew that she got in too deep, and that she was killed for it.

I also heard that the scream from her husband pierced the universe it was so loud, and that the families knew it was a scream for our blood, our heads.

I remember the day because it was the first day I was locked in my room.

Today was the first day in a year and a half I was given a shower without someone standing by the door making sure nobody got in and that I didn't escape.

I thought he was protecting me.

I even accepted that it was the only way my father knew how.

And yet he always let my brother in.

I grabbed the only body wash in the shower and started running it all over my body. It smelled like him, the blond fallen angel who wore gloves and was scary attractive.

His flawless complexion alone would make anyone do a double take, but it wasn't just that or the icy blue eyes, or even the thick hair.

It was the way he carried himself, like the world should know who he was, and thank him for existing.

I shivered even though the water was hot, and rinsed off, taking my time not knowing if I would get the luxury again. It took me forever to get the knots out of my hair and I used probably half of the conditioner in that shower in order to do it, but finally I was able to rinse and run my fingers roughly through it.

I'd always loved my hair.

Funny how the things I loved the most about myself were the things my brother had hated.

My lips.

My hair.

He always commented on how both were too pronounced, like I was begging for attention.

Attention he always said he hated to give me.

I shut off the shower and reached for a towel and wrapped it around my naked body, feeling better than I had in years. I was alone. Safe and alone. For now.

I looked around for a bathrobe or something to put on and stared at my dirty clothes. I could always wash them, but putting them back on after that shower, after feeling like my old life was gone felt wrong.

So I put them in the trash and opened the door, looking both directions like someone was spying on me, before walking down the hall. The room he said I could sleep in was on the right. It had a bed, a dresser, a closet, and no windows.

I prayed the closet would have clothes.

It didn't.

I couldn't walk around in a towel, and I knew he wasn't the sort of guy, at least from what I could tell, who would be amused by it. If anything, he would probably ask me why I didn't logically just wear a curtain or something.

I chewed my lower lip and made my way farther down the hall, stopping at another door and slowly opening it.

It smelled like him.

I walked in.

And gasped.

The room was absolutely phenomenal, it had a flat screen TV in the corner, a huge king-sized bed, a fireplace that nearly took up the whole wall, and an attached bathroom bigger than the one I'd just used. It was in dark navy and browns and it seemed to fit him so much better than the living room.

Not that I would know.

Right?

I was ready to leave when his closet caught my eye, the door was slightly ajar, and I could see clothes hanging, expensive clothes, no not clothes, suits, what looked like dozens of suits, some with price tags still on them.

Maybe he would have a tank top or something I could put on? Boxers? At this point, a suit would be fine, but it would probably get me killed.

Mind made up, I walked over to the closet door and flicked on the light.

The closet was massive. Almost as big as the room, and that was saying something.

Suits galore.

Expensive shoes.

Sunglasses had their own space in the middle of the room, where a table stood with a decanter of whiskey and crystal glasses.

A chandelier hung in the middle right above it.

How loaded was this guy?

I didn't see normal clothes, street clothes, jeans, or anything that a normal person who looked my age would wear.

I did a small circle and spotted drawers in the corner. I pulled open the first and found a pair of boxers that felt soft and expensive. Then I opened the next to see nothing but white and gray T-shirts. I grabbed a gray one and prayed it was the right choice.

It was either this or the towel.

Maybe it was a test.

Maybe the last thing I would do would be putting on these boxers and that T-shirt.

I sighed, dropped the towel and did just that, and prayed I wasn't wrong.

"They have more guards out today," Chase said in a bored voice.

The iron gate that led to where she used to live was locked up tight. Two men in suits stood behind the gate. I imagined they had guns with them, and I wondered how many men were still in that house waiting to be killed.

"You got in the first time." I nodded to the gate. "What did you do? Just waltz in and say I'm Chase fucking Abandonato?"

"Something like that." Chase held his Glock close to his face. "It was either shoot them all on sight including the dirty girl or make a trade. She was already half dead, but you know how Phoenix is. With his past he can't—"

"I know." I wanted him to stop talking about it. My past and Phoenix's past were too identical for words.

Both of us raised by complete monsters who took joy in hurting women, only Phoenix was forced to break those women.

While I was forced to watch while my father did the honors.

I squeezed my eyes shut.

"Watch, son," Alexander Petrov was a big man, the way he held the girl down, a girl who looked at me like I was her only saving grace when I was thinking of shooting her so she didn't have to endure any longer while he fondled her breasts and laughed. "She's used goods, won't get a good price for this one." He tore her shirt.

Bile rose in my throat.

His hands on her skin.

Her eyes locking on mine practically begging for death.

I pulled out my gun and fired two shots into her head.

I made it quick.

Blood splattered all over the small room, and my father jumped to his feet. "Son of a bitch! I was enjoying her!"

"You were suffocating her," I said in a cold voice. "And yesterday her tests came back positive for syphilis, you want in on that or are you gonna say well done?"

He shuddered. "Syphilis, you say?"

"And God knows what else, she was a prostitute." I'd alter the records later, wouldn't be the first time. "Plus, I don't like seeing half dead women get raped, there's no pleasure in it when they don't fight back, don't you agree?"

His eyes flashed with an unholy gleam. "I don't think I've ever been more proud to call you son."

I gave him the dutiful smile I always did while I mentally wrapped my hands around his neck and strangled him.

Him… I would kill slowly.

"Hey!" Chase smacked me in the shoulder. "You still with me?"

"Let me go in alone."

"The hell I am." Chase was already grabbing more ammo and strapping it to his chest. His sleeved tattoos gave him away to anyone who knew about the man they now called the executioner.

The right hand of the Abandonato Family and the Capo.

Last year someone shit himself, literally, when Chase got out of his car.

It was one of the best days of my life since joining forces with the ridiculous Italians and being forced to kill with them as well as eat at their table.

"Please." It was a word I rarely uttered. A word so rare that tangible silence crackled in the air with awareness that I wouldn't utter it again, not to an Italian, especially not to Chase.

"I counted an additional six men last time, not including two De Lange captains, and you want to go in there and just, what? Ask for a meeting?"

I smirked, already opening the car door. "You forget, I'm Russian."

"And?"

"And my balls are bigger." I shrugged, earning a glare from him. "They think I'm their friend, they think I play both sides and that my loyalty is only to myself."

"Good, because that's all true, you jackass." Chase shook his head slowly. "Just try not to die. It will completely ruin my good, mood, yeah?"

"You? Good mood?" I snorted. "I'll get the gates open, try not to hit any plants on your way in, when you hear multiple gunshots from inside you'll know it's safe for you to reveal yourself to the masses."

"Be quick about it."

"If you're so worried, time me." I winked.

"Record's four minutes, Phoenix won't be happy to see someone take the title from him."

At that, I smiled wide, finding immense joy in torturing Phoenix the way he constantly tortured me with his weekly meetings and trainings on how to be a good boss to a family that didn't even want me.

"Ready?" Chase held up his Rolex.

"Set." I cocked my gun.

"Shit." Chase muttered as I walked up to the com and pressed the button.

"Yes?"

"Andrei Petrov, I have business with the family."

"You're not expected."

I smiled at his idiocy. "That's kind of the point, let me in."

The gate buzzed.

It was too easy when people thought you weren't the enemy.

It was easy when you made them think you were their friend.

I was good at that, being what I needed to be to anyone and everyone. I was a true chameleon and I knew that's why Chase and the rest of the bosses didn't trust me.

Because they knew I could and would play them.

I was with them until they were against me; at least that's what I told myself. As long as Luca Nicolasi roamed this earth, I'd taken an oath.

And I'd see it through.

As I sauntered right onto De Lange property, the two men

inside the gate approached me.

I had a bullet in each of their foreheads before they could utter one word. Another man opened the door and pointed his gun at me.

Idiot.

No wonder the De Langes were getting killed off so easily, he didn't even use the door to hide behind, just ran out into the fucking sunshine waving his gun like a jackass.

He fell against the doorframe and slumped to the ground. Sighing, I lifted my gun, and stepped over his large body and into the house.

Come out, come out wherever you are.

Blood rushed through my body, pulsed, pumped like I was high on the best drug. I could see clearer, smell better, I could sense everything around me like I'd just taken a hit of heroin.

I saw movement in my peripheral vision and shot down the hall. Voices shouted.

There were at least a few more men — that I knew. The De Langes weren't known for having many men at their homes, it was too easy for us to pick them off.

Which meant…

"What do you want?" a voice yelled.

"Surrender, and I'll tell you."

"We don't surrender."

"I'm Russian. I'm afraid I don't care," I said in a lethal voice. "I give no mercy, I torture for sport, and I'm seconds away from blowing up the entire house. You may as well come out before you're holding your own intestines and scrambling to shove them back into your miserable bloating body."

A man moved into the hall, gun in his hand holding it high in the air. "What the hell do you want? We made a trade, gave you the girl, and were told we'd be left alone for a few more days so we could regroup. I think that's what you call… grace? Artful warfare?"

"I don't give a fuck what they call it. I don't know the meaning of the word mercy." The guy froze. "One question, and if you answer correctly I'll let you live."

He gulped.

"The other night, the girl you sent to me to sell. Who is she to you?"

His grin turned lethal. "Why? She not performing well enough for the members of your club?"

I shrugged. "I only care that I get paid, and she's been… difficult. I just wanted to make sure she wasn't holding a candle for someone and plotting her escape. I hate paying for product and finding out it's used goods, so tell me, who is she to you?"

He narrowed his eyes at me. I could see the relation similar dark hair, similar skin tone. It was him. I just needed him to say it.

"I'm her brother."

I grinned and lowered my gun. "Good answer."

I had maybe one minute before Chase came storming in, gun raised, shooting anything that moved.

"Come here." I tossed my gun to the floor, barely registering the thud it made against the hardwood.

He sighed in relief and walked right up to me.

I grinned.

"What?" He frowned. "What's funny?"

"You." I licked my lips. "Hand me your knife, the one you're hiding in your left hand. Now."

He cursed and handed over the silver knife.

"Stick your tongue out." I gritted my teeth as anger pulsed

through my body, murder, monster, savior, saint. I had no idea what I was.

Maybe I was finally losing my grip on reality.

He laughed. "My tongue? No. I don't think so."

I held the point of the knife to his jugular and pressed the blade against his skin. "Open your fucking mouth. Now."

Shaking, he parted his lips.

I grabbed his tongue with my right hand, gripping, twisting, and then I sawed it off with his own knife.

Blood spewed from his mouth as he screamed and fell to his knees in front of me.

I tossed the tip of his tongue just as Chase walked in, gun raised.

"Son of a bitch, Andrei, could you stop doing weird shit?"

"Sorry." I wasn't, sorry that was. "His voice was annoying me."

"He's no use to us if he doesn't talk." Chase pointed out.

"There's ways to get him to talk. After all, he still has his hands." On second thought, I tilted my head as his right hand was pressed against his mouth.

I picked up my discarded gun and fired a shot into his left hand.

"He's right-handed, and we have time, maybe we'll get lucky and he'll learn sign language."

"Crazy Russian." Chase seemed both offended and pleased. "I'll call for some clean up, we'll take him to the club for questioning."

That's what I was afraid of.

That he would confess that the girl they were keeping was his own sister, that she was a De Lange, a walking abomination to our family.

To Chase especially.

I knelt down, picked up the tongue, and stuffed it in my pocket while Chase grabbed his cell, cursing into it like it was the first time he'd seen me do something crazy, which it wasn't. I was known for shooting off body parts people didn't need, I really didn't see the point in murderers keeping things that weren't necessary to their survival.

Suffering, I knew well.

Killing was too easy.

While Chase was on the phone, I leaned over and kissed six thirty-two's brother on the forehead and whispered. "Mention her, and I'm going to shove this piece of your tongue down your throat and watch while you choke to death, understood?"

He whimpered.

I patted his cheek. "Good talk."

"Yeah, no he did it in…" Chase checked his watch. "Three minutes forty-seven seconds. Yeah, yeah, I'll give you proof. No Nixon, just shot off his hand, cut out his tongue… I'm never eating tacos again, thanks for that visual." He clenched his teeth and then nodded to me. "Nixon wants him alive."

"He's alive." I shrugged.

Chase just stared at me like I was losing it.

"What?" I wiped my gloves on my pants and shoved the guy's knife into my pocket.

"I got this." Chase hung up the phone. "Take the car and go get cleaned up. The guys and I will figure all this shit out and head over to the club tonight for drinks and torture."

The brother whimpered.

I gave him a cruel smile. "Good, we just purchased some new cat tail whips, can't wait to see how much flesh we can pull from his back before he talks."

"Crazy bastard." Chase shook his head at me. "Do you just come up with this shit on your own or do you Google ways to peel flesh off people's skin without killing them?"

"Google..." I slapped him on the back. "...is your friend."

"Google, he says, as his name tops every list in the FBI."

"Hey, they love me over there. I almost gave them you guys." I laughed. "They can't touch me, and now they can't touch you. You're welcome."

"You're an annoying little shit."

"I'm only five years younger than you, and a lot more..." I tilted my head at him and lowered my eyes. "Endowed."

"I may kill you in your sleep one day, just thought you should know."

I shrugged. "I may just let you so you can put me out of my misery."

It slipped.

Chase's smile fell.

"Leave it," I snapped and walked out of the house with a knife in one pocket and her brother's tongue in the other.

CHAPTER ELEVEN

Alice

I was in the process of wiping off the sparkling countertops when the door to the apartment opened and shut.

I jumped when he locked it.

He wasn't looking at the kitchen. He was staring straight ahead like he was lost, or maybe like he didn't want to be found. I couldn't decide which.

But it gave me time to take in his form. He had blood splatters all over his suit. He shrugged out of his jacket, keeping the leather gloves in place, then jerked open his white button-down shirt. Buttons flew everywhere. I held in my gasp at his ridiculous body.

I wasn't attracted to men.

Men terrified me.

Men like my brother.

But this man was built like he never ate a carb in his entire life. He looked like he'd been cut from stone. His stomach was so muscular that I had a hard time understanding what he did to get it that way.

His shoulders were huge, something I hadn't noticed in his jacket but saw now, I'd thought him lethal before.

He looked like he was barely holding onto his own sanity as every muscle flexed and he leaned his head back against the door and cursed.

I was afraid to say something.

Afraid I would make him angry or angrier. Afraid that he had forgotten I was even there and needed a moment.

He kept his leather gloves on, peculiar, but other than that, he had no clothing on except for trousers that molded to an even more perfect bottom half.

I gulped not recognizing the feeling at first, and then I nearly burst into hysterics.

I was losing my mind.

Because I found him attractive.

Not just attractive.

He was one of the most beautiful people I'd ever seen in real life.

And he said he would keep me safe.

What sort of mind games was he playing?

I took a step backward.

I didn't think about the floor creaking, or that the guy would hear my heavy breathing, but he must have.

His head snapped in my direction.

His eyes locked on mine with cool indifference, and then slowly he drank me in like he'd never seen a woman before in his entire life.

I crossed my arms. I wasn't wearing a bra, and I wasn't flat chested either.

I gulped, suddenly insecure and worried he was going to hit me or raise his voice.

My gaze locked on his gloved hands.

I didn't realize I was shaking until he took a step toward me, and I tried to grab onto the countertop and missed because my hands wouldn't stay still.

And yet he kept walking.

Every muscle in perfect view.

Every muscle growing before my very eyes.

How had I thought this guy was lean?

Lethal. Yes.

Lean? Hard no.

His blue eyes flickered with something as his lips parted like he was going to speak and then he whispered with barely controlled rage. "Are those my clothes?"

Shit.

I gulped. "I figured you would want me to throw away my clothes, and I didn't exactly have any other choices, and you hate it when I ask stupid questions."

"Know me so well already, do you six thirty-two?" He tilted his head.

I could see a few splatters of blood still on his neck.

Whose blood?

My brother's?

Another De Lange family member?

How many of us had to die for them to be happy?

He reached into his pocket and pulled out a knife I recognized. It was covered in blood. He slammed it onto the counter, the sound slicing through the silence between us. "For you."

"That's Rome's knife," I whispered in disbelief. "Where did

you get it?"

"Oh, he handed it to me, and then I cut out this." He reached into his other pocket and placed a piece of what looked like tongue next to the knife. "You can thank me now."

I couldn't move.

Couldn't breathe or think.

"Y-you cut out his tongue?"

"It was either that or chopping off his dick, and I figured you'd want to do the honors. I wasn't wrong, was I?" He crossed his arms across his perfect chest and waited.

"No." I cleared my throat. "No, you weren't wrong."

"Excellent." He swept past me, leaving the tokens of whatever he'd just done sitting on the counter I'd just cleaned. I couldn't look away. "You need clothes that are clean."

"That's why I grabbed—"

He held up his hand without turning around, silencing me immediately. "I said, you need clothes that are clean. What you don't understand is that I may have a ridiculous amount of clothing, but all of that clothing has been touched by me. Nothing is clean, you need clothes that are clean."

"You make it sound like you don't shower." I tried teasing.

It was a very bad idea.

He looked over his shoulder and scowled. "The proper response is 'yes, great idea, by the way thank you for torturing my rapist and saving my life.'"

"Yes." Searing tears filled my eyes. "Great idea."

He tapped his foot impatiently.

"And thank you for torturing my rapist and saving my life."

"Better, six thirty-two, better." He nodded and then pulled out a cell phone. "Yeah, I'll need everything. For a female." He walked back to me and without blinking, cupped a breast.

"D cup," His hand slid around my side, I was too stunned, too angry to move. He had no right to touch me! I hated my response to it almost as much as I hated the fact that he had no physical or emotional reaction other than a blank stare. "Thirty-six," That same hand slid down my ass. "Medium, some small," I squeezed my eyes shut, praying his clinical inspection would be over soon. He looked down. "Seven and a half."

He dropped his hand and slid his cell back into his pocket like nothing had happened when I was shaking like a leaf.

"I'm not a rapist, six thirty-two, I was just trying to get you clothes, so if you'd stop standing there looking like I wronged you, I'd appreciate it. I've been surrounded by beautiful women my entire life. Believe me when I say, nothing about you tempts me to finally act on it."

He jerked away.

Something crashed in the other room.

Loud cursing ensued for a few minutes.

And that's when I realized he'd said finally.

As if he'd never once acted on it in his entire life.

CHAPTER TWELVE

Andrei

I slammed the bedroom door closed and leaned against it, my body still shaking from the touch.

I stared down at my gloved hands. My fingers were trembling, I watched in fascination as they refused to still.

So that's what it felt like.

To feel human.

To touch someone and have no choice but to respond.

I willed them to stop shaking.

I pulled the glove from my right hand then slipped the other from my left. Every time I stared at my bare hands, I saw blood on them.

A therapist would have a fucking field day with me. Rationally, I knew blood wasn't there, but that didn't stop me from wanting to wash my hands a dozen times a day.

Or from wearing gloves so people didn't see the stains.

So they didn't see the death.

Hands were tools.

Mine were covered in blood.

And I'd been tempted.

To take off one glove, to see if her skin was really as warm as it felt beneath the leather, if she would respond. If she would take that lip between her teeth and bite, would her eyes dilate the way grown women's did when I walked past them?

I'd had my fair share of encounters.

But when a man feels nothing.

He stops trying.

Did it even matter?

I laughed to myself. It sounded wrong coming from my lips. Men like me didn't laugh, and if we did it was usually out of cruelty.

I stood in front of the mirror, blood splattered all over my chest, my neck, what possible reason did I have to think that this girl, born in the wrong family, at the wrong time, would be the one person capable of breaking the curse?

The one person able to touch me.

To make me feel anything other than the slippery tendrils of death as it choked me on a daily basis.

I was an idiot to think that she would be different.

Just like she was an idiot to think that this was anything other than me keeping her safe from those who wanted her blood for no other reason than it was De Lange.

I shoved my hands back into the gloves and stared at my reflection in disgust as I reared back and punched the mirror with my right hand sending glass crashing to the floor.

Glass crunched beneath my boots as I did a slow semi-circle. I ripped off my gloves again and hurled them against the bed, kicked off my boots hitting the wall and then jerked off my pants and threw them against the ground, leaning over the dresser completely nude, wondering what the hell I was going to do with six thirty-two.

Alice.

No.

She had no name.

No names.

No names.

I felt the name in my head, though, like a drum beat, Alice, Alice, Alice De Lange.

Chase wouldn't understand. He would kill her.

Tex already wanted her blood.

I would need to find a replacement.

And in the meantime, I would figure out a way to keep her safe and keep myself sane.

This was probably one of the most suicidal things I'd done in my entire life, keeping an enemy under my own roof, feeding her, clothing her… like a fucking pet.

Yeah, a therapist would just love to get in my head, wouldn't he?

A knock sounded on my bedroom door. "I heard a crash, are you okay?"

I jerked my head toward the door. Was she serious?

I stomped over to the door and jerked it open. "Unless you hear gunshots, I'm fine, and you really only need to worry about that on August third."

She frowned her cheeks heating. "It's August third."

"August third at one a.m. You'll be happy to know the reason I'm not dead is because the gun didn't go off, so save your worry for next year when I try again. Now go be useful somewhere else. And six thirty-two, knock on my door again and I'm going to take one of your hands as a souvenir."

I slammed the door in her face.

Why did she have to be so provoking?

And beautiful?

And why the hell would me being naked cause her to blush? It made no sense; so much so that I wanted to ask her what sort of girl was still able to blush after what she'd been put through.

I stomped into the bathroom and flipped on the shower. Then I grabbed a brand-new piece of wrapped soap, discarded the paper, and hopped into the shower.

Fresh soap every time.

And no matter how many times I ran that soap over my body, I saw red. All I ever saw…

Was red.

CHAPTER THIRTEEN

Alice

He'd been completely naked.

Still covered in blood splatters.

And if I heard him correctly, he was talking about killing himself. What sort of guy attempted — according to him — suicide once a year?

My heart constricted.

I tried not to think about how selfish I was being by wanting to see a window, by wanting to be useful.

A knock sounded on the door. I put the remote down and went over to open it, but it opened on its own.

"Hey there." A woman who looked old enough to be my grandma held out her hand. "I'm Georgie, I have clothes for you."

"Oh." I shook her hand firmly, as she sized me up and then winked. "He was right about your sizes. Astonishing, the man's never been wrong. It's in his hands. He just feels a woman body and knows what would look good on her. Well, we don't want to keep him waiting. You know how Andrei gets, impatient little shit—"

Like some kind of ninja phantom, he appeared in the doorway.

"Andrei, we were just talking about you." She beamed.

He actually smiled at that. "What was it you said? Impatient little shit? Is that my nickname today, Georgie?"

"Someone needs to humble you." She beamed like she was proud of him, and he seemed intent on ignoring her positive attention. She turned and reached for something in the hallway then pulled in a giant rack with dozens of bags hanging on it along with enough clothes for ten women. "All right, I'll just leave this here, keep what you like, let me know if you need more, and I'll bring it back tomorrow." She leveled him with a sly smile. "If you're hoping to get a good price on this one, I'd suggest the white dress."

I felt my body sway.

Price? As in sell me?

To who?

For what?

I tried to keep my expression closed when my heart was squeezing painfully in my chest, he said I was safe.

And I believed him.

"Not selling her, not yet," he said in a bored voice. "That will be all, Georgie."

"Bye, handsome." She winked and closed the door behind her leaving us blanketed in silence.

Andrei was wearing a pair of designer jeans and a long sleeve black shirt that molded to his body like a second skin.

He went to the rack and started looking through it. At

that point, I noticed he still wore his leather gloves, these ones were clean.

It was on the tip of my tongue to ask why when he tossed a bag to me. "Keep the heels. I don't like the Nikes — color's too loud, and you won't be needing them. The Prada are nice if you don't fall flat on your face in them…" He sighed and then pulled down a beautiful black cocktail dress. "This will be perfect for dinner."

"Dinner?"

"Dinner."

"With you?"

"No, with a ghost," he deadpanned. "Do you see anyone else in the room?"

"No."

"Logic. Try using it," he snapped then shoved the dress in my hands. "We leave in an hour."

"We're leaving?" Why the heck was I repeating everything he said like I was mentally handicapped?

His eyebrows shot up. "I imagined you would learn quicker than this. I don't owe you explanations, six thirty-two, only my protection, right? Ergo, turn your ass around march into the bathroom, put on the clothes, try not to break your leg in those shoes and do something with that mop of hair on your head—" He frowned and then he went over to the kitchen and grabbed a pair of scissors.

I backed away.

He took another step toward me.

I put a bar stool between us.

"Scissors are the worst weapon to use. The handles get caught on your knuckles. If I was going to hurt you, I'd use a serrated knife. Stop backing away and hold still."

Shaking, I didn't move as he walked behind me. His body heat radiated against my back, and it was playing with my head, with my emotions, with everything because I had this weird reaction to his nearness. Like I wanted to lean back against him even though he had scissors in his hands.

Like I wanted him to hold me and tell me it was going to be okay.

But I knew I was nothing more than a prisoner to him.

A new toy he could dress up until he was bored.

That's probably why Georgie didn't seem surprised to see me in there.

He'd been surrounded by beautiful women all his life, and he was right. I had nothing special that he wanted.

Hadn't my brother said the same thing?

I hung my head just as Andrei whispered behind me. "I'm adding a layer."

"So you cut tongues and hair?"

He tugged harder than he needed to, making me wince. "Are you actually teasing the man with the weapon?"

"Are you actually cutting a whore's hair?" It was out before I could stop it. I meant it as a way to deflect what I knew in my heart was true.

My brother had made me a whore.

My dad had allowed it.

And this man was going to sell me for it, wasn't he?

Big fat tears collected in my eyes.

I refused to let them fall.

A gloved hand touched my shoulder, I was being slowly turned around to face him. I didn't want to look at his cold ruthless eyes. I knew what I would see there.

Indifference.

I hated it more than the rage I saw in my brother's eyes, because at least I could react and plan.

With Andrei I just hoped and waited.

"Look at me," he snapped.

I lifted my head, and when I wasn't lifting it fast enough he shoved two gloved fingers below my chin and gripped it tight. "Call yourself a whore again, and you won't like the consequences."

"Isn't that what this is? Georgie said something about being sold."

"Do you have chains around your ankles, six thirty-two?"

"No."

"Do you have a tattoo on your ankle with a lock on it?"

"No," I rasped.

"Then you aren't one of the women being sold. And in order to stay that way, in my good graces and in God's, I'd suggest you stand still so I don't accidently give you bangs. You would look shitty with bangs."

I frowned. "What sort of—"

"Shhh..." He smirked, then, like he was enjoying himself. "It's been a while since I've cut hair."

"Alarming," I muttered, earning another small smile that was gone too soon as the sound of snipping filled the air.

He was gentle.

It was strange.

The man with the leather gloves who cut out tongues had a gentle touch.

I would have preferred rough.

I had no idea what to expect when he pulled away with pieces of my hair clutched in his hand.

He held my hair up to his nose and sniffed and then he

tucked the cut pieces into his jean pocket and crossed his arms. “Not bad.”

“Not bad but not good either?” I asked in a small voice.

“Asking for compliments?” He was so close I could almost taste the cologne he wore — it was warm, spicy.

“N-no.” I ducked my head.

“Pity, because I would have given you one.” He jerked his head toward the bathroom. “Go dress, you’re about to be thrown into a den of hungry lions, only worse, they’re Italian and they hate vodka. Mention your name and you won’t make it out of their cave alive, understand?”

“Yes.” I straightened my shoulders and locked eyes with him. “I’m six thirty-two… I don’t have a name.”

“Good girl,” he whispered. “Very, very, good.”

CHAPTER FOURTEEN

Andrei

She had two minutes before we were supposed to be leaving.

When she had one minute left, the bathroom door swung open. She had her hair in a high ponytail, and the black cocktail dress did wonders for her already curvy body.

It was a simple little black dress that had a high neck in front and a scooped back. It was form fitting and it looked perfect with the nude spiked Valentino heels.

I grabbed a long fake fur coat from the rack and held it out to her. “Time to go.”

Her eyes widened as she slipped into it and then held it close like the fur was comforting to her skin.

Hmm.

I held out my hand to her.

She stared at the gloves.

New gloves.

Ones that didn't that have blood on them, not that it mattered since blood followed me wherever I went.

After a brief hesitation, she placed her hand in mine. I held it tight, mainly because I wanted to show ownership when we walked down the halls and through the bar.

People needed to know they couldn't touch her.

Not without my consent.

"Don't make eye contact with anyone. They'll think it's an invitation, and I've already hit my quota on murders today."

"Okay." Her voice was weak; her skin was pale.

Shit.

She looked like she was walking to her death.

They needed her to look… alive.

Content.

Not scared for her life.

Those men, they smelled fear. They lived for it. They wanted the ones that were scared because they fucking got off on it.

Shit.

"You need to look more excited than that," I said once I pulled the door open. "More confident. I need you to play a part, do you understand me?"

"Yes. I think… so." Her eyes darted to the hallway than back to me. "You said I was safe, right? I'm safe?"

I didn't want to soften. No good would come from me getting attached or being the person in her life that lied and said everything was going to be okay when it wasn't.

Her father was dead.

Half her family was dead.

And her brother I would let her kill.

This wasn't a safe life or a happy one.

This was war.

This was the mafia.

"You're safe." I locked eyes with her. "With me, you'll be safe."

I didn't add that I was more dangerous to her than any of the men out there. I didn't tell her that I was a monster that couldn't feel anything.

I just let her believe I would use my gun for her.

And that's all that mattered.

I was disgusted with myself then, horrified that as I dragged her through that club, I felt nothing, I was so fucking tired of being numb, of turning it off, of having women touch me and laughing because it amused me that they thought they could seduce me when I was much more tempted to kill them for trying.

I inwardly cursed my dad for making me that way.

For making women objects.

For trapping me in my own prison.

We walked down a separate hall that led to the clubs. She clung to me tightly, and I found I liked the way she held onto me, like she was afraid I would let go, like she didn't know that just because I would keep her safe, didn't mean I was safe.

We walked down a long corridor that led to a black door. I slid my card over it, and it buzzed open.

The sound of music filled the place. We'd been open an hour and already we were at capacity. Men and women were scattered everywhere, all over the couches, in the VIP section kissing, touching, flirting.

One of the Italians, now my man, eyed me with curiosity as I brought her through and then his eyes flickered with amusement before he turned away and spoke into his wrist.

I would hear from Ax later, that much I knew. Bastard rarely kept to himself when he wanted information and he was only too happy to report everything to Nixon Abandonato like a good puppy.

I wondered what she thought, then, as men parted for us, as women stared at her with open-eyed jealousy.

I pulled her toward the bar near the front entrance and held up two fingers. Manny nodded at me and filled two shot glasses with Stoli's.

I picked up one and handed her the other. "*Ypa*."

With trembling fingers, she took the shot from me and repeated. "*Ypa*."

I almost smiled when she took the shot and then made a face. "I didn't just ask you to kill me in Russian, did I?"

I admired her ability to joke in the circumstances she was in more than I should. "No that would have been *ubei menya*," I shrugged. "Just in case you ever feel the need to beg for it."

"It wouldn't matter."

"Pardon?"

"I said it wouldn't matter. I've begged for it before, I begged for it every night since I was fourteen, so even if I screamed it at the top of my lungs—"

"Don't." I put my hand over her mouth silencing her, putting an end to the conversation. I didn't want to hear about her pain, her struggles. I didn't want to care that her brother touched her where no brother should touch, and I sure as hell didn't want to know that the woman in front of me, begged for death the same way I did for entirely different reasons.

No, I didn't want to compare pain.

I was too afraid our scars would match.

And it would be all I saw.

I held up two fingers again and handed her a new shot. "Here's my promise to you, *dorogaya*. Say those words to me, and it will be over with before you take your next breath."

Her lips parted, and then she reached for my hand and squeezed it, never taking her eyes off of me as she whispered, "Thank you."

It was the first genuine thank you I'd ever heard from someone.

And all because I promised I would kill her if she asked.

She didn't know then how seriously I took my vows. She had no way of knowing the power behind those words and the brutality behind my gun.

Something shifted in the air, with Post Malone blaring through the speakers, with Stoli's vodka on her parted lips.

I realized it wasn't my surroundings.

It wasn't even her.

It was me.

I'd felt her thank you down to my damned soul.

Funny how you forget, how painful it is to feel, until your dead heart thuds loudly to remind you, you're still human.

"Let's go." It came out rough, as I grabbed her arm and led her to the front entrance where my Escalade was waiting for us.

She scooted across the leather seat. I followed.

And when we were blanketed in silence, I exhaled out our destination.

"Nixon Abandonato's house."

Six thirty-two stiffened next to me.

She knew the name.

Then she would know that it was important that she did exactly as I said.

If I hid her in plain sight, they wouldn't ask questions.

If they showed up at the club and saw I had her with me and never introduced her, they'd suspect her.

I hoped that none of the girls knew who she was.

I hoped that none of the men would recognize her as the girl who was taken from the De Lange's a few days ago.

And I hoped that she'd forgive me, if for some reason they did.

Because if they did.

She wouldn't make it back to the car.

If they did, she was riding to her own funeral.

I turned to see if she was wringing her hands together, or if she was biting her lip, tapping her heels, and I almost smiled when I noticed she was doing all three.

"Deep breaths," I said in an amused voice. "You're with me."

"But you're Russian."

"How astute of you to point out the obvious."

"No." She gulped and turned her body toward me. I enjoyed the way the fur hugged her body, protecting her, keeping her safe from the elements, keeping her safe from watchful eyes. "I mean, you do realize who he is? Boss to one of the most powerful crime families in the world, his second in command went on a killing spree with you today. Don't think I didn't recognize him. The four families are powerful, and they hate De Langes. You aren't Italian."

I smirked at that. "Oh, you'd be surprised what I am."

"You aren't listening." Her voice shook. "Again, you're Russian. You don't understand… they'll kill me."

"They'll have to get through me first."

She looked like she was minutes away from turning

hysterical, so even though I rarely had to tell people why they should fear me, why they should run in the other direction, I put my hand on her thigh, stopping the incessant tapping of her foot.

Her body tensed beneath my touch.

Her warmth seeped through the leather of my gloves, and my fingers tingled as I held my hand there, wondering for the first time in years, if I would like touching her skin or if I'd have the ever present aversion to it.

It had been getting worse over the years.

The gloves hadn't been necessary a few months ago.

And I hated that it was one more thing that I did, following in my father's footsteps, leather gloves, always leather gloves.

"Listen carefully, six thirty-two, we're almost to the compound Nixon calls a house." I dug my fingers into her thigh a bit, she let out a whimper of fear, one I put there, not on purpose, but because I wanted more heat, I wanted… just more.

I jerked my hand back as we pulled up to the gate.

"My name is Andrei Petrov. I am the last living heir to the Petrov crime family. I am worth more money than you will ever see in your lifetime, I was taught to kill when you were watching cartoons with a fucking sippy cup. I kill without a second thought, I feel nothing, and when I tell you that I'll keep you safe, know that I'll keep you safe. Those men in there won't know your last name because I won't give it. If any of them find out who you are, my suggestion is to say one last prayer because even my gun won't be fast enough against six of the most dangerous men on this planet, seven if you count the old man, eight if you count my mentor. I say this not to scare you but for you to understand that your survival depends on this."

"R-right. Yes. Okay." She nodded her head what felt like a dozen times and then whispered. "If I'm not a…" She shook her head. "Who do they think I am?"

The SUV pulled around the front and stopped.

The door opened and I called over my shoulder. "My new girlfriend."

CHAPTER FIFTEEN

Alice

There was no time to hyperventilate as the cold spring air hit me square in the face. It was a chilly Chicago day, not that I'd been outside much in the last year.

Not since every De Lange Family member went into deep cover.

My family was too involved to walk the streets.

Meaning I was both target and bait.

Seeing the sun, feeling it on my face, well that wasn't something I'd been allowed to feel in a while. I was pulled from school, pulled from every extracurricular I was involved in, not that it was a lot, but still, being pulled from dance wasn't fun.

Being pulled from Eagle Elite was even worse.

They'd shown up in black cars.

Students had watched while I was walked to the car and told I wouldn't finish my junior year.

And the rest was history.

You'd think I'd be used to stress.

But this was next level stress.

I would be walking into the most dangerous house I'd ever been in. This was worse than my brother, this was worse than my father. Worse than facing the barrel of a gun.

This would be torture if they discovered me.

And Andrei just wanted me to do what? Look pretty on his arm and try not to hurl on the dinner rolls?

I imagined that everyone was armed.

I took another faltering step in the unfamiliar heels as Andrei wrapped an arm around me. He felt warm, his breathing was even, calm. And he looked almost annoyed that I wasn't walking fast enough.

Annoyed that I was petrified.

Then again, now that I knew more of who he was, I figured, I should be just as scared of him as I was the rest of the Italians.

Because he was their friend, wasn't he?

Which meant I was his enemy too.

My stomach sank as we approached the large immaculate house, with its water fountain in the middle of the driveway and its gorgeous brick stature.

Two men were standing in front of the door.

One looked angry at me for existing, while the other looked curious.

The one with the angry look gave Andrei a long stare and sighed. "They let you out tonight?"

"Cute, Vic, you kill any puppies today? Strangle them?"

The guy named Vic looked like he was ready to smile, but then he muttered. "Pain in my ass, every day of my life… damn babysitting duty."

"The door." Andrei winked at him. "You should probably open it for us."

"How's the finger healing up? Hmm Andrei?" This time he did grin as he opened the door. "What has it been? Ten months? A year?"

Andrei stiffened. "Remember, tit for tat. One day when you're sleeping on the job, I'm going to take your pinky."

Vic barked out a laugh. "Just make the cut straight so I can sew it back on, crazy bastard."

"Swear." Andrei put his free hand on his heart as he pulled me through the door.

What sort of people joked about stuff like that without breaking out the guns and getting into fights? In my own family joking like this only got you a black eye but these guys? They laughed! It was so unexpected I couldn't stop staring at Vic or at Andrei and the exchange between them.

To be honest, I wasn't expecting a dungeon per say, but I was expecting a lot of men sitting around staring at their guns, talking about their hatred for my family or the impending war between all of us.

Instead, the first thing that happened was an adorable little toddler ran up to me and hugged my legs. "Pretty dress!"

Stunned, I just stood there and then she looked up at me with these beautiful crystal blue eyes and repeated it again. "Pretty dress."

"Thank you." I smiled down at her. "I like your doll. What's her name?"

Andrei didn't leave my side, but I suddenly felt eyes on me.

Slowly I looked up, and anyone might think I'd just waltzed in there and announced I had a bomb strapped to my chest.

The guy from earlier, the one who wanted me dead, Chase,

had an apron on and had stopped stirring what looked like sauce in the kitchen, his smile extremely amused while a woman who looked pregnant stood next to him a similar look on her face.

And then slowly I exhaled as I looked around the room while the little girl still clung to me like I was a Barbie doll.

I recognized all their faces.

Including their wives.

They were the monsters I had begged to save me.

The monsters that never came.

The ones I prayed would destroy us all so it would stop.

So he would stop visiting me in my room.

So the pain would stop.

Nixon Abandonato approached then, all six feet two inches of him, muscles on top of muscles, enough ink down his arms and legs to make a person dizzy, lethal, beautiful, dangerous.

He bent down and picked up the little girl.

She wrapped her arms around his neck and nestled her head beneath his chin. “Daddy, don’t you like her dress?”

Daddy?

This beautiful little creature was his daughter?

I felt suddenly dizzy as Nixon tilted his head to the side, his eyes narrowing. “Yes, it’s a beautiful dress, one you won’t be wearing until you’re thirty, all right Serena?”

“Yes, Daddy.” She beamed, apparently unaware that a tight cocktail dress wouldn’t be in her future for a very long time, or, if the look on his face was anything to go by… ever.

“Wow.” A voice came from the right, and there he was stomping into the kitchen looking every inch the rumored Italian Godfather, only young, so young and attractive it almost felt like a sick joke. “When I said to bring a girl… I didn't think you'd take me seriously."

Andrei shrugged. "Maybe I'm tired of your constant shit."

"You love it."

"Pink cupcakes." Andrei actually looked relaxed as a grin spread across his face. "With sprinkles."

"Knew you'd like that touch." Chase laughed from his spot in the kitchen. "Would have paid to see Tex bring that in on the plate."

"It had polka dots, the plate."

"Don't worry we have a Hello Kitty card for you too, all of us signed it," Nixon joined in, a smirk on his face.

Andrei grumbled a curse.

"Happy birthday, man," Nixon held out his hand.

Andrei tentatively shook it.

Wait. Was this a meeting?

Dinner?

Birthday party?

And then a gorgeous woman came around with a giant cake, two more women followed.

The wives.

Nixon's wife Trace, Tex's wife Mo, and Phoenix's wife, Bee. The other women that were scattered around the room were already sitting drinking wine, Dante's wife raised her glass to Andrei and grinned.

What sort of warped universe did I just walk into?

My father told me they tortured people at night.

He said the monsters drank blood.

He made me think they were this thing of fiction, like a vampire or werewolf, with no soul, no heart, just killing.

"Well?" Nixon pointed to the cake. "Blow out your candles, old man."

Andrei's hand gripped on my hip.

I flashed him a quick smile. "You know if you don't, they'll probably just pull a gun on you."

Nixon's expression shifted, and then he narrowed his eyes on me. "Told her a lot about us, haven't you?"

"Well." I gulped. *Here goes nothing.* "I am his girlfriend, so…"

Everything happened all at once.

Trace tripped, the cake slid from the tray, Mo tried to grab it just in time for Chase to lean in and accidently shove them forward and then another guy standing behind Nixon turned.

Cake went flying across his face.

Candles included.

Oh shit, shit, shit.

It was Phoenix.

He used to be a De Lange.

My stomach sank.

He would recognize me.

He would.

I used to play at his house when my dad had meetings with his, when I was little and curious and had a stupid crush on him because he was five years older and looked so… pained.

Cake dripped from his face as he glared at Trace.

And then Trace stepped forward with a smile on her face and ran her finger down his cheek and sucked off the frosting. "Perfect, you like chocolate right, Phoenix?"

He glared and then went for her. "That's it." He pulled her into his arms and swung her around while she laughed and then rubbed his face all over her back. She lunged for Nixon who used his child as a shield, and Tex grabbed a bottle of wine and chugged directly from it while another tiny toddler came running with a wooden mallet screaming, "Thor, GOD OF THUNDER!"

Phoenix dropped to the ground. "Get them, Junior. Get Aunt Trace!"

He went running toward her.

And then Serena fought to get down and jumped in front of her mom. "Captain America attack!"

"Aw man!" Junior dropped his hammer and started yelling and convulsing on the ground.

"What's he doing?" I asked under my breath.

A chuckle fell from Andrei's lips, and I blinked up at him. He was beautiful when he smiled, absolutely gorgeous. I sucked in a shocked breath and quickly looked away.

He leaned in, his lips tickling my ear as he whispered, "Little man's hulking out. It's best to just let him finish."

Sure enough, he jumped to his feet and yelled, "I'M GREEN!"

"RUN!" The little girl shouted and then ran behind Chase, who pulled out two knives from sheathes on his back.

The knives were actually real!

"Samurai!"

"Iron Man!" Dante, a guy close to my age and someone I'd seen at school a few times and given a wide berth, jumped onto a chair.

"Spiderman beats both Samurai and Iron Man!" Someone else came running into the room. His hair was longer, pulled into a man bun that made him look downright sexy.

"Noooo, Uncle Sergio always picks Spiderman!" Serena wailed

"Forfeit." He winked and started making spewing noises at Junior and Serena who both fell into fits of laughter and hugged his leg, pieces of cake and all.

Yup, warped universe.

This was so opposite of what I'd grown up with that I wanted to burst into tears. It didn't match with the stories.

Phoenix De Lange, or now Nicolasi if the rumors of him cutting the De Lange brand from his arm were true, was smiling at his child, not trapping him in a room. Not yelling at them for deciding they wanted to hulk out and play in front of the adults.

In fact, the entire scene was unreal.

Because my every dinner — my entire life, in fact — had been spent being seen not heard.

An older man walked into the room; a glass of wine held against his lips. A black fedora sat on his head, and a matching scarf was wound around his neck. He sighed heavily and then held out that same glass in the air.

Immediately, Chase was there pouring into it, and then Trace was kissing the old man's cheek.

"Who's this?" He was pointing at me, and then looked down at the cake. "That Andrei's dessert?" He pointed down at the mess all over the living room and kitchen.

Andrei released me then, walked over to Phoenix, and swiped his finger across his jaw and then licked the frosting the way Trace had done previously. "You make this frosting just for me, Phoenix?"

Phoenix glared.

I hid my smile.

Because I liked that Andrei tested him.

I liked that he was an equal.

More than I should.

"Just call her Black Widow." Andrei piped up answering

his question with ease.

"Well." The old man clasped his hands together and gave us both a funny look before grabbing a towel. "Should we clean up and eat before Chase pulls his gun out over the mess."

"Not my house." Chase held up his hands and eyed Nixon. "You may want to Google how to get frosting out of the hardwood."

"Google this," Nixon flipped him off.

Junior did the same.

Nixon shot an apologetic look to Phoenix who was already looking up at the ceiling for God or someone to deliver him.

And then an arm was getting looped in mine. "So, Black Widow, do I know you?"

"Uhhh," I smiled at her as bright as I could, my fur coat suddenly feeling like a death trap on my shoulders. "I don't know."

"Sorry." She frowned and then looked at me again, really looked at me, her hair was cut to her chin, she was gorgeous in a flirty romantic way. "You just look really familiar."

"El, stop pestering her." Dante came up and wrapped an arm around the woman's shoulders. The woman who I knew was his wife.

I hadn't stayed at University long.

But I remembered them.

And then another fuzzy memory shot to the forefront of my mind.

Of Dante and Andrei of all people.

Of a fight in the middle of the quad.

Of long stares, whispers of a war between the Russians as they tried to overtake Eagle Elite University.

And then I sucked in a breath and found myself swaying

a bit.

Andrei.

I knew he looked familiar.

We'd had Bio together.

I had sat in the back.

He was in the front, often seen taunting teachers, and frequently known to throw ridiculous parties where there were rumors of gambling, shootings, and so much sex that they became legendary.

Then there was an accident…

"So, you're his girlfriend now?" El kept our arms looped and led me to a chair, good because I really needed to sit and try to figure out how to navigate. I wasn't just in over my head, I was already drowning, gasping for air, and Andrei was doing nothing to help. At all.

"Uh, yes." I needed to sound more convincing.

More memories surfaced.

They'd closed the spot where they held all the parties. Chase's wife had died there.

Phoenix had shot her.

That much the De Lange Family knew, that much they'd told me.

After making a deal with the Russians.

I shot a look toward Andrei. Her pact with that man, our enemy, was the reason that we were getting hunted, and yet he was… breaking bread with them?

Was it not true then?

Any of it?

I numbly found my seat. El was on my right while Andrei sat on my left shooting daggers with his eyes at Phoenix, who seemed to be telepathically asking question after question about who I was and what I was doing there.

"So, girl whose name we know isn't Black Widow, you work at the club?" Tex asked once we were all seated around the table, once the older one said grace, once they started passing around food like it was Thanksgiving.

Sheep in wolves clothing.

These people were killers.

And they were sharing a meal like it was normal.

I shivered in my seat. "What do you mean? The club?"

Tex stopped chewing and shared a look with Nixon who was staring me down like I had two heads. "You know, the club, where Andrei holds court?"

"Oh," I forced a smile as my mind trudged up visions of being chained to a bed while I was given bathroom breaks. "Sorry, I guess I just never really thought of it that way." I scrunched up my nose. Try prison. Dungeon. Cell. "I'm actually new."

"New?" Chase piped up his eyes were so intense that I wanted to look away but knew I couldn't. "So new she still looked unrecognizable beneath all that dirt and scum, good to know you discovered showers, and so soon."

That earned him an elbow from Luc, his wife.

"What?" He mouthed then ripped off a piece of bread and kissed her on the cheek.

She blushed and rolled her eyes while I exhaled in relief. He didn't know who I was.

Otherwise, I wouldn't still be breathing.

And I wanted to keep breathing.

I noticed a flicker of movement to my left, Andrei was very slowly peeling off the ever-constant leather gloves, from his thumb down to his pointer finger, he tugged until they were free.

So he took them off for dinner?

I waited for him to do the same to his left hand.

He didn't.

The hand stayed covered.

And his right hand, from what I could tell was completely flawless just like the rest of him.

Even his nails looked manicured, not covered in blood like I assumed, nor scarred, just, perfect.

He reached for his wine.

And cleared his throat loudly making me jerk away, making it so I was staring directly into Chase's cold expression again. He didn't even blink. Just reached for his wine, his tattooed arms flexing with the motion. I gave him a small smile as a trickle of sweat ran down my spine.

"So," Dante began. "How's business, Drei? Things looking good?"

"No business during dinner," Tex interrupted gruffly, "Though I have to say I'm curious. This is the first time you've brought a girl. Was it the sprinkles on the cupcake that did it? Or the way I smacked your ass afterward that convinced you to listen this time?"

A few of the guys snickered like they were in middle school, while Tex kept his rapt attention on Andrei like he really cared about his dating life.

"Well…" Andrei sounded annoyed. "You know how much I love pink frosting… and since none of you jackasses can keep a secret, I knew family dinner would most likely be a surprise party with a cake since last year I showed up and almost shot Chase when he suggested pin the tail on the donkey." He leaned back, cool, composed. "Besides, why spend your birthday alone when you can spend it with someone like this…"

I almost choked on the piece of bread as his arm snaked around me and squeezed. Did he realize that he was gloveless on that right hand?

He rarely touched me, and if he did, it seemed like he hated every second of it.

I leaned into him and smiled, playing my part even though the bread was sitting like a rock in my stomach. Even though I could feel his fingertips almost tremble against the fur I was still stupidly wearing.

Tex flashed us a grin. "Playa, playa."

"Please never. Ever, again, again, ever…" Chase grumbled. "You can't say Playa. You're too Italian, you sound like a white rapper, but like a really really shitty one."

Tex chucked a roll in his direction.

Chase snatched it midair and grinned. "Still got it."

"So." Trace drew out the word louder than necessary as her eyes darted around the table and landed on me. "If you don't work at the club what do you do?"

Nixon gave her a drop-it look.

I opened my mouth to say something, anything, like I clean toilets, wonderful manicure is that new?

When Andrei said in a bored tone, "What do you think? She's a whore."

Everything dropped at once.

Tex, his fork.

Nixon, his knife.

Chase, multiple F-bombs.

Phoenix's hands over his son's ears.

And multiple wine glasses.

Tears burned the back of my throat as I watched the

shocked expressions. All looking at me to nod my head, make a joke. I could kill him. I wanted to strangle him for hurting me, for embarrassing me.

For making me play a role I never wanted to play.

But he said I had to make it believable.

So through tears of hurt and humiliation, tears of anger at the man who said he'd keep me safe, I whispered. "Good thing I come at a cost, huh Andrei?"

His eyes flashed with fury.

And then I kept eating, my fork scraping against the plate, filling the uncomfortable silence with the precision of an atomic bomb.

I imagined what they were thinking about me, and about him, our relationship.

My brother had made me feel used.

Dirty.

Unwanted.

This stranger, Andrei had made me feel worse. He'd given me hope, he'd dressed me, fed me, he'd made me think I was safe.

Only to announce I was none of those things in front of the monsters I'd begged to kill me.

No. I was going to be a whore.

Not his girlfriend.

His whore.

Until I imagined he got bored and killed me.

At least the death, I imagined, would be swift. After all, hadn't he promised I had only to ask and I would not draw my next breath?

I lifted my wine glass to my lips and drank.

I didn't cry.

I didn't hunch my shoulders.

I was trained for this.

I was a motherfucking De Lange woman.

I drained my glass and held it to Andrei for more, and then I turned to Chase and beamed. "Lovely pasta."

And in that moment, I could have sworn, the Capo saw me, really saw me, and smiled a real smile of approval.

As if it had been a test, and I had passed with flying colors.

CHAPTER SIXTEEN

Phoenix

It was nearing midnight.

I sent Junior home with Bee and waited for the inevitable. I sat in the shadows of the living room as Dante finally approached with El by his side.

I knew what was coming.

I saw the way their eyes flickered with recognition before glancing to me and only me.

Because I knew everything, and they knew that.

There were no secrets to me, nothing hidden.

I was a Nicolasi now.

I owned secrets.

Traded in them.

And I would have the answers.

Dante was playing with one of his many knives while El was smiling a smile I knew was fake all the way down to her toes.

"Headed back?" I asked without looking up.

"In a few. Some of the guys decided to have a glass of whiskey while they plotted world domination…"

"Too bad I've already dominated, then, huh?" I joked while El sat on the stool in front of me, followed by Dante on my right. I sighed heavily. "You don't need to ask."

"Figured." Dante shook his head. "I feel like I'm betraying someone here. I feel like you know that too, so just tell us how we're playing this because that woman should not have walked out of here alive."

I squeezed my eyes shut and sighed. When would it end? This, this was why I liked war. War I could predict. But peace? Peace felt a hell of a lot more chaotic in my dark soul.

"You would be correct." I lowered my voice "Andrei's our friend, that's all you need to know. He swore a blood oath of fealty to us, and us to him. He has his reasons, just like we have our reasons for keeping secrets."

El put her hand on my knee. "She's a year younger than Andrei."

"Yeah." I licked my lips, tasting lingering wine there. "We see how this plays out." I stood, "And you say nothing. We trust Andrei to do his job, all right? If he has her there, if he's pretending she's his whore then there's a fucking good reason for it."

Dante snorted in disgust. "Pretending? The guy's probably already had her—"

"Doubtful," I interrupted.

Dante's eyes flickered to my face. "How could you possibly know that?"

"Because," I whispered. "Andrei's a virgin."

I left both of them gaping at me and smiled to myself as I

left the house and walked to my waiting Maybach.

I smiled wider when I got in and the engine roared to life.

Andrei was in for a hell of a surprise if he thought he could just announce something like that to the family and make us believe it.

I knew him in and out because I kept him in check.

And I knew that if he brought her around they'd get suspicious of why he wasn't touching her.

Something that he clearly hadn't thought about when he was trying to throw everyone off her scent by being his usual crass self.

It was a mistake on his part.

And Andrei Petrov did not make mistakes.

I snorted out a laugh as I imagined a world where Andrei understood that while painful, physical touch also has the power to heal, and I wondered if there was another woman in this life, like my wife, who had the patience to teach him just that.

"Good luck, crazy bastard, good fucking luck," I whispered into the air as the gates opened and I slammed the accelerator.

CHAPTER SEVENTEEN

Andrei

For the first time in my life, I panicked.

How had I not looked past the title of girlfriend and given her a job? Hell, bartender would have even been better than whore.

But with the way she looked in that dress.

With the reputation I tended to like an obsessive-compulsive freak.

They wouldn't believe I'd taken a bartender to dinner, would they? Or a waitress. No, I was too dirty. Too far gone. I would bring a whore to a family dinner in front of their children.

I, Andrei Petrov, would do that, because I laughed at their silly Italian code, because I didn't care about love or family or any of the things they found necessary for survival.

But her face.

Fuck, her face killed me.

And then she'd asked for more wine, and I had the most intense need to either laugh or kiss her senseless for being brave when she needed to be, despite being angry and hurt, despite wanting to strangle me with the napkin on her lap.

And I didn't make a habit of kissing women when I could avoid it.

They were always disappointed I didn't do more.

Disappointed that I didn't follow up the kiss with my mouth everywhere else, with our bodies moving in sync.

When I kissed a woman it was for a reason.

Not for a want.

Or a damn need.

We were driving back to the club when my phone rang, I wasn't surprised it was Phoenix, he knew me better than most. I was, however, surprised he was calling so soon.

Six thirty-two had scooted all the way across the leather seat and was staring out the window like a shooting star would solve her problems.

How she was able to even sit there with her head held high was beyond me. How she kept that look of wonder in her eyes.

And I was the bastard that was making it worse.

"She's not a whore." The first thing Phoenix said when I answered the phone. He was quiet after that, reading the tension across the phone as he always did, gauging my breathing to see how I'd react. He was the mentor I'd never asked for, the man who had taken over for Luca, who watched over me and made sure I kept to my shit and didn't lose what was left of my soul in the process.

He was also the only man alive who understood the pain of being raised in a prostitution ring. Only he had been forced to break the virgins in, while I was only forced to watch while my dad did the honors.

"No." My voice was clipped, my answer short.

"She looks familiar." Bastard was baiting me, I almost smiled.

"She's a new acquisition, haven't decided if I'll let her go with the other girls in a few weeks or keep her for myself."

Six thirty-two stiffened, her hands gripped the leather seat like she was trying to calm herself down or maybe keep herself from grabbing her heel and impaling me with it.

Phoenix sighed. "Right, keep her for yourself, so what? You can stare at her? We both know how you are; you can't hide that shit from me, I was born in it, I breathe it, I'll die in it."

I squeezed my eyes shut. "I don't want to talk about it."

"Tough shit," he snapped. He rarely snapped with me. He knew that anger only made me more indifferent. "You can't go on like this, you're worse than a sexless robot."

I barked out a laugh. "What the hell does that even mean?"

"It means, one day you're going to lose it, and it's going to be ugly, and you're going to hurt whoever is on the other end of your rage, I would hate to hear that it's that pretty girl who looks like she'd rather play with Serena and Junior than talk with the wives. A girl whose strength is completely born out of necessity, and whose eyes hold no hope whatsoever when she looks at you. That, would be tragic."

Her brother had done that to her, not me. I wasn't the guilty one. I hadn't taken her innocence, and I never would.

"Calling the kettle black a bit, aren't you?"

"I own my darkness." Phoenix stood. "I embrace it with both arms. You, my friend, justify it."

He hung up on me.

I wanted my knife.

I wanted to justify throwing it into his back.

Phoenix just had to offer up his advice, didn't he?

I wondered if she knew that I'd made a pact to keep the families safe, that I would die to protect the wives, the children. That I had two jobs: figure out how to take down this club, the last club my father owned, once and for all, and make sure that the wives were never left unprotected if anything happened to their husbands.

I secretly loved them.

I secretly respected them.

And I would take that secret to my grave. My intense need to protect them from a fate she'd already faced.

It's why I'd taken time out of my busy schedule to warn Luc of Chase's darkness, of his need to kill every last remaining De Lange.

I tried to save Luc.

And I almost failed.

"You did good, tonight, six thirty-two, very good." I reached for her, put my hand on her thigh only for her to jerk away from me.

"You should have told me from the beginning… that I'd traded one owner for another, one master for another… you shouldn't have cleaned me, shouldn't have fed me. You should have let me bleed while I serviced you. He was right you know… I'm nothing but a whore."

"Stop the car." I was barely in control of my rage. "Stop the fucking car!"

The car jerked to a stop along the highway. I grabbed her by the arm and pulled her out to the gravel road and slammed her against the side of the vehicle.

She squeezed her eyes shut.

And turned her head away.

I cupped her chin, forcing her to look at me as I reached for her breasts, shoving my other hand inside her coat and running it down her hips until I gripped her ass.

She let out a shriek before I slammed my mouth against hers, I wasn't thinking beyond teaching her a lesson as I dug my fingers into her hair, deepening the kiss, forcing her to open her mouth while I drank.

I jerked my head away and whispered coldly in her ear. "A whore would have moaned, not shrieked, a whore would have given me a price. A whore would have spread…" I gripped her thighs and stepped between her legs spreading them apart. "Just like this." I rested my head against her neck. "You're not a whore. I just needed them to think you are." I stepped back. "Satisfied?"

I didn't see it coming.

Because I didn't expect her to fight.

Not until I felt the sting of her slap across my cheek as her fingertips burned into my ice-cold skin.

"Now I'm satisfied," she hissed.

We locked eyes; hers were filled with barely restrained blue fury as she stared me down.

"I can't decide…" I trailed my gloved finger down her jaw and dragged it across her bottom lip. "What I enjoyed more. The kiss or the slap."

"I can demonstrate the slap again if you want."

I smirked. "No, that's okay."

Her lower lip trembled.

Shit.

I hung my head and muttered. "Get in the car, Alice."

It wasn't until we pulled up to the club that I realized, I

didn't say "six thirty-two."

And as the door opened to let me out, I realized.

I'd suddenly done the unthinkable.

And made it personal.

Fucking Phoenix.

CHAPTER EIGHTEEN

Alice

My hands were shaking as Andrei led me back into the club, back to the prison, back to the place where he'd most likely take advantage of me just like my brother did, then toss me when he got bored.

His kiss proved nothing.

It was to punish me.

To show me his place.

To remind me of mine.

And I hated that I liked the way his lips felt.

The way my body responded when it absolutely shouldn't have. It's why I slapped him, because I was angry and embarrassed that he would use it against me when he had to know what it cost me to give it.

What it cost me to even reveal it.

I kept my stare straight ahead as he grabbed me by the hand and led me past couples making out in the hall. The women all wore black and red, and on their ankles were the little lock tattoos, something every single one of them had in common.

A reminder that they were owned?

Chained without actual chains?

"The tattoos," I whispered. "Do I get one?"

Andrei stopped walking, causing me to crash into his back. I recovered just in time for his icy blue stare to lock on mine. "Is that what you want?"

I gulped. "What I want is to be free, and I don't like pain so no I don't want a tattoo. I'm just asking so I can mentally prepare myself."

He let out a sigh that sounded more annoyed than angry. "We'll discuss this later."

"No." I stood my ground.

A muscle twitched in his jaw as he raised his right hand and gripped my chin, the leather gloves felt hot against my skin. "I said," he whispered coldly, "we'll discuss this later."

I didn't realize people were staring until he dropped his hand, and then he flashed me a smile so seductive, so endearing I almost turned around to make sure I wasn't mistaken that it was for me.

I frowned.

Only encouraging him more.

"Come." He pulled me roughly into his arms and kissed my neck.

I sucked in a breath as his hot kisses moved down to my collarbone, pulling my fur to the side while he toyed with the material of the dress. My knees almost buckled as he assaulted me with something so simple.

A kiss.

He sucked on my collarbone, his tongue swirling along my skin and causing goose bumps to erupt up and down my body.

I trembled in his arms, and then his lips were on my ear. "Remember what I said… they need to see ownership, or you're fair game. And if you're fair game, you can expect one of those ugly tattoos within the hour, so decide…"

"Decide?" I said it too breathlessly.

He chuckled darkly. Bastard. I hated him. I hated him.

"Are you mine?" He pressed his body against mine and walked me backward toward a wall then grabbed my hands, pinning them over my head as he continued his assault on my left shoulder. My fur coat dropped to my waist as he used his teeth and tongue to kiss along my other collarbone.

"Do I have a choice?"

"It's me or them," he hissed, then bit my skin enough to leave a mark as he stopped kissing me and pressed his forehead to mine. "That's as bad as it gets with me, *dorogaya*."

My body swayed as he pressed against me, making it hard to breathe, hard to think. He was solid muscle and radiating sex like he was used to getting exactly what he wanted and knew all the tricks to get there.

"Come," he snapped, releasing my hands and wrapping an arm around me. We walked through the VIP section of the club, past a security guy with dark hair and light blue eyes. He looked from me to Andrei and then stepped in front of Andrei when he tried to open a solid silver door.

"Boss." He crossed his arms. "We have men entertaining in the vault."

"Better she see it now than later, better she know now," he muttered. "Open the damn door."

"Right away, Boss." He pushed away from the door and slid

a card over it. "Did you want me to bring you champagne?"

"We won't be staying long, Ax."

"Hmm." Ax eyed me up and down again and then nodded. "Am I adding to my list of secrets and favors, Russian?"

"May as well." Andrei grumbled. "We all die someday."

"That we do." Ax sighed. "Blood in, no out."

"*Sangue in non mai fuori,*" Andrei repeated.

Blood in, never out. His Italian was flawless, like he'd been born speaking the language.

I gaped and then was pulled through the dark corridor and into a small space with nothing but windows overlooking a huge concrete area. The glass looked super thick, and when I looked to the left and right there were several other boxes that looked like this one, like something you'd see at a theater, with full red curtains ready to pull in front of the window.

"That," Andrei said in a lethal voice, "is what you get with them."

He pointed down at the cement looking stage.

"Nobody's down there."

He sighed, grabbed a small silver remote with two buttons, and hit the red one twice.

Slowly a curtain was pulled from the back of the stage and a woman hung there by her wrists bound over her head, wearing nothing but a ripped dress. She had a gag in her mouth, and the man in front of her had a cat tail whip in his hand.

Rock music blared in the sound system as the woman struggled, blood streamed from her face, making a trail all the way down her body as it dripped down her toes. Her eyes were wild as the man hit her across the thighs again and again, then dropped the whip and pulled off his blood stained shirt and jerked his pants down.

He had a similar remote to Andrei and hit a button, the woman was suddenly lowered, her hands still tied above her head.

The man walked up to her and flipped her around and started thrusting into her, as her blood caked his hands, the same hands running up and down her body.

"Enough." My voice shook as tears slid down my cheeks. "Make him stop!"

"I'm afraid I can't do that, *dorogaya*. He's paid for his time with her, and she's signed a contract she can't get out of."

"But he's raping her! He's going to kill her!"

"We have good doctors."

"That's what you say?!" I roared. "That you have good doctors? Are those doctors going to sew up her broken heart? Are they going to give her back her decency? Take away her humiliation? Her shame? Are they going to wipe her memory of this, so she doesn't wake up every night screaming?"

"No." Andrei pressed the red button as the curtain started moving around the window blanketing us in near darkness. "Our doctor will make her comfortable as she takes her last breath."

"You're a monster," I hissed, hating that I'd enjoyed his kiss and the way I felt in his arms when I'd already seen my fair share of horror at my brother's hands.

What the hell had I been thinking?

Letting this man touch me?

With blood on his hands.

This man who owned a place where women were sexual objects and looked forward to death!

"Make your choice, six thirty-two."

"Wh-what?"

"You have three seconds."

"What are you saying?"

"Monster." He gritted his teeth and took a step toward me, then pointed at the window. "Or man."

I sucked in a sharp breath, squeezed my eyes closed and whispered, "Monster."

CHAPTER NINETEEN

Andrei

I could feel her trembling next to me even though I wasn't touching her. I had to show her what her choices were, and yet, I still didn't give her the third option.

Death at the point of Chase's gun.

We made it back to my apartment quickly.

I shut the door.

I locked it.

And I watched as she dropped her fur coat on the back of the couch and then leaned over it, visibly trembling, like she needed to catch her breath, maybe say a prayer to a God who clearly wasn't listening all those times she was being touched by her brother.

A God who never listened when I begged for my own death, for solace every birthday.

We were a pair of souls that were never heard, lost, forgotten.

More in common than not.

As much as she would hate to know that.

"There is one more option..." I walked up to her and rested a gloved hand on her right shoulder slowly turning her body toward mine. "One that I haven't given you."

"What?" Her voice was hollow, her eyes dead as she stared down at the floor. That's when I knew: her brother hadn't stolen all of her hope. No, I had done that, I had stolen the last piece of hope in her body in order to keep her safe, in order to make her mine.

In order to save a life she seemed to not even want.

"Ask me," I whispered, my body straining to do something other than rest a fucking leather glove against her skin.

Like kiss her.

Tell her the words no one ever told me.

"It's going to be okay."

"It has to be."

Because that would be a lie.

And I couldn't do that to her.

Just as much as I couldn't live with the lie on my lips, released into the universe manifesting itself, twisting around us in its dark ugliness.

A tear slid down her cheek.

I caught it with my finger and cupped her face. "Ask me."

"If I die, he wins, and I can't let him win. You gave me his tongue after all... I'll see it through." She swayed toward me, I caught her with both hands and held her there, afraid of what would happen if I was pressed against her again, if I had to smell her, if I tasted her. It was ruining my calm facade, because she was so fucking good.

And I wasn't, was I?

I had a sex club where men killed women for pleasure.

And even though I saved who I could.

I fully damned the rest.

I was that man.

I wasn't a savior.

I was the monster she believed I was, and it would be cruel to make her think otherwise.

"And after you see this through, *dorogaya*?"

"What does that mean?" she snapped. "Whore in Russian?"

I would take that to my grave.

My very early grave.

Because a part of me, the part that still craved… something, couldn't call her six thirty-two all the time. But I couldn't utter her name again, not out loud, not when it felt so innocent falling from my lips.

And wrong, so wrong that I would do anything to protect her from what it meant… when a man like myself said a name out loud.

She finally lifted her head, glaring at me. Her anger was back. Good. It would help her survive. "Are you calling me a whore again?"

"That depends, are you spreading your legs for me?" I gripped one of her thighs with my hands. "It's an easy answer, since you're willing to bite off my ear before letting me pull any part of you apart, and believe me when I say, you'd enjoy it… immensely."

Her eyes searched mine. "I can't."

"Can't what?"

"Enjoy anything…" She gulped as her cheeks flushed. "That way."

My nostrils flared as I leaned in and whispered, "He should

die for that."

"According to you, he will."

I leaned back. "I'm not calling you a whore. It's a term of endearment."

Her eyes widened. "What sort of—"

I covered her mouth with my hand. "Your questions are exhausting. You," I said pointedly. "Even more so."

The fierceness of her gaze would feed me for days, the way she stiffened beneath my touch, ready to bite my fingers off.

Her fight.

It was her fight, wasn't it?

That and the way she lay on her bed like a fucking queen taking court, waiting for her loyal subjects to serve her.

She was magnificent, and she didn't even know it.

Better that way.

Better that she couldn't reach pleasure from a man.

Because I wasn't a man capable of giving her that.

"Tomorrow," she said in a quieter voice. "Are you just going to keep me locked up in here indefinitely? Now that I know I don't spread my legs for the great Andrei Petrov?"

I hated my last name.

Hated the memories it conjured up.

Men addressed my father by Petrov.

They addressed me by Andrei.

Putting the two together put me in a completely shitty mood, and I was already all the way there.

"Do whatever the hell you want, just stop asking so many questions. My trigger finger's been feeling… aggressive." I smirked.

She scowled and looked down.

I wanted more than anything for the fire to be directed at

me, not our shoes, but I was all out of demands to give and I knew if I kept engaging her, she'd never stop, and I needed sleep.

With a sigh, I stepped away and walked down the hall to my private room. I heard footsteps stomping after me around one second later. I made it as far as my door before I leaned against it and uttered. "What the hell could you possibly want?"

"A job."

I stared at the wood paneling and wondered if I'd ever been stunned into silence like that in my entire life.

And then I stared some more as I looked over my shoulder at the fire in her eyes. "A job?"

"I can't just sit around, that's what my brother and father did, they locked me, they—" Tears filled her eyes. "I'm not stupid, if I'm not your whore that means that I'm something, that means I'm either already dead or you're keeping me hidden to use me later, I get that, but until later happens, until I breathe my last breath, I'd like to do… something, anything! And if you say clean the kitchen…"

I smirked at that. "What? You don't like cleaning dishes?"

"Your dishes are spotless, and you know it."

"I like order."

She snorted.

"I also like being alone, and yet here we are."

"Yes. Here we are." She swallowed, gazed at my mouth for a few brief seconds, and then her eyes flickered away like she'd been caught doing something she shouldn't.

I ignored my own racing pulse right along with the fact that for some insane reason, I wanted to pull off my gloves and cup her face, hold her close and feel her pulse beneath her skin.

Shaking with rage that she would try to conjure that out of me, I spat, "What useless thing were you doing before they locked you up?"

She frowned. "I'm only twenty-one."

"I know."

"I was in school."

I grinned. "Eagle Elite?"

She sucked in a sharp breath. "They pulled me out."

"Because they wanted to keep you alive," I said plainly. "And we all know who runs the University."

"My family used to."

"Your fucking family is lucky to still be breathing, parasites, every single one of them."

"Better a parasite than a rapist and murderer," she snapped back at me.

I grabbed her by the throat and shoved her back against the wall. "I'm not the rapist." I released her throat and adjusted my jacket. "Get some sleep. I'll take care of everything."

"Everything?"

"Are you seriously going to question everything I do to keep you safe? Now I have to keep you entertained? I liked you better when you were afraid."

"I'm petrified!" she yelled. "But I'm out of options! I don't think I have anything left to lose!"

At that, I sighed. "Oh, sweetheart, you have no idea how much you have left to lose, not yet, and hopefully for you, not ever. I'd say a prayer tonight if I were you. Because the minute you were brought into this club, your clock started ticking, and one day time will run out. I'd pray for a miracle because even I can't protect you from them if they find out and decide to shoot."

She was silent then.

And for reasons I refused to contemplate, I leaned in and pressed a soft kiss to her cheek. "Be ready by eight."

She put a hand to her cheek and then dropped it.

My smile was smug as she jerked open the door to her bedroom and then slammed it in my face.

"Goodnight to you too," I said into the darkness, and then I went into my own fortress and stupidly stayed up too late wondering how I could make it so she was here a bit longer.

If only to aggravate me to death until I tried killing myself next year.

So much anger in those eyes.

So much life.

Huh, that's what it looked like.

Being human.

CHAPTER TWENTY

Alice

I didn't sleep.

I was too confused.

Too hurt.

Upset.

I had no life anymore, not that I'd had one before, I just didn't know how to navigate not only Andrei's mood swings but the fact that I knew if I pushed him too far he wouldn't hesitate in shooting me or torturing me. He gave off this vibe that humanity meant nothing to him, and looking at what he ran, I understood it, finally understood why he called himself a monster.

I shivered under the covers and finally threw them over and got up. I'd slept in the stupid dress because I didn't have anything else to sleep in, and I didn't want to piss him off again by asking to borrow a shirt.

I was just about ready to walk across the hall to the

bathroom when I noticed a note on my closet door.

"Open."

That's all it said, "open."

Creepy. Was he in there last night? Watching me sleep like Twilight gone bad? I shivered again then walked over to the closet door and swung it open. Immediately, a light turned on.

I gasped.

Tons of jeans, leggings, shirts, sweaters, dresses, enough clothing that it would have taken someone at least an hour or two to hang everything.

How had he done it in the middle of the night?

I walked into the closet and did a small circle. Heels, Nikes, sandals. Did that mean I was staying longer than a few days? Did that mean he was going to give me a job or something to do?

I didn't have time to think beyond that, because there was a knock on my door and then Andrei was letting himself in.

"Good, you found clothes." He sounded bored.

I put my hands on my hips and then realized I probably looked like I'd been run over by a truck, dark circles under my eyes and messy hair, wearing last night's tight dress.

Perfect.

He stared at my toes then slowly made his way up, his expression somber, and then a small smile. "Trouble sleeping?"

"You could say that," I said through clenched teeth.

"I have a doctor in the family. I'll grab you something to help you sleep."

I narrowed my eyes. "Would I wake up?"

"Depends." He leaned against the closet door. "Would you want to?"

I scowled, irritated that he always had to make everything

about death and darkness and couldn't just have a normal conversation.

Then again, nothing about him was normal.

He was wearing black skinny jeans, a V-Neck shirt that showed off an expanse of tattoos on his chest and his blond hair was combed a bit to the side, he looked.

Nice.

In fact, I hated it.

He looked approachable.

Like the really hot guy you see at the mall and daydream about after you make a fool out of yourself stalking him and trying to snag a picture for Instagram.

He held out a hanger.

And on that hanger.

Was my freedom.

Or as much freedom as I would ever get offered.

I stumbled toward him and grabbed the hanger. "An Eagle Elite uniform?"

"Mmm." He tilted his head. "Wouldn't want the princess to get bored in her dark tower."

I instantly felt guilty. "Look, I appreciate what you did, rescuing me from—"

He moved so fast I didn't have a chance to prepare for it. He cupped a hand over my mouth, his eyes flashing with fury. "Never, *ever* say that again. I'm not the hero. Remember that when you close your eyes, when you want to say thank you. I'm as selfish as they come, as lethal as can be, and nothing on this godforsaken earth is free. Do. You. Understand?"

I nodded.

He didn't move.

His face suddenly paled as he looked down.

What was he looking at?

And that's when I realized.

He wasn't wearing gloves.

His hand was touching my mouth.

Skin on skin.

He was warm.

Why did I expect him to be so cold? Why did I assume he'd be unfeeling? Instead, he was buzzing with warmth, his fingertips giving off zaps of pleasure that made absolutely no sense as we stood there at a standstill, me trying to figure out if he was going to lose it and him probably trying to keep from doing exactly that.

He inhaled slowly.

Exhaled.

And yet he didn't move his hand.

Tension built between us. His body had grown taut with something I couldn't really define, but there was a violence in his stillness, like a storm ready to rain hell.

I wasn't sure what to do, so I stared him down, and I breathed, I kept in cadence with his breaths and then the little light in the closet turned off, probably from our lack of movement.

His hand stayed, he lowered his head, then slowly slid his palm across my face. It fell to my cheek as he cupped it. His fingertips were soft, his movement silky.

"You're too warm," he whispered like it was a problem, like he didn't understand why it was a problem, just that it was. His head ducked again. This time, his cheek pressed to mine, his lips parted.

I closed my eyes.

Berating myself for feeling anything other than horror that

he was touching me, the man who would kill me, the man who was both savior and Satan.

"So fucking warm." He nipped my lower lip.

I gasped as he pressed his hard body against mine and slid his tongue past my lower lip.

This wasn't him.

This kiss.

This was something else.

This was almost tender.

This felt scorching and heartbreaking all at once, as he tilted his head and deepened the kiss, his hand never leaving my face, his body pinning mine to the wall. I felt him everywhere, through his clothes, the heat of his body, the strength of his muscles, and the way he seemed to control even the air around us as he kissed me deeply drank even deeper, made me react in a way I wanted to be embarrassed about as I gripped his shirt, wondering what I was doing when I hated any sort of male touch.

But his touch was the first touch I'd had from the opposite sex that wasn't mocking.

It was tender.

And it was breaking my heart more than the other kisses ever did.

The light flickered on.

He stopped kissing me, stepped away, ran shaky hands through his hair, and snapped. "Put on the damn uniform."

And then he was gone.

And everything went back to normal in my mind. Because I knew, it was my fault. I was the one that had that effect on men, wasn't I?

That's what my brother said.

It's what my dad said was my curse.

I was doing this to him, right?

My fault. My fault.

My only solace was that he didn't try to touch me, and that for once in my life, I could imagine, I could dream, and I could lie to myself that the kiss was real.

When I knew, he would hate himself for it, the way he hated me.

Just like everyone hated me.

For being nothing but me.

A woman born in the wrong family.

With the wrong name.

And pretty hair.

With tears in my eyes, I grabbed the uniform shoved into my hands then very slowly hung it up and started to change.

CHAPTER TWENTY-ONE

Andrei

My hands wouldn't stop shaking as I grasped my phone between them and sat on the couch, my knees bumping up and down like I needed another hit of something before I lost my mind.

I couldn't stop shaking.

Couldn't stop feeling her warm skin.

No matter how bad I wanted to.

I tasted her.

I felt her on me.

On my skin.

In the air I breathed.

I didn't know how to handle it.

Because in all my twenty-two years it had never happened before, I'd never had such a violent reaction to another human, so aggressive that I would hurt her, I would hurt her to get more, so I yelled, so I stepped away to protect her from me.

Shit.

My phone lit up with a text from Phoenix.

Phoenix: How goes hell?

Me: You tell me.

Nixon, Chase, Sergio, Dante, and Tex were added. Perfect. Just Perfect. I was having a midlife crisis at twenty-two, and they wanted me in on another group text?

Phoenix: You seem... strained. Doesn't he, guys? Like his whore maybe isn't giving him what he really, really, really needs.

Me: Don't make me kill you.

Phoenix: Huh, you're probably already dead inside, or did your heart do a little... flutter?

Tex: Flutter? What the hell is a flutter? It should do a hell of a lot more than flutter, my man, like think of your dick as a...

Sergio: The fact that I have to interrupt this and explain human anatomy should shock me. It doesn't. And Tex re-read, he was talking about his heart, you ass, not his dick. Though, I get why you'd be so focused on yours since it's so small...

Chase: Burnnnnn

Nixon: Yes, let's bring that back, burn... Are we twelve?

Me: Is there a reason you guys decided to come in and ruin my day by traumatizing me about Tex's dick or is this just another Wednesday?

Phoenix: Wednesday.

Dante: I can't get flutter out of my head.

Nixon: Same, man, same.

Me: I've never fluttered, not once, and I'm pretty sure flutter and dick shouldn't be in the same sentence. I'm leaving gossip hour; I have shit to do.

Phoenix: We know... because as of midnight last night the Eagle Elite computer system was hacked, and a girl by the name of Alice was added as a junior.

I thought I'd have more time, good thing I hadn't added in her last name yet. They'd think it was a clerical error and then I would lay out my cards.

Me: Oh?

Chase: It's almost insulting when you play dumb, dumb ass, besides thought her name was Black Widow?

I grinned down at my phone, my shaking subsided just barely when I thought of pissing Chase off.

Me: She was bored. And the idea of her cleaning toilets and sucking dick wasn't very appealing.

Phoenix: Oh, so she's been servicing you and your toilets? Interesting.

Sergio: I don't buy it.

Nixon: You barely touched her.

Chase: You literally kept your gloves on the entire time you were touching her, and I know why, we all know why you don't like human contact but when you have a beautiful woman in your arms that reasoning kind of dies a very quick death.

Tex: Between boobs.

Dante: I don't think his hands should be just like, laying between her boobs, guys. Don't give him false information. Plus, we all know he's an ass guy.

Phoenix: Do we, though?

Me: Is there a point to this?

Sergio: Just that if you wanted her enrolled it would make sense to come to us and get it done.

I sighed, hanging my head a bit as I typed back.

Me: Full disclosure, we got in a fight. I was trying to make it better by doing it faster than your grandpa hands could.

Tex: Haha get it, because he's old as fuck!

Sergio: Can someone put a muzzle on Tex?

Phoenix: You should have let us know, given us a heads up.

Me: Well, I figured I can't fly under the radar anymore, may as well ask for forgiveness than permission. Plus, you know I don't like using too many words. Hurts my throat, and I'd rather have something else that deep if you get my meaning.

Chase: It's really no shock that you're single.

Dante: None at all.

Tex: How deep?

Sergio: My. God. You're an asshole.

Nixon: Look, just shoot us a text next time. When are you going in? Phoenix set up the new dean at the beginning of the semester. It's one of the Abandonato cousins who doesn't have a stomach for blood.

My eyebrows shot up.

Me: And they think they won't see blood at EE? That's hilarious. What did you do? Lie to him repeatedly and promise him nothing but staff meetings and teacher luncheons for the rest of his days?

Nixon: Er, something like that.

Me: Let me know how that works out for you when he runs away screaming from all the bloody bodies and guns.

Chase: It's more refined now that the De Langes are less of a problem.

Me: Right.

Phoenix: Let us know if you need anything, and for future reference, if your girl's mad at you, it's probably because you called her a whore during family dinner.

Me: Why would I lie to you?

Nixon: Why... indeed?

Me: Nixon, I say this out of both love and hate, go shoot something before you lose your temper. We get in a fight, and I end your life.

Tex: This I would pay to see.

Me: I don't have all day to take out all the Italians, that would take more planning, but I do have time to take a girl who's still pissed off to school where I'm going to piss her off more.

Phoenix: Fingers crossed she doesn't draw first blood.

Too late, she already did. I stared down at my phone and almost typed those words.

It was an odd thing to think.

Me: I have it under control.

Dante: Doubtful. Highly doubtful.

Dante might have gone to school with me for a few months but he didn't know me, not in that way. He only knew me as the part I played, his enemy, to flush out the double-crossing.

He had no clue the sort of man I was now.

The things I would do.

The guilt I felt.

I tossed my phone against the couch as Alic—six thirty-two made it down the hall in her short black skirt, black and red jacket, and white shirt. She had a pair of black nylons on and high heels that made her legs go on for days.

I licked my lips and stood, looking away and fishing my phone from the couch. "Ready?"

"Yeah, I was…" She sighed. "Wondering if you had a protein bar or something—"

She covered her stomach with her hand.

I immediately felt like shit, again.

Her hand was shaking.

Did she have low blood sugar?

Why the hell did I care?

She was a product.

A thing.

Barely human.

So fucking warm.

I squeezed my eyes shut and leaned against the countertop, sucked in a few deep breaths and then rasped out, "Yeah, one sec."

I went to the cupboard and grabbed a few protein bars then realized that she'd probably need lunch too.

How the hell had I turned into this guy in the span of twenty-four hours? From calling her a whore to making sure she had a sack lunch?

Phoenix would shit a brick and then break a rib from laughing so hard.

"Thanks." She took the bars.

I grabbed the bag I'd had Ax buy for me first thing that morning, I was trying to go for something that wouldn't look too expensive and had probably failed since it was Gucci, but I liked things that looked nice, that complimented each other, and I liked the idea of her with white leather. She had everything she'd need in there except—

With a curse I reached for my wallet and pulled out two crisp hundred dollar bills.

Blood money.

Stained with mine and theirs.

"Here." I held it out.

She stared down at it and then swallowed slowly. "Nothing's free."

"Pardon?"

"You said that last night. Nothing's free, everything has a cost, what's my cost for this? For your kindness? For the clothes? For lunch money? I need to know, so I can process what it means I have to do. I know I'm in deep. I know this is my life now. The least you can do is just tell me. Please." She lifted her head; her gaze was unwavering.

I had a sudden image of her dropping to her knees and was so fucking appalled I stumbled backward and turned away from her.

"Dinner," I said smoothly. "You're in charge of cooking dinner, every night, at six o'clock, until I tell you it's been paid off."

I could hear her exhale. "Okay, I can do that."

"We're going to be late." I grabbed the keys off the counter and walked ahead of her, opening the door and waiting.

She took one look at the door, then her gaze flicked to me, and she held her head high and walked out.

So regal that I found myself smiling after her.

Her posture didn't change as we moved through the near-empty club, and when we reached outside, Ax was already at her side opening the door to my black and silver Aston Martin.

She hesitated a minute and then slid into the seats while

I walked around to the driver's side and got in, roaring the engine to life.

I'd missed driving lately.

And I didn't want to show up in a giant Escalade that screamed mafia, better to show up in a car worth three million dollars and scream wealthy.

Money was safer.

Money looked dangerous.

Money made me look more normal, and when mafia showed up it was typically in all black with guns strapped to their bodies.

I'd show up with my knife and still do more damage.

The sound of Avenged Sevenfold filled the air as I hit the accelerator and whizzed past two cops who both waved. We flew by an ambulance.

She gripped the sides of the seat as I peeled around the corner and pulled in front of the iron gate at Eagle Elite.

Why hadn't Dante burned the place down?

The question I think all of us asked once he was done doing his duty, the question I asked myself when I was told I could leave.

The gates opened.

Trees lined the sides of campus as I sped down the lane and then took a right for the registration building.

He would be waiting for us.

It would be easy.

She would be protected here.

From everything.

My bare hands included.

The guys would look the other way. They'd be curious but they wouldn't think I would hide her in plain sight like I was doing. According to them I still had a De Lange girl prisoner, and Alice was just someone I had an interest in.

It would be fine.

I gripped the steering wheel and wondered why I was sacrificing so much… for so little.

After all a woman was a pawn.

An object.

And yet.

This one reminded me of them.

Of the wives.

Of their strength.

And I couldn't stop.

Just couldn't fucking stop.

The rabbit hole had me sucked in its grasp, and I was still falling without a clue as to what was at the bottom.

I parked the car and got out then went and opened her door. She seemed confused by this as I held out my hand.

My gloves were gone, they would look ridiculous with what I was wearing, and again, it would look too conspicuous.

I wasn't a boss here.

Here I was just another rich guy.

Not that every single staff member wouldn't know who I was, just like the dean was probably already holding out his prayer beads and chanting.

Students walked around, some stared, others looked away like they knew it was dangerous to be too curious.

And the whole time, I clutched her warm hand.

Felt her palm pressed against mine.

Warred with the need to do something about it.

With the strange tingle in my chest that made its way down my arms and legs like I was slowly burning from the inside out.

"Walk faster," I snapped. I couldn't hold her hand forever, I couldn't even hold it for a few seconds without losing touch with reality.

We finally made it to the front steps and walked up. The building was solid brick, three stories, and looked completely innocent despite all the crimes that it had been involved in.

I grinned when a staff member opened the door to us and then quickly jogged away like I was going to impale him with my knife.

And slowly as we walked down the hall, doors closed. No, they slammed like they were afraid I was going to stop and ask for directions or just stop and start shooting.

My reputation, it seemed, preceded me.

Nice.

We finally made it to the dean's office.

The secretary, Mrs. Derullio, looked up, eyes wide. "We weren't sure if we should be expecting you or not."

"Do you not have a phone?" I asked just as one started ringing.

With shaking hands, she answered and nodded. "Yes, sir, yes, I'll tell him." She hung up. "The dean says he's expecting you."

I winked. "Thought so, nice sweater." It was horrible but she didn't need to know that. That shade of green would make anyone look sick.

"Oh, thank you." She smiled wider.

I grinned and led six thirty-two to the door just as it opened. Bear Abandonato stood on the other side. I wasn't really sure what his real name was. All I knew was that he had a reputation for being like a big teddy bear, hated confrontation, and wasn't for the life, despite his height of six-foot-seven, and weight of three fifty-two pounds.

The guy was a beast.

"Come on in." He beamed down at Alice. "I'm so happy you could join us this semester..." He looked briefly at his paper. "...Alice." And then he frowned. "I'm sorry, it seems we don't have a last name for you," He grabbed a handy pen and looked up at her with hopeful eyes.

Alice stiffened.

Her hand gripped mine so tight I was ready to outwardly react.

Woman had grip strength that was for sure.

"Petrov," I volunteered. "Alice Petrov."

"Oh!" Bear's smile could not, manage to get any bigger, "Didn't know you had another sister, Mr. Petrov."

I smiled mockingly at him. "Oh, I don't."

"Cousin."

"Most of them are dead."

"I see." He frowned. "So, she's... a niece?"

"No. Actually." I beamed at Alice and very slowly lifted her hand to my lips, inside shaking with... something. "She's my wife."

Alice gaped and then shut her mouth. The minute my lips touched her skin, she sucked in a breath.

"Ah, in the honeymoon phase still, I see." Bear winked.

Alice snatched her hand away and nodded. "Yes, it's new..." She shot me a glare. "Some might even say, hardly any time has gone by that we've been... together."

"Seems that way, doesn't it?" I laughed, enjoying her obvious hatred toward me and the idea of being my wife. For some reason it gave me pleasure just as much as the touch of her skin.

"Yes." She clenched her teeth. "It really does."

I leaned in and whispered in her ear. "Don't burn my dinner tonight… Alice."

She put a hand to her chest when I said her name out loud, like it did something to her heart, like she didn't want to hear me say it, because it conjured up a reaction.

My instincts told me it was a way to control her.

While what was left of my heart, told me it was a way to win her.

"All right, then," Bear pulled out a folder. "Here's your schedule for the semester, you should report to Econ, it's starting in the next ten minutes, right across from here in the tan building."

"Okay." She took the paper and stood. "Thank you, Mr. Bear."

"Bear, Abandonato, whatever you wanna call me." He smiled brightly while I felt her stiffen again.

"Thanks again." I shook his hand and then escorted her back out of the office and down the hall. Her body was tense, too tense.

When we made it outside, I grabbed her hand and jerked her down the stairs and to the side of the building. "Listen," I barked and gripped her chin between my thumb and forefinger. "You said you wanted something to do. This is better than cleaning toilets. Finishing your education, right in front of your enemy, they won't suspect it and you've already passed the test with flying colors last night."

"Why are you telling me this?" She licked her lips. "I'm not scared."

My eyebrows shot up. "So, you're petrified of being in

my apartments back at the club, but here, in the middle of a swarm of enemies who want nothing more than to see you dead, you feel… fantastic?"

She just shrugged.

"Clearly, I need to try harder. Buy more clothes, offer more freedom, tell you how beautiful you are, is that what you want? Compliments? Things?"

"I want a life."

"You can't have a life," I said through clenched teeth. "And what you have is what I give you. Do you understand?"

"Y-yes."

"The minute they brought you through those doors, you lost every option given to you, the only ones that are left I control. Last night you chose me, don't make me regret asking."

She snorted out a laugh. "That wasn't asking! That was threatening!"

"That…" I narrowed my eyes. "…was more efficient than begging you on hands and knees…"

"Perhaps," She lifted a shoulder. "But one would have given you much more… pleasant results."

It was on the tip of my tongue to ask her what she meant.

And then I realized she was smiling at me.

A dazzling, controlling smile.

Manipulation.

I leaned in and kissed the side of her neck. She went stiff in my arms, her hands shaking. "I'm the king of manipulation, of every single game you could possibly conjure up. The day I'm in front of you, on my hands and knees, will be the day I take my last fucking breath. I submit to no one."

She leaned up on her tiptoes and brushed a similar kiss to my neck and then turned her head and pressed a soft kiss on the corner of my mouth and said. “We’ll see.”

I gripped her arm.

We both glared at one another.

“Don’t play games you can’t win, six thirty-two.”

“Don’t start what you can’t finish, Petrov.”

And then she was gone.

CHAPTER TWENTY-TWO

Alice

I was completely out of my element, my old friends had already graduated and were off to bigger and better things, and at the time I'd been so completely freaked out and isolated that even the teachers hadn't known my full name.

I was that girl.

The one in the back.

Always in the back.

Or the one you waved at because she looked familiar but never really hung out with because she looked too lonely.

Fun.

But at least I was doing something.

And I was outside.

I smiled to myself as I made my way to Econ, partially because I was excited he was giving me what freedom I had, and partially because I felt the control between us slip, not by much, only enough for me to hear the slight intake of breath when I kissed him on the mouth.

Everything about Andrei said stand down and make sure you put at least three feet of distance between us, and every time I got close, he either physically pushed me away or yelled.

There was meaning behind everything he did, everything he wore, the way he spoke to people, the words he used. He was right in saying he was a master manipulator, and I wondered if anyone had ever been brave enough to utter the word no in his presence and actually mean it.

Yet another reason why when he claimed me as his wife, I knew I was stuck, and as long as it wasn't real, I was fine.

I shivered. The very fact that he gave me his name enraged me, and then it filled me with a feeling I refused to acknowledge, one that told me I meant something. I was important enough for him to take an identity and place it on me, claim me as his.

I tried not to think of his kiss, his reaction, the way his lips slid across mine in a way I'd never experienced before.

I could count the tiny breaths he took between each assault, the way his muscles flexed beneath my fingertips like any second he was going to slam me against the wall harder and rip my clothes off.

The thought should terrify me.

Except it was different; his kiss was different.

Or maybe I was just glamorizing the fact that I was being held hostage, sold by a family who used me, to a new master who would end up doing the exact same thing.

The idea deflated me as I made my way into class and sat down in the very back.

Students trickled in.

Nobody looked my way.

And I wondered what made me so invisible to the people

around me. When I was punished by those closest to me by being seen?

To everyone else I was a nobody.

But my own family? They punished me for things I couldn't control.

And Andrei, seemed angry at his own reaction.

What was so special about a girl with blackish brown hair and blue eyes? What's so special about me?

And sadly.

Even after two different classes.

I came up with absolutely nothing.

CHAPTER TWENTY-THREE

Andrei

I drove like hell back to the club, pissed that she saw it, the slip, for one brief second she'd shocked the hell out of me, and she knew it too.

Well played, six thirty-two, well played.

I got out of the car and made my way into the bar, waving Ax over. "Any changes with the girls today?"

He sighed and jerked his head to the right. "New batch came in around two a.m., same blacked out plates, same make and model of the car. With so many people living in this area, hell people living outside it, we still can't place the car, but…" He shifted on his feet a bit. "We did get some intel from one of the girls…"

"What?" I crossed my arms. "Other than screaming, what did she offer?"

Ax paled a bit and then whispered, "She said she's known your father since she was seventeen."

I didn't move. Didn't flinch, even though somewhere, deep down, I knew who it was, I knew she would have bright blond hair and a pretty smile, I knew she would have icy blue eyes. I knew she would be older. I knew she would look like Andi, and I knew why.

"Tell no one," I snapped. "And take me to her now."

"Already have her waiting in the purple lounge by herself, Boss."

"This is why you're my favorite," I muttered under my breath. "You don't wait to get told shit."

"Waiting gets you killed, Drei. You know this, I know this, and you'd start a war with my family if you killed me. I'm sorta fucking useful."

I rolled my eyes. "And there's that Abandonato arrogance."

"One of our best traits." He grinned. "You want the cameras on?"

I bit my lip. "Not this time."

He gave me a funny look. "If you're sure."

"I'm sure you should go take a break."

"You're not gonna kill her?"

"Why would I kill someone valuable?"

"Oh, I don't know, Drei, because you've lost your temper over a fucking french fry before."

I rolled my eyes. "That was a year ago, and I was hungry."

He sighed. "Let me call one of the guys."

He was being rational.

Then again, he hadn't just been kissed and played by a woman who should be dead. Who had a giant target on her back.

I exhaled through my lips. "Fine, call Phoenix."

"I call Phoenix, Phoenix calls Tex…"

I pinched the bridge of my nose with my fingertips. "Call them all but tell them I won't wait. They have twelve minutes."

I heard a sound behind me and went still.

"I may have already told them." Ax grinned. "See? I'm needed."

"Go be arrogant somewhere else where I'm not tempted to strangle you, mmkay?"

"Good talk." He slapped me on the back just as all the Italian bosses walked in with a few of their men and captains.

My bartender looked ready to duck under the table.

It was rare to have all of them here at once.

Then again, we'd been trying to take down the ring for a decade. So, it was necessary, especially if we had information.

"How was school?" Tex asked wrapping an arm around me tight, as he pulled a toothpick out of his mouth and grinned.

"How's the tiny dick?" I snapped right back.

Dante strolled up. "It could be there but nobody has seen it, kind of like bed bugs… you wake up with a bite, but if you can't see them, are they really there?"

Chase smirked. "Dante comparing Tex's dick to bed bugs, I don't think I've ever been so proud of my protégé."

"Except that one time when he killed two people with one bullet." Nixon held out his hand. "Ax called us right away figured we should do this as a team, since that's what we are… right Andrei?" He narrowed his eyes. "A team… that shares information? Regardless of how damning?"

He knew threatening me only made me more indifferent. I raised an eyebrow and smirked. "Someone not getting any?"

Sergio and Phoenix were talking about something in hushed tones before giving me equally blank stares. Where Sergio had a man bun and was wearing black slacks and a dress shirt, Phoenix was in ripped jeans and a black tank top that matched the black tattoos on his arms. His hair was a little longer than usual and he looked just as cold and callous as ever. "We all here?"

"Vic's got the front." Phoenix crossed his arms. "Who's asking questions?"

"Me," I barked. "My club, my rules, and try to keep your guns in your pants, we're a bit more civilized."

Tex bit out a curse. "I'll believe it when I see it."

I shoved the metal door open.

And there she was.

Looking every bit as pretty as she had when I saw her the first time, when she forced me to watch. Two. Hours.

"Son," Alexander Petrov wasn't a small man. "One day you'll do the honors, one day you'll get to feel how tight this is, how ready this woman is for me, see her face? You see it son? Watch her, watch what I steal from her."

She held me there for my own father, made me watch the way he made her watch. Like if she was going to be punished, so was I.

I learned how to see without seeing that day.

How to stare at something and see nothing at all.

Feel nothing at all.

She was seventeen.

And I was ten. I watched it while I was ten.

And all I remember thinking after it was done… Would he someday get angry enough to do that to me too?

I prayed that very night for God to take my soul.

And woke up completely crushed that I was still breathing.

She had cuts on her face, dirt marred the red streaks of the blood that had dried against her skin, her ice blue dress looked more like a slip than a dress making it painfully aware that she was pulled from bed. And since my father was currently a rotting corpse, that meant they either finally found her, she gave herself up, or she slept with the wrong guy.

"Elena." I said her name like the curse it was. The curse it had been to my life.

Her head lolled forward, a tired smile crossed her face. "Is that any way to talk to someone who used to hold you tight?"

I flexed my hands into fists. "Why are you here?"

"Does it look like I volunteered?" She spat blood on the concrete floor. "Ever since your father died, I've been in hiding, thanks for that by the way."

"Tragic, you should have just ended your misery and drank poison."

Her eyes narrowed into tiny slits as she nodded to the men behind me. "Friends of yours, traitor?"

"Traitor?" I barked out a laugh. "I have over a billion dollars at my fingertips, enough manpower to take you down without doing so much as sneezing, and you call me traitor? I can see it now, Alexander Petrov's paramour, sleeping her way through the brotherhood in order to survive. I hope they've been wearing a condom."

"Enough," she snapped. "I can't go to the FBI, so I came here."

"Because you think they hold me in such high esteem?"

"Don't patronize me. I know you have pull." She sniffled as blood dripped down her chin. "I want protection."

"You can buy condoms at the store. We done?"

"Don't be a smart ass. I remember when you used to kiss me with that mouth—"

I felt the tension pounding in my chest, the ache of being abandoned, the fucking need to have something human love me, touch me, and then her cold brittle hands, slapping the tears from my face, when all I wanted was their warmth.

"Only out of respect. I preferred your lips to his knife. Don't flatter yourself."

She glared up at me. "I know who's bringing in the girls, but I want protection. I want you to swear you'll give me protection. He still has men out there, men trying to run this crumbling empire, men who want nothing more than to take the remaining heir down and start up the rings again."

"I'm sure you do." I grinned. "But they'll have to come through me, and since none of them have the balls to even stand in the same room, it looks like I'm safe…"

"Offer me protection, damn it!" she roared.

I could feel the restlessness behind me. The guys liked to speak with their guns. Typically, I wouldn't tell them not to. Violence got us answers, but not out of a woman who was born into it, a woman who fed it, who encouraged a young boy to watch it.

A gun wouldn't faze her.

Blood was almost like her natural color.

And as much as I wanted to lie and say I would offer her protection; my word was everything.

Besides, I didn't want her near me.

I turned and gave the guys a curious look. "Did you know that the Bullet Ant gained its name because the pain is so severe it feels like you've been shot? A tiny miniscule bite and scientists say you'll beg for death." I walked to the opposite end of the room and spread the purple curtain wide.

Four glass cases stood waiting.

"Naturally, some men prefer extreme pain when they're having sex, so I like to keep some of the best around, just in case." I sighed and put on the leather gloves next to the case. "Twenty-four hours, that's how long you suffer, and the best part, really the best part of the bite?" I reached into the cage and grabbed one tiny ant and held it between my thumb and forefinger. "It's hardly noticeable and what police officer would believe you anyway? Oh, I got bit by an ant, the Russians are coming." My voice was detached, my emotions gone. All I felt for this woman had been slapped out of me every time she told me she wished I wasn't born.

Every time I asked her to pick me up and she said I was dirty.

Every time I froze in my room and she refused to give me an extra blanket.

My father created me.

She molded the clay.

The guys all backed up against the wall, equal parts amused and curious as I held the ant out to Elena. "Who's dropping off the girls?"

"Give me protection."

I sighed and stood. "You had to have known I wouldn't just let you make demands in my club, on my turf. I'm the fucking boss of the Petrov Family, I make the demands, the decisions. You…" I leaned in and whispered in her blood-caked ear. "Are lucky I'm even speaking to you without cutting off a finger first." I leaned back and tilted my head. "Who?"

"Protection!" she screamed.

I reared back and placed the ant on her leg.

And then I watched.

She went completely still.

"It won't bite unless provoked." I grinned. "Must be hard since you like to scream at things, hit them." I examined my gloves and shrugged. "Just try not to be yourself and you should be just fine."

"GO TO HELL!" she roared.

And then she let out an ear-piercing scream so loud that I was suddenly thankful the room was noise proof.

"It BIT ME!"

"I warned you." I smiled at the guys. "I'll let you know how things progress. We'll question her when she's able to speak without yelling, when she learns her manners, and most of all, when she learns who runs the fucking world."

I shoved the door open and waited for everyone to walk out, then I turned and locked it, leaning my body against it while the guys all faced me. "What?"

"The hell?" Tex roared. "You just keep those things? Like pets?"

I snorted. "Hardly. Sometimes customers use them. Don't ask me why, I'm not into that shit, I have more painful ways if this doesn't work, but she's always been petrified of ants and spiders, so, if this doesn't work, I'll go grab Mary and see if she can do better."

Nixon made a face. "I'm almost afraid to ask this."

"Mary's the grandma tarantula we keep behind the bar when we want to scare away the wrong customer so the right one walks up and spends more money than they should on alcohol." I checked my phone. "Mary gets a lot of screams, probably the best whore we have here."

Chase whistled. "Well, now that I'm completely creeped out by all the creepy things you have here—"

"Say creep one more time," Dante teased.

Chase gave him the finger. "You don't have any… tigers or shit in here do you?"

"Oh, I'm sorry did you want a tour?" I asked in a bored tone. "Or can I get back to work?"

"The club doesn't open for another few hours," Phoenix pointed out, damn it.

"I'm aware of that. I'm still busy." I clenched my teeth. "Go."

The guys slowly filtered out. Tex rubbed his arms like he had ants on him, and Dante grazed his finger down Tex's neck earning a hard shove and a reach for his Glock. Nixon gave me a middle finger salute before joining them.

And then I was left with Phoenix.

"I don't buy it." He crossed his arms. "You and I both know you like to read in the mornings so you don't kill anyone at night."

I swore violently. "That was private information."

"Nothing's private between us, you ass. Now tell me what you're going to go do. Better yet—" He put his hand on my shoulder pissing me off more. "Show me."

"Make me."

"I'm not afraid of ants. Furthermore, I'd fight to the death before you got near those or Mary. So help me God, let me in or I'm just going to keep fighting until you have no choice but to surrender, and we both know that word isn't in our vocabulary. Don't make my wife a widow. What shit are you working on?"

"Why can't you just leave it?" I roared stepping up against him until we were chest to chest. "Why?"

"Because I made a promise to a man we both respect and won't ever admit out loud that we love. That's why."

I blew out a tense breath and snapped. "Follow me."

I went back outside to my car.

And I drove it all the way to Eagle Elite and parked it on the far end of campus, where I knew she would be walking out to her next and final class.

Phoenix looked confused and then he did a double take, from me to the grass and buildings, back to me. "Holy shit has this turned into a sting operation?"

I pulled out my binoculars. "Hilarious."

There she was. Walking by herself. A guy tried to come up beside her, she walked faster.

"You have binoculars." Phoenix pointed out.

"I'm making sure she's safe. I'm keeping my promise."

"You could keep your promise by sending Ax, you know."

"Ax isn't me. I'm better than Ax, I'm better than every single one of you except Chase because he has more rage."

Phoenix gave me a murderous stare. "Oh, I think I could conjure up some rage, don't forget who you're talking to."

"Same goes for you."

"Shit, you're young," he muttered like he didn't want me to hear him. "I always forget that."

"Because…" I lifted them back up when she stopped walking. "I look so old?"

"No because you were forced to grow up too fast."

Pain filled my chest.

I ignored it.

I shoved it away just as a guy wrapped an arm around Alice's body and pulled her against him.

She put her hands against his chest.

I was already out of the car.

"Don't kill him!" Phoenix shouted after me.

"No promises," I yelled right back as I jogged across the lawn and then slowly walked up to his side.

I tapped him on the shoulder.

The minute he turned, I clocked him in the jaw so hard he'd need to call his dentist to replace at least three teeth and if I was really lucky, four.

"Son of a bitch!" He roared from the ground. His looks screamed all-American football, sandy brown hair, a few misplaced freckles, athletic and dimples.

Fuck me.

The kid probably had a nanny growing up, wanted to go to Harvard because his dad went to Harvard but got sent here because it's harder to get into.

He probably wore white briefs, peed sitting down, and had a pet parrot.

"What the heck was that for?" Grass stained his black slacks as he tried to stand. We were naturally gaining an audience, but all I could seem to focus on was the fact that he was wearing white tube socks.

White. Tube. Socks.

With black shoes and black pants.

"Let me guess, you dress yourself?" I joked.

"So, you punched me?" He pressed the back of his hand to his mouth. "Ish thah a tooth?"

"Andrei." Alice grabbed my arm and pulled me to her side. "What are you doing to my new lab partner?"

I smirked down at her. "Saying hello."

"And a handshake was too easy?" Her eyes were bright, her cheeks pink like she'd been out in the sun too long, and something about her expression made me want to pull her against me, to see if her skin still felt warm from the sunlight, to see if she would hug me back.

One minute in Elena's presence and I questioned things.

She was a menace to my sanity.

"I don't shake hands." I turned on my heel as Jackass of the Year got to his feet and swayed a bit. "These are the rules tiny dick. She's mine. Touch her and I cut off the finger that committed the offense, breathe too close and I'll take a piece of your tongue, and if I ever hear a word against her, I'll make sure you can't get a job until you're forty. Do we have an understanding?"

"Wh-ho are you? Her father?"

"Do I look old enough to be her father?"

His mouth dropped open, then shut, he shook his head wildly.

"She's mine," I barked. "Do we have an understanding?"

"Yes."

"Sir," I prompted.

"Sir, yes, sir."

I rolled my eyes. "Please stop saluting me, you're embarrassing yourself. Now go."

He stumbled away. A few of his friends helped him grab his bag and a discarded book, and the remaining students gaped like they'd never seen violence before.

"Why are you here?" Alice said through clenched teeth.

"What?" I tucked her hair behind her ears with both hands. "Not happy to see your husband?"

"You are not…" She leaned in; her eyes furious. "My husband."

"You have my last name. You're mine."

"I didn't sign anything."

"That's cute… your innocence that is."

"I haven't been innocent in a long time, and you know it." She heaved, her chest rising up and down like it hurt to admit.

Shit.

Without thinking, I reached for her hips and pulled her hard against me, then lowered my mouth to hers. I kissed her softly, I explored her with my tongue, and she let me, she opened up like she hadn't experienced hurt before or pain.

And she let me take what was mine.

I pulled away searching her eyes. "Innocent. Trust the man who owns a club like the one I do. That kiss… is innocent. Don't believe anything other than that."

Her eyes darted back down to my mouth. "Okay."

"And don't let guys grab you."

"You're grabbing me."

"I'm different."

"You're awfully protective for a keeper."

I smirked at that. "Yeah, well, I don't like people touching my things."

"Things." She deflated, "Right."

I knew I ruined what seemed to be a moment for her, and admittedly for me, and she detached herself from me, putting distance between us. "I'm going to be late for class."

"I'll pick you up in an hour."

"Great, I finally get the father I never had, and he's the most overprotective human on the planet. Fun!"

I glared. "Call me your father again, and you'll finally understand what it means to be spanked."

Her cheeks flushed as she ducked her head and started walking in the opposite direction.

When I finally made it back to the car it was to see, with utter horror that Phoenix had his phone up like he was filming the entire thing.

"Please tell me you didn't record that."

"I didn't record it." His lips twisted into an amused smile. "I went live."

I grabbed the knife from my boot and threw it at the nearest tree, only to hear him say. "That too."

CHAPTER TWENTY-FOUR

Alice

Damn, Andrei made such a ridiculous scene that nobody would talk to me for the rest of the day, and poor Mitchell my new lab partner tried to quit! One day in! I needed a partner to pass things!

Now I was alone.

And while I appreciated the over protectiveness, while it made me warm inside for a nanosecond, now I was just pissed.

I'd always wanted someone to watch out for me. Someone to care for me. I mean wasn't that what brothers were for? Fathers? To be the guy that threatens all your boyfriends with a gun? Or gives you a curfew? I never had any of that, and admittedly it felt good to have someone care.

What didn't feel good was being socially ostracized because he was worried about a guy who still lived at home and played Fortnite until one a.m.

My last class wasn't very exciting. It was a four hundred

level business comm class that I wanted to yawn my way through, but I was still thankful, thankful that I was doing something, not being trapped in my room waiting for the worst and not being trapped in my own closet battling my own feelings against the monster who owned a club that raped women.

It didn't matter that he wasn't a rapist.

He supported it.

I checked the clock and grabbed my things as the professor dismissed us. Nobody made eye contact with me as I weaved my way through students and finally exited the building.

My breathing stuttered when I saw Andrei leaning against the side of the building closest to me, his V neck so low that I saw a swirl of tattoos, his golden blond hair was combed messily to the side, his jeans were tight against his legs, tucked lazily into his jeans, his maroon shirt was thin enough that I could see the tight corded muscles of his six pack and the bulging biceps every stupid time he texted on his phone.

It didn't help that his aviators were low on his face, or that I could see the small diamond piercing in his nose as it twinkled toward me as if to say, come and get me.

It was irritating.

My own reaction to a man who I knew was bad.

To a man who cut out my own brother's tongue. He was both hero and villain, and I didn't know how to mix the two together.

Apparently, I wasn't the only one staring either.

Several girls held up cell phones and snatched quick pictures, while a few guys sneered in his direction out of pure jealousy. The man looked like a Viking god. Of course, they were jealous.

I held my head high as I made my way over to him.

He didn't look up. When I was a foot away, he just tucked his phone back into his pocket and grinned, all white even teeth, a small dimple in the corner of his left mouth made itself known. How had I never noticed that before?

"I'm disappointed."

"Huh?"

"So many girls were taking pictures I almost started posing, and yet you're not even appreciating the goods by doing the same thing."

"I don't have a cell phone."

He crossed his arms and grinned. "Did you check your bag?"

"What?"

He motioned for me to turn, then very slowly unzipped the front pocket and pulled out a brand new iPhone. He handed it to me then lifted the hair by my ear and chuckled. "My number's labeled Satan."

"Would have guessed that." I barely got the words out; it was like I couldn't get air into my lungs. He was too close, he smelled too good, and it was confusing. It didn't help at all that he wasn't wearing his gloves.

I liked them. In a way it was a barrier between us, a visual way for me to understand that there was distance separating us.

I needed that.

Maybe as much as he did.

"Shall we?" He held out his hand.

Frowning, I took it, noticing that he seemed to clench his teeth like my touch was painful.

"You don't like touching me." I said it like a statement.

He stared down at our hands and quickly looked away;

a forced smile fell across his full lips. "For reasons I'll never share. So, don't ask."

"Is it me or all women?"

"All humans," he said quickly. "Skin is too warm, I don't like it, I don't like to feel it… drives me fucking crazy."

"And yet you're not wearing gloves."

"Maybe I'm conducting an experiment," he said in an amused voice. "Hold your hand for longer than five minutes and prove to myself that I can handle the pain."

I tried to jerk my hand away.

He held my fingers firmly in his grasp. "I'm not being an ass, I'm being honest. Maybe that does make me an ass, but it is painful, make no mistake about that. Touching you is like holding my hand in the flames as they lick my skin and singe it off, as they promise warmth only to burn me alive."

We reached the car.

He dropped my hand like it was hot and opened my door. "You hungry?"

"No." Yes, but I didn't like this weird version of him, where he cared, where he picked me up from school. I preferred scary, scary I knew how to deal with, not that he wasn't petrifying.

Case in point, there was a dagger on his seat and it still had blood on it. His gaze followed mine, and he quickly picked up the knife, cursed, and wiped it off with a black cloth he drew out of his pants pocket, and then finally put both in the back.

I gaped. "Do I want to know?"

He was silent for a couple of breaths, and then he started the car. "Probably not, it's just business."

"I've heard that before."

"Doubtful. The business your father and brother do isn't just illegal, it hurt my friends, my alliances. Ergo, that's not just business, it's fucking war."

"Who drew first blood? You or them?"

He hesitated and shook his head as he pulled out of the driving spot. "Does it really matter? She made a deal with me, a deal she shouldn't have made, and I did what I could to protect her, but she went in too deep, tried to go over my head, it's not my fault Mil De Lange is dead, it's hers."

I hung my head. "That's not what I was told."

"Well…" He turned the car to the right. "You weren't there."

I stared down at my hands. "You were?"

"I was the one who set it up, who drew them out, drew her out. Of course, I was there, had Phoenix not shot her, it was my job to follow through."

"She made a mistake. People make mistakes."

"Her mistakes cost the De Lange Family everything. Her mistakes had to do with greed. Just curious, but did you know the worth of the Abandonato dynasty?"

I bit my bottom lip and shook my head.

"Twenty billion dollars." He said it slowly. "Not million. Billion. And Chase offered her part of, not just that fortune but his private fortune from his own mother, from her fashion line. Mil refused to take anything. Her biggest sin was her pride."

"And yours? What's yours?" I asked a bit breathless as I leaned in.

He gripped the steering wheel with both hands. "Right now?"

"Yeah."

"Betraying myself and the Italians by protecting a dead girl because I can't seem to get her out of my fucking head." He took another turn and then queried, "Burgers?"

I snapped my mouth shut and jerked back against the leather seat as he pulled up to a local burger place and actually proceeded to get out of the car and then open my door for me.

What game was he playing?

My heart was still hammering in my chest from his words. I couldn't even read the menu by the time we made it back inside, for once I was thankful he was so bossy and controlling, he ordered me a burger and then a milkshake like I was twelve.

I wanted to be insulted but I was hungry.

We sat in silence.

Him on his phone.

Me sucking down the shake like I really was his kid.

It was painful.

The silence.

"So." That's what I filled the void with. So. "What did you do today?"

He didn't look up just shrugged and said. "Had a visit from the past. One of the sluts my dad married and forced me to call 'mom' said she had info. Wouldn't talk, so I made her regret coming to me for protection."

I sucked harder on the straw, gulping, "What did you do?"

"She's alive."

"I wasn't asking."

"Your body language was all over the place, interested, closed off, then embarrassed that you were actually curious." He still wasn't looking at me.

I reared back.

"And now you're wondering how much I've noticed up until now. Did you want me to read you, or is it too early in our marriage for that?" Again, he didn't look up.

I glared. "We're not married.

"Until you're safe, you say, 'why yes husband, I would love to know more fascinating details about my body language and blatant curiosity when you put your hands on me, tell me more.'"

I almost threw my milkshake in his face.

He grinned down at his phone. "Don't throw it, I like this shirt."

"I don't."

"You stared two seconds longer than normal this morning, then another ten seconds this afternoon before you approached me, you didn't take a picture, then again you didn't really need to, did you *dorogaya*?"

I narrowed my eyes. "Maybe I was thinking of all the ways I could escape from you."

"Doubtful." He finally set his phone down and placed his forearms on the table, they were strong, muscle on top of muscle, with smooth skin. "You know the consequences if you run. I won't hesitate to kill you before they do. They'd torture you. I'd put you out of your misery."

I shuddered and looked away. "Is that where I say, 'thank you for your mercy'?"

"No. I just don't feel the need to lie to you about everything. The truth may be more painful, but it's more real, and I think you need real as much as I do."

"Now you open up? After two days with me? Are you sampling the drugs you sell at the club now?"

His eyes flashed. "I don't do drugs, nor do I sell them." He shrugged. "I may move them here or there, but that's only because someone has to do it, and I'd rather be that someone than one of the cartels."

Our food came.

He'd ordered giant burgers for both of us and started immediately setting out ketchup, fry sauce, and mayo.

I watched in fascination as he dipped a fry into each and then ate it.

It occurred to me then, I'd never seen him do anything so human.

He was eating and I noticed that I hadn't seen him really devour his food like this in front of me before.

It felt strange, watching him do something I imagined he never took part of, what did I think? He drank people's blood.

"Watching me eat can't be that entertaining," he said between bites. "Unless you just like watching my mouth and imaging what it would feel like sucking one of your—"

I threw a fry at him.

Then froze. Literally held my breath.

He didn't reach for his gun.

He didn't move either.

Slowly, he lifted his head and tilted it to the side in a graceful catlike manner, his face hard as stone. And then he picked up the offending fry and very leisurely dipped it in ketchup.

I felt my body heat in all the wrong places as he held it in front of his lips, his eyes at half-mast as his tongue slid out and licked the bottom of the fry.

I gripped the edge of my wooden barstool, unable to look away as he twisted the fry in his mouth, his tongue swirling around it, and then his lips sucking so perfectly that it was a crime. An actual crime, his mouth. He shoved the fry in and licked his lips then went about licking his thumb slowly, then his forefinger.

"Do that again and I'm not using a fry."
"'Kay." And I meant it.
I wouldn't survive his touch.
I wouldn't even know how to.
And I'd hate myself, wouldn't I?
If I gave in.
If I let him touch me that way.
I'd be exactly what my brother and dad called me.
What he'd called me at dinner.
Not his wife.
His whore.

CHAPTER TWENTY-FIVE

Andrei

I was either suffering a mental breakdown.

Or I needed to take up a hobby.

I couldn't stop thinking about her.

It was driving me insane.

I had to work that night. I worked every night, but I had to play my part, and I wouldn't be able to see her innocent reactions to things like sucking a french fry.

I laughed at that as I tucked my half-open black linen shirt into my low-slung leather pants. I grabbed my family crest, placing it firmly on my right hand. A sickle with three bleeding stars hanging over it.

The Petrov Dynasty.

Broken.

Bleeding.

The last remaining star.

That's what I was.

That's what it represented.

I'd been the smaller star because I was the youngest heir, and now? Now the only one left. I couldn't count Maya, Nikolai Blazik's wife. She was a half-sister and that was it, and she wanted nothing to do with the Petrov name.

Not that I could blame her.

I should probably update the good doctor about the happenings in the club, and the mysterious arrival of Elena.

I'd checked on her twice.

Both times she was still writhing in pain.

She was weak, had always been weak. My father chose her because he liked her face and he knew he could control her and in return she could control me, his youngest child, his protégé.

I'll never forget the days I had to fight her away from me.

The days she'd try to kiss me, to force herself on me when I was sixteen and finally started looking like a better option than my own father.

He should have killed her on the spot.

She carried a scar on her right thigh from my knife.

Maybe I'd extend it down her calf then burn the wound closed to remind her who she was dealing with.

Later.

Tonight, I was a club owner.

Tonight, I was the devil himself.

Tonight, I couldn't get distracted by past enemies or Alice.

Six thirty-two.

Damn it.

She was starting to be more than a number, and I hated that when I thought of her I said her name in my head… and I said it softly.

Like I had a heart that actually cared.

I put on my silver Rolex and grabbed my cell then made my way out into the kitchen.

Alice was there.

And she was wearing a pair of shorts that showed too much creamy thigh and a sweatshirt that looked vaguely familiar. I did a double take. Son of a bitch. I leaned over the couch. "You really need to stop stealing my clothes."

She looked up from the book she was reading and then eyed me up and down, "Are you going out?"

"Out the door." I pointed. "To do my job."

She scrambled to her feet. "Can I come?"

"I don't know," I tilted my head and smirked. "Can you?'

She threw the book down on the couch. "Stop being crude. May I come?"

In theory she would be safe, but I couldn't give her all my attention and she would want that and more.

I sighed and held up my hand, reaching for my phone to send out a quick group text.

> **Me:** Party at the club tonight, Cristal on me, bring the wives. Say any shit to Alice, and I strangle you with your own tie.
>
> **Nixon:** Who the fuck is Alice?
>
> **Phoenix:** Thought her name was six thirty-two?
>
> **Dante:** Black Widow, remember? Making things personal?
>
> **Tex:** I've waited for this moment my entire life.
>
> **Chase:** Wait, Alice... why does that sound familiar? Same chick you randomly enrolled? Hmmmm things heating up?

A chill washed over me.

Sergio: We were going out already, see you guys there in an hour.

I sighed in relief.

Me: Great.

Chase: What's her last name?

I hesitated, eyed her, then stupidly typed into my phone.

Me: Petrov.

Tex: WTF?

Sergio: Wait.

Chase: That's not how this works... guys tell him, you date, you eat food, you propose.

Dante: Um, this coming from the guy that tried to kill his own girl?

Chase: I had my reasons.

Phoenix: Interesting development. I think we need alcohol for this conversation.

Me: Not enough, on this planet.

Phoenix: Even better.

Nixon: I've never gotten dressed so fast in my entire life.

Me: Gotta go.

I looked up to Alice. "The guys are bringing their wives and their own security as per usual. Ax will be roaming the VIP area, and I'll have Vic stand guard at the door with Mateo."

"Really?" She smiled so bright I almost dropped my phone.

"No, I'm getting your hopes up on purpose."

Her face fell.

"Joke. That was a joke."

"You don't joke."

"Mmm..." I leaned in and whispered into her ear. "You

don't really know me, now do you?"

I pulled back.

Her eyes narrowed. "I think that's the great question isn't it? One day you can be terrifying, and in a second you can be the most charming guy in the room, albeit the most deadly. Which of you is real? The club owner? The fierce protector? The fake husband? Bodyguard? Who are you?"

Stunned, I could only stare. Not many people saw the chameleon tendencies, the need to blend into every situation with flawless precision.

But she somehow did.

"All of them," I snapped. "I'm whatever I need to be, when I need to be it."

"And with me?" she asked, stopping me in my tracks as I turned toward the door. "Who are you when you're with me?"

Anger swirled inside my chest, that she would demand an honest answer from me, that I would even debate whether or not to answer in the first place.

"Who I could have been," I finally settled on, "if I wasn't a man possessed with darkness."

"Andrei—"

"Wear something conservative. The last thing I want is to have to kick out paying customers because they think they can have you."

"So I'm still yours."

"Funny that you think I would ever let you go," I called over my shoulder then slammed the door behind me and leaned against it for a few heartbeats as I tried to regain the control of my breathing.

Who the hell did she think she was?

She was in no position to barter, to demand, to even

converse with me, and yet, it was impossible not to engage, not to tell her things, not to want her to ask them.

I walked down the hall, my steps decisively angry, and realized with blatant clarity, that I, Andrei Alexander Petrov, was well and truly.

Fucked.

CHAPTER TWENTY-SIX

Alice

The thing about finally being given freedom, you actually want to start to take it.

Freedom is like waking up from a long nap, you stretch your arms, then your legs, and suddenly you realize you can actually get out of bed, so you stand, and then you walk, and then you run.

Despite his millions of faults.

He'd given me that, a gift.

It hit me when I was standing in my closet trying to pick from the hundreds of dresses he'd purchased for me, for no other reason than he was intrigued.

I wasn't going to dive into what that meant.

I was just going to be thankful, that I wasn't locked in a room on a Wednesday night.

And that I was going to be able to wear a pretty dress.

Well that, and the fact that he hadn't said no.

I wasn't sure what had shifted. He was still scary as hell, and he still made me want to back away and hide against the nearest sturdy structure, but something in the way he looked at me now, like maybe he trusted me? Or maybe he was just like he said, curious.

Whatever it was.

I was going with it.

It had taken my father years to destroy my trust.

It had taken Andrei Petrov, two days to earn it.

There was something extraordinarily scary about a man who could take someone so broken, terrified, and bruised, and make her want to put on a dress and heels.

He was something monstrous.

And something beautiful.

All wrapped up in one.

I ran my hands along the lines of dresses and stopped when my fingertips grazed a beautiful Valentino black dress with a white little collar, it screamed innocence except it had a lace overlay that had only two small stitches of fabrics over the breasts.

I thought about his outfit.

Leather and red.

Why not match?

It would either piss him off or make him laugh. I was hoping I would earn another one of his rare laughs or french fry shows.

I picked up a pair of tall red heels that tied all the way up to my knee and managed to zip my dress by myself.

It fit snug.

I did a twirl in the mirror, the length was mid-thigh, a bit short, but I could work with it.

I couldn't, however, wear a bra.

The small pieces of black fabric covered a small area of chest and the lace did the rest, running down my arms in tightly fitted sleeves.

The white collar stood out, I decided I liked it. A lot.

I made my way into the bathroom and stared at the makeup that he'd purchased.

Something about putting too much on just didn't sit well with me. Was I getting dressed for him or me?

I put my hair up in a high ponytail, the edges of my hair grazed mid-shoulders making the look a bit mod.

I decided to go understated the whole way, a bit of foundation, no shadow, and dark eyeliner with mascara. I finished off the look with a Charlotte Tilbury liner that boasted it would make my lips look bigger and the matching bright red lipstick.

"Well, into the lion's den," I whispered to myself as I rushed back into the closet in search of a purse. I finally found a tiny clutch next to two more designer purses I would never be able to afford and felt instantly guilty.

And a bit sick.

He hadn't made me his whore.

But there was something very Pretty Woman about my situation.

I chose not to focus on the things.

And shoved my phone into the black beaded clutch and told myself to be brave, not make eye contact, and make sure everyone knew who I belonged to.

Even if the thought of being owned by anyone made me sick.

His club. His rules.

Tonight, I was Andrei Petrov's.

All his.

I chanted this in my head the entire way down the dimly lit hall, and then finally at the already open door to the club.

I hesitated a minute. Was the dress for me or him? For both of us? To prove I wasn't broken? I was suddenly more nervous than I'd ever been in my entire life, I ducked my head in.

Rap music pounded through the speakers so loud I was amazed clothes weren't coming off.

There were at least a few hundred people there already, and it was only ten.

I knew he'd be in the VIP section, but I wasn't sure how to exactly get there without…

"Alice," a voice said to my right. "Let me take you to him." Ax held out his elbow and gave me a warm smile. "Please don't take away the one and only chance I'll ever have to see Andrei Petrov fall to his knees."

A searing blush flooded my face as I took his arm and tried to tuck my hair then realized it was in a ponytail. "Thanks."

"I should be the one thanking you." He grinned wider. "So glad I'm on shift tonight."

I laughed a bit. "Me too, otherwise I would have been lost."

"Nobody gets lost in this club," he said pointedly. "Cameras everywhere."

"What about the apartments?"

Ax didn't even blink. "Those are his private residence. No cameras anywhere in that place, boss's orders."

"Hmm."

"Good information, yes?" He winked.

"Oh no, it's not, it's not like that, not even a little bit it's not—"

"Yeah okay, sure." He shrugged as we walked up about a dozen stairs and into the VIP section with table service and couches. It was draped in blacks and reds just like the rest of the club but the seating was divided by curtains that could be drawn around for privacy.

It wasn't very full yet, the section. When we rounded the corner, I had no time to prepare myself for the wives.

I was attacked.

With perfume, smiles, hugs.

From each and every one of them.

Trace was first. "That dress!"

Mo groaned. "I used to look sexy."

"She's pregnant," Bee pointed out, air kissing each of my cheeks. "She feels fat."

The woman looked like a freaking supermodel. "Uh, how far along?"

"Six months." Mo made a face. "Water for the win." She held up a water bottle. I smiled.

El was next on the hugging, Dante's wife. "You're stunning."

"Oh." I pressed a hand to my stomach while Val gave me a knowing look. "Thank you. I'm so glad you guys all came."

"You kidding?" Val laughed. "I wouldn't miss this for the world."

"Same," the girls all said in unison while I tried not to laugh. What did they think was gonna happen anyway?

I noticed his boots first, the red sticking out from the main couch, his legs spread like he owned the place, which I guess he did technically.

He looked like a Russian king.

A Czar.

Regal.

I sucked in a breath as he seemed to actually laugh at something Chase said, and then his head moved.

The wives, no joke, took one giant step away from me.

His smile fell.

Crap.

I should have chosen a different dress, worn more makeup, done something, anything.

His face looked like granite as his eyes lazily raked over me. Tex started choking on something while Chase whacked him in the back.

The only one not grinning from ear to ear in my direction was Andrei.

I almost turned and ran.

Almost.

Andrei finally lifted his hand and crooked one finger at me.

Great, now I was being summoned.

Punished.

The air suddenly felt smoky, choking as I took a step and then another. He didn't even blink, his ice-cold eyes locked on mine like a tractor beam, and so I walked. I walked right up to him, stepped between his legs, and held my head high.

It felt like the entire club was watching him, waiting for his next decision. I kept the tremble from my body, barely, as his eyes slowly moved from my face down my chest, my hips, and then my shoes.

His leg was shaking like he was tapping his foot.

His eyes flashed.

And then his hands were on my hips, pulling me onto his lap. The dress was too tight, so I collapsed against his chest, my legs dangling over the side of his. And then his lips were on my neck, sliding up until he said with deathly calm in my ear. "I like your dress."

I licked my lips. "Thank you."

His hands didn't move from my hips. He had his gloves back on, but I could feel their heat and I knew what his fingertips felt like against my skin, I could almost imagine them there now, digging into my flesh, tugging me hard against his lap.

Wait.

No.

What was I thinking?

I couldn't.

Not with him.

Not ever.

What happened to not being attracted to powerful hurtful men?

And why was I still sitting on his lap like it was Christmas? I moved my hips against him and settled in more comfortably.

He flinched and then shot me a glare as a waitress dressed in a slinky red cocktail dress brought us all a round of shots.

Vodka, of course.

"*Ypa*," He handed me a shot and then clinked his glass against mine while everyone else raised theirs with laughter, like they weren't natural born killers.

Even the women.

A flash of knife showed against Mo's thigh. She took a drink of water and winked.

Right.

"*Ypa*." I repeated and downed my shot.

I'd need a lot more than one vodka shot to survive that night, wouldn't I?

Thankfully, the waitress returned, this time with drinks,

some wine, whiskey, a few Moscow mules that looked like heaven, and more shots.

Andrei immediately took the shot. I suddenly had this insane need to know how much vodka he could down while playing darts and attempting to hit a bullseye, and then felt stupid for being curious.

"So." Tex stood and faced us, wrapping an arm around Mo. His mere presence was imposing, like he was too big for the room, knew it, and used it to his advantage. His dark reddish hair seemed to glisten underneath the pulsing lights. "Are we celebrating tonight?"

"Celebrating?" Andrei narrowed his eyes and then stared at the empty shot glasses like there wasn't enough alcohol in his system yet.

"Yeah." Tex grinned and lifted his drink to his smirking mouth. "Your marriage, of course."

I could have sworn Andrei choked on the shot as it went down, and then he winked at Tex. "Oh we've already been celebrating, you weren't invited."

"Trust me, the very last thing I want to see is you trying to find your prick and win a prize when you find the right — oomph."

Mo smacked him in the chest. "So, this is exciting, right? Another girl to add to the gang!" She shared a look with me that said I'd better be explaining later what the hell was going on, and I knew without a doubt I had to lie.

I had to freaking lie.

Because I couldn't tell her the real reason.

No, that seemed like a great way to get killed in this really pretty dress and end up buried in it.

"Come on." Trace reached for my hand and pulled me to

my feet. "Let's go dance, and we want details…" She peeked over my shoulder to Andrei.

"Oh, I'm sure it's nothing special." I gulped, still within earshot of Andrei. "I mean, nothing different from all his other girlfriends."

The guys silenced.

The girls shared obvious looks of intense curiosity.

And then Trace looped her arm in mine and said loudly, "Andrei doesn't have girlfriends. In fact, you're the first girl he's ever brought to family dinner, let alone, to hang out."

I stole a glance at Andrei.

His expression was unreadable.

But he did reach for another shot.

And when I looked down.

His foot moved.

Tap.

Tap.

Tap.

CHAPTER TWENTY-SEVEN

Andrei

There are many definitions of Hell.

My list was exhaustive, my definitions tragic.

Tonight I was adding something new to the very top.

That. Fucking. Dress.

I hadn't purchased her clothes, I was too busy running the club, and trying to keep her alive.

The wives seemed thrilled to have someone to take under their wing. Inside of a week, she'd know how to throw knives and render a man unconscious with her thumb and forefinger.

Great.

"So, what gives?" Tex kicked my tapping foot. Shit, how long had I been doing that? I stole a glance at Alice, but she quickly looked away.

"You're going to have to use English." I scowled.

"The girl." His arm hung around Mo. "The De Lange girl, shit for brains brother, you cut his tongue out, dad's most likely gone to ground, when are you letting her do the honors of killing her brother before we kill her? She still suffering in one of the holes you call a room here?"

I could feel the tension pulsing from Alice's body.

"Do we really need to talk business?" Mo patted Tex's cheek. "Besides, does it really matter? It's not like anyone can escape this place."

It was on the tip of my tongue to say that even I couldn't escape it. Physically its walls kept me here; mentally I was imprisoned by the screams of people I couldn't help.

Chase adjusted his position next to me and looked up at Tex. "What day did you say she was exchanged for her father's life; all the killing gets a bit fuzzy."

Shit. Just another thing I left out for Alice to find later.

She was traded.

Meant for dead.

Surprise.

"Few days ago." I sighed and motioned for another round. "I'll look at the ledger. She was fed three times a day, on constant watch, and at the time was so sick we thought she would die."

Chase flinched. "Then don't let her."

Luc put her hand on Chase's arm.

His jaw ticked. "She's a De Lange."

"So is your wife," I said softly. "And you don't see me pointing a gun at her face."

He jolted to his feet. "That was different, and you know it. She took a blood oath."

"Yes," I said, nodding to Luc, who looked ready to pull Chase into her arms and kiss away his anger. "She did. It's the only reason you're still living and not out on a killing spree."

"To be fair," Phoenix pointed out. "He's still on a killing spree."

"A controlled one," Nixon added in, his eyes sliding from mine to Chase's and then he shifted in his chair and glanced at Alice.

Shit.

"Mo's right." I stood. "Let's drink. We can talk business tomorrow."

"You're hiding something." This from Chase.

I went stock-still and then looked over my shoulder, irritated that he would call me out in my own club. "And you're lucky I didn't take your wife before you had the chance."

He lunged for me.

Nixon held him back.

I winked. "Sometimes, Chase, it's just too easy," I slapped him on the cheek lightly. "Keep it in check before I get security to escort you out of here."

"Or Mary," Tex mumbled under his breath.

"Who the hell is Mary?" Trace asked.

Nixon groaned. "Don't worry about it."

"Is she another one of your…" Trace gave me a sheepish look. "Girls that, you know…"

I grinned. "No, actually I don't know. Did you want to draw me a diagram?"

Phoenix started coughing.

I sighed. "Mary's a tarantula. We keep her at the bar."

Trace's eyes widened. "Is she in a cage?"

"Of a sort." I grinned. "Why, you want to meet her?"

"I do." Alice piped up.

All heads turned to her. Most of the men looked shocked while the women took a step away from her like she was diseased.

"What?" She smiled wide. "I never had a pet growing up, and tarantulas are so cute. I've heard they're really gentle."

"Gentle my ass," Sergio said under his breath.

I crossed my arms. "You're bluffing."

She shifted on her feet. "Oh? Why would you say that?"

"Your eyes darted down to the left at the exact same moment you shifted weight, and then you licked your lips, fast not slow. You're lying."

"Does he do this to everyone he likes?" Bee asked out loud.

"I think I feel a bet coming on." Dante rubbed his hands together. "If she can hold Mary for say… one full minute without panicking, what are you going to buy your new… wife that not one of us knew about?"

I shot him a death glare.

"What?" He shrugged. "I just wanted to make sure we didn't drop the very important subject of you suddenly being married to a woman we don't know."

"I have questions." Chase gritted his teeth. "Loads of them…"

"Pleasure," I rasped, lifting my hand to cup Alice's face. "Not business, not tonight."

God, it hurt to touch her, even with my gloves on.

I was numbing myself with alcohol.

And even then, I still felt her.

I took another shot and swallowed. "Deal."

She held out her hand for me to shake it. "Deal."

I tugged her against my chest. "That's not how I make deals."

"Well, shit," Nixon muttered under his breath as I pulled out a small knife from my pocket and flicked open the blade.

"Andrei..."

"What?" I called over my shoulder. "She's the one who agreed."

Alice's eyes shot to the knife then back up to me. "What's the knife for?"

"Give me your hand." I answered to no one.

The guys went quiet, the women watched like we were the newest drama to hit Netflix as they downed their drinks over the exchange.

Slowly, Alice lifted her hand. I turned it over, palm facing up, and imagined my mark on her, my tattoo on the back of that wrist. I wanted to mark her, so anyone who saw her knew.

But not here.

Not now.

I made a tiny cut on her thumb.

And then I pulled off my glove and made a cut above the bottom star, my star. She wouldn't know what it meant, to take a blade to your own skin, your own family tattoo.

It meant she was my blood.

I was taking it too far.

I didn't care.

It was the dress.

The ridiculous see-through lace dress.

I pressed my thumb to hers and then clutched her hand and whispered. "I guess you're going to have to prove you can take it."

"The spider or you?" she mused.

Two of the guys burst out laughing while it sounded like Tex started taking bets. Fantastic.

Still holding her hand, we walked over to the bar. It was hard enough concentrating on the task at hand let alone putting up with the guys laughing. Her ass looked incredible.

I wasn't the sort of guy who stared.

Because nothing held my attention.

Until her.

I wondered if it was a defining moment, already it was an out of body experience, the knowledge that for twenty-two years women didn't turn my head. They were objects. Things. I knew how to please them, I had studied that topic extensively thanks to my father, just like I knew that sex started with the kiss, but I'd never wanted anything beyond that.

Because it was all of my soul that I had left.

And the thought of sharing it with someone was unthinkable. The damage insurmountable.

I had one thing no one could take from me.

And I refused to be weak enough to give it.

Despite the dress.

My eyes lowered.

I used to burn people alive. I could handle a dress.

She moved ahead of me; my hand slid down to her ass.

I would rather burn a body.

She was the fire wasn't she?

And I was burning from the inside out.

I exhaled. "Rico." My voice sounded funny, like it knew the rest of me was teetering out of control. "I need Mary."

Rico was another Italian transplant. he loved working the bar because he got the most action when people got out of trouble.

He also heard the most secrets.

His head was shaved bald, and he had at least a million different colored beanies. The guy was almost too hipster to walk down the street without at least an organic coffee in hand.

"Sure thing, Boss." He winked at Alice. I tugged her closer to me. He just shook his head and smiled. I was being possessive. I knew Rico had a crush on Ax, even though Ax was married, but still, I was ready to fight for what was mine.

Alice stilled next to me when Rico disappeared behind the bar and then returned with what could only be described as the oldest tarantula in existence.

When I held it in one hand, its legs almost draped over the edges of my fingertips. She was mostly gray and black with a few bits of red fur.

Alice smiled down at him and held out her hand.

"Keep it flat," I instructed.

"Okay."

Was she really excited? About holding a tarantula? It was against humanity to like spiders, right? Didn't women run away screaming when they saw spiders? Snakes? Mice?

She looked ready to kiss him.

I growled low in my throat, suddenly aware that I was making Mary anxious as she lifted a leg toward me, then another.

I refused to apologize to a thing.

So, I stared her down and waited for the transfer.

Rico held her out and she crawled slowly onto Alice's hands, she had both out since Mary was so big.

I heard hollering from the guys, and the girls all looked ready to pull out their guns and shoot the poor spider.

"She's beautiful," Alice said reverently.

I stared at her, really stared at her. "You're surprising in more ways than one, *dorogaya*" I itched to touch her neck, to smell her skin, to climb inside her head and ask her why she was so intrigued by something so simple, by something that most people would say was evil.

She held Mary closer to her face. "Look at those eyes."

I wasn't looking at Mary at all.

And I would bet that the entire establishment agreed with my assessment of Alice's eyes.

Stunning.

Like cut ice.

Perfect in every way.

I jerked my attention away from her face and down to Mary. "She's very old."

"I like her," Alice said in a soothing voice. "You probably think it's strange, but I've always liked things I don't understand. Things that people cross out as evil or scary are just misunderstood, don't you think?"

I opened my mouth, but nothing came out.

The spider slowly started crawling up her arm.

Mary never crawled up anyone.

She kept moving until she rested on Alice's shoulder like a fucking parrot, and then she seemed to just… relax against her skin.

The hell?

I eyed Rico.

He just shrugged. "Animals are good judges of character."

"It's a spider," I pointed out.

"Actually, tarantulas are considered part of the crab family," Alice piped up and held out her finger to Mary, who proceeded to lift her leg and touch her finger like they were high fiving.

That was when I noticed every one of the guys was watching in stunned silence while the girls held up their phones taking pictures and videos.

Somehow, she'd earned their respect through a tarantula.

Somehow, she'd distracted them from the obvious.

And she'd done it by showing love and affection to something most people would shoot first and ask questions of later.

Too close to home.

My stomach clenched.

This woman, this girl, was doing things without realizing it, making me feel when I didn't want to.

I wanted the pain.

And then the numbness.

But she kept pulling off the bandages and poking at the scars.

One day, I feared I'd get up and explode every fucking one and fall to my knees in hopes she'd accept them.

It couldn't happen.

Not now. Not ever.

Submit to no one.

Submit to no one.

No. One.

"All right, you've proved your point," I said in an aggravated voice "Rico, take Mary?"

Alice was too close.

I was seconds from reaching for her.

From doing something that I couldn't come back from.

It would alter me.

I wanted nothing to do with it.

The minute the spider was out of reach, I grabbed Alice by the arm and led her away from the guys.

"Another round," I called to Rico, "Let them know I'll be right back."

"You got it."

"Andrei?" Alice's voice was sweet. She wasn't even worried that I was dragging her half across the club by her arm. "Are you okay?"

"Am I okay?" I laughed without a hint of humor "Are you?"

"Yes?"

I pushed her against the dark corridor that she had walked through. "Who did you wear this dress for?"

She reared back. "Does it matter?"

"Yes."

Her eyes searched mine. "I thought… I don't know, I wanted to look nice, and then I thought you might like it."

"You thought…" I chuckled darkly. "That I might like it?"

She gulped. "Yes."

I gripped the fabric at her thighs and slowly pulled it up. "And what did you imagine would happen if I liked it too much?" My hand stilled.

She sucked in a breath her eyes panicked. "I don't know."

"Yes, you do." I pressed my body against her, my hand still on the bottom of her dress. "Did you think I'd fall to my knees? Or maybe that I'd strip you out of it later, lick my way down your body, give you multiple orgasms until we're both exhausted?"

She shook her head. "No, that's not—"

"Drive me crazy on purpose, and I may just take you up on that offer. Then again, I figure you're not the sort of girl to dress for a man she doesn't like. So why did you wear the dress?"

"Why does it matter?"

"It matters." I needed to know she wasn't thinking about seducing me. I needed to know she was different. I needed to know it wasn't about me.

"I wanted," she said in a thick voice, "to make you proud."

I jerked away from her. "What?"

She pressed her lips together and shook her head. "You heard me."

"You don't need my praise."

"And yet I wanted it."

"Why?"

"Because sometimes girls like to be told they're pretty, and because I knew you called in a favor to get everyone here so I wouldn't feel trapped. I wore this dress because I thought it would complement what you were wearing, and I wanted you to be proud," Her eyes lit up with tears. "Proud of your whore."

"Damn it, Alice!" I roared slamming my hands on either side of her head as she squeezed her eyes shut. "You're not my whore!"

"But—"

My mouth crashed down across hers so fiercely I almost lost my footing. As she wrapped her arms around my neck, I slid her body against the wall, shoving her skirt up past her thighs, then pulling her legs around me as I gripped her ass, deepening the kiss.

She moaned my name.

I was not myself.

I was undone.

Out of control.

Crazed, as her nails dug into the back of my shirt and tried to pull it over my body. I rocked my hips against her core, she was hot everywhere, molten lava, ready for me, ready for this.

It was unnaturally right, the attraction I had for her, the way her body molded against mine like our souls had been separated and only just found each other again.

I angled my head to the left, deepening the kiss, my tongue pressed against hers, dominating and submitting all at once, her hands moved to my hair tugging on it, mussing it as I turned us around and shoved her against the opposite wall her hands moved down my chest pulling my shirt open as her fingertips touched my chest.

A throat cleared.

I was going to kill whoever that throat belonged to.

Slowly I pulled back and looked to my left. "What?"

It was Phoenix. He had a knowing look on his face. "Oh, I was just looking for the bathroom."

My nostrils flared.

He didn't smile.

What? He went from my mentor to my babysitter.

"Wrong hallway," I snapped.

"Oh, I wouldn't go that far." He sighed.

Slowly I released Alice. As she slid down the wall, her face ducked into my shoulder, I held her there. "Phoenix…"

"The guys want to talk about the De Lange girl that was brought in… they won't let it go, so I figured you'd want to know that information… hmm?"

"Yes," I rasped, then fully released Alice and ran my hands through my hair, my chest still heaving. "Fine."

"Go ahead." Phoenix said with deathly calm. "I want to talk to Alice for a minute."

I knew she was safe with him.

I didn't want to leave.

"Andrei, I rarely use any sort of authority with you because I consider you a friend. Right now, I need you to go sit with the guys and talk."

"Kill her, and I come after your entire family."

"I know," Phoenix said seriously.

I shared a look with Alice, nodded, and walked off.

The only thing I heard was Phoenix's first sentence. "He will be the death of you."

I wished I could say that he was wrong.

He wasn't.

CHAPTER TWENTY-EIGHT

Phoenix

"I'm not going to kill you." I said it softly even though it didn't look like she believed me. She was plastered against the wall; her lipstick smudged her pride probably a bit bruised. "I am, however, going to help you."

That got her attention. "What?"

"You know who I am?" I crossed my arms and leaned on the opposite wall.

She swallowed. "Yes."

"You know there isn't anything that happens in this godforsaken world without my permission? Without my knowledge?"

She lowered her head. "Yes."

"You know I'll snap your neck before letting you hurt him?"

Her head jerked up. "*Me* hurt *him*?"

"Ah you thought I was here to talk about your real last

name. No, Alice, I'm not here to discuss you, I'm here to discuss him."

"But—" She held out her hands in front of her like she was trying to use the air to brace herself. "I don't understand?"

"He's…" I searched for the right word. "Unfeeling."

"What?"

"When you touch him, it hurts."

"I know."

"No," I said through clenched teeth. "You couldn't possibly know the pain associated with human touch for Andrei or the sacrifice he makes when he holds your hand or kisses your body. He's at war with himself because for the first time in his life he wants something, but he doesn't know how to do anything except… hurt."

Her face fell. "You're saying he'll hurt me."

"I'm saying he has twenty-two years of pent-up rage and sexual aggression; I'm saying if you want him, want whatever this is between you two, you go all the way. You half ass it and he will murder you and sleep in your blood. And the man who still finds a way to smile even when he has no reason to will be gone, and I'll blame you. We will all blame you for taking the last part of his soul with you because you couldn't seem to control yourself around a man with his looks, his power."

"He terrifies me," she confessed. "I feel like I should be running, and every time I start on the path away from him, it ends up leading exactly back to where I shouldn't be. In the monster's arms."

I smiled at that. "Yeah well, sometimes the monsters are better in bed."

She laughed.

"I'm not kidding." I shrugged. "Men are mortal, and

monsters…"

She locked eyes with me. "They're more."

"So much more," I whispered. "You need to decide, and soon. Once you're in deep with him, I can't do anything."

"And my other option?"

I stared through her. "I make you disappear, give you a new name, new identity, I give you everything you need to start over. Away from this life."

Her eyes lit up

Shit, he was going to hate me.

"Really?" She was going to take me up on it.

Fuck.

"Really." I nodded.

"Can I think about it?"

"You have twenty-four hours."

She gave me one final small nod.

I started walking away and then stopped. I knew she was watching, listening to me. "Something to think about…"

"What?" she asked in that soft voice of hers.

"You would be his first."

"First?"

"Everything."

"I don't understand."

"His only."

"What are you saying?"

I looked back over my shoulder and made sure I had her full attention. "Deep down, you know."

"Maybe you should just explain it so—"

"The first woman to bring him to his knees, the first woman to keep him there, the first woman to touch him where no one's allowed to even look, the first woman to take what's left of his innocence while handing him the remnants of yours," I whispered. "He would give you the final pieces. And if you took them and left, you would be doing more than leaving a monster — you'd be unleashing on the world absolute fucking chaos."

I walked away.

I didn't want to see the shock on her face.

Or the truths etched there.

Because I wasn't sure what would happen if she did walk away.

If she chose herself over something with Andrei.

And when I made it back to Bee's side, I knew she saw the strain in my face, the energy that had left me completely exhausted.

"You okay?" she whispered, laying her head on my shoulder while Andrei and the guys ordered more drinks.

"Never," I answered honestly. "I just learn how to deal."

"I know."

"What do you love about a man like me?" I wondered out loud in a moment of temporary weakness, vulnerability.

And then my wife turned to me and kissed me softly on the lips. "I love the man. I embrace the darkness, I feed it, I soothe it. You ask me what I love about a man like you? You're not merely a man, Phoenix Nicolasi. You're so much more than that. I love every dark twisted part of you, and I would search the depths of Hell for your soul if I had to. It would be easier to ask me what I don't love…"

Stunned, I stared for a few seconds then said, "What don't you love?"

She grinned up at me. "You steal the covers."

I burst out laughing and pulled her into my arms. "Is that all?"

"Well you haven't kissed me in an hour, that's pissing me off."

I kissed her.

And then I earned a glare from Tex.

I just shot him a middle finger and kept kissing his sister, my wife, wondering if Andrei would ever find the same happiness, when he was so hell bent on pushing everyone away.

CHAPTER TWENTY-NINE

Andrei

Alice returned around ten minutes later, her skin a bit flushed and her eyes distant. Whatever Phoenix told her; it wasn't good.

"Did you kick her after you killed her spirit or before?" I mumbled under my breath reaching for another shot.

What was that? Seven? Eight?

I eyed her damn dress again.

Did it even matter at this point? I downed the shot and waited.

"I just gave her some…" He shrugged. "Perspective."

"God save us when you're the one giving perspective," I grumbled and then felt myself smiling.

Phoenix stared at me a bit longer than necessary. "How much have you had to drink?"

Alice laughed at something Trace said as I reached for another shot. "Not enough, not even close."

"Alcohol makes it hard not to…" He started using his hands why the hell was he using his hands like that? "I wouldn't suggest it."

"You didn't even finish your sentence and I'm the one drinking too much?" I snorted into my vodka shot.

It was smooth.

Clean as I tossed it back.

"We're headed home." Nixon approached, hand outstretched. "Thanks for the interesting night. We'll talk next week about the De Lange girl."

Shit.

"We will," I agreed, shaking his hand while Trace gave me a drunken finger wave. One by one everyone left, finally, including Phoenix and Bee.

"Water." Phoenix tossed me a bottle. "And try to just…" Why was he looking at me so damn funny. "To just trust… the moment."

I gave him a blank stare and then burst out laughing. "The fuck? Are you giving me sex advice?"

"No." He looked away.

I squeezed my eyes shut. "You should go before you embarrass yourself."

"I don't have the ability to get embarrassed." Phoenix shrugged when I opened my eyes. "And I'm not the one purposely trying to get drunk."

I glared, felt my jaw click as I ground my teeth. "I'm fine."

"You're playing with fire." Phoenix stood. "Trust me, I wrote the book on it, fucking still living with the feeling of dancing with the flames." He reached for Bee's hand.

She grinned up at him like he was a god.

And then she stood on her tiptoes and pressed a kiss to his

neck.

He locked eyes with me. "I hope you know what you're doing."

Alice was at the bar, bending over so far that I could almost see all the way up her dress. I shot Phoenix a pained expression. "I think for once. I don't know whether to run or fight."

"Maybe," Bee piped up. "You do a little bit of both."

I tilted my head at her, my vision blurred a bit before I shook it off and stood. "I can't imagine that going over well."

"You never know," she said softly.

The rest of the group walked off just as Alice approached with a drink in hand, it was clear and had a lime twisted in it.

"So." Her cheeks bloomed with color as she sat down on the empty couch, I slid in next to her, overlooking my kingdom while people drank, danced, partied, and left through the side door to get high off whatever product my family had brought in over the last week.

I had pot readily available for every customer.

Cocaine if they needed to stay awake.

Molly when they wanted a shared sexual experience.

But I drew the line at heroin.

I wasn't a complete monster.

I told myself I only gave them good drugs.

I lied on a daily basis.

I ignored the feeling in my chest, of Alice seeing what was beneath the surface of my calm facade.

I started tapping my foot again.

And then her hand was on my thigh.

I stilled. And slowly looked up at her. "Something on your mind, *dorogaya*?" I was having a hard time focusing on her, an even harder time looking away from the expanse of leg as my vision continued blurring.

She seemed to think about it and then leaned back.

I rested my arm on the back of the leather couch and motioned for more shots from the waiter.

I wasn't near numb enough if I could feel the heat of her body on my fingertips, if I could still taste her mouth on my tongue.

"Phoenix, he just said some things." She stared down at her hands.

"Phoenix likes to talk."

"What if he's right?"

I snorted. "What if he's wrong?"

She sipped her drink through a black straw.

I felt nothing but rage for the plastic that was touching her lips. Before I could stop myself, I reached out and grabbed the straw from her drink and very slowly lifted it to my mouth.

Would I taste her there?

I licked my way down the straw and winked at her. "Beefeater Gin?"

Her jaw dropped. "How'd you know?"

"Can you keep a secret?" I teased lowering my voice.

I ignored how damn adorable she looked when she nodded her head with big wide eyes and scooted closer.

I crooked my finger.

Another scoot.

And then I purposely grazed her ear with my lips and whispered, "I own a club."

She stilled and then burst out laughing like it was the funniest thing she'd ever heard.

I couldn't stop smiling.

Either the vodka was doing the trick.

Or I was insanely drunk off her laugh.

Both were a probability.

"Okay, I deserved that." She turned to me, then, lifting the cool glass to her mouth and drinking deeply.

I flinched.

Ready to grab the glass.

To pull her across my lap, punish her for making me want her so violently that the only way I was keeping my hands off of her was through keeping my hands on vodka shots.

I was in control.

Barely.

Another tray of shots was placed in front of me.

I checked my watch. It was closing on midnight.

I needed to question Elena in the morning, and in my current state, I was already questioning all the alcohol I'd consumed.

Alice yawned, her eyes fluttering closed a bit before she set her glass on the table. "I'm going to go to bed."

She stood, swayed a bit on her feet. I wasn't sure if it was exhaustion or drunkenness. God knew I wasn't one to judge. How long had it been since I'd actually drank more than a shot or two? Especially with all the Italians?

She was messing with my calm.

With my business.

With everything.

I stood with her, waiting for the room to right itself as Ax approached with a grin on his face. "Calling it a night, Boss?"

"Make sure nobody dies," I said in a bored tone, and then I wrapped an arm around Alice. "But if they do, only disturb me if the body count's higher than three."

Alice stiffened beneath my arm.

I almost rolled my eyes.

A loud chime sounded.

Shit.

I'd completely forgotten.

All the tattooed women slowly moved through the room in a sea of red dresses, and then they went through the open black door as my men waited on either side.

Alice looked up at me. "What's going on?"

"Bidding hour," Ax answered before I could get a word out.

"Bidding." Alice scrunched up her nose. "Like a silent auction?"

Ax's lips twitched.

I shook my head slowly.

I narrowed my eyes as a few De Lange men made their way through the crowd, including Alice's brother, his lips swollen and expression sullen. Clearly, missing part of his tongue was not a huge impairment. Maybe once other parts were missing…

"Who let them in?" I clenched my teeth as Ax followed my gaze. "I want whoever it was, fired."

"They're paying customers," Ax pointed out. "And you always keep your enemies close."

Alice shrunk next to me, like she wanted me to shield her body.

I knew if we walked back to the apartment they'd see her.

"Shit." I hung my head. "Guard my bidding room. No one comes in, knock twice once they've had their drinks and are seated in the auditorium."

"Right away." Ax nodded.

"Come on." I led Alice to the room I'd brought her to days

ago, the one with the red and green blinking lights, the one that exposed her to the truth.

My truth.

A sickness washed over me as I unlocked the door and gently shoved her in then locked the door behind me.

It was dark except for the single light on in the auditorium.

All of the women in red waited in the middle, standing on the concrete like goddesses.

Lights flickered.

And then a single woman stood there, head held high.

I didn't know her name.

The number flashed above her, six thirty-six.

Alice gasped.

"Don't look…" I said through clenched teeth.

"This," She touched the bulletproof glass. "How often does this happen?"

"Every night." I walked up behind her, thankful that nobody could see in, wishing that we couldn't see out.

I didn't want her to look.

Damn it.

I flipped her around and kissed her shoving her body against the glass, my mouth tasting hers as cheers erupted around the auditorium.

She didn't see the blood splatter the glass next to us.

She didn't see the trail of it running down the cement mixing with the woman's tears.

Another light flashed.

Alice pulled back from me, her eyes locked on mine, and then she very slowly turned, even though I gripped her tight.

The woman was dead, her throat in the process of getting slit after she was shot in the head, execution style.

Alice gagged and covered her face with her hands. "What was she guilty of?"

"Existing," I whispered lifelessly. "Breathing." I shrugged. "Take your pick."

Alice shoved against me. "I need to get out of here, I need to leave, I need—"

"Shh," I tugged her back against me. "You're hysterical. Running out of this room gets you put in that auditorium. You want to know how you get a tattoo? By not choosing me!"

"Great!" she roared. "So, I either suffer at my brother's hands, or you get bored with me and throw me down into the auditorium!"

"Have I even touched you?" I shoved her against the glass, my hands on either side of her face, pressing the glass so hard that my fingers hurt. "Have I fucked you?"

"N-no." She lifted her gaze to mine. "But you want to."

The denial built up in my throat.

And never came out.

Her face grew harder. "And when you finally do… is that what happens to me?"

"No," I rasped. "Never."

"And yet you let it happen to others. To women who have done nothing wrong!"

"Raise your voice at me one more time," I seethed. "And I'll lock you somewhere nobody will hear you scream."

She slapped me.

Hard.

I jerked back in shock. Nobody touched me without my permission. And nobody struck me more than once.

Nobody.

My nostrils flared as two knocks sounded on the door.

I had her by the wrist and out the door in a flash, dragging her down the hall.

She screamed.

And I let her hate me.

I let her scream at me.

I let her curse me to Hell.

I let her.

Because it was like throwing cold water over my burning body.

She was right.

I wasn't hers.

She wasn't mine.

This wasn't a fairy tale.

I killed innocent women.

I'd always killed innocent women.

And she was right.

I would tire of her once I took her, just like my father had tired of his women; I was his son, after all.

She'd revealed my biggest fear without even knowing it.

That I was just like him.

That once I had sex with someone, I would need more and more until it turned violent like it had for him.

Until I needed them younger and younger.

Until I needed more.

Always more.

I jerked open the door to the apartment and shoved her in, then locked them, and stomped past her.

"Andrei—"

"Six thirty-two," I interrupted without turning around.

I could have sworn I felt her heart drop to the ground and shatter at my feet as she sucked in a sharp breath.

She was nothing.

Just a pretty thing I would destroy.

Something I would take off the shelf and mar with my darkness, she might as well be Pandora's box.

I would open her once.

And be lost forever.

Tragic.

True.

I hung my head. "Get some sleep. I'll have Phoenix grab you in the morning. I'll provide a strung-out stand in for the Italians. You can take your clothes; I don't want them here. Take the shoes, the purses." *Take my fucking soul.* "I don't want anything in here that would ever remind me of you."

It hurt to say out loud.

More than I thought it would.

My chest was tight as she hurried past me with a whispered "I hate you." On her lips.

And when the door slammed, I hung my head and said. "Good."

CHAPTER THIRTY

Alice

My tears stained the pillowcase. I felt irrationally angry over him sending me away. All I'd ever wanted was my freedom.

And he was giving it to me.

I should be thankful.

Giddy even.

He was going to give me a fresh start.

I'd been in his presence mere days, and the thought of not having him looming after me, arguing with me, kissing me, made me physically sick.

That's how demented this whole thing was!

Falling for Andrei was like mental warfare.

I knew it was wrong.

And yet touching him always felt so right, I'd never felt more safe in my entire life.

I thought back over the night.

Over what Phoenix had said.

Andrei would give me everything.

But what if it wasn't enough?

What if by taking the last part of him… I created an even bigger monster?

Was I really debating this?

I threw off my covers and walked across the room, opened my door and stared across the hall at his.

Everything about Andrei was too big, too unreal.

Too much.

I raised my hand to knock, changed my mind, and just opened the door.

His bedroom was beautiful, just like him and eerily different late at night. Dark navy was offset by shades of white and pale blue, with understated accents in creamy tones. Subtle, classy. A few art pieces hung on the wall, all abstracts with hues echoing the room itself. A chaise of slate gray leather sat in a nook that looked… cozy, inviting. The mahogany bed with a plush mattress was topped by a snow white duvet. In stark contrast, a black fur blanket lay folded across the foot. Everything was high-end but… comfortable, lived in. Not a red, black, or gold in sight. This room was a sanctuary except for the large flat screen TV in the corner.

A roaring fire blazed in the fireplace.

And the man who I hated.

The man who I couldn't stop thinking about.

Was on his knees in front of the fireplace.

He was wearing a pair of black pajama pants, silk.

And he was staring at the fire like he knew what it felt like to let the heat singe him.

The flames licked higher and higher.

His gloves were off.

He didn't acknowledge that I was in the room, but I knew he heard me, sensed me, could have killed me in less than three seconds if he wanted.

I was out of my element.

Funny how the hero in my story should have been my own family, my brother, my father.

But because of that mistrust, because of the twisted way they showed love, I'd fallen for the dragon that protected the castle.

I'd fallen for the beast.

I'd fallen for darkness.

Preferred it to light.

I'd fallen for the devil himself.

"Don't test my self-control, not tonight." His voice was raspy, deep. If I closed my eyes I could hear the slight Russian accent, just like I could feel the warmth from his body even though he wasn't touching me.

When I finally made it to him, my knees buckled.

He was kneeling in a pool of blood.

"Andrei…" I dropped in front of him, searching for the wound, only to see that his left hand, the one with the star tattoo, was completely mutilated. "What happened?"

"He's in me," Andrei whispered. "The devil himself."

"No." I reached for his bloody hand. "That's not true."

"In my blood." He stared straight ahead. "At least I can cut the reminder from my skin, cut the tattoo away from my bone and pray it's not a premonition of things to come, the final star in the dynasty, falling…"

Maybe he was still drunk.

"That would be the cruelest trick of all you know." His eyes watched the flames behind me. "My father, he's laughing from his Circle of Hell, watching, waiting, mocking me."

I didn't know what to say, so I ran to the adjoining bathroom, grabbed a towel and ran back, then wrapped it around his hand, shocked he let me touch him.

Angry that I'd slapped him when he'd never lied about who he was.

Angry that I'd want him to be something other than the man kneeling in front of the fireplace bleeding out his truth.

"Listen to me." I held the towel against his hand. "Just because you're his son, doesn't mean you're like him."

"Lie," he whispered, finally locking eyes with me. "I am exactly like him."

"Prove it," I challenged.

He blinked slowly, his eyes landing on my mouth. "I'd rather prove you wrong than prove him right. You have a big day tomorrow. Go to sleep."

"No."

He scowled. "Could you for once listen to me the first time?"

I smiled. "No."

He stared me down. "One day, *dorogaya* you'll have beautiful children. They'll laugh, they'll be free. When you close your eyes, you'll be thankful you ran away, thankful that you started fresh. For some of us, it's too late, but for you?" He pressed his good hand against my cheek, his hand was alarmingly warm, soft. "You will have a beautiful future."

"And if I choose an ugly present and uncertain path?"

"You were never mine." He said it like it killed him inside to admit. "Your name was never written down in the book here at the club, you weren't purchased, you're free. This is the part where you say thank you."

"If you bought me, would you let me stay?"

He swore. "Do you hear yourself? Is this what three days in my presence has done to you? Degraded to the point of being an object for fucking sale?"

"Answer me!" Tears welled in my eyes.

"*Dorogaya*" His voice was thick. "I'm a very rich man, but even I couldn't afford you."

I gasped.

He leaned in and spoke the word against my lips. "Priceless."

Our foreheads touched then, they pressed together while tension built between us.

"Go." I flinched at the pain in his voice, the sheer vulnerability of the way he said such a simple word, like releasing it into the air between us felt like stabbing himself in the heart. "Please."

I didn't kiss him.

Kissing wouldn't fix this.

Fix him.

Me.

I was traumatized, broken, I'd suffered by those who loved me.

And the problem between us.

He had too.

We were abused by those who were supposed to protect us. Its unnatural for a parent to go against instinct, so it's only natural that the object of their hate, of their hurt, turns to darkness for peace.

Because you can no longer trust the light.

I knew that feeling well.

I stood.

He didn't look at me.

But as I walked toward the door, I heard him whisper, "Goodbye, *dorogaya*... Alice."

I called Phoenix first thing.

He didn't answer.

So, I sent him a text.

> **Me:** I'm going to need a new social for Alice, new last name, a job, maybe something in retail. She likes clothes. Have her dye her hair blond so she's unrecognizable, talk to her about the risks of wiping her prints from her skin. I'll have her ready in an hour.

Phoenix replied back quickly.

> **Phoenix:** I'm confused, I gave her twenty-four hours. She has yet to contact me. Did she tell you she wanted this?

I frowned down at my phone.

> **Me:** What are you talking about?

> **Phoenix:** I offered her, her freedom last night. She said no.

Hands shaking, I read the response over and over again. He had to be wrong. Mistaken. Confused.

Because it was often that Phoenix Nicolasi was confused? He was in his twenties, not his eighties.

Me: Whatever. I made the choice for her. It's not worth it. I thought I could control it, thought it would be different.

Phoenix: So, what you're saying is, you're a coward?

Me: Take that back or I'm burning down your house with you in it.

Phoenix: Promises... whoops, I just added everyone in on this conversation. Guys Andrei's scared.

I almost broke my phone in half.

Barely stopped myself from throwing it against the wall as texts came in.

Nixon: He does realize that he's the monster he sees in the mirror... right?

Me: Speak for yourself psycho.

Nixon: I love it when you compliment me.

Chase: I was scared of the dark too when I was a kid, but then I put on my big boy pants realized I have a dick not a pussy and got the hell over it!

Me: We sure you have a dick?

Dante: Don't make him show us.

Tex: Like the camera can really capture things that small.

Sergio: Why are we talking about dicks again? It's seven a.m.!

Phoenix: Trouble in paradise. Andrei's scared of his wife.

Me: I was interested, now I'm not. Because I don't do attachments. She'll be fine. She has my name.

Nixon: Did you pass her a note to break up with her? Or are you waiting until recess? Shit man, you can't just marry someone one day and break up with them the next.

Me: Setting your house on fire too, guess I'll be busy tonight.

I hated that he was both wrong and right. She'd be safe because she'd have my name, they didn't know it wasn't real. It didn't matter. My name was all that mattered.

Nixon: Could you start the fire in the kitchen? Trace wants to do a remodel, would save me a shit ton of time.

Chase: I love setting things on fire.

Tex: People. You love setting people on fire, oh wait that's Andrei.

I rolled my eyes.

Me: It was necessary at the time.

Sergio: Setting a human on fire when you could just shoot them? Mmmm, okay. Sure.

Phoenix: We're getting off track. He wants to send her away.

Chase: Hell no. I'm enjoying this. Let's lock him in his apartment and spike everything with Viagra.

Nixon: We don't want to kill him, can you imagine the erection?

Dante: Erection, erection, erection. I love our texts, they make me feel so mature.

Chase: Small fry, the adults are talking, shhhh.

Tex: Rock a bye baby on the tree top...

Me: The day Tex sings me a lullaby is the day I give up on life, or maybe it's the day life has given up on us?

Sergio: Deep, Drei, so deep.

Chase: Word.

Nixon: Look, we took blood oaths to protect you. That means from yourself when necessary, I mean look at Chase! He was miserable!

Chase: Thanks man, really.

Tex: Nixon's right. Don't send her away because you're scared of a bit of nakedness.

Me: I'm not scared of her.

Phoenix: Take it from someone who refused to eat certain colors because I didn't think I deserved them... you're not good enough for her. You'll never be good enough for her, but you try, every day, that's the difference maker.

Tex: He's right. He's not who I would have picked for my baby sister. Anyone, I would have literally chosen anyone but him.

Phoenix: Thanks man.

Tex: It's true.

Phoenix: She screams when she—

Me: STOP

Dante: Voice of reason here, arch enemy, person who almost shot you in the face and took great joy in sitting on your throne at Eagle Elite.

Me: You're not missed.

Dante: Don't do it. You'll regret it.

Me: I already regret this entire conversation.

Phoenix: My answer, as you've already guessed, is hell no. If she reaches out to me and wants it, that's on her, but I'm not doing this favor for you, because it's not in your best interest.

Tex: Dad put his foot down, nice.

Me: You swore fealty to me and my family.

Phoenix: I'm protecting you from losing your soul. You're welcome.

Nixon: Sex does solve a lot.

Tex: He's not wrong.

Dante: Besides... you're a whore, shouldn't be hard.

They didn't know.

In their eyes I was double dipping.

Running the club and screwing anything with legs and a healthy appetite for life.

Fantastic.

Phoenix: Guys...

Me: Phoenix say one word...

Phoenix: I hate to be the one to do this.

Me: Phoenix I will MURDER YOU.

Phoenix: Andrei's...

Nixon: Dying?

Tex: Secretly Italian?

Dante: Been married for a year?

Sergio: Russian, he's Russian. I win.

Chase: He's a virgin.

Phoenix: You knew?

Nixon: I'm sorry, what?

Tex: WTF?

Dante: You justify setting people on fire and sex is what? Too adventurous for you?

Nixon: What?

Tex: I'm confused.

Phoenix: How did you know?

Chase: Last night, so much sexual tension, not the kind where you know they're boning, but the kind where you know they're not, put two and two together, noticed he acted a lot like he flinched when women did touch him, it was always brief... Oh, and I overheard Phoenix talking to Bee about it.

I exhaled in relief. At least I was a better actor than that.

Me: I'm running myself over with my car now. See you in Hell.

Tex: Wear a condom!

Nixon: Don't go too fast.

Chase: It will be over in five seconds. Maybe two.

Dante: I can come over and—

Me: Finish that sentence and I strangle you.

Tex: That's what she said.

Phoenix: You aren't your father.

I stared at the screen.

The guys stopped texting.

Maybe they knew I needed a minute.

Maybe they didn't know what to say.

Me: I have work to do. I'm going to break Elena. I'm not going to have sex. It's all I have, all I have.

I hated being vulnerable.

I hated admitting that.

And then Nixon replied.

Nixon: I respect that.

Tex: Same.

Dante: She wouldn't be taking it, Drei, you'd be giving it.

Sergio: We're here if you need us.

Phoenix: I get that more than you will ever know.

Me: Then try to understand why I want her to leave.

Phoenix: No, I think I like the idea of you being tortured and finally facing your demons, they'll come knocking a different way, and there are worse ways to conquer your fears.

Nixon: He's right.

Me: I'm leaving this chat group now.

I tossed my phone on the bed and ran my shaky hands through my hair, then stood, grabbed my phone, and stomped out of my room.

Alice was waiting in the kitchen. She'd made bacon.

I stared at it.

Then at her. "You packed?

"No." She swallowed a piece and reached for another. "I'm not."

"Why?" I leaned against the granite; it cut into my hip as I waited for her response.

She eyed me up and down. "You need me."

"No." Rage filled me, how dare she! "I really don't."

"We'll see."

"Yup, guess we will."

Was everyone going to drive me insane today?

I slammed my hands on the countertop and tried to breathe in and out, in and out. "I'm off to torture my stepmother. Don't know when I'll be back."

"Wait!" She reached for my arm, touched it.

I flinched. "What? What more could you possibly want from me?"

"Can I come?" Her eyes searched mine.

I had to have heard her wrong. "I'm sorry, what?"

Was she drunk?

"Can I come with you?"

"You," I said slowly, "want to come with me and watch while I torture a woman for information and bring her as close to death as physically possible?"

She shivered and then paled. "Is she bad?"

"Does it matter?"

She nodded.

I bit back a curse. "She used to hit on me when I was a kid and tried touching me in the shower multiple times, would tell my dad I was the one hitting on her and made it so that I had to kill my own puppy when I was a child. Does that answer your fucking question?"

Alice's eyes lit up with rage. "I'm coming."

"Just make sure you puke in the corner and remember she's the enemy."

"If I'm staying, I need to learn how this works."

Exhausted already, I sighed. "You're not staying, six thirty-two."

"Back to that, are we?"

"Alice." I said her name with warning when my heart sped up that she would even fight to stay. "Don't."

"Do I need to bring like a weapon or something?"

I smirked. "Wow, you're actually serious, aren't you?"

"Yeah, I mean you cut out my brother's tongue. I'm assuming I need a knife or—"

"I'm keeping you far away from all sharp objects. With my luck you'd actually injure yourself and distract me. Besides, do you really think I would be so boring as to use a knife when I want information?"

Was it my imagination or did her eyes light up? "No. I

would think for a man who has a tarantula at the bar, you'd be far more… adventurous."

I barked out a laugh. "You have no fucking idea."

At least one good thing would happen from today.

Alice would watch what I did.

And because she was a good person.

Because she was more than good.

She'd realize just how much she didn't belong in my world.

I was the prince of darkness.

She may as well be an angel of light.

CHAPTER THIRTY-TWO

Alice

The room was purple.

I imagined more of a jail cell or dungeon sort of situation, something cold and dirty. Instead, the room seemed almost flirty, nice.

Though I did notice that the door was thick enough the room had to be completely sound proof.

There were multiple curtains covering something in the very back.

And tied to a chair was the woman who should have protected Andrei from the devil but instead tried to seduce him.

She was part of the reason he'd become the man he was.

And I hated her.

I hated how pretty she was.

How her hair was thick, luscious.

How even after staying up all night writhing in pain, her

face held a ghost of a smile for her stepson.

Rage filled my soul as she eyed him up and down like she owned him.

Bull. Shit.

I clenched my hands into fists.

Andrei turned to me and looked down. "Feeling a bit… aggressive?"

"Very."

He looked puzzled. "Is there a reason for that?"

Elena sighed loudly. "I'm right here!"

"I'm not speaking to you." Andrei said in a bored tone.

I almost stuck my tongue out at her.

Instead, I wrapped my arms around Andrei and whispered in his ear. "She hurt you, so I want to hurt her."

When I pulled back, his eyes flashed. "I should be completely disgusted with how erotic that actually sounds."

I felt myself blush.

"And that—" He tapped a gloved finger to my cheek. "—is just another reason you need to go. Today."

"We'll see."

He just shook his head like he didn't want to argue, and then he turned to Elena. "How's the ant bite?"

"How's the limp dick?"

He burst out laughing. "Only when you're in the room. God, I can't even imagine how many poor souls got the syph because of you."

She clenched her teeth and tried lunging for him, but the metal chair must have either been heavy or anchored to the floor.

I watched as he circled her, his smile amused, calm. He was in his element, it felt like I was watching something personal, vulnerable, he was hunting.

She was his prey.

I crossed my arms and shivered as his muscles flexed beneath his tight, long, black shirt.

He was wearing jeans that looked expensive, and his nose piercing seemed to make him look more predatory as he smiled at her with perfect white teeth.

He was mocking her without even opening his mouth.

"Who's supplying the women?" he asked stopping behind her.

"Offer me protection.

He sighed in annoyance and then winked at me like he was enjoying himself. "Alice, tell me, do you like fish?"

"Um… yes?"

He grinned and crooked his finger.

I followed him to the far side of the room. He pressed a button, and the curtain spread revealing several tanks of different sizes.

I noticed the jellyfish right away.

Rats of different sizes.

A few smaller spiders that looked exotic.

A snail that looked completely harmless.

A puffer fish that was cute but, I knew, deadly.

And then a sleek looking fish that had a sharp fin.

"That one," I pointed to the sleek fish. "What's that?"

"Surgeon fish." He grabbed a pair of metal tongs and a net. As he dipped the net into the water and scooped up the fish, he grabbed the tongs and clasped the fish as it flopped around. "Some say that its fins are as sharp as a scalpel."

"Are they?"

"No." He grinned. "Sharper."

"So, you're saying don't touch it."

"Exactly."

He turned to Elena. "You like fishing, right Elena?"

She glared. "Protection for the names."

"No," he barked and then looked to me. "You see that bucket in the far corner? Can you fill it in the sink and bring it over?"

I located the yellow bucket, filled it in the sink next to the bathroom, and walked toward Elena.

"You his assistant or his whore?"

I narrowed my eyes at her. "Both."

"Enjoy it while it lasts, sweetheart. Soon you'll be in this chair."

"No. I won't. He promised he'd kill me and make it quick if it ever came to that, so no, Elena, I won't ever be in that chair."

Her face turned a bright red as I dropped the bucket in front of her, water sloshed all over her jean-clad legs.

Andrei had a remote in his hand. The floor below the chair suddenly lowered, he slid the bucket under her dangling feet and dropped the fish in.

I watched in fascination as he pressed another button, bringing the bucket closer and closer to her feet while the fish swam around in agitated circles.

"Now." Andrei cleared his throat. "I either leave you in here for an hour with this fish while he cuts your feet to tiny ribbons and bone, or you can tell me who's sending the girls."

"Your father's son," Elena spat. "You'll have to do more than torture me with your freaky zoo."

"This…" Andrei grinned. "I do for fun. I do for free. Because killing you is too easy, because slitting your throat is pretty painless, because I want to see how much blood of yours, I can spill. You'll tell me because you value your life. But that doesn't mean I can't enjoy it while I can."

"You're sick!" she yelled. "Just like him!"

"You're right about one thing." He pressed the button until her feet dipped in the water, she let out a scream. "I am sick, but sorry to disappoint you, I'm nothing like him, I would never have fucked you."

He pressed the button all the way.

The bucket went all the way up to her knees.

The water went from clear to crimson in seconds.

I couldn't look away.

Andrei, however, yawned. "Names?"

"P-protection!" She shook in her seat as she tried to jerk her body free and kick over the bucket.

It seemed to just piss off the fish more.

Andrei reached for something on a shelf and then walked over to the bucket. "Good enough." He reached the tongs in, put the fish away and then dumped what looked like an entire box of salt into the bucket.

I cringed.

She screamed so loud my ears rang.

I covered them briefly and then lowered them as tears ran down her cheeks. She looked ready to pass out.

"No?" Andrei sighed. "That's too bad."

He grabbed a bottle with a fine-tipped nozzle and squirted it down one arm in a circular motions as though writing something, and then did the same on the wooden plank floor.

"Last chance before you pass out," Andrei said in a cold, detached voice.

"GO TO HELL!" she roared.

"Already living there. Even have a nice flat screen and king size bed, but your concern—" He grabbed a pack of matches from his pocket and lit a stick. "—is noted."

He dropped it.

Instantly, the floor erupted in flames.

It was writing.

Petrov.

It didn't touch her body.

He grabbed another match, lit it, and grabbed a bottle of vodka that was sitting near the bed.

"Give me a name," he demanded.

She stared down at the floor.

He took a swig of alcohol and blew across the match, lighting her entire right arm on fire.

Amidst her screaming, he pressed a button, lowering the floor again. He grabbed the bucket filled with blood and salt, then dumped it over her burning flesh.

Her screams pierced the air.

It smelled like blood and alcohol.

Like salt and acid.

Like the fires of Hell.

He nodded to her arm. "So, you don't forget who you're talking to."

And then he pointed to the floor. "So, you never forget who runs this family. I'll be back tonight."

Her teeth chattered and then her eyes rolled to the back of her head as she slumped in her seat.

She'd passed out from pain.

Covered in her own blood.

In salt.

And still smoking from where he'd set her on fire.

With a burned inscription on her arm.

Andrei.

A sick part of me was glad.

A sick part of me.

Was proud.

Because I would have given anything to be able to do that to my brother for laying his hands on me, for daring touch what wasn't his.

I didn't realize how much I wanted vengeance.

No… revenge.

Until Andrei led me back down the hall and into the apartment.

"You're shaking," he whispered. "Good."

I nodded.

"You're afraid," he added after another minute. "Even better."

"No," I said quickly.

"No?" he repeated, hesitating briefly before putting his hands on my shoulders and turning me toward him. "Is this your first lie?"

"Not scared." I exhaled roughly and met his gaze. "You gave me his tongue."

Andrei nodded slowly.

"If I asked for his still beating heart?"

He showed no surprise as he said. "Consider it done."

"And if I wanted to do the honors?"

"I'd hand you the fucking knife."

"That would be murder."

"No," he whispered harshly. "That would be justice."

I kissed him then, stood up on my tiptoes and crushed my mouth against his. He was warm, every hard part of his body.

He pulled me into his arms, pressing me against the counter top as he deepened the kiss, digging his hands into my hair, the same hands that had just tortured another human being.

Maybe I was as depraved as he was.

Maybe he'd awakened something inside me.

Because I wasn't sorry.

No. I wanted more.

Because I was on the other side.

And for once, I was empowered.

No longer the victim.

CHAPTER THIRTY-THREE

Andrei

The room crackled and hissed around me. It laughed at my pain while she kissed it away.

She should run.

I warned Chase's wife.

Told her to run.

Now it was my turn.

To tell her that she was kissing poison.

Getting too close.

I slid my tongue into her mouth. I tasted, I took, I was greedy with each kiss. With blood on my hands, I held her.

With death in my soul, I drank from her.

With the devil in my heart, I coveted her.

I wanted closer.

More.

My gloves felt too hot for my hands.

My hands too big to contain the weeping leather as I pulled

away from Alice and stared into her big blue eyes.

"You don't want this," I whispered.

She bit down on her swollen lip and reached for me, I stood still as her warm hands touched both of my cheeks. "Lie."

I let out a hiss of air at her touch. "Walk. Away."

"Kiss me again."

"I can't do that." I needed to stop doing that.

"Can't or won't?"

I told myself one more kiss, one more touch. I told myself it would be okay, that I was still in control.

That I was above this.

That no woman had ever owned me.

No woman had ever taken everything.

My chest heaved as I stared at her mouth, unable to move, completely rooted to the floor.

Alice moved her hands to my jeans and slowly unbuttoned them. I didn't stop her, I needed to fucking stop her, but it was like I'd drank this paralyzing poison from her lips and couldn't function, could only watch her as my soul floated above my body, mocking my inaction, telling me that this would be the end of me.

The very end.

Letting her in.

Keeping her there.

I would give her everything.

And then I would lose control.

Lose my mind.

Lose my heart.

I would lose.

So would she.

"Alice..." My voice cracked. "I wish..." Her hands stilled

on my jeans like she was ready to pull them down. "I can't. I wish I could. I can't."

How could she possibly understand?

How could I explain the gut-wrenching fear of looking in the mirror and knowing that one choice kept me sane. One choice.

And that was sex.

He'd made that choice.

I wouldn't.

I couldn't.

I couldn't trust myself, couldn't trust it wouldn't happen to me too, and hurt someone like her.

Someone so very… perfect.

Without blinking, Alice gripped my jeans, indecision etched on every pretty part of her face.

She was beautiful.

So damn beautiful.

I gripped her wrists with my hands and pulled them away from the very real temptation of getting completely naked and sinking into her, feeling her clench around me, her tight heat.

Shit.

I pulled her into my arms, and she rested her head on my shoulder. Just because I couldn't let her touch me, couldn't cross that line, didn't mean I couldn't make her happy, I would kill to watch her face in the throes of multiple orgasms.

I quickly gripped her by the hips and put her up on the cold granite countertop.

"Andrei what are you doing?" She looked down at me uncertainty in her blue eyes.

I moved my hands to her ass and pulled down the black leggings she'd been wearing, all the way down to her ankles, right along with a pair of lacy underwear that were bright pink, and perfect.

"Andrei?"

"Yes?"

"Seriously, what are you doing?"

I gripped her knees with my hands and then spread them wide. "What's it look like I'm doing?" I smirked. "I'm feasting."

Her eyes widened.

Never underestimate a virgin with an extremely vivid imagination and heightened sexual appetite.

I wasn't a fucking monk.

I would like to think I knew more than most men, because I'd seen it all, watched it, inadvertently studied it.

If someone gave me a diagram of a woman, I could point out over twenty-two ways to get her off — with my tongue, a feather, my fingers, take your pick.

"You don't have to—" She let out a gasp, gripping the edge of the granite, turning her hands white.

I chuckled darkly against her right thigh and bit. "I'm sorry, what was that? I don't have to?"

"I've never, nobody has ever… done. This."

"Tell me," I asked gently before I dipped my tongue inside her and flicked.

Her entire body jerked.

"Tell me he never touched you like this, tell me nobody has ever touched you like this."

"Never," she rasped. "You." That word was like a gunshot going off in my soul. "Only you, Andrei."

"Me." I flicked my tongue again, and gripped her by the ass, pulling her almost completely off the counter while I sat beneath her and sucked her off in the most primitive aggressive way I knew how.

With every ounce of energy I had in my physical body.

With my soul.

I used every weapon in my arsenal.

My tongue relaxed her, made her entire body quiver, my fingers splayed her open and teased every pink part of her.

I breathed her in.

Inhaled her scent.

Exhaled a heated breath against her sensitive swollen flesh.

"This is too much. It's too much I can't." She gripped my hair.

I pulled back, slowing each stroke, licked her like she was chocolate and vanilla swirl.

"Oh, God." She jerked against my face.

And I fucking drank.

Quenched my thirst on her orgasm.

And swore to do it again.

Her entire body quaked against me, her heartbeat pulsed against my tongue, and when I drew back, when the after effects finally settled… I gazed up at her, wiping my mouth down her thigh to her knee, and locked eyes with her. "I'm not even close to being full."

CHAPTER THIRTY-FOUR

Alice

"What if I'm hungry?" I asked innocently, still fully exposed to Andrei with his swollen, wet mouth, his smug as hell mouth.

He smirked. "I'll make you dinner."

"Not that kind of food."

"I'm spicier than you," he fired back with an amused laugh.

"What? And I'm cake?"

"I didn't get a good enough taste test. I'll come back to you on that, once I feed you. The only rule is you have to sit on my face. Otherwise… no deal."

I almost hid behind my own hands. "You…" I had nothing.

"Me." He shrugged. "You like stir fry?"

I almost smacked him. "You can't just say things like that out loud and then offer stir fry!"

"Fine." He leaned in; his lips moved up my neck. "Steak?"

"Meat. I could do meat." I reached for him.

He dodged me.

"When are we going to talk about the fact that this isn't an even playing field?" I asked out loud while he moved around the kitchen island, still so obviously aroused I had trouble not staring.

The man was… incredible.

And he still had pants on.

Unbelievable.

I wasn't attracted.

Was that the lie I was telling myself?

"It's cute that you think there's a chance things will ever be fair between you and me." He seemed so amused I wanted to smack him.

"You can't just do things like that to people and then just offer stir fry and then walk around so aroused you'll probably poke your own eye out in the next five minutes!"

He barked out a laugh. "First off, if I was that hung, I'd be a horse. Second, I'm still in possession of both eyes, but it's good to know you're concerned."

"I'm not." I gritted my teeth, pulled up my leggings, and jumped off the counter in a final tug to get them to the right spot. "You're avoiding this discussion."

"I'm trying to feed you." He moved around the kitchen, opened the fridge.

I slammed the door closed. "I'm not leaving."

He sighed. "You think after that I'd let you?"

"What was your plan? Barring the door and chaining me to your bed?"

He leaned against the fridge, his eyes scanning me from head to toe. "Close. I was planning on chaining you to your bed and then feeding on you whenever I got edgy…"

"So, like every five minutes?"

He leaned in and whispered, "Three."

"If I agree to that will you at least take off your gloves when you're around me?"

He'd touched me intimately without gloves on.

And it hadn't seemed hard.

Yet I knew it was. I knew it was painful.

I knew because Phoenix said it was.

Before I lost the nerve, I reached for his right hand and clutched it in mine.

He bit back a curse.

His entire body went stiff.

When he was in control it didn't hurt him, that's what I'd noticed, but when it was forced on him, he reacted.

I almost gave up then.

Because I knew that there was no way I could let him take control during sex, could I? I'd spent years being abused by a brother who tried everything under the sun to try to get it up so he could have sex with me, so he could debase me.

Being at Andrei's mercy.

I gulped.

And yet, the only way this was happening.

Was if I submitted to a man.

When I swore never again.

Andrei stared down at me.

He was so beautiful. With his fierce blue eyes, chiseled jaw, perfect complexion. My fallen angel.

I wondered what it would be like to just drop to my knees.

"You should eat." He broke the staredown, his jaw flexing as he gripped my hand tighter and then very slowly brought it to his lips and kissed the back of it.

I almost swooned all over the floor. "I like it when you kiss me."

His face softened. "You're impossible not to kiss."

"My dad said I was too tempting, my lips too big, my eyes too wide, he said I tempted men and—"

Andrei gripped my chin with his left hand, still holding my right. "Listen very carefully to what I'm about to say."

His eyes flashed with so much anger I was actually afraid. "Okay."

"It's. Not. Your. Fault."

Tears filled my line of vision until finally spilling over onto my cheeks. "It is, they say—"

"Alice, if you hear nothing else, believe nothing else, believe this. You are precious, and they will burn in Hell for hurting you, for telling you lies. The value you have, your life, your soul, your beauty, your intelligence, never let them make you think it's worthless. That's their shame talking, their anger, their bitterness, their jealousy. The truly ugly of this world have one thing in common and one thing only… they want the truly pure and beautiful things to believe they are less than. Don't let them win."

My throat felt tight.

My tears too hot for my cheeks.

"Now…" He released my hand and pulled me against his chest, hugging me so tight that I wanted to cry more because it felt so right, so good.

Devil mine.

I instantly relaxed.

"Let me make you food," he whispered against my hair.

"As long as it's not that weird fish with the sharp fin. He was really pretty."

He barked out a laugh his body shaking against mine. "We won't kill Speedy."

"Stop." I jerked away with a smile, wiping my tears from my cheeks. "Please tell me you don't name all your torturous animals."

He just shrugged and said, "The jellyfish's name is Bob."

And just like that, I, Alice De Lange.

Fell in love with Andrei Petrov.

CHAPTER THIRTY-FIVE

Andrei

She promised me she would eat while I went and checked on Elena. The last thing I wanted was to leave that apartment with her scent on my skin, her taste still buzzing across my tongue, numbing my mouth.

I jerked open the heavy door to the purple room. The odor of Hell wafted out. Burnt skin, blood, and fear.

Her clothes were still soaked with blood and salt, and the angry red and pink slashes across her right arm were already starting to swell.

Good.

"Names," I said in a harsh whisper.

"P-protection." Her teeth chattered.

"You're going into shock." I made my way toward her, circled her chair, and stopped when I was directly behind her. "It's normal for your body to shake, for your teeth to gnash against each other in search of relief, relief that won't ever come." I ran a finger down the side of her neck.

She flinched.

Even her skin felt evil. "Tell me." I removed my finger. "Is it worth suffering over? Dying over?"

"I tell you, you don't protect me, I die."

"Fine." I snapped. "I'll offer you protection inside these walls, how does that sound?"

She snorted. "Like a trick."

"It's all you'll get."

"Swear to me!" she screeched "Swear that you'll protect me here, in these walls."

I walked to the door and opened it, then hit the comm button that was on the outside, dialing up Ax.

"Boss?"

"Bring in Lennie."

"Yup."

I walked back into the room and faced her with a calm smile. Mascara ran down her cheeks, her teeth clenched together like she was a feral animal.

She would be the sort to feed on her own young.

Hadn't she tried?

"Just once, Andrei, he doesn't have to know! You're growing up so fast…" Red nails dug into my thigh.

I shivered.

She deserved exactly what was coming. "I swear."

She hung her head. "It's Oscar De Lange and his cousin Aldo. Before your father was killed he gave them the contract. Their only job was to bring fresh girls to the clubs, use the same cars, drop 'em off, and do it again. They still had connections with the old prostitution rings."

My blood chilled. It would make sense. How Alice's

brother knew about the club, why he visited, why he thought bringing her here would get rid of her.

Or possibly…

Distract me.

I jerked my head toward the door. It opened, and Lennie made his way in, black briefcase in one hand, black plastic gloves in the other.

"You can set up right there." I pointed to her feet.

He grabbed a stool and started opening his kit.

"What's this?" Elena glared at me.

"This is me keeping my word." I snapped my fingers. "Eyes up here. How long has Oscar been working the trade with Aldo?"

She sighed. "Oscar's old. He needs a family he can trust. The De Langes are a bunch of psychopaths without any leadership, so he went to the first family that had no issues with selling women — Aldo's."

I clenched my teeth. "Who else knows about this?"

Elena rolled her eyes. "It officially became the family business after Mil De Lange's death. Aldo has been helping Oscar for the past year and a half."

"I've been locked in my room for a year…"

My stomach clenched.

She didn't know.

She asked so many questions, though.

I let her in.

I let her into my apartments.

I let her into my life.

I let her in.

I let the enemy inside.

And handed her the keys.

Fuck.

"You look pale, Andrei." Elena grinned. "Something to do with that beautiful girl who was in here earlier? I must say she looks… extremely familiar—"

"Keep talking and I cut out your tongue the way I did Aldo's," I barked.

Her eyes widened and then she threw back her head and laughed. "You know, it was a good plan. He sells his sister and she gains access to the whole underworld he's trying to take from your very hands."

"He was here last night," I admitted.

"He wants the club. He will kill you for it. Your father promised more money, more clubs. Your father died. So, you either carry out the contract he started or eliminate everyone who wants to take what's rightfully yours, as boss."

I snorted out a laugh. "I keep him alive because I find it amusing that Aldo shits himself in his sleep wondering when I'm going to come back for the rest of his tongue. He lives because I allow it. What could he possibly do to me?"

She was quiet as Lennie pulled out his tattoo gun and ink. "Oh, I don't know, Andrei, what could he possibly use against you?"

I could still taste her.

Betrayer?

Was she a De Lange loyal to me? To the Italians?

Or to her abusive brother and father?

That was the problem with the De Langes.

You never knew where they stood until it was too late.

"Go ahead and get started Lennie." I looked away from Elena, couldn't stand the thought of her trying to read my face.

The buzz of the gun filled the room.

"What the hell is he doing?" She tried fighting against the binds of the chair.

"Offering protection," I called over my shoulder. "Welcome to the club, I think the gentlemen will enjoy very much having some older Italian blood in the mix. Try not to ruin the tattoo before it begins. Oh, and you'll want to shower before your first customer. I'd start praying you don't get called to start the bidding this evening. The woman sacrificed is always the one who refuses the men who want her. This isn't the time to get shy, and I'd pull out everything in your sexual arsenal. Would hate to see you get your throat slit."

I shut the door behind me and leaned against it.

I knew she was screaming even though I couldn't hear her.

Just like I knew I needed to test Alice the minute I got back to the apartment.

Friend or foe.

Enemy or lover.

I didn't know.

I was too in over my head.

Shit.

I sent a quick text to Phoenix.

> **Me:** We may have a problem.
>
> **Phoenix:** We?
>
> **Me:** Us. She's... potentially compromised. Her brother knew exactly what he was doing in bringing her here. She's either supposed to infiltrate from within or distract me enough to become a pawn in a bigger game. Aldo and Oscar De Lange behind the women. Get Sergio on it now.
>
> **Phoenix:** Shit.
>
> **Me:** I'll get some answers out of her.

Phoenix: And ruin what could be the best thing that's ever happened to you? What are you going to do? Tie her to a chair?

Me: Something like that...

Phoenix: Think this through.

Me: I'm going dark. And I already have.

Phoenix: Shit, Andrei—

I turned my phone off, slid it into my pocket and stared at the apartment door, then very quietly let myself in, shut the door and locked it behind me.

Alice wasn't in the living room.

I made my way down the hall, slowly measuring my steps until I reached her room. She was curled up on her side, sleeping.

I squeezed my eyes shut.

Two days ago, I wouldn't have thought twice.

Today I was hesitating.

Making excuses.

Justifying.

She was in me now, in the air, in my blood, in my lungs with each inhale, each shuddering exhale.

I ignored the pain in my chest.

She was just another object sent to either distract me or bring me to my knees.

That's the lie I told myself.

The lie I wanted to believe.

To make it easier on myself.

I left the room and returned with rope and a few cable ties.

"Alice," I hissed. "Wake up."

She jolted awake her feet made a kicking motion as she pressed a hand to her chest. "Do you often stand over people holding rope while they're sleeping?"

Her dark hair spilled over her shoulders.

I wanted to twist it around my fingers, tug her close, kiss that swollen mouth.

"Is there a wrong answer to that question?" I wondered out loud. "I need your hands."

"I was kidding." She held out her hands in front of her body palm down. "The whole me being chained to the bed…"

"Uh-huh," I slid the zip tie around her wrist and jerked it toward the headboard, pulling it tight against the post so she couldn't move. I kept her left hand free.

"Legs," I barked.

"Wh-what?"

"Pull them straight."

"Andrei?"

"Do it," I snapped.

She quickly straightened her legs. I wrapped the rope around her knees and kept wrapping tight until I got to her ankles, I made a figure eight and knotted it, then stepped away.

"Andrei?" She said my name again, her voice shaking.

"Elena has been taken care of." I tried to sound bored, but she looked so innocent, so crushed.

I looked away and shoved my hands in my jean pockets. "She was very… helpful in her information about your family."

Alice paled. "Do I want to know?"

"Maybe you already do?" I suggested. "How would I know? Maybe you were sent here for a reason? Seduction, perhaps?"

"Seduction?" she repeated, her eyes wild. "Are you hearing yourself? My brother touched me, touched me!" Her eyes filled with tears. "I have next to zero sexual experience, and the only time I've ever found pleasure in it was an hour ago and now

I'm tied to a bed!"

I flinched as she jerked her hand against the headboard. "There is another possibility…"

"What?" I'd never seen a woman look so pissed, alive.

I loved it more than I should.

"You're working with him," I suggested, circling the bed and finally sitting on the opposite side. "He's your partner? He wants the club, you know, the money that comes from selling girls. Fact, in one day this club makes more than three million dollars in sales and prostitution, that's not including drugs or private parties. And he's just desperate enough to think he can take that from me."

She shook her head and looked away. "I would never help him do that. I would never be on board with him owning anything as evil as this." She clenched her teeth and stared at me when she said it.

"A few hours ago you were screaming my name, and now I'm evil?" My grin was cruel. "Which is it? Heaven or hell? You can't let me give you heaven then damn me to hell in the same breath, Alice, that's not how this works." I reached into my pocket and pulled out my knife, flicking it open. "I need to know that you're telling me the truth."

"What possible reason could I have for lying?"

"Money. Greed. Power." I shrugged. "To name a few."

"Fine." Her lower lip trembled. "If that's what you really think. That I would live up to the De Lange name, kill me, turn me over to the Italians." Tears filled her eyes. "It's not fair." A tear slid down her cheek. "To give me hope like you did, and then rip it away." She choked on a sob. "I will never forgive you for this, Andrei. Never."

I sucked in a breath. "Put yourself in my position."

Her eyes darted away.

"What would you do?"

She licked her lower lip and hung her head. "I don't know."

"Yeah, you do."

Her head snapped up. "Fine! I would torture them for information. I would make sure the people I loved were safe, and I would do everything in my power to keep it that way, even if that meant I had to kill. I would do whatever it took and never look back!"

I crawled up the bed and straddled her body.

And then I held the knife to her throat. "Are you working for your brother?"

"No." She sobbed, her neck straining. "I'm not."

"Were you sent here to get information?"

"No." Tears slid down her chin onto the blade of my knife.

"Were you sent here to seduce me?"

Her eyes searched mine. "No."

I wanted to believe her.

My past told me she was lying.

All women were liars.

All of them.

Don't trust them.

They use their bodies.

My chest heaved as I stared her down.

She didn't look away.

Her eyes were bright with tears. My hand shook as I pressed the blade against her soft skin.

Our foreheads touched, our mouths inches apart, as I sliced the plastic binding her wrists.

I grabbed the tip of the knife and then twisted it so that the hilt was pointed toward Alice. "Take it."

"What?" Her chest heaved. "What do you mean take it?"

"It's yours." I searched her eyes, measuring, weighing her reaction. "It would take seconds for me to bleed out," I pointed to my neck. "Or you could just stab my leg and pray you hit the femoral artery."

"You're insane," she hissed.

"Why yes, I am," I agreed. "You could probably get through the club without anyone asking questions. Hell, you could probably take my SUV and meet up with your family without being stopped. Because I claimed you. Because no matter what I say, I can't stop thinking about you, wanting you. Because I'm the insane man, who would still want that, even if you stabbed me in the neck right now. That's how insane I am. That's how crazy I am. That with my last few breaths I would think to myself… fucking worth it."

I didn't know what to expect.

That she would stab me.

Drop the knife.

Or yell.

Maybe cry some more.

She was perfectly still and then she shoved me away from her and fucking drove the knife directly into my right thigh.

And maybe I was insane.

Because my first response.

Was to kiss her senseless.

Our tongues tangled as she shoved me back against the mattress, I was bleeding all over the white duvet, could feel the tip of the knife lodged in my muscle, twisting the fibers.

And I still kissed her.

She pulled back, eyes blazing, lips puffy. "Doubt me again, and I'm aiming higher."

I bit down on my lower lip to conceal my smile, then reached for the knife, pulled it quickly out of my thigh, cut the rope off her legs and threw it against the wall.

The tip stuck above the dresser, blood dripping from the metal making a gruesome red smear down the white wall.

"You should put something on that." She suddenly looked nervous, licking her lips, looking down at my leg, when all I could think about was the fact that she'd stabbed me and how erotic it had been.

The pain, for once.

Was good.

My hands weren't covered in black gloves.

They weren't shaking.

The pain was in my leg, not in my hands as they touched her.

The pain throbbed, it numbed, it consumed.

I nipped at her lower lip and flipped her onto her back against the stained mess of the duvet as more blood dripped from my thigh. "Later."

"You're bleeding everywhere," she pointed out.

I kissed her harder and came up for her. "Then maybe you shouldn't have stabbed me."

"You told me you didn't trust me to my face and tied me to a bed an hour after giving me the best orgasm of my life. And then you gave me a sharp object. What did you think would happen? A parade?"

I barked out a laugh. "Yeah, something like that, only you were supposed to be naked, and the parade was you walking in front of me while I watched and judged."

"You're." She made a face and shoved at my chest.

I kissed her again, making my way down her neck, licking

behind her ear while she bucked off the bed. "I'm what?"

"Evil."

"Thank you." I bit the soft spot between neck and shoulder then pulled the simple white shirt over her head.

"Wasn't a compliment."

"Maybe not to a sane person…" I countered, reaching for her breasts, cupping them, and imagining a world where I could lock myself in the bedroom with her and do nothing but touch, taste, feel.

My excitement was short lived.

Because she was suddenly reaching for me.

I batted her hands away.

She was persistent.

"Do we need to get the knife again?" I threatened.

"Did you want the other thigh to match?" she countered through clenched teeth.

I smirked. "Maybe."

"You like me." She said it like it was a statement not a question.

"Yes."

"You like kissing me."

Where was she going with this? "Yes."

"You like touching me?"

"Is this a test? Am I passing or failing?" I wondered out loud.

"I like you too. I like kissing you. I like touching you. The only part of the test that's pass-fail is if you let me make you feel good."

"Can't." I shook my head. "Your brother… what he did, what you… I can't imagine a world where you would ever be okay with touching me and not being completely disgusted."

"Disgusted," she repeated. "Do you really believe that?"

"I know that," I rasped. "I've lived that. I've seen it all. Women, the only way they come back from it, the only way is through the fence."

"You're not making any sense…"

"The American dream, the perfect doting husband, who turns off the lights during sex, buys her a dog, tells her they don't need sex unless it's his birthday or even Christmas. There's exactly one position they do it in, and he almost always gets off within a few minutes while she lays there and mentally counts down the seconds until he's done."

"What are you talking about?" She cupped my face her hands were so soft against my skin.

"All I'm saying…" I locked eyes with her. "…is that I am not the sort of man who helps you get over your fears in the bedroom. I'm the reason for them."

"Lie," she whispered. "And my brother he never… he tried, multiple times, but he never…"

What exactly was she saying?

"I'm a virgin."

I jerked away like she'd stung me. "What was that?"

"Virgin." Her cheeks pinked. "He tried, and he touched me, and he did horrible things, but the actual act of sex, he could never do it. And then he'd blame me for it and call me a whore and other things…" She shuddered.

"I'm going to cut off his dick and feed it to him." Damn! I meant to think that not say it.

She just stared at me and smiled. "Such pretty promises."

I knew she wasn't going to take no for an answer, just like I knew I was going to bleed even more if I kept jerking away from her.

Her hand inched up my thigh and then she was unbuttoning my jeans.

I wasn't wearing boxers because my jeans were tight and I didn't want to be constricted.

So, she had no preparation for me.

For the size of me.

For what she thought she was going to do.

Her eyes widened. "I've never felt more like a virgin in my entire life."

Makes two of us.

I leaned over and pressed a kiss to the side of her mouth. "I'm currently bleeding out on your bed, you've proved your point — son of—"

She gripped me with her right hand.

I ducked my head next to her shoulder and tried not to draw blood as I bit down on my bottom lip. Her hands were velvet.

Smooth.

She explored every inch of me.

And I'd never been more at anyone's mercy than I was in that moment.

Bleeding all over a girl who wanted nothing more than to pleasure me the way I did her.

"Alice—"

"Do you realize you say my name now? No more six thirty-two… even though I was getting really attached to that number." She squeezed harder. "And the way you said it."

"Fuck." I was dying. I braced myself over her and shook my head slowly. "The knife won't kill me. This, however, might."

"I don't want you dead." Tears sparkled in her eyes as she moved her hand back and forth and whispered, "I want to give you life."

I growled against her mouth, trying not to crush her hand as she moved, trying not to rush what I wanted to last forever.

Trying not to think about pulling down her leggings and sinking myself into her.

I told myself this was justifiable.

Sex wouldn't be.

This was okay.

This would be fine.

This was everything.

I moaned her name.

I was so damn close.

I wanted it to last longer.

Gently, she pressed me onto my back, her eyes raking over me as she very slowly lowered her head.

I flinched. "Alice, don't, seriously don't—"

The word died on my lips.

And I, Andrei Petrov, heir to one of the deadliest mobs in history.

Fell.

CHAPTER THIRTY-SIX

Phoenix

His damn phone was off, which meant she was either alive or dead.

Perfect.

I tapped my fingers against the black folder and weighed my options as I sat alone at the kitchen table, drinking a glass of wine, wondering when the other shoe was going to fall.

If the De Langes were the ones locating the girls and dropping them off at the clubs, then the world finally made sense again.

We would need to send in Chase. Fast.

And we would need the FBI to raid the club in a way that made it look like the Italians and Russians weren't ratting each other out or working with each other.

Shit.

I stared into my wine glass as the sound of feet hitting the hardwood gave me pause.

"Junior." I smiled as a I said his name. "You were supposed to be in bed."

"I was in bed." Smart ass. He was wearing Spiderman pajamas and had a shit-eating grin on his face. "I just wanted a drink of water."

"You have a glass by the bed." I pointed out.

"It's not my Batman one."

Patience. Patience. Patience. "Oh, I'm sorry does the water taste different depending on the cup?"

"YUP!"

Dear God.

"So, your dinosaur cup?"

"Poop." He laughed. "It tastes like poop!"

I grabbed him and pulled him onto my lap while he fell into a fit of giggles.

Three children were out there waiting to be pulled into the protective fold of our family.

The only problem was the name associated with them.

The only problem was the De Langes wanted them as much as we did, and Andrei didn't even know they existed.

The grandfather clock chimed midnight.

There was only one thing we could do.

After all, Andrei would need his family. He would need people he trusted, people he could rely on.

Fucking hell.

I kissed my son on the head. "Off to bed, Junior, I'll be in there in five minutes."

"All right." He skipped away.

I grabbed my phone.

I was creating more chaos.

We were supposed to be at peace.

I was inviting more war.

But if it helped us destroy what was left of the De Langes, if it gave Andrei the support he needed, the family that he never had the chance to have.

I would do it.

I dialed the number to Italian royalty.

The pure bloods.

I called in the Sinacore Family.

"Yes?" A heavily accented voice said smoothly into the phone. "What is it, Nicolasi?"

"The missing Sinacore heirs." I bit down on my lip. "I have one, as well as the location of the other two."

He was silent and then, "In the States?"

"Chicago."

"How long have you known this?"

"Long enough."

His sigh was long, hard. "You risk war bringing the children into this. They are the rightful heirs."

"We risk war either way. It's their birthright."

"Where is the boy?"

"Man." I grinned to myself. "He's a man… You know him by the name of Andrei Petrov."

I will never forget the amount of cursing that occurred before arrangements were made.

Or the feeling of sickness in my chest that I was about to make life for him a hell of a lot harder.

"Strap in, Andrei, strap the hell in."

I wanted him.

More of him.

All of him.

I felt like I was on the edge peering over it, terrified to jump, wishing I was smart enough to swing to the other side and avoid danger altogether.

That's what Phoenix had offered me.

Was I really ignoring the help and just closing my eyes and falling into darkness? By choice?

He trusted me.

And I was almost scared to admit, I trusted him too, Andrei Petrov, murderer, monster.

Lover.

Friend.

Ax interrupted us holding up what looked like his cell phone. I was ready to throw it across the room, but the look on his face told me it was important, so when he apologized by kissing me on the forehead and walking out of the room.

I sighed and lay back against the bed.

That was an hour ago.

And I had class that afternoon, a lab actually, I wasn't sure if he was going to drive me again or give me some freedom to go to and from the school.

My bet was on guard duty.

I waited a little longer.

He wasn't coming back, was he?

I crawled to the side of the bed, threw my legs over, stood, stretched, and decided to go put on a movie and plan out dinner before I took off. It was the least I could do, right?

Every cell that made up my body buzzed with the awareness of him, of the way he smelled, tasted.

I was high on a drug I didn't even know I had taken until it was too late.

The kitchen was empty.

The door to the hall locked again.

Another prison.

Only I would have liked to stay in this one, if it meant Andrei stayed. I probably wouldn't look back.

I made my way over to the fridge and pulled it open, but I wasn't really seeing anything. My mind was too filled with what-ifs when it came to Andrei.

I felt different with him.

Alive.

Free.

I shut the door and leaned back against the counter. Phoenix's words seemed to stamp themselves into my consciousness.

I wanted to ask Andrei what it meant.

I felt stupid having that conversation. Then again, how else were we supposed to get past the point of him wearing gloves, or being able to receive a touch, a kiss that wasn't started by him?

My body shivered.

The sound of the lock turning and then the door opening had me turning toward the entrance.

My body gave a jolt when it wasn't Andrei who stepped through but Ax. He grinned over at me and then tossed a pair of keys in the air and swiped them. "I've been sent to take you to class."

I deflated a bit and nodded. "Yeah, I wasn't sure if he was going to let me drive myself or if I was going to get a babysitter."

"More like bodyguard," Ax said softly. "He worries."

"Does he?"

Ax's expression sobered. "You really don't understand, do you? What people would do to you if they knew? You'd be begging for death, and Andrei is under strict instructions if he's ever in contact with a De Lange."

I froze. "Wh-what?"

"Maim them first, kill a few days later so their anxiety spikes, or kill on sight."

I gulped and looked down at my feet. "He took an oath?"

"Every one of the Italians, myself included, and Andrei, took a blood oath to each other, and to Chase, executioner of the De Lange line. According to the five families, we are now four, and the De Lange arm does not exist."

It was like getting told my history was gone. Even though it wasn't a proud history, it still existed, I was still a part of something, no matter how horrible or debasing it was.

And now, I was a walking contradiction.

Sleeping with the enemy.

Close enough.

No wonder Andrei didn't trust me.

I wasn't even supposed to be breathing. He'd warned me, he'd gone to great lengths to protect me.

And I still hadn't fully grasped the situation until now. "What if I turned myself in?"

"Don't!" Ax snapped. "Then I would be a dead man."

"How so?"

"Andrei would slit my throat for failing to protect you even if it was from yourself." He shrugged. "Now, grab your shit so we aren't late."

He pulled out a gun, his hand on the trigger as it hung at his side. His expression went from friendly to killer in seconds.

I quickly ran into my bedroom and donned my uniform, including thigh-high boots, then ran out to meet him. "Ready."

"Let's go." He opened the door and put his hand on the small of my back as we walked down the dimly lit hallways into the main part of the club.

Andrei was sitting at the bar with a man who looked vaguely familiar and a gorgeous woman with sharp features and her hair cut to her chin. Bright red lipstick painted her lips, and she was wearing leather pants and a loose sweater that fell over her shoulder. Her heels were spikey and looked expensive.

My eyes darted to the scene.

They all had vodka shots.

And I was going to college.

It was just another reminder how different our worlds would always be, and how he would always attempt to shield me from the darkness.

Andrei looked my way and lifted his glass in the air and then returned his attention back to the man and woman.

My heart squeezed.

The things we'd shared.

Done.

Together.

My memory flashed, his hands touching my skin, burning from the inside out, so sensual and slow that I almost went mad with it. And touching him, feeling his strength between my fingertips as I brought him to his knees.

It meant something to me.

Sharing that with a guy when before it made me cower.

I stumbled a bit, lost in my thoughts. Ax had me by the arm in seconds. "You okay?"

"Uh, yeah." My weak voice gave me away, along with the tears that were gathering in my eyes. Would it have killed him to at least have checked on me himself?

I sensed Andrei before I turned around.

It was like he'd appeared out of thin air.

His hand touched the door just as I was about to get in the car, I turned to him and suppressed a wince. The heat from his body was almost too much.

I lifted my eyes and let out a frustrated sigh.

Fallen angels had nothing on this guy, even his swagger had swagger as he locked eyes with me and gave the smallest of smiles.

Being on the receiving end of his smile was like staring directly at the sun; it almost hurt my eyes, but it was too pretty, too bright to look away.

For someone so dark, he knew how to smile well.

And somehow, his smile made me feel worse.

"You all right?" he whispered, leaning in.

Now he asks?

"Yeah, I have class." I was already turning.

His hand was on my waist before I could get into the car.

And then he was pressing me against the Escalade, his hands on my face as he leaned in and pressed a soft kiss to my lips.

My knees went weak.

He tasted like vodka and honey.

My mouth trembled.

He thumbed my lower lip. "Be safe, *dorogaya*."

"I'll try not to run into any murderers during Econ," I countered, searching his eyes, wishing he would tell me more, admit that I was surrounded by murderers on a daily basis since being with him.

Surrounded by threats.

Not just from the Italians.

But from him.

From anyone and everyone who knew what my line had done.

I almost hung my head.

But I wasn't guilty of anything but being born in the wrong family.

"See you later." I finally found more words and quickly crawled into the car.

In my peripheral vision, I noticed his eyes flicker with something as his expressionless face seemed to darken.

I almost asked Ax to hit the accelerator for fear that Andrei was going to jump into the car and do something crazy.

Ax slowly put the SUV into drive and off we went.

I exhaled in relief only when we were closing in on campus.

"He means well," Ax finally admitted as he drove through the open gate. "He just doesn't know how to execute his feelings in a way that doesn't scare people shitless."

I smiled at that. "Yeah, I've noticed that."

"Try not to worry about it." He parked the SUV in a spot close to the Econ building.

I hopped out, expecting him to stay in the car and wait for me.

Instead, Ax moved around the vehicle and held out his hand. "Let me carry your bag."

I stared him down. "Is carrying my books really in your job description?"

"No, I'm just a gentleman." He flashed me an easy smile that showed off yet more Italian genes that should be used to sell sunglasses or clothes, underwear — hell, laundry detergent.

I handed him my bag as we slowly walked into the building. Students stared. Andrei's previous outburst probably hadn't helped.

I didn't really think twice about the stares. I knew what people thought. That I had a psycho boyfriend — or husband, whatever, I had his last name — it did matter.

I. Was. Safe.

I quickly found my seat as Ax waited outside the lab, cell phone in hand like he was going to read or check out CNN for the next two hours.

With a sigh, I looked down.

On my desk was a piece of paper.

In bold black letters it read, *Russian Whore.*

I quickly grabbed it, crushed it between my hands as I made my way over to the trash can and threw it away.

The professor had yet to show up.

More students filed in.

And as I made my way back to my seat, I noticed several more signs being held by students.

Russian Whore.

Petrov Prostitute.

Spread Eagle at Eagle Elite.

I was shaking by the time I made it back to my desk and the students didn't seem to care just laughed amongst each other while taking pictures of the signs and posting them who knows where.

Facebook.

Instagram.

Snapchat.

The signs of course disappeared five minutes later.

And I sat, in absolute hell minus one lab partner.

Staring at a paper that I couldn't seem to read because I was so sick to my stomach over what I'd seen, over the way they'd treated a stranger.

So, he scared my missing lab partner. Big. Deal.

How was I the whore?

My stomach clenched more as a girl walked by me and placed a drawing on my desk.

I assumed it was me.

And I was bending over in front of him.

I shoved it away.

Tears slipped down my cheeks.

Because hadn't that been the truth this morning?

And then he'd ignored me.

Only to kiss me again when he thought I was hurt.

I was so confused, so upset that I almost didn't notice the

hush that descended over the room twenty minutes later.

My hair stood on end as I slowly turned.

Andrei walked through the door, a look of complete rage rendering his features terrifying as he locked eyes on me, and then he crossed his arms and stood in the middle of the room.

The door opened again.

Tex Campisi walked in.

If a pin had dropped, it wouldn't dare have made a sound.

I could have sworn the guy next to me started praying.

Nixon was next, his smile cruel as he stared at everyone like they were his next meal.

Dante sauntered in.

The room erupted in mad whispers.

Phoenix followed.

The whispers stopped.

Sergio was next, his swagger confident, his eyes locking on mine with purpose I didn't understand.

And then finally, Chase Abandonato.

The murderer of my family line made his way into the room with blood splatters on his shirt and a knife in his hands.

The professor didn't blink.

He yawned and pulled out the newspaper and read as if the most powerful men in the crime world weren't just hanging out in Econ.

Andrei raked the room with his gaze. "This isn't a game."

People looked away.

"Fucking look at me when I'm talking!" he roared.

A girl in front started bawling.

And the guy who Andrei had stopped next to shook so violently his desk started to move.

"Insult what's mine again, and we'll be transporting you in

body bags. Do. You. Understand. Me?"

Heads nodded.

"Chase." Andrei said his name through clenched teeth. "A demonstration."

Chase's eyes roamed across the room until he finally stopped on a guy who was looking down at his lap. "You. Stand."

The guy blinked up at him, his face pale. Slowly, he stood on shaking legs.

"What's your name?"

"P-Peter." The guy's voice cracked.

"Peter." Chase crossed his arms over his chest. "All right Peter, I'm going to give the class thirty seconds to tell me who started the signs or I'm going to cut off a finger. It seems to be a fair trade to me… One."

As he counted, people shied away.

"Fifteen."

Nobody was standing.

"Sixteen."

I didn't want them to suffer because of me.

It was my fault.

"Twenty."

Shit.

Tears filled my eyes as I glanced around the room. This wasn't their world; this wasn't their war!

"Twenty-eight."

"Me." I jumped to my feet.

An explosion of shocks and whispers filled the room. "I didn't start it, but it's my fault for being who I am. It's always going to haunt me like it haunts you, don't involve people whose blood will never be worth spilling. The cost is too great… even to someone like you."

And to my utter surprise, Chase Abandonato… smiled. "That will be the lesson for today folks. The reason she's with us is because she's the only fucking person in this room willing to make the hard choice. The only girl in this room who gives eye contact. And the only girl in this room worthy of the Petrov name."

Andrei stepped forward and put a hand on Chase's shoulder. "Beautifully said."

"I practiced."

"It shows." Tex barked out a laugh. "Let's go, Little Petrov. Class is dismissed early, and I have a hankering for a burger."

"Oh shit, I could use some fries," Chase grumbled.

I wasn't sure how to respond.

The rest of the class seemed frozen.

So, I grabbed my things and slowly made the achingly painful walk to the front of the room. Andrei wrapped an arm around me then pulled me against his chest and kissed the fear and shame right out of my body, replacing it with something else, something that felt a lot like acceptance and hope all wrapped up in love.

Something that was… warm.

"Let's go, *dorogaya*."

I'd arrived at Eagle Elite with a guard.

And left.

With an army.

CHAPTER THIRTY-EIGHT

Andrei

We'd driven separately.

I sent Ax with the rest of the guys.

Mentally thanked them for standing by my side when I forwarded them the text Ax had sent me as he scrolled through the Eagle Elite social media accounts.

The anger I felt in seeing those words directed at her.

At mine.

Was enough to set me off for the next decade.

It was enough for me to pack enough ammo to take out the entire city block.

It was enough for me, Andrei Petrov, to humbly ask for help.

They didn't ask questions.

They didn't mock me.

They said "done" and minutes later, we walked in together, as a team, as a family.

I would take it to my grave, the way it felt to have the Italians ready to shoot on sight for offending what was mine.

I would never admit that I didn't say thank you because I wasn't sure I could get through it without trembling, without tapping my foot, without looking weak.

So, I nodded my head at them.

Got a few middle fingers back.

And got into the car.

Alice was quiet as she sat next to me, her face ashen, her thigh-high boots kissing her skin with their smooth leather making me want to dip my hand between her legs and shove her skirt up past her hips.

Whore.

Petrov Prostitute.

Those bastards should count themselves lucky that I didn't want her to see all the blood I would spill and hold it against me.

Because I had driven to that school with the purpose of killing.

And the only person that was able to stop me, to talk me from the ledge, was Phoenix, followed by a gruesome looking Chase who just shrugged and said, "It was messy, didn't have time to clean up."

The old me would have mocked him, said something to insult him and make him feel less than.

But I couldn't see past the rage.

Couldn't feel anything but the hard rhythm of my heart as it thudded angrily against my chest with the need for retribution, to hurt them the way they hurt her.

Some of the anger was misplaced, and maybe misdirected at myself, because I'd called her a number, I'd called her a whore. I had done those things, justified them because I was trying to protect her.

I swerved my black Maybach to the side of the road, my hands still gripping the steering wheel as I stared ahead.

Alice didn't move.

I clenched my jaw so hard that pain shot down my neck. "Are you okay?"

Slowly she turned to me and laid a hand on my shoulder. "Are you?"

I counted her soft breaths.

One, two, three, all unhurried, all patiently waiting for me to fill the silence with something other than her breathing, something other than the painful beat of my heart.

I felt too much with her.

And all at once.

Her fingertips, I focused on her fingertips, in the way they dug softly into my shoulder, watching, waiting, comforting.

I got out a hoarse "no." And finally released my grip on the steering wheel and turned to her.

Pink cheeks, full lips, wide green eyes, measured breaths, and worried posture.

She was everything I wasn't supposed to want.

"You saved me again." Her hand was still on my shoulder.

"No." I shook my head. "I think you have that backward, *dorogaya*. It's you who has saved me."

Her eyes widened.

And I acted.

I unbuckled my seatbelt, leaned over the center console, and jerked her against me, swallowing any protest she might have on her lips, tasting her with my whole body with every sense on fire.

It was passion.

It was painful.

It was us.

A chaotic mixture of all of my nerve endings firing too fast, too intense, but I didn't want to stop it anymore.

Maybe because I couldn't.

I was losing the war.

No, I wasn't losing.

I was forfeiting.

And winning all at once.

She moaned against my mouth as my hands roamed down her shoulders, pulling open her white oxford shirt. I kept one hand on her trembling body while I moved the other down to her skirt.

Her hips bucked as I slid my hand up her naked thigh. "I'm keeping you."

She softened against me, kissed me again, dragged her lips across mine over and over again. "Good."

She spread her legs for me.

And I nearly died.

So trusting to a man who promised he'd murder her if she asked.

To a man who didn't deserve to be touching anything so pure.

To the devil himself.

"Alice..." Her name felt like worship. Maybe for someone like me, it was.

I didn't know how to navigate what I was about to ask her, what I was about to take from her.

Or what I would give her.

All I knew was that if I couldn't hold her anymore, if the

warmth, the life, left her body.

I would die.

I'd never loved anyone before.

And I'd never loved myself.

Maybe it was love.

Maybe it was obsession.

Lust.

Maybe a little bit of all three.

I didn't care.

"Alice." I said her name again because it felt like being baptized.

New.

Pure.

I moved my hand from her thigh and pulled away.

And then I reached into my pocket and pulled out the knife Luca had given me when I agreed to go under cover with the FBI for him, when I agreed to turn against my own blood, when, according to him, I became my own man.

"I bled against this blade," I whispered. "So did Luca. A blood oath isn't just a promise. It's a completely unbreakable bond."

Alice licked her swollen lips and nodded in understanding.

"So, when I tell you that I'm binding myself to you," I continued. "I want you to know that the only thing that will keep me from you is death."

Tears filled her eyes, and one spilled down her cheek. I caught it with my finger and lifted it to my mouth, tasting the salt of her tears, pledging a silent oath to make sure that she never spilled them because of me or her family again.

With shaking hands I let the facade slip.

I let go of the control I so desperately felt the need to have over everything.

And I took off both gloves and dropped them onto the console.

She sucked in a sharp breath like she'd just seen monster and man fuse or maybe she just saw vulnerability I refused to let anyone else see.

This was it.

This moment.

On the side of the road.

With Alice De Lange.

My gaze didn't waver from hers. "The Italians cut across the hand."

I peeled my shirt over my head. "The Russians…cut across the heart."

I sliced across my chest, felt my heart beat against the metal blade as I carved a bloody A into my own skin.

Her eyes widened as I reached for her right hand, slicing across the palm and pressing it to my chest.

I kept it there.

More tears filled her eyes as she stared at me in wonder.

"I, Andrei Petrov, pledge my life, my heart, my soul to you."

I didn't realize that I was shaking until she wrapped her free arm around me and held me tight.

Our blood flowing, mixing, making love, as it dripped down my body.

CHAPTER THIRTY-NINE

Phoenix

"Nice swing." I pulled off my aviators and watched as Luca stiffened and then turned toward me and cursed. "Not happy to see me?"

He grabbed his club, his fingers tight. "Was thinking about throwing this around four minutes ago but figured Bee would be mad if you came home with two black eyes."

I grinned. "She's seen worse."

"Haven't we all." He sighed and slowly walked over to me, he was wearing black trousers and a black long-sleeve shirt that looked a bit out of place on a golf course. Then again, the gun shoved in the back of the pants didn't exactly help things.

"Your gun's showing." I pointed.

"I don't play well with others."

"And that extends to your golf retirement as well?"

His eyes narrowed. "I don't believe we had a meeting today."

"We didn't."

"And yet here we are."

"Here we are." I jumped into the golf cart. "I'll drive."

He sighed and got in on the other side while I drove us to the next hole. "I need you to be there when we tell Andrei."

"We?"

"Yes, we."

"Did you have a plan outside of just shocking the hell out of him?"

"No, I thought ripping the band-aid as aggressively as possible would be the best way to get myself shot so I decided to bring you in to soften him up."

"Andrei doesn't understand the word soften."

"And you do?"

He barked out a laugh. "You've made your point."

I slowed down to the next hole and stared ahead as the sun started to set. "He's not going to take the news well."

"You could always bring in Nikolai and Maya."

"Thought about that, but then we'd be asking Nikolai to fess up and let her know he's been working for Andrei ever since Alexander's death."

"Your point?"

"I think he'd like to stay married. You know, regular sex and all…"

Luca shrugged. "He will need family."

"He has us," I found myself saying even though half the time I wanted to shove him in front of the nearest semi. Something shifted today, though, something I didn't expect.

He showed a bit of humanity.

Along with self-control I wasn't sure I would have if someone had said something like that about Bee.

And by the looks of him, he still hadn't slept with her.

He was too uptight.

"You done thinking in my golf cart?" Luca whispered, sarcasm dripping off every word.

I rolled my eyes. "I didn't tell any of the guys."

"It was your call to make."

"Yeah, but what the fuck am I going to do when the Sinacore Family shows up for family dinner? You know they'll move the entire family here. They'll have no choice, not with Andrei and the others here, and you know what they'll want."

Luca sighed long and hard. "They'll want to take the place of the De Langes."

"They'll have a right to."

"We would once again be strong, five families strong," Luca said more to himself than to me.

"And the De Langes will officially be exorcised." Andrei would fight us on that, but of course he would, because unless he made her his in all the ways that matter, legal and physical, she had no protection.

And if the Sinacore Family ever found out she was from the De Lange bloodline.

They'd kill him before letting him sully their blood.

Bad enough that he was half Russian.

Even worse, to fall in love with a De Lange.

"Does he love her?" Luca asked the question I'd been pondering for the last week.

"Andrei doesn't know how to love. I know that, you know that, the very fact that he's fallen this hard this fast tells me he could, but it may be too late for him." I hated admitting it. "If he hasn't given in now… then I'm left to assume he's intrigued, and he likes her that's as far as it will go."

"And if you're wrong?" Luca asked.

"Then I'm completely fucked because even I don't want to get on Andrei's bad side. Like I said, I made a judgement call because it's what's best for him, and what's best for the families."

Luca patted my shoulder. "You better hope you're right."

"What would you have done?" I looked up at him.

He winked. "I chose well."

"What the hell does that mean?"

Luca got out of the cart and grabbed a driver from his bag. "Wanna play?"

"Luca."

"What?"

I crossed my arms.

"Phoenix grab a damn driver and stop staring at me like I'm the devil. We both know he rarely visits me anymore now that he's off torturing Andrei. Temptation must be hell for that boy." He pointed his club at me. "The only other person I've ever seen that needed to get laid more than his next meal was you and at least you weren't a virgin."

I rolled my eyes.

"And for the record." He grinned. "I would have done the same thing."

It didn't make me feel any better.

Then again, I rarely felt good about decisions that could ruin lives or end up killing people.

"Grab a damn club."

I flipped him off and grabbed a club. And tried to forget about what was coming in the next week.

And the many lives that would be taken.

All because a Sinacore woman fell in love with the devil himself, Alexander Petrov.

CHAPTER FORTY

Alice

It had been exactly two hours since we'd made it back to the apartments. Since Andrei had walked through the club bloody and shirtless for everyone to see. An A across his chest.

Me… across his heart.

Written in his skin.

He'd wrapped my hand in his shirt and my first instinct was to take it off, to let myself bleed too, to feel the raw intensity of blood pulsing out of my body at the same time his was.

Knowing that what he had done could not be undone.

There was something holy about the entire conversation, even his expression had changed. Like he chose to remove his mask.

He'd told me to change into another dress and to do my hair and makeup and then he'd just left.

He didn't tell me when he'd be back.

Or if he was coming back.

Nothing.

I slipped on a white Versace that hugged every curve, the neckline had a slight sweetheart dip while the straps wrapped around my neck then hung loosely down the back as another set of straps kept the dress in place. My shoes were a nude heel from a brand I didn't recognize but knew was Italian.

And I was once again wearing a fur coat, wondering how many fake animals were sacrificed in order to fill my closet.

I had just sat down on the barstool, wondering yet again if I should text him when the door swung open.

I couldn't keep my expression calm as he swaggered his way toward me, dark skinny jeans, boots, and a black T-shirt with a few holes was tight against his body, his camel colored leather jacket completed the effect.

His nose ring almost glistened in the light, his hair was swept to the side, and I could see every inch of his chest and neck tattoos as they danced along his skin.

His lips looked so soft.

So kissable.

His mouth absolutely delicious.

Mine.

This man had pledged himself to me.

I started shaking with the reality of it.

I slid off the barstool and walked toward him.

Andrei held out his hands when I reached him and then he tugged me against him and kissed me softly, hungrily. "You ready to go?"

"Where are we going?" I wanted to stay right there in his arms.

"We'll put in our time at the club, be seen, and then we'll

go have dinner…"

I grinned. "Dinner, hmm?"

"Dinner." He kissed me again, his hands dipping tenderly into my hair as he licked my lower lip.

I gasped as he tugged it and pulled away. "Is this… a date?"

His hands slid down my ass as he held me prisoner against his rock-hard body. His head tilted as a small smile formed across his mouth. "Did you want it to be?"

I felt my cheeks heat. "I've never been on a real date."

His expression hardened, and then he whispered. "Good. That means I'm your first. I want to be your first everything."

My knees trembled. "That's a big undertaking."

"Good thing I'm a big guy," he fired back with a wider grin. "I like your blush."

I looked away.

He gripped my chin. "Don't, Alice. Don't look away when I give you a compliment. Your blush is everything. It reminds me that this…" He pressed a hand to my chest. "…is beating, is pumping blood throughout your body. Your blush is a gift, it's a reminder you're alive. I need that, possibly more than you could ever imagine."

I pressed my hand against his as my heart raced. "Do your friends know that you're romantic?"

"I'm not romantic." He squeezed my hand. "I was merely being honest."

Well then!

"Okay."

He turned and draped an arm around my shoulders. "Rumor has it, your brother's going to come again tonight."

I stiffened. "Why are we going out there, then?"

"To put on a fucking show." He said through clenched

teeth. "And then, I'm going to make sure he never sees daylight again. Tonight, we celebrate."

"Celebrate?"

"I'm bringing him down. Should I give you his head as a gift? His eyes?"

I gulped. "No. His life is enough."

"No." He his jaw flexed. "It's not."

I didn't argue with him. I could feel the anger roll in chaotic waves off his body as we walked down the hall again and made our way into the main VIP area. People were dancing, drinking, the music was pumping and most of the women who were with the men, getting paid for their services, were still sober, still laughing, enjoying themselves until they were once again forced to stand in that horrible place and get sold off to the highest bidder.

"Andrei?"

"Hmmm." He led me past one of the couples making out on the black leather couch. "Do they all get sold? Eventually?"

He didn't hesitate. "Some are sold, some make too much money to sell and prefer to make this their home, and others don't stand a chance."

"What do you mean they don't stand a chance?"

He stopped walking and stared straight ahead. "They're the fighters that don't give in, the women who won't sell their bodies for the sake of their soul. They are the ones I try to save."

"You can't save them all…"

"One day, I will," he rasped. "One day, I'll raze the walls of this place and never look back."

Andrei Petrov didn't make empty promises.

So, when he said he would never look back.

I believed him.

Ax suddenly appeared in front of us. "They're here."

"Good." Nervous energy pulsed from Andrei's body. "Call the guys, make sure we have security at every exit, make sure he doesn't drink too much, water down the liquor in his drinks so he feels everything."

"Yes, Boss." Ax winked at me and then pulled out his cell and started firing off instructions as he walked off.

"Here." Andrei pulled out a barstool for me. We were still in the VIP area but not on the couches like last time. He held up two fingers.

Two shots of vodka were poured.

He held his up and smirked. "You ready for your revenge?"

"Will it make me feel better?" I took the shot and clinked it against his glass.

"Absolutely not." He threw the shot glass back and slammed it on the table. "But it will make me feel better knowing he's no longer here to claim you, to touch you, to think about you when he has no right to invite you into his thoughts. You're mine. Mine."

"Yes." I leaned toward him.

He gripped my chin with his thumb and forefinger holding me there like he was memorizing every plane of my face, and then he tilted his head and pressed a kiss to my neck. I felt his teeth graze my skin as I gripped the side of the bar table, and then he kicked my legs open, shoving his knee between them. I let out a shocked exhale at the contact of his knee so close to my center, so invasive and public

And then the corners of his mouth tilted up into a smile. "Wanna play?"

I looked from him to the shot glass and held it up. "I may

need one more of these."

"That intimidated?"

"Why, yes..." I leaned in and pressed a kiss to his parted lips. "The great Andrei Petrov just asked if I wanted to play..."

Heat surged between our mouths as he deepened the kiss, tugging at my hair with his right hand.

Magically, two more shot glasses appeared.

And as we clinked them together, he winked. "At least we both win."

I let out a laugh and took the shot just about the same time a shadow cast over us. No, not just one shadow. Two.

I knew it was my brother before I even looked up.

"Well," the word sounded funny with a piece of his tongue missing. "You wasted no time."

I gripped Andrei's thigh. "I don't understand."

"I wasn't talking to you," he spat.

I almost stood.

Andrei's expression was calm. "You're in my club again. See something you like?"

"We both know this should be mine. It belongs to the De Lange Family as much as the Petrovs!"

Andrei frowned. "What are you talking about?"

"I know you know." He clenched his teeth. "Without us you wouldn't even have this. I want a higher cut and I want partner."

"It's never good to reach above your station." Andrei shrugged. "Have some drinks and we'll talk."

My brother must have been surprised because he stepped back a bit and put his hands on his hips. "How can I trust you?"

"That's just the thing." Andrei grinned. "You can't. Take

it or leave it. My offer to discuss your terms expires in thirty seconds."

"Done." He held out his hand.

Andrei took it and then pulled him forward. "I forgot to say thank you by the way…"

He frowned; his eyes flickered to me. "For?"

"For your familial sacrifice of course," He grabbed my hand and kissed it. "For my wife."

My brother gaped. The man I didn't recognize behind him went completely pale. "You never asked my permission."

"I did, the day I cut out your tongue, did you need a reminder? You gave me her, so I let you live. You're welcome."

Aldo looked ready to murder me.

And I hated that he was angry because it was someone else that was touching me, someone else that belonged to me, someone else that wasn't him.

I started feeling sick to my stomach as he turned on his heel and walked off toward the opposite end of the room.

I exhaled when he was gone but felt his eyes on me still. "Now what?"

"Now." Andrei gripped my hips and then lifted me effortlessly off the stool so I was straddling him in my short dress, the slits riding up to my thighs. "We kiss."

"What do you mean?"

"I want him to burn." Andrei nipped my lips and then tilted his head. "I want him to burn with so much jealousy that he forgets himself, that he doesn't look at the exits for his enemies, I want him to go mad with anger and then when his blood pressure is through the roof, when he's purple with rage, I'm going to slit his throat and dance in a river of his blood."

I had no time to respond as his mouth came down on

mine hard, I could feel his arousal through his jeans as he tasted me, and I couldn't help but rub my body against his in a vain attempt to get closer.

He felt so hot.

So good.

I whimpered against his mouth when his hands jerked my body harder against him. The friction was almost too much.

I was ready to rip off his jeans and beg him for it.

And he knew it.

He didn't stop.

I started to sweat, tried to control the building pressure between my thighs as his tongue moved behind my ear. "I'm imagining you naked."

I squeezed my eyes shut. "Yeah?"

"Mmmm, I'm imagining putting my mouth on you and drinking you dry, I'm imagining thrusting deep."

I clenched my teeth as my most intimate places pulsed in rhythm with my pounding heart.

"Your thighs wrapped around my neck…"

I gripped his hair and tugged, hard.

"Maybe I'd finish with you on your stomach… no, I would want to see your face, so I'd flip you over and put your ankles on my shoulders, I'd grip your thighs so hard your skin would bruise, and then I would do it again and again." His tongue licked my ear. "And again." His breath was hot on my skin.

My body shuddered, needing release that he refused to give. I pressed a hand to his chest and lowered it until I touched the front of his jeans, my palm pressed against his length.

He smirked at me like he knew I wasn't just losing my mind but all sense of propriety as I wondered if we could get away with it, if we could just, undress in a dark corner.

What was I thinking?

I was in a haze.

A seductive haze he'd created, with images I couldn't stop thinking about, us sweaty, writhing together, in his bed.

I jerked when he suddenly moved my hand away, his knuckles grazing my thigh as his fingers inched beneath my skirt.

I stiffened.

"Don't lose your nerve now, Alice."

"But we're in public." Was that breathy voice mine?

"That..." He grinned seductively. "...is the entire point of the game."

"People will see."

"Good."

"They'll know."

"Even better." He moved his hand higher. "Let him see your response to me, let it be the last fucking thing that miserable excuse for a human sees."

I nodded as our foreheads touched as his hand gripped the inside of my thigh beneath my dress, as his thumb pressed against my lacy underwear.

I didn't feel shame at my response.

At the fact that I was so ready for him it was almost embarrassing.

His thumb grazed the material so softly that I wanted to smack him on the side of the head.

"I like your anger." He wrapped an arm around me. "Now lean forward so I can give you exactly what you need..."

"You." I kissed his neck as his thumb moved inside me, one finger, a small amount of pressure and I was completely set off, lost to him and every sensation he gave me.

Mine. He was mine.

Maybe he'd always been mine.

But tonight I felt it.

Tonight I saw it.

Tonight we were an *us*.

My body shuddered all around him.

I was still feeling aftershocks when Andrei moved his hand and ran his thumb around the rim of his shot glass, lifted it in Aldo's direction in a mock salute and took the shot.

I smiled down at him. "You don't do things halfway, do you?"

"It seems I can't with you." His gaze was lazy, his eyes hungry. "Tonight, *dorogaya*, I'm taking you."

"No." I leaned in and whispered, "Tonight, I'm taking you."

He bit down on his lip and smirked. "So, it's going to be a bloodbath?"

"Isn't it always when it comes to you?"

"No weapons." He winked. "In the bedroom."

I stared down between us. "Then what do you call that?"

"Hard. So. Damn. Hard."

I burst out laughing as he pressed another kiss to my mouth and then Ax appeared again. "Nice show. Aldo got on the phone like he was calling in reinforcements."

"Let them in. Are the guys here?"

"They are. Phoenix said you were doing it wrong."

Andrei rolled his eyes. "Phoenix should take lessons."

"Heard that." A dark voice coughed behind us. "Hello, Alice, nice dress." Was it my imagination or was he possibly blushing?

The rest of the guys filed up toward the bar.

Panic seized in my chest. What if my brother said I belonged to him? What if he claimed me in front of them? What if?

"Don't worry." Andrei held me close. "He doesn't speak well, can barely understand him as it was..."

"He's on the move." Ax said in a bored tone. "Toward the first exit."

A security guard blocked it.

Aldo frowned and then went to another one.

All exits were blocked.

He pulled out a gun, people started screaming.

And that's when I saw an older man walk right in and shoot Aldo in the kneecaps along with the guy I didn't recognize with him.

People screamed but didn't run toward the exits, which made me wonder if this was common.

Tex was on the move with Chase. they each grabbed a body and started toward the opposite end of the room.

The elderly man who'd shot them made his way toward us. His black scarf was wrapped tightly around his neck, his black matching fedora gave him a very GQ look. "Don't suppose you have any Italian wine here?"

Andrei smiled. "Flew some in last week just for you, Frank."

"Knew I was liking you more and more."

Andrei motioned the bartender.

Frank turned his blue gaze to mine. "Seems you were a lion tamer in another life, mmm?"

"Or an angel sent from God," Nixon muttered. "Let's go chat with him about the girls so I can get home. We shut this down tonight."

"Agreed." Andrei helped me off his lap. I wasn't sure how

he could go from that to ruthless killer in seconds. Then again, there were a lot of things I didn't understand about Andrei, but I wanted to, more and more every day.

Nixon put his hand on Andrei's shoulder. "We should go back there."

Andrei nodded and snapped his fingers at Ax. "Keep Alice safe."

Ax nodded.

Andrei leaned down and kissed my cheek. "Last chance. You want to pull the trigger?"

I shook my head no.

I didn't deserve to have his blood on my hands and live with the nightmare or the guilt. Because no matter how horrible he was, he was still family.

"Is that a no to your souvenir as well?"

I smiled at that. "Leave his body intact. You've already given me his tongue."

He scowled. "Where's the fun in that?"

"All right, Dr. Doom." I shoved his chest. "Hurry back to me."

His eyes flashed. "You can guarantee it."

CHAPTER FORTY-ONE

Andrei

I could feel her on my skin.

I tried not to grin in triumph as I walked with the rest of the Italians, large purposeful steps toward the back room.

Not the purple room.

No, this room was special.

It had cement floors, sound proof walls, and chains that hung from the top of the ceiling.

Both men were chained, standing on metal chairs, bloody and a bit beaten already.

Aldo spit out a tooth.

I sighed. "Really, Chase?"

He just shrugged. "He was talking too much."

The other man eyed me and then looked away.

"Ivan." I crossed my arms. "I see you've been playing well with others in the sandbox."

He struggled against the chains but said nothing. His light

hair had spots of blood in it and his eye was already turning black.

"This is what we're going to do," I said sternly. "We're going to torture you, and then we're going to kill you if you don't give us the information we need. If you give us what we need and Sergio can prove that the locations to your cells are accurate, along with your contacts, then we'll simply shoot you. Make your choice gentleman, I have a date."

"Fuck you!" Aldo screamed. "How dare you think you can do that to my—"

I sucker punched him in the gut.

He couldn't say her name.

Or that she was his sister.

Regardless of the way he talked, he could still make out the name enough for the Italians to question me.

Phoenix cleared his throat behind me.

"Make your choices," I demanded as the door shut, keeping us all in.

"You are weak." Ivan gritted his teeth. "Your father would be ashamed of you!"

I grinned up at him. "Do you really think I live for a dead man's approval? That would be a wrong assumption, considering I was recruited against him the day I turned eighteen."

Ivan paled.

"Ah, now you understand, these men are more family than my father ever was. It would be wise to stop talking before I take another tongue. I've developed a sentiment for taking pieces of every man I conquer, and believe me, before your dead body leaves this room, I'll take something, maybe your eyes, your tongue, maybe the tip of your nose, or a finger, as a reminder to those who know me, who fear me, that I don't fuck around when it comes to my business and my empire."

Ivan stared straight ahead and whispered, "Death. I choose death."

"And you Aldo? What have you picked off the menu for the evening?"

Aldo glared. "I won't tell you shit."

I tsked. "Chase, did you want to do the honors?"

Chase grinned. "With pleasure."

Aldo struggled as Chase punched him across the face, and then kicked the chair away so Aldo hung by his bloody wrists. He screamed out in agony.

And I watched.

I enjoyed it.

Because I couldn't protect her then.

But I could save her now.

I could get her revenge.

I could take his life.

And I would.

"We know it's you. Elena was very informative. We just need a name for your contact, an address even of where you keep the girls before they're delivered and then we'll make it as painless as possible."

Ivan opened his mouth. "We're dead anyway."

"Smart man."

The Italians waited in silence.

It was my club after all.

My business.

My respect for them grew tenfold.

"Well?" I crossed my arms.

Ivan hung his head. "Viktor Stasevich is our contact, an

old friend of your father's. He keeps the girls until we make the pick-up. He and his team work with a—"

"Shut the hell up!" Aldo roared.

Ivan barked out a laugh. "We're dead men! Do you know who these men are? We will not walk out of here alive, and I will not have my eyes lost to me when I am dead!" He was superstitious, interesting. "He and his team worked with Alexander, the De Langes took your contract Andrei, and when they started making more contacts within the family…" His eyes flickered from Chase back to me. "They asked for a meeting."

"They?" Chase said with clenched teeth. "Or she?"

"Sh-she." Ivan hung his head. "I gave it to her behind Andrei's back and gave her Viktor's number. The money the operation brought in was tens of millions. Alexander made sure that even in his death, the family would be taken care of, but he could no longer trust anyone, so when she—"

"Mil," I corrected.

Chase looked ready to kill every single man in that room.

"When Mil met with him, she was promised protection along with the money and the new contracts."

I knew Mil had gotten in deep.

I didn't know it was that deep.

And by the look on Chase's face, neither did he.

"What else?"

Aldo barked out a laugh. "This is rich. You don't know, do you? For being so powerful, you don't know shit that went down in our family!"

"We're about to." I glared. "Ivan continue…"

"Mil knew it was dangerous, and she didn't want anyone finding out. She just wanted the money to funnel back into the De Langes, but it was too much money all at once..." His face was ashen like he was afraid of what we would do if he said more. "...so she reinstated three of the prostitution rings that her father had connections with and laundered the money with drug trafficking."

The room went silent.

And I could feel the hate for every single De Lange in the bloodline build into a boiling point that even I knew I couldn't control.

I needed to get Chase out of there before he did something like start blindly shooting.

As it was, his chest rose and fell, his eyes crazed.

Out of the corner of my eye, I spotted Tex grab his gun. Nixon did the same and pointed it directly at the back of Chase's head.

"Ivan," My voice was hoarse. "One more question before I give you that bullet you've easily earned."

"Yes." He hung his head.

"This Viktor... who did he report to?"

Ivan's lips trembled. "Mil De Lange."

Phoenix swore under his breath. I knew this was hard for him; it was hard for every single one of the men who'd trusted her. Chase, her ex-husband and Phoenix, her half-brother, the one who had pulled the trigger.

Warfare and blood seemed to consume that room. Past regrets, things left unsaid, situations we should have all dealt with differently.

I hung my head for a second as a few beats went by.

As the rage and hurt from the Italians twisted and fused into a furious bomb ready to go off.

"I'll need your cell phone." I walked over to him and pulled a cell from his pocket then tossed it to Sergio. "Does Viktor have control of the rest of the rings along with distribution of the girls?"

"Yes."

"Does Viktor have protection?"

Another gulp. "Yes."

"The De Langes?"

He looked to Aldo. "Yes."

"You understand this means you are hereby charged with turning against your own family, your own Russian blood?"

"Yes."

"And with that understanding, do you ask for forgiveness?"

"Yes, Boss. Please forgive me for turning my back on Russia, on you, for forging an alliance with the De Langes."

"Got his number and address." Sergio held up the phone. "Aw, how cute he had find a friend turned on…"

A few of them chuckled. I imagined Phoenix and Chase were both standing still, hatred dripping from their stares.

I pulled out my gun and pressed it against Ivan's chest. I fired one shot. "You're forgiven." Two more shots rang out, and then I pointed the gun up and shot him beneath the chin as blood rained down over his body and mine. "May you rot in Hell."

I turned to Aldo. "Anything you feel like adding?"

He grinned over at Chase. "Yeah, I do."

Shit.

"Your wife spread her legs for the Russians, she spread her legs for me!"

Chase didn't move. Didn't flinch. His eyes blazed with unchecked fury.

Aldo burst out laughing. "You think you were so special?

You think you gave her what she needed? What she needed was power!" He was hysterical. He was a dead man. "She needed her family! Not a rich Abandonato with everything handed to him! You think you're so untouchable and you don't even know what's been planted in your own family!"

I froze and glared at Aldo willing him to stop talking.

"That's right, kill me and you'll never know." He smiled. "You'll never know a damn thing."

"He's lying." I bit out. "Desperate."

"Says the man who's been—"

I pulled out my gun and shot him between the eyes before he could expose her, expose us. "Sorry he was pissing me off."

Chase narrowed his eyes at me. "Was he? Because I would have liked to do the honors, no I would have liked to rip his tongue from his throat and watch his eyes bulge out of his head while I drove my knife directly into his heart, but instead, you fucking *shoot* him?!"

"I made a call. My club. My rules. We're done here." I shoved my gun back into my pants. "Let me know what results you get, Sergio."

I bypassed Nixon and Tex both of them oddly silent as they stared me down.

Shit, shit, shit.

Chase seemed relatively calm despite what I'd said, what I'd done.

So why was I panicking?

Phoenix gave me a funny look when I walked by Frank, and then Dante was standing just outside the door. "A word."

"Kinda busy running a club and playing both sides, brother." I tried to move past him, but he shoved his hand against my chest and slammed me into the wall.

Phoenix appeared behind him.

"I know who she is," Dante said in a lethal tone. "And I also know what just went down in there. You tell him, soon, otherwise none of us can protect you from his wrath."

"And who would protect *him* from *mine*?" I sneered. "You?"

Dante glared and shoved me away from him. "I mean it, Andrei, don't play this game. Just tell him so it's not a surprise later on, all right?"

"I'm not ready."

"I guess it doesn't really matter anyway," Phoenix sauntered forward. "It never has."

"What?" I snapped. "What doesn't matter?"

Phoenix crossed his arms. "I made a call you may not like."

"Phoenix." I gritted my teeth. "What the hell did you do?"

"You're a Sinacore, though I think deep down you knew that and were trying to deflect. Maybe you didn't know just how important your role was or you just didn't want any of us to ask questions. You joke about being half Italian because it's true."

Dante let out a string of curses.

"They're coming," Phoenix said slowly. "Here."

"Why the hell would you invite that family here? They're narcissistic Italian scum who think they're fucking royalty!"

Phoenix stared me down. "Actually, they've been waiting for their prodigal son to return for close to twenty-two years now. Then again, they weren't made aware that you had no clue until now. A man divided cannot know who he is, until he knows where he came from."

He reached into his pocket and pulled out a ring with an Eagle holding a fish in its hands. "This ring belonged to your mother, for her to give to you on the day you took your place as boss for the Sinacore crime family, royalty as you put it."

"I'm Russian. I'm a Petrov."

"Your father was a Petrov. Your mother was the daughter of Heraldo Emmanuel, from the house of Savoy — the last living royal family of Italy." He tossed the ring in the air.

I didn't make any move to catch it.

It bounced on the ground, once, twice, and then Dante reached down and picked it up, resolutely placing it in the palm of my hand.

Phoenix's next words were damning, as they drove a knife straight into my heart. "If you don't love her, don't put her through this war, Andrei. The Sinacore Family does not mix bloodlines."

"I'm mixed." But even as I said it, I knew. I knew all about the Sinacore Family, I'd saved Renee from a similar fate. I had killed in order to keep her hidden here.

I'd double crossed my own family.

I didn't acknowledge it at the time. All I knew was that I didn't care.

"Phoenix." I leaned against the wall, clutching the ring in my palm. "How many are coming?"

"All of them." The words were a blow to my soul. "And they will finish the job we started. The De Langes are exorcised — and the new arm of the five families will rise up under their new leader. You."

CHAPTER FORTY-TWO

Alice

I was starting to get nervous. Not that Ax wasn't extremely distracting. He had two kids now, both of them under the age of four, one of them just started pre-school and managed to sneak out of the house in the morning and start his car.

Ax added more locks.

Same thing happened the next day.

Suffice it to say his family life sounded so normal it was almost strange. He held guns most of the day, helped torture people and then at night read Goodnight Moon to his two boys.

I stirred my straw around in my drink and yawned just as Andrei stomped toward me with so much aggression in his eyes I actually shrunk back a bit.

"Thanks, Ax." His voice was off.

Something was wrong.

"Andrei?"

He pulled me against him, held me there so tight that it was hard to breathe, and then he leaned back just enough for his eyes to lock on mine. "I missed you."

Why did it seem like he was saying goodbye?

Like he would miss me when I was standing right there?

"Ax." Andrei's piercing gaze didn't leave mine. "No interruptions, especially the Italians, things can wait… just a while longer."

I frowned. "What happened?"

"We got the information we needed, and I shot your brother between the eyes because he was about to attempt to say your name only after bringing Chase to the brink of mass homicide. So, I'd say it went well." He pressed a kiss to my cheek. "Are you ready for our dinner date?"

I let the truth wash over me.

My brother was dead.

The monster had finally killed him.

And I was relieved. I was more than relived. I was grateful, thankful, and I refused to feel like a bad human being because my brother's evil was no longer present on earth.

I sighed in relief and clung to Andrei.

He exhaled against my body and pulled away. "Dinner?" Again, he prompted, like he wanted to get out of there. He seemed fine on the outside, as normal as a man like Andrei could be, but his eyes were distant, his body language stiff, aggressive.

Afraid. He seemed afraid. Maybe that's why I didn't recognize it at first, because he'd never shown me that emotion before.

"Actually…" I held him close and kept him there. And in all the scenarios that had played on repeat in my head, I would have never guessed that this would be one of them I would take, the road I would take.

I was going to seduce Andrei Petrov.

I was going to take every last inch of him and breathe life into him.

I was going to give him the control he so desperately needed.

And I would give him everything.

Not because he asked me to.

But because I suddenly realized he needed me to, he needed it. His eyes were unfocused again as a few people walked by us, the Italians.

I nodded to them.

Phoenix gave Andrei a look that I couldn't discern.

Dante stopped while the rest of them walked past and said their goodbyes, his eyes met mine and then Andrei's.

Before I knew what was happening, Dante was leaning in and pressing a kiss to my cheek and whispering. "Make it count."

I had no idea what it meant.

All I knew was that they knew something I didn't.

And that Andrei's death grip on me intensified to the point of pain.

"Let's stay in." I turned around abruptly. "Let's order pizza or something?"

Andrei's frozen face morphed into a frown. "I promised you a date."

"A date just means we're doing something together. Let's do something together here… home."

His blue eyes softened. "Home?"

"Our home." I nodded, feeling the word in my soul as it

continued to repeat in my head over and over again. Home. The monster had given me a home.

Tears filled my eyes.

He leaned over me and pressed a searing kiss against my mouth. "Even if I was killed tonight — I would never regret you, Alice."

"See." I leaned back. "Romantic."

"Shhhh," He winked. "Don't ruin my sordid reputation, *dorogaya*."

I reached up and patted his cheek. "Nothing but a teddy bear."

He barked out a laugh. "Tell that to Ivan."

"Ivan?" Did I even want to know?

Andrei wrapped an arm around my shoulders as we walked side by side out of the club and down the hall to the apartment. "Shot him twice in the chest, and under the chin just to make sure it was quick, lots of blood. Used to be a good man until he turned."

"Why do men turn?" I asked, genuinely curious. "In this business I mean. Is it just for money? Power? I mean what's the point when your life is on the line? Or when you suddenly gamble with your life and those you love just because you can't help but want more?"

Andrei didn't answer. He silently unlocked the door, his face a mask of indifference as he showed me in, closed and locked it behind me. "You really want to know?"

"Yeah." I crossed my arms and shivered, despite the fur coat. "I do."

"Contentment."

It wasn't the answer I was expecting.

"I surprised you." He flashed me a half smile as he leaned

back against the door. "You expected me to agree with you?"

"Maybe?"

His gorgeous smile grew. "You have a lot to learn Alice. A man with idle hands, a man without a purpose, is not a man at all. He is less than and he knows it, so he will do anything to fill that hole. The consequences no longer matter, because a man was built with purpose and when you lose your purpose, you lose everything."

It was so deep, so wise that I didn't have an intelligent response other than to lean toward him, wishing he'd say more.

Andrei held out his hands like he was getting ready to cup water. "In my world, a man was built to do two things." He reached for my hand, and then he held his other hand out and turned it over. "To hold those he cares for closer than his own heart, and to work to the bone for their happiness, their contentment. A man who has lost this, has lost his purpose." He dropped my hands and shrugged out of his leather jacket. "Elena belonged to Ivan first. They were married, in love, my father took one look at her and stole her, said it was just business. She became my stepmother, a young stepmother, and Ivan let him because he lacked the power to stop him. So, he did what any man would do when a wrong was done against him. He figured out a way to get back his contentment by taking what he could from my father and aligning himself with the De Langes."

"And Elena?"

"She was never the same. Then again, neither was he." Andrei hung his head and whispered something in Russian before turning to me. "Enough talk about death and purpose. I owe you a date. A nice date, without a blood-stained shirt," He tugged at his tight black T-shirt.

I didn't see the blood on his shirt, but I'd noticed it on his cheeks and on his neck. "It doesn't bother you? Other people's blood?"

He smirked like it was a cute question. "It means they're no longer a threat."

"Well I guess that's one way to think about it."

"I don't waste energy thinking about the dead, they don't matter. The living, however, do." He took a step toward me. "Any more questions or can I shower?"

"I remember a time when you yelled at me for asking you questions," I pointed out with an arched brow.

"I remember a time when I would have done anything for you to ask more. Wait, that was thirty seconds ago. I would talk to you until my voice was hoarse, but I can't. Because as much as blood doesn't bother me, I know it bothers you, it reminds you of things you shouldn't have to see, so I'm going to shower and then we're going to eat and then I'm going to kiss you and I'm not going to stop."

"I like that plan," I whispered.

He kissed the top of my head. "Good."

And then he was sauntering away from me, his lean muscled body moving through the living room like a freaking panther.

I exhaled and shook my head. He was too much and not enough all at once, because when he was with me I wanted more, and when he left me, my heart threw itself into chaos, worry.

I looked down. If he was changing, should I too?

Frowning, I went to my room and flipped on the closet light. Everything was either too fancy or not nice enough. My hands grazed the pieces of clothes hanging, the tags that went along with them, and then I stopped when I got to the end of the room.

Hanging behind a few dresses were silk pieces of lingerie.

They were blood red.

One of them was a gorgeous red baby doll nightdress. It went to my mid-thigh and wasn't see-through but definitely looked like it wasn't for going out.

With a smile, I looked over my shoulder and then back at the silk. I touched it with my fingertips and imagined how it would feel against his skin, maybe instead of hurting he'd feel pleasure.

I was doing this.

I wasn't the same woman who had walked in these doors.

He'd made me different.

And I wondered as I slowly stripped out of my dress, if I knew all along, if that's why I smiled when I was held captive.

Because I knew I would fall in love with my jailor.

Madly.

Deeply.

Irrevocably.

In love.

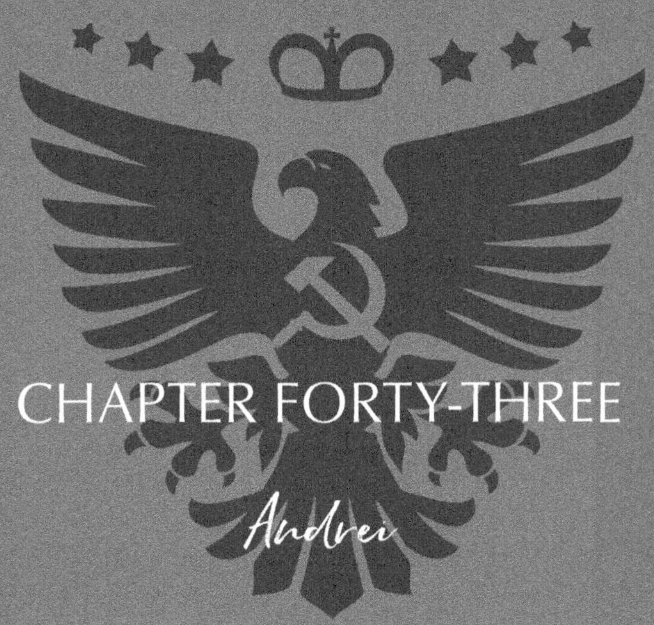

CHAPTER FORTY-THREE

Andrei

I pressed my forehead against the cool tile and squeezed my eyes closed as the searing water pelted my back.

I heard him then.

My father.

"You will never be pure enough. Good enough. Never."

I didn't listen to him then.

But it *had* affected me — so deeply, so traumatically that I figured that's how others saw me, that I was less than. That I wasn't deserving of human touch, and then it turned into this desire not to touch people, because when I touched someone they were warm.

It was a reminder they were real.

And it was a reminder that I was a monster. A killer.

I pounded the side of the shower, I wanted to scream. I clenched my teeth to keep myself silent, poised, controlled.

I couldn't lose control with her.

Not now.

Especially not now.

Because now I had no choice.

The Sinacores would kill her if they knew, just like Chase would.

My choices were limited.

And I was selfish enough to want her and damn the consequences.

I wanted her.

I didn't deserve her.

But I couldn't stop wanting her no matter how hard I tried.

With a curse, I turned off the water and grabbed a towel, wrapping it around my body as I quickly dried off in the bathroom and walked naked into my bedroom to grab a pair of jeans and a T-shirt.

She was waiting for me.

She was starving.

So was I. Not for food; food wouldn't sate this feeling I had in my soul, this feeling I had every time my heart beat and reminded me I was alive.

I threw on a vintage Henley and a pair of ripped jeans and ran my hands through my wet hair.

I was in too much of a hurry to care about anything else. I stopped when my hand touched the bedroom door.

My gloves.

My black gloves were on the dresser.

I hung my head in shame as his words washed over me again.

"You will never be good enough. Never."

I swallowed the annoying feeling in my throat, the one that told me I was choosing emotion over logic, and grabbed the gloves, shoving my hands into them.

I would need them tonight.

Sadly, I would need them for the rest of my life, especially if I was doing this…with her.

Nobody else.

The Sinacores could go to hell.

Because tonight, she was going to be my heaven.

I rounded the corner to the kitchen, not finding her right away. I wrongly assumed she'd already be snacking on something. I loved that she actually ate.

Instead, the light strains of Tchaikovsky filled the air, quietly, in the background.

A smile played at my lips as I walked farther into the living room.

And then the smile died a quick death as I gripped the nearest counter space and swallowed.

She'd been sitting on the couch.

I wasn't the only one who'd changed.

She didn't make a big show of standing or even turning around like she needed attention or wanted me to say anything.

Sometimes the best compliments are the ones made in complete and utter silence.

If I spoke, it would ruin the moment.

And the moment was perfect.

Because she was being vulnerable. And I knew that she might as well be standing there naked, asking me to love her, take her, pleasure her.

I sucked in a shaky breath and almost laughed. *So, this is what fear feels like?*

I didn't like it.

I didn't like the temptation I had to shake, or to kill the

moment with my own insignificant speech.

Fucking hell, she was gorgeous.

Her hair hung past her shoulders, dancing with each step she took. A piece had fallen between her cleavage, trapped exactly where I wanted to be.

I clenched my hands, the leather suddenly too binding, too constricting for what I had in mind.

But I couldn't do it.

I couldn't be inside her and touching her all at once with everything I'd seen. It wasn't fair to expose her to my demons when all I wanted was to give her heaven.

Hell wasn't part of the bargain.

My eyes roamed lazily over her body as she took another step, her thigh causing the flimsy material to billow up as she moved.

It was pure torture as my body pulsed with temptation and need. It erupted from my fingertips as I gripped the countertop harder. Imagined myself breaking it in a million pieces as she finally stopped in front of me, not close enough, not by half.

I never knew that one word would be my downfall as she leaned up with a teasing smile on her face and whispered. "Hungry?"

My body completely seized.

It was like every single nerve ending fucking exploded, and all I could do was blink down at her and wonder how the hell I was supposed to be the guy that took control when for once, I wanted to give it completely up to the vixen standing in front of me with her red lingerie and her open smile.

Maybe she knew.

Maybe she was just as desperate as I was, because she pressed her hands against my chest, softly, and then drew slow circles with her fingertips making her way to my shoulders, gripping them, as she wrapped an arm around my neck and pulled me down. "You can kiss me now."

"I wasn't waiting for permission," I growled.

"Then what were you waiting for?"

"My heart stopped beating; I was waiting for it to catch up."

She sucked in a shocked breath, I took advantage, molding my lips to hers as I pulled the rest of her against me. The material didn't hide her body heat. Rather, it seemed intensified, it made her skin like molten lava as I drove my tongue inside her mouth, imagining the time when it was all of me touching her, inside her, not parts.

Me.

Her pulse beat erratically beneath my touch as I cupped her neck, making it easier to kiss her, to deepen the kiss so much that I tasted heaven on her tongue and wanted to confess every fucking sin I'd ever committed in order to taste more.

She broke off the kiss. "I had a plan."

I smirked. "Oh yeah? What was this plan?" I toyed with the straps of lingerie near her neck already mentally calculating how fast I could rip them from her body, already thinking about the knife around two feet from my right hand. It would be an easy cut. Too easy.

She let out a light laugh and shook her head as her cheeks bloomed with heat. "I forgot."

"So soon?" I teased.

"Your kiss does a good job of making me forget."

"Seems I need to work on my kiss, because I need you to remember this… more than I need my next breath, *dorogaya*." I kissed her hard, gripped her by the ass and pulled her against me. "I need you to remember us, always, forever. Promise me."

"Why—"

I cut her off with another kiss then whispered against her mouth. "Promise."

She nodded, her lips moving against mine soft like velvet, stirring a slow burn in my body as I tried to regain control of every single instinct I had to run the other way. "Promise."

"*Dorogaya.*" I said it softly this time. "I think, you are the only thing on this earth that could actually terrify me."

She stopped kissing me and wrapped her arms around me.

My love.

My sweetheart.

My life.

Was hugging me.

I hugged her back, my heart in my throat, my future uncertain. All I knew was that she was the reason.

For everything.

"Please, Andrei," she said in a hoarse voice. "Let me give myself to you."

"I don't think I'm worthy of that gift."

"And I don't think you're in a position to say no," she fired back softly. "Unless that's not what you—"

I kissed her soundly, picked her up by the ass and set her on the counter. As our tongues tangled, I was moaning, growling, gasping for air; then again, so was she.

My body tightened in all the wrong and right places, needing release, feeding off each kiss like a drug bringing both of us to the point of no return. A kiss here, a kiss there, biting, nibbling… It was like taking hit after hit of heroin and knowing that I would get so high off her that I wouldn't think.

I would just do.

And she would see it.

She would see all of me.

Have all of me.

She would hold the one thing no one else did.

The last pure part I'd been left with.

I broke away from her, chest heaving, body on fire as my length pressed against my jeans. The problem was my body knew what it wanted, and my mind got in the way. It always got in the way.

Alice licked her lips where I'd kissed her, then hopped down from the counter and grabbed my hand.

I blindly followed as she brought me into my own bedroom. Darkness descended.

And I was reminded of where I was birthed.

In Hell itself.

I flinched when she closed the door.

It was dark, so dark.

And then her hand was back on my chest.

I exhaled as I wrapped my fingers around hers.

There was enough light coming in from the bathroom to see her face, her perfect body, and the small smile that teased her trembling lips as she backed away from me and reached behind her.

My lips parted in a rough exhale followed by a dirty curse as the lingerie very slowly fell from her body to a pool by her bare feet.

She was completely naked.

I expected to feel nothing.

The expectation was so strong that I was devastated before the last inch of silk hit the ground.

It didn't happen. The sadness. The mocking. The vision of

using her as a means to an end.

All I saw in her eyes was terrified vulnerability.

And all I felt in mine looking back at her, was unsurmountable holiness at what she'd just done.

A woman raped.

A woman used.

A woman now naked in front of me, offering control when it had always been hers to take.

She shed her dress.

She did that for a monster.

The least I could do was show her the man.

I took off my right glove first, tossing it on the floor, and moved to my left as it fell by her nightdress.

My shirt was next.

Her eyes drank me in.

With shaking hands, I started unbuttoning my jeans. She moved forward before I could finish, on her knees, in front of me. Where I didn't want her to be, it was too wrong, for someone like her.

She batted my hands away.

I swayed on my feet, drunk off the moment, off her.

It felt like my soul was floating above my body as I watched her slowly unbutton my jeans, and free me.

My dick strained toward her in a way that bordered on indecent.

Her eyes met mine as she leaned forward and swirled her tongue across the tip before slowly standing in front of me and wrapping her arms around my neck. "Bed."

I smiled against her mouth. "Are you making demands now?"

"I figured we'd still be standing here if I didn't."

I burst out laughing and smacked her slightly on the ass as I backed her toward the mattress, I rubbed where I'd hit and then I bit down on her neck and licked my way up to her lips. "You taste like salvation."

"You taste like damnation. Heaven and Hell," she whispered, interlocking our fingers together as she fell back against the bed, me hovering over her, like I was waiting to strike when really all I wanted to do was memorize each feeling, even the way my tongue felt between her lips each time I dragged another kiss from her.

Alice's chest rose and fell as she lifted her hand and pressed it against the A carved out of my chest over my heart. "Where's your knife?"

I stared her down. "There's one under the pillow, why?"

She reached behind her and came back with the knife my father had given me, the one that I kept on me at all times.

It was impure, that knife.

It represented our family.

Him.

Us.

Darkness.

Her skin glistened as she took the tip and pressed it against her chest, right across her heart. "I don't want to be like the Italians, Andrei."

My eyes stung as they filled with unshed tears. I never cried. I didn't think myself actually capable of it… until that moment, when she offered me both pain and pleasure, sacrifice, body and soul.

My voice shook. "What are you saying?"

"I'm saying, you cut my hand, I want you to carve yourself into my heart."

I was losing control.

Fast.

My body roared to life in a way that felt violent as I sucked in breath after breath. "You're saying…"

She dug the knife into her skin, a whimper escaped her lips. "Make it fast."

"But you're perfect."

"So are you."

"No." I shook my head. "You don't understand… You're pure… I'm not."

"Maybe I'll just be your sacrifice, the one you've always needed, the blood that's always needed to be spilled," she said with tears in her eyes. "I'm yours, Andrei Petrov. Take me."

With a growl, I took the knife and carved a small A over her chest. As her blood flowed from the fresh cut, I threw the knife against the wall.

Blood trickled down her chest, her blood, my name.

And then I was kissing her, out of control, an animal as I rocked my body against hers, shrugged my jeans down and kissed her, drank her, pressed my hand against her bloody chest and felt her heart, her soul between my fingertips.

Mine.

She was mine.

Every inch of skin I touched was on fire as her hips lifted, our bodies slid against each other, a mixture of sweat and blood.

Our foreheads touched, our breaths short as I positioned myself at her entrance, my fingers danced along her thighs, feeling her life, feeling every part of her pulse in a rhythmic cadence for me and only me.

"Andrei," she whimpered.

"You will always be mine," I promised.

"Always," she agreed.

I drove into her, knowing it would hurt, knowing she would curse me later, both hating and loving the feeling of her body as she convulsed around me. I sunk into her heat.

And I knew.

There would never be any going back from this.

She had undone me.

Maybe I had undone myself.

This was what I had been waiting for my whole life.

For someone to accept the ugly and call it pure.

Our eyes locked as I moved inside her.

She spread her legs wider and hooked one around my hips as I measured my pace, wanting it to last longer than the three seconds that seemed most probable.

She clung to me, gripped my hair. "How it should be."

"Yes." I bit down as I sank deep, feeling every intimate part of her heat, wanting to stay there forever as she clenched.

Fingertips against my scalp.

Parted lips breathing against my neck.

I gripped her ass and angled her higher. She let out a shriek as I drove faster, harder.

I wouldn't last at that rate.

We were both shaking, maybe in shock, maybe because it was so new. Whatever it was, it was perfect.

"Fuck." I kissed her neck and found her mouth, tangled my tongue with hers, kissed her like it would be my last time, spoke against her mouth in Russian I knew she wouldn't understand.

I said my wedding vows.

She would never know.

That I was promising everything.

And would take nothing in return.

"*Ya*, Andrei Petrov, *daru tebe svoyu zhizn', svoye serdtse, svoyu dushu.*"

I reached between our bodies, wet heat washed over my fingers as I pressed into her, sending her over the edge.

And for the first time in my life, a woman screamed my name while I was inside her, while I loved her, while she loved me back.

And that was enough for a man who had been damned to completely lose his mind and fall into a pit of ecstasy as I pumped into her and left years' worth of darkness, directly into the light.

"*Dorogaya.*" I kissed her softly.

She kissed me back. Her lower lip was wet from our kiss, slippery as she asked, "What does that mean?"

"It's a term of endearment," I panted. "Like sweetheart, honey, my love…"

She stilled. "You called me that the second day you knew me."

"No," I corrected. "I called you that the minute they brought you in. I just didn't say it out loud."

CHAPTER FORTY-FOUR

Alice

I didn't realize I was shaking until Andrei pulled what else but a black fur blanket over my body and kissed me on the side of the mouth. "Stay."

Like I could even move after that.

My heart was in my throat.

My body was sore.

He'd called me *Dorogaya* since he first knew me, since he even used my number instead of my name. What did that mean?

I heard water turn on in the bathroom, and then he was back, completely naked still, looking every inch the perfect fallen angel with his rock-hard body, still hard… I averted my eyes. He was just hard everywhere and smiling and just…

Mine.

He was mine.

He very gently pulled the fur back and ran a soft hot cloth

up my thighs. I moaned in pleasure as he pressed it between them then swiped down the other side.

"Careful," he whispered. "You're not ready, but I feel like I could stay between your legs all night… don't encourage me…"

I felt myself melt a bit at his adoring gaze, his eyes focused only on me, his hands on me, his concern for me.

I wanted to cry and laugh all at the same time.

I reached for his hand and grabbed it tight. "What were you saying? In Russian… during…" I licked my lips and didn't finish my sentence.

"You'll have to be more specific," he said seriously, his eyebrows knitting together like he was both concentrating and amused at my expense. "Which part?"

I glowered.

Earning a laugh before he got up, tossed the cloth somewhere, and joined me back in bed. Even the way the bed dipped under his weight had me sighing and wanting, wanting more of him, to touch him. So, I did.

I turned on my side and rested my head on his chest, threw my right leg over his body trapping him like a maniac, and pressed my palm against his chest. "I'm so glad it was you and only you."

He seemed to hold his breath and then exhale it in a shudder. "Me too."

"Andrei?"

"Yeah?" He wrapped my hair around his fingertips and lifted it to his lips like he wanted a part of it too, like it wasn't just my body but every part of me that he needed.

"I love you."

He went completely still.

I didn't need to hear him say it back.

And I knew in that moment, I would do anything, anything to one day be able to say that Andrei Petrov gave me not just his body, but his heart too. His soul.

"I can't—" He started and stopped. "Alice you have all of me, and I care for you more than anything in this godforsaken world. You mean more to me than—"

"Stop." I pressed a kiss to his chin. "I didn't expect you to say it back. I just wanted you to know how I feel, how I will always feel about you."

I saw it then, the shift in his gaze like he was hiding something, like things weren't as okay as he'd told me they were.

"Andrei?"

I will never forget the minute — the second — he went from being vulnerable to the man I'd met before, the one with the masks and the faces. Only this time I could see the visual struggle, could feel every muscle tense in his body like his heart was fighting his mind.

And all I kept thinking was *don't. Don't give in. Stay with me, Dear God please stay with me.*

But this was Andrei.

He didn't.

He left.

It was the most terrifying thing I'd ever seen, watching Andrei Petrov look at me with an empty smile and whisper, "Let me make you food and we can talk about this later."

I had given him everything I had.

And he was dismissing me.

Dismissing us.

The mattress moved, just enough for me to pay attention

as I glanced down at our feet and noticed his tapping against an invisible surface.

And all I could think about was one word.

Lie.

CHAPTER FORTY-FIVE

Andrei

I had wine and cheese delivered and brought it into the bedroom, a room I never wanted to leave.

And that was the problem.

The minute you expose every vulnerability you have to someone, you give them every fucking tell and you can't hide, and you don't want to because when they accept you, you feel safe.

And I felt safe.

With her, I felt the safest I'd ever felt.

And I both loathed and loved her for it.

She had no idea the power she had, the struggle I was dealing with in trying to stay sane and not tell her the whole sordid mess I was in.

Because I knew it wouldn't end the way either of us wanted it to, I knew if I fought for her, she could die. I wouldn't risk her life. Only mine.

They wouldn't accept her.

Would rather kill her than let her marry me even though they had no idea I'd never marry, because I'd already pledged my vows to her, it didn't matter that it wasn't legal, because in my heart, my soul, it was as real as marriage would get.

I was hers.

She was mine.

"You'd tell me, if something was wrong, right?" Alice took a long sip of wine and stared at me over the glass rim. "Andrei?"

"No," I said honestly, my voice felt cold, off. I was protecting her. I was doing the right thing. "I would not."

Her eyes narrowed. "Can I ask why? Do you still not trust me?"

I loved the way her eyes flashed with anger. God, I loved it even when her anger was directed at me. Damn it, I was gone, wasn't I? If I would accept a slap from that perfect hand, smile afterward, and beg for more?

"Because telling you too much puts you in danger, so no I won't tell you if something's wrong because I want you to trust me to protect you the only way I'm capable of protecting you. Everything I do is for you, that's all you need to know."

Her shoulders slumped as she looked away. "You put it back on."

"What?"

"Not your gloves, and I can't explain it, but it's like when you were with me, you're with me, mind, body, soul, and then afterward you just slipped into something not you. Something indifferent. I don't like it."

I hung my head. "Come here."

She didn't move.

I set her wine on the nightstand, moved her plate, and

pulled her into my arms. "What if I told you we have twenty-four hours? Would you panic or use them?"

"Both."

I felt my body seize with the truth as I slowly glanced over at the clock by my bedside. I did the mental calculations. I hated math. I hated this war. I hated everything but her. "We have eighteen. Eighteen hours and this ends, not because I want it to, but because it's the only way to keep you safe. Forgive me, please, for wanting you too much. Forgive me for wanting it to be you, my one and only lover. Mine."

She turned in my arms and pressed her face against my neck. "Why?"

"I can't tell you that."

"What do you mean?"

I sighed as the truth fell from my lips. I couldn't do it. I couldn't lie to her face. She had taken that from me too. I was glad. I didn't want to be known as a liar like my dad. I was glad she had taken away at least one mask. "I'll be sending you away."

She reared back and slapped me across the face. Deserved. Very much deserved. I flinched, but I knew she needed to get it out, so I faced her again and waited for another slap.

Tears filled her eyes.

I gripped her hands between mine and rubbed my thumb across her skin. "I will not apologize for keeping you safe."

"You can keep me safe!"

I felt my face fall, my facade crack. "*Dorogaya*, not from this, not from this." Tears stung my eyes. They made me hate my own bloodline, both of them, they made me hate despite the love staring back at me. But I couldn't start another war. This one… I knew I would not win. Five families against a broken Russian one.

They would have to choose.

And it would not be me.

"Why?" Tears streamed down her cheeks. I caught them, damning myself to Hell that I was the reason for them when I swore I would never let that happen.

"I can't tell you that either. Just know it's for the best. I'm not doing this lightly, Alice. I'm doing it because I see no other option, because my hand has been dealt, because I love you too much to not let you go."

It slipped.

The *I love you.*

I didn't think she would notice it.

Instead, she launched herself against me sobbing. "I love you too much to let you go."

"And I love you too much to see you killed."

"You promised!" She beat against my chest. "You promised you would kill me if it ever got to that point! You PROMISED!"

I froze and then I pulled away and tilted her chin toward me. "What did you just say?"

"You." Her lower lip trembled. "Promised."

An idea formed as I took her mouth with mine. "I'll never let you go." I pressed her palm to my chest, to the scarred A while I pressed my free hand to hers. "Never. Never."

"Never," she repeated as she shoved me down against the mattress and straddled me.

I gripped her thighs; she'd be bruised in the morning.

I'd mark her with pleasure again and again.

I pulled her closer, and then she moved onto me.

I thrust up the minute she sank down.

"More," I growled.

She was beautiful the way she rode me, the way her hair hung like a curtain giving us privacy when our bodies moved with each other.

The most beautiful thing I would ever see was this.

Us.

Together.

I jerked her down as our pleasure built, I sucked her bottom lip, bit down, and moved to a sitting position, wrapping her legs around me as her body convulsed tightly around me, sucking me dry.

"It's going to be okay," I found myself saying and believing. "Trust me."

"A monster." She nodded as she kissed me again. "I always wished they would save me. Don't let me down."

"I won't," I vowed.

And for the first time since feeling abandoned by every spiritual being ever worshipped.

I prayed.

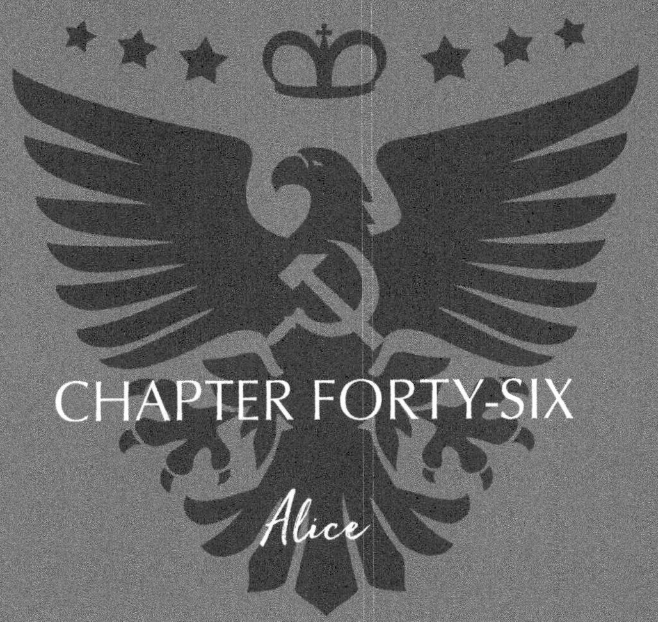

CHAPTER FORTY-SIX

Alice

The countdown had started.

We slept another three hours before I woke up with a hot Russian mouth between my thighs.

I spread my legs, my back arching as I gripped the sheets. "Don't stop."

I could feel his smile against my thighs, my body buzzed with each touch of his tongue. He pulled away too soon.

And then his hands were on my hips, slowly moving up to my breasts, like he wanted his bare hands to memorize every inch of skin, to ingrain them in his memory.

I sucked back the knot in my throat as he moved with catlike grace up my body, until he cupped my face with one hand and just stared at me, his eyes piercing, his lips swollen from the last few hours.

I knew it was almost time.

I'd been keeping track.

Or maybe my heart just knew without having to look at the clock.

We had two more hours before whatever was going to happen… happened.

He still kept me in the dark.

Maybe it was better that way.

Maybe it wasn't.

But he asked me to trust him, so I did.

Blindly.

"I watched you," he confessed. "When they brought you in, I watched you, and my response to you hurt, it fucking hurt, like something had zapped my heart forcing me to notice it again. And then I hated you for making me feel anything. Now I can't imagine being numb again." He squeezed his eyes shut for a few seconds, and when he opened them, they were glassy.

I did that.

I was making the monster cry.

My lips trembled.

He kissed them then, pressing his mouth to mine. "I promise I'll try. I promise I'll try, but if I can't… if I can't do it, I need you to ask me."

"Ask you?"

"I need you to ask me to kill you."

My stomach dropped. "What?"

"I can't take the risk that they would torture you, that they would gang up on me, I'm not their blood, so in this scenario I don't have the pull that Chase does. Just promise me."

"Kill me." I locked eyes with him. "*Ubei menya.*"

He sucked in a sharp breath. "It sounds too beautiful, too wrong coming from your lips."

I smiled and made the mistake of glancing at the clock again. Ninety minutes with a man who should have always been mine.

"No more talking." I wrapped my arms around his shoulders and pulled him down, only to have him adjust his position and flip me onto my stomach. "What are you—"

"Hmmm?"

"Never mind," I said against the pillow as I felt his heat against my ass, the backs of my thighs. His body was so hard, so hot settled against my skin, like this is how my fairy tale was supposed to end.

I guess it made sense.

I'd always dreamed of an escape.

I just didn't realize mine would be death by the very monster who saved me.

"I'll be okay. No matter what, Andrei. I'll be okay," I promised.

He kissed my back, his hands spread wide across my skin. "I'll follow you."

"No." I shook my head. "You won't."

"I will."

"Don't ruin these last moments we have together by saying something like that." I almost turned back around, but he had me pinned down with his body weight. "Don't. I can't bear it."

"Tears." He swiped them with his fingertips as I turned my head to the side. "You shouldn't shed your tears for a man like me."

"Someone should, Andrei. Someone should shed tears for a man like you. You have years' worth of unshed tears, unfulfilled promises — let me decide who I'll sacrifice my tears for."

He pressed a kiss to my shoulder. "I will love you forever."

I squeezed my eyes closed as more tears slid onto the pillow.

And then he was inside me, causing me to come up from the bed in pleasure as he pressed my hands down against the mattress, he was wild in his passion.

His hands bruising my wrists.

His body heavy and perfect against mine.

I would remember this for as long as I still had breath.

And I would be thankful that I was given at least a few short moments of perfection.

I could feel the intensity of this moment as it built up between us, as he whispered my name like a vow.

"Andrei," I whimpered. "You're my everything."

"Alice…" He let out a growl. "You're my fucking soul."

CHAPTER FORTY-SEVEN

Phoenix

There weren't enough curse words on the planet for what was about to take place.

It was early, around seven a.m. when I got the call I was expecting.

I drove, with my hands gripping the steering wheel like a vise, and when I made it to Nixon's and saw all the nice cars parked — the suits; the what seemed like hundreds of suits…

I questioned my own judgement.

I was helping bring down my old family.

I was helping build a new strong arm of the five families.

This was what it was about.

Because at the end of the day it wasn't just about a love affair for Andrei, it was about keeping my blood safe, my friends, my family, my wife, my child.

I would not apologize for that.

For using the knowledge I had to force their hands.

To force his.

I slammed the door to my car and casually made my way into Nixon's. Wine was already on the table despite the early hour.

Several black suits seemed out of place against the old Mediterranean style furniture. A sea of them, all waiting for me, waiting for the final call. Everyone was tense, rigid in their posture despite the wine that was waiting on the table. I imagined half of the men in there had twitchy fingers ready to reach for their guns, I also imagined that this was the moment that would define the next generation. And if it failed, if he failed, it would be on me.

The rest of the guys gave me a knowing look, probably because I wasn't surprised. I had, after all, made the call to the Sinacore Family.

And there they were.

The underboss, who had stood in for the last decade, because it was said that he would stand in until the rightful heirs took their place, he refused to step up regardless of the outcry to be named boss. He was surrounded by a few of his made men and captains.

"Drinking already?" I nodded to the bottle. "Must have been some flight."

Louis Sinacore, the underboss, gave me a placating smile. "Where is he?"

"Probably sleeping like everyone else at this godforsaken hour," Tex said under his breath.

Louis said nothing. Tex was still the Capo; even the Sinacores reported to him, and even more so now that they weren't in Sicily.

They were in the US.

They were of equal power to each of the families in the Cosa Nostra. The only difference was the blood that ran through their veins.

It was ridiculous that people would think they held extra power just because they hailed from the last living royalty in Italy, but people were superstitious. Not just that, they wanted something to believe in.

Needed it.

And the Sinacore Family had given it.

"Phoenix," Nixon said through clenched teeth, his lip ring glistening in the early morning light. "Care to explain why we have visitors?"

"Sure," I said slowly. "I made a call."

"Obviously." This from a tense looking Chase.

I sighed and crossed my arms. "The De Langes were working with the Russians, with Alexander Petrov, with Ivan, one of his last men. They re-opened their prostitution rings. Three of them. They went back on their word, we'd given permission for Chase to do a cleansing of the lines, but we weren't going to eliminate all of them, it made no sense at the time, we just wanted them to believe we were going to in order to keep them in line." I swallowed. "And now…"

"Now…" Louis nodded, his expression inscrutable. "You need a replacement."

I swallowed the knot of anxiety in my throat. "We're always stronger as five families. They'll keep trying to enter into the fold every time, unless we replace them with someone stronger, scarier, more…" I shrugged. "Royal."

"So that's where they come in?" Nixon talked like the Sinacores weren't even in the room, arrogant bastard. I loved him for it. "Why couldn't we just call a hit on every last

De Lange?"

"A massacre?" I nodded. "Yeah, we could do that, and then our own people fear us more than they already do, which isn't necessary. Let the new family come in and create a reputation for themselves, let them create the bloodbath. We call a commission when it's done, ordain the new arm of the Sinacore Family into the Cosa Nostra, and the problem is officially solved."

Dante raised his hand. "Not to put a damper on world domination here, and no disrespect..." The kid just oozed disrespect, but whatever. "But they have no boss."

Louis shifted in his seat.

It was common knowledge that they'd been without a boss for years.

Because they'd been inactive.

They'd been laying low in Sicily, they'd been a figurehead.

"It's time to wake the beast," I said with deathly calm.

Louis's jaw tightened, the men sitting stood.

"It's time," I said again. "To remind the rest of the world who the Sinacore Family is, and what they will do to those who defy them."

I reached for a glass of wine and twisted it in my fingers. "To answer your question, they have a boss, a powerful one that will combine two families who desperately need it."

Sergio stilled.

I could see the shift in Chase's stance.

Nixon gave me a curious look.

"Andrei Petrov," I whispered, "is their heir."

The drop of a single pin would have sounded like an explosion in that room.

So, I lifted the glass high. "To the new Cosa Nostra, may

she be as strong as she once was, to the new arm of the five families, The Sinacore—Petrovs."

"Fuck," Tex muttered under his breath.

As we toasted to the families.

I knew.

We'd just done something we could not undo.

We had taken the oldest family in mafia history.

Poked them.

And forced them to rise again.

May the De Langes rest in peace.

Because we'd just ended the war.

CHAPTER FORTY-EIGHT

Andrei

It was starting.

Don't ask me how I knew.

It was in my blood.

I was born of violence.

A son of war.

I felt it in my bones as I slowly put on a pair of jeans I would later have to toss in the trash because of all the blood, and paired it with a black V-Neck.

She was sitting up in bed watching me.

I let her.

And I wordlessly went over to my dresser and grabbed two knives, shoving them in the back of my jeans, another in my boot.

My Glock was loaded.

I wasn't sure how much I would need.

I wasn't sure how this would even happen.

All I knew was that something was happening.

"Get dressed." I didn't recognize the sadness in my own voice as I stared her down. "I'm going to escort you to the SUV, and you're going to get in, and then you're going to promise me that you won't do anything until I come for you."

She nodded her head quickly, jumped out of bed, and ran across the room, throwing herself into my arms. "Tell me it's going to be okay."

"It's going to be fine," I lied, kissing her hair. "Pack a small bag just in case, you never know, this may be me being dramatic." It wasn't, she didn't need to know that.

She was De Lange.

I could lie all I wanted.

But we took records of everything.

Phoenix knew.

Dante knew.

Which meant El, his wife, knew.

Too many people knew.

People I couldn't kill.

People I couldn't control.

People that were most likely done lying to their own blood, especially after discovering what the De Langes were doing. And how they were supplying me.

Alice pulled away and ran across the hall.

My phone buzzed in my pocket.

It was Tex.

> **Tex:** Shoot on sight. De Lange bloodline. Men. Women. Children. Official cleanse of the family line.

My stomach sank.

It wasn't like the Italians to do that. Kids? I was obviously growing a heart. Then again, there was a reason for the warning text, it would be sent out to every family member, and if the De Lange adults were smart, they'd hide their kids until the cleansing was over. That's one thing the mafia did not do.

Kill orphans.

Tex, as the Capo, would place them with other families, they would be forced to pledge allegiance to them for life.

But they would live, unless their parents decided to be selfish pricks and use them.

Phoenix texted next.

Phoenix: You at the club?

Me: Where else would I be? Disneyland?

Phoenix: Ah, he has jokes.

Me: He's happy or WAS.

Phoenix: We're on our way... have you made your choice?

Me: Not that easy.

Phoenix: Life is hard. You're either with them and us, or you're against. She can't help who she is. I'm not stupid. You're not legally married, she has no protection of your name, none. She's on her own unless you can convince them. That's all the advice I can give.

Me: I'm sending her away.

Phoenix: To die?

Me: What else do I fucking do!

Phoenix: You're smart. You'll figure it out.

Me: I told her I would kill her if it came to that.

Phoenix: Then aim low, or high, and make them listen, because they're about fifteen minutes out, and they're ready to crown you mafia king.

Me: If I told you I'd rather live in complete poverty with the woman I love?

Phoenix: I'd say you just grew a pair. Twelve minutes.

Me: I hate you sometimes.

Phoenix: Good.

I shoved my phone back in my pocket and cursed, slamming my hands against the dresser, and then rage like I'd never felt before took over. As if it had been building since I was a kid under my dad's reign.

I threw the dresser over then took my knife and dug it into the mattress, ripping the sheets, pulling them from the bed.

I wouldn't sleep in that bed ever again.

Not without her.

I let out a roar of outrage as I fell to my knees and lowered my head. I'd tried to run away from my father, from his family, only to be the only one left standing to lead it.

And now? Now my past was knocking.

The only way out was death.

I gripped my knife in my hand.

I stared at the way the metal glistened.

It would be easy.

Why hadn't I thought of that before?

My blood would stain the room in seconds.

It would be their fault.

They would have no leader.

But…

They would still kill her, wouldn't they?

I didn't realize I was shaking until a soft hand wrapped around mine, slowly lowering the knife to the ground.

"Let go," Alice whispered.

"Can't," I said through clenched teeth. "I can't…"

"You must." She shook me.

I didn't move as I lowered my head and a solid tear fell from my eye.

"Andrei?"

This was my ending.

Saying goodbye to the one person, the one reason for any happiness in my soul.

I blinked up at her. "We need to go."

I felt like I left my soul in that room as we walked out. I sure as hell left my heart with her.

My body went through the motions as I grabbed the bag she'd packed and escorted her through the dimly lit hallway one last time.

Maybe if Hell froze over.

This would have ended differently.

But Hell was very much alive.

Because I was living in it.

And soon, I'd command it.

We made it through the club and outside in record time.

One of my black Escalades was out front.

Ax was in the driver's seat.

I opened the door and tried shoving her in.

"Wait!" Alice turned in my arms, pressed her mouth to mine with such ferocity I experienced pain and pleasure simultaneously. I sucked in a deep breath. I would remember her.

I would remember everything.

"Thank you," I whispered. "For giving me twenty-four hours of heaven, after twenty-two years of hell."

Tears streamed down her cheeks.

I brushed them away. "Stay safe."

"Where am I going?"

I hesitated and then, "You'll see."

I kissed her forehead and shoved her in the car, then slammed the door before I could do anything stupid.

I fired off a text to Ax.

> **Me:** Don't tell me where you take her. You know our options. If you tell me they'll try to get it out of me. I'll die before giving her up.
>
> **Ax:** Good answer, Boss. And try not to worry too much.

I snorted. Right, try not to worry too much?

He pulled out of the parking lot around one minute before ten different vehicles pulled into it, the scores of tires kicking up loose gravel.

I waited patiently.

She was safe.

She was gone.

I'd never felt such hatred for another human being as I did for the ones slowly getting out of their cars to face me.

On the outside, I was calm.

On the inside, I was a fucking hurricane ready to wreck everything in my path.

The guys approached first.

Tex had two guns strapped to him, and a stupid grin on his face like this entire situation was hilarious. He was wearing a black beanie for shit's sake.

Nixon wore combat boots that looked like they would easily crush someone's windpipe if he so chose it. His lip ring glinted in the sun as he ran a hand through his messy hair and narrowed his eyes at me like he wasn't sure if he should kill me or congratulate me.

Dante stood on the other side of Nixon, and Phoenix looked like he was exceptionally bored.

Great. I was the only one losing it.

Gravel crunched beneath Chase's boots as he folded his arms across his chest. "Got any De Langes in there?"

"I'm sure I do. They like to sell women, remember?" I snorted. "Feel free to start your bloodbath while I stand out here and get a tan."

He let out a little laugh. "Sure you don't want to join?"

"I would, but it seems I have business."

Chase tilted his head and then put a hand on my shoulder. "You look pissed."

"Good, I feel pissed."

Tex barked out a laugh. "Did we interrupt play time?"

Son of a bitch, my fingers itched to shoot him.

"Does it really matter?" I fired back.

Phoenix let out a sigh as a few men I didn't recognize got out of their cars and made their way toward me.

The Sinacore Family.

I'd met one of their men this last year, and I'd made him look like a fool to his own father.

He'd wanted his trust fund, and I'd allowed him to access it early. His father wasn't exactly thrilled when his perfect son returned home without the bride that had been promised to him since birth — along with her inheritance.

My response?

Whoops.

After all, Renee and Vic were married now. And Italians didn't break vows of any kind. Marriage was sacred, so they were fucked.

But their memories were long.

And I knew they weren't pleased to welcome me into a family that could trace its heritage back to when they sat on thrones and wore crowns.

Sergio bumped into me while I was watching the men, and then he slipped something into my pocket.

He pretended like he didn't do anything.

I pretended right along with him.

What the hell was he doing?

"Morning." I crossed my arms. "Are we doing this here or do we need alcohol?"

The man who approached was at least six inches shorter than me, and his gray pinstriped suit did nothing to make him appear taller. He had silver hair and was wearing dark Ray Bans. In his right hand, he held a single white rose.

"So, this is the great Andrei Petrov," he said with a thick Italian accent.

"I would shake your hand but I wouldn't want to taint your skin with my Russian blood." I sneered.

"Half!" he barked. "Half Russian. We will need alcohol for this." He motioned toward the club and then sidestepped me.

The hell just happened?

Chase had already disappeared into the club, and from the filtered sounds drifting from behind the doors, he was doing what he did best. Killing.

I wondered if his loyalty was deep enough to me, to not kill her if the time came.

And then I realized that rules were rules.

And his job was to carry out the orders of the Capo.

With an inward curse, I walked into the dim club and made my way up to the bar, it was too early for most of the staff to report, which meant if there was blood, they wouldn't have to witness it, not that they weren't already immune to it.

Everyone sat in the VIP section, on couches, bar stools. I reached behind the counter and grabbed, a few bottles of wine, along with a few bottles of whiskey and vodka. At this point we'd need the entire damn bar.

I knew what was coming.

I knew it.

"Your mother's a whore!" my dad yelled. "An Italian whore! That's why she's dying!"

I winced as I reached for her hand.

She looked so frail.

Weak.

She gave me a small smile as he stomped out of the room.

"Come here, Andrei."

I climbed up to her bed and touched her face.

It was cold.

I hated it.

It was death.

My hands shook as more of the memory surfaced.

I wore gloves because I didn't want to feel warmth.

Because it reminded me that she was cold.

So fucking cold.

The memory surged forward.

I grabbed a blanket to cover her, but she was still shivering.

And then she said very softly so that only I could hear as men moved around the room.

They said words like torture.

Water boarding.

Skin grafting.

I didn't know what they meant.

"She knows too much. He wants his time with her first though, wants to shame her…"

Another man left.

And then my mom crooked her finger with tears in her eyes. "Andrei, I love you more than life itself."

"I love you." I didn't understand love much. My mother wasn't often around me, my dad wouldn't allow it. But I felt something inside my chest for her. Something important.

She pressed a finger to her lips and then revealed a knife out from under the blanket. "I need you to do this for me, Andrei."

My eyes widened in horror.

What was she asking?

"He will kill me regardless. This way I feel no pain. If you love me, you will help me."

It was unfair to ask your own blood for that sort of mercy.

I shook my head.

"Please." More tears streamed down her cheeks.

I shook my head again. "No, I can't."

"You can."

"I can't!" I screamed, not realizing I was sobbing over her body, not realizing that the minute I'd tried tossing myself onto her, she'd aimed the tip of the knife to her chest.

My weight sent it directly into her heart.

I was seven.

"You know why we're here." The silver-haired man grabbed a bottle of wine and began pouring in the glasses I'd grabbed.

I knew I looked pale.

Maybe it was his face that triggered the memory.

Maybe it was his smell.

Something about him was familiar.

Something about him looked like my mother.

He was old, at least eighty.

"Do I?" I finally answered, still trying to put the pieces together.

"You look like her." He shook his head. "We thought she ran off with her lover — instead we found out he purchased her from the De Lange Family. Her price was three million dollars, something Alexander Petrov bragged about to the world. He bought his Italian bride with blood money and said he loved her, but his love was a lie."

"So, the treachery goes all the way back…" I mused looking around the room. "I'm sorry he took her. He wasn't a good man. Then again, are any of us?"

"You defend him?"

I snorted. "I'd stab him in the heart then beg God to give him life again just so I could watch his face as I drove the knife deeper into his skin, again, and again, and again. You want to know what I hate? I hate that I wasn't the one that did it."

His eyes widened briefly. "Do you know who I am, son?"

"You're Sinacore," I whispered. "And you're here for me, of course."

The rest of the guys were silent, but each of them was tense like they were waiting for a shot to go off.

Or maybe waiting to restrain me.

"My name is Louis Sinacore, I have been underboss ever since your mother and her sister were taken. One day they were playing in the field, the next…" He shook his head. "A parent should never have to survive their child."

My eyes narrowed. "Parent?"

"I'm your grandfather." He said it so factually that I almost laughed.

"What?" I felt like I couldn't swallow, like the room was imploding, or maybe that was just my brain. "What do you mean my grandfather?"

"Does he still need the sex talk?" This from Tex.

I shot him an annoyed look.

He held up his hands in mock innocence.

"And you're here now because?" I gritted my teeth. "What? You wanted a fucking family reunion?"

I knew what he wanted.

I just needed him to say it out loud.

I needed it to be over.

"We didn't know she was your mother, not until a few months ago, we had no idea. We would have come sooner."

"I did just fine," I said through clenched teeth.

His face was remorseful. "Don't lie, son."

I shot to my feet.

He slowly got to his, and then he held out his white rose and nodded to the man next to him who stood as well, he grabbed a knife from his pocket and sliced Louis right hand.

Louis closed his eyes and squeezed his hand and then opened it as three drops of blood splashed against the white petals.

Before I knew what was happening, every single one of the men I called friend, restrained me, while Louis approached.

I let out a shout.

It was no use.

Me against them.

I'd never felt more betrayed in my life as Louis held the rose in front of my face like a bad omen and then with the help of his men, moved to his knees.

I struggled against the guys.

Chase grabbed my left hand.

And cut what was left of my Russian tattoo.

The sickle, the bleeding stars.

But he left the crown.

Confused I looked down as Louis held up the white rose in his left hand, an antique crown tattoo wrapped around the back of his hand.

It was identical to mine.

Chase squeezed my blood onto the rose.

Drip. My old life was gone.

Drip. My new life wasn't given, it was forced.

Drip. I would never forgive them.

Drip. I struggled as one more drip landed on the rose.

And then Louis was helped to his feet. As he pulled the petals one by one, they dropped at my feet.

"If we spill your blood, you may spill ours. We honor the new Sinacore boss, blood of his mother, cut from his father. You are no longer Andrei Petrov, you are Andrei Sinacore, and you will rule this family until the day you leave this earth. *Sangue in no fuori.*"

The guys released me.

I stood there in shock.

I wasn't given a say.

I knew I didn't have a choice.

I didn't know it would be like this.

Louis pulled out a card, the patron saint of Edward the Confessor, only people in a line of Kings were given that saint.

I opened my mouth to tell him to stop the ridiculous ceremony, to tell him I didn't want anything to do with my father, my mother, with anyone but the woman who owned me.

I locked eyes with Louis as he pressed the card to my forehead and then very slowly lit the edge on fire with a lighter, only to blow it out immediately.

"As burns this saint, so burns my soul."

Chase elbowed me in the side while someone else kneed me in the back.

With clenched teeth, I sealed my fate and whispered. "As burns his saint, so burns my soul."

"It is finished." Louis beamed. "All is as it should be." He raised his hands into the air and let out a long exhale that sounded like it had been trapped inside his body since my mother's disappearance.

The guys let me go.

Chase's shirt had speckles of blood.

Seemed I was hiding more than one De Lange.

It was over.

In more ways than one.

Louis took off his ring, it was identical to the tattoo, and with great force, he shoved it onto my left hand like a fucking wedding ring.

"Now," Louis clasped his hands. "Before business, we drink."

Finally, something I agreed with.

But I couldn't move.

I was rooted to the ground as the guys all walked around me and started talking about the weather, their kids, the new Maybach that was just announced.

I stood there.

Completely fucking empty.

CHAPTER FORTY-NINE

Alice

I've always heard that every person, at one point in their lives, experiences a crossroads.

I was at that point.

Ax had brought me to a private airport.

The jet was pitch black and looked expensive.

I had my bag in my right hand as I stepped out of the SUV and stared up at it.

A man I didn't recognize, a beautiful man started walking down the stairs to greet me.

He was tall, muscular, extremely familiar despite the fact that I'd never met him before.

"Nikolai." Ax held out his hand.

Nikolai shook his hand firmly and looked to me. "Any issues?"

"Issues?" I repeated.

"With getting out of the club before it was infested with

more Italians?" His lips quirked like he said something funny.

"No," Ax answered for me. "I just got a text. Everything seemed to go as planned… Unfortunately."

Unfortunately? What did that even mean?

Both men gave me a pointed look.

I wanted to back away, I wanted to steal the SUV and drive it back to the club.

"Is Andrei—" I licked my dry lips. "Is Andrei okay?"

"He's alive," Ax said quietly. "Then again are you ever really living when you don't have those you care about by your side?"

"Deep for a made man," Nikolai teased. "All right then, so I guess this is the choice you're going to make?"

"Choice?" I almost shrieked. "I wasn't given a choice."

"She's new," Ax pointed out like I was an idiot.

I almost smacked him. "What do you mean I'm new? I wasn't given a choice. Andrei shoved me into the SUV, basically making me think I was never going to see him again and looked like he was marching off to his death!"

"In a way he was." Nikolai shrugged. "The death of part of his past, the rebirth of a new future. The question is, where do you fit in Alice De Lange?"

I sucked in a sharp breath and started backing away from both of them. "H-how do you know?"

"Then again," Nikolai ignored me. "He did lie and tell everyone you were married so you were safe."

"He's an idiot," Ax pointed out. "Should have just done it and apologized after the fact."

"I'm lost," I whispered. Did I need to grab the knife I'd tucked away in my bag, or not?

"You can get on the plane with me. Fly to New York, disappear, new name, new identity, I'll even let you work for me."

"Huh?"

"He's kind of a big deal." Ax nodded. "In case you're wondering why he looks familiar; he won a Nobel Peace Prize for his research with AIDS and other STDs." He shrugged. "Then again of course he was able to study it closely since he's known as The Doctor or Dr. Death. He's Russian in case you haven't noticed the tattoo on his left hand, and he works for Andrei on the side."

"It's good that you work at the club." Nikolai shook his head. "What if she tells?"

"She won't." Ax winked at me. "She's in this now."

I was in something all right.

My heart was breaking.

They were talking in riddles.

And I just wanted to know he was okay.

"What's my other choice?" I asked quietly staring down at the asphalt. "You said I have two choices."

"Your second choice is a bit more… adventurous."

"Adventurous?"

"You stay and let him fight for you," Ax said confidently.

"I'm a De Lange." I gulped. "Chase will kill me, and if he won't, one of the other ones will."

"Chase's wife is half De Lange." Ax shrugged like it wasn't a big deal. "She sacrificed herself for him. Blood must always be spilled."

My head shot up. "What was that?"

Nikolai's lips twitched. "Blood must always be spilled. Especially after Mil's betrayal. Like I said, staying is more adventurous, dangerous, and you may not live. But something tells me that if you get on that plane, you're already dead."

"Figuratively." Ax cleared his throat. "He means

figuratively."

Tears welled in my eyes.

Could I do it?

Could I get back in that car and face not just the monster I loved, but the ones who would kill me without a second thought?

He'd killed for me.

Spilled my own brother's blood for me.

He had given himself to me.

I nodded at Nikolai. "I think I'd rather die than get in that plane with you."

"Good answer." His dark eyes flashed.

"You were hoping I'd say no?"

"I was already in the city for business when Ax called. You may need me later anyways. It seems I'm staying."

"Why would I need you later?"

"Doctor." His face fell.

Great.

I refused to lose my nerve now.

"Are you going to come with us then?"

"Wouldn't miss it for the world." He grinned and then shoved Ax. "I'm driving, you're a lunatic."

"You're not wrong." Ax winked and opened the SUV door for me. "After you, Alice."

The door shut with finality behind me.

I had promised him I would leave.

I had promised him I would be safe.

I had promised him I would ask him to kill me.

And it seemed I might have to follow through with it if things went wrong.

"Blood must always be spilled." I repeated out loud.

"Nikolai, how much blood does the human body have?"

"Around seven percent of your body weight is blood, why?"

The car turned as he drove us back in the direction we came.

"How much blood would appease Chase?"

"All of it," Ax said without thinking. "You'll need a different plan, stabbing yourself isn't going to work."

"I wasn't going to stab myself." I wrung my hands together.

We were back at the club too soon.

A dozen expensive black cars were parked out front. "What's going on?"

"Oh." Ax turned around as he loaded his gun. "The Sinacores are here to wipe out the remaining De Lange blood line and take their place, and the love of your life is their new boss."

I froze. "What?"

Nikolai's face softened in the rear-view mirror. "He's half Italian, he's the heir to one of the oldest mafia dynasties in the world. And his first task is a mass cleansing."

I squeezed my eyes shut. "And if he defies his first task?"

Nikolai locked eyes with me. "To defy your own blood, or direct orders from the Capo, means death."

"I'm walking into my own funeral." My voice shook.

"Oh ye of little faith." Nikolai winked.

I'd been at a crossroads.

I had chosen the road less traveled.

The one with signs that said beware.

The one with the broken bridge and enchanted castle.

The enchanted castle filled with bloodthirsty monsters, and no princes riding in on white horses.

"I need a minute." I grabbed my bag and took a few

soothing breaths then very slowly got out of the SUV with Nikolai and Ax flanking me.

The club was loud when we walked in.

Men were laughing.

Drinking.

And my heart was breaking.

He'd known, hadn't he?

Andrei had known.

And he'd chosen blood.

Over love.

CHAPTER FIFTY

Andrei

For once in my life, the vodka didn't do anything except remind me of Alice. I had sent a text to Ax to make sure she made it safely to wherever he was taking her.

He had yet to respond.

I trusted him with my life, but he was still Italian.

Then again, so was I.

Shit.

"No offense, but you look like hell." Chase sat down next to me while more laughter erupted from the corner where Louis and Tex were talking. Nixon and Phoenix had joined, and Sergio was currently on his laptop trying to locate every last De Lange in the Chicago area.

Most of the families had fled.

As long as they didn't come back they wouldn't be killed.

But we didn't want to leave any stone unturned.

And I had no choice in the matter.

If the Sinacore Family was to take its rightful place, there had to be no question that another family would challenge.

And the De Langes were stupid enough to do just that.

Sergio cursed and jerked his head at us. "Vic said a group of De Lange men just left one of the known locations downtown, heavily armed and headed this way."

"Good." I could taste blood on my tongue. "I need to kill something."

Next to me, Chase chuckled. "Knew that you wanted in, it's probably why you look like shit, unless something's happening with that wife of yours?"

Wife.

My stomach sank like a rock as I kept my face indifferent. "She left."

Chase's eyes narrowed. "That's not how marriage works typically. You get that, right? Why the hell did she leave?"

"This isn't the life for her." I looked away.

"I'm calling bullshit." Chase grabbed a bottle of water from behind the bar and sat back on the stool. "When you find someone you don't just let them go to protect them. Been there done that, the T-shirt fucking sucks, and it's depressing as hell."

It was strange that I was having this conversation with Chase of all people, with De Langes pissed off and headed our direction.

With the taste of another De Lange still on my tongue.

The universe was clearly out to kill me today.

I was about to say exactly that when the room fell silent.

I knew it was her before I craned my neck toward the door, I could smell her, feel her. Rage took complete control of my body as I slowly stood. She walked into the club like she wasn't going to get killed.

She couldn't be that stupid.

Ax was on one side of her, Nikolai the other.

What the hell kind of game were they playing?

"Nik." I narrowed my eyes as he casually crossed his arms like sunshine was sprouting out my ass. His smile wasn't welcome. Not now. "What's going on?"

"Missed you." He snorted. "Found this one hanging out by my jet and asking for a ride."

"Your jet." I clenched my teeth so hard that I could have sworn I heard a molar shift. "Ax just happened to be at your jet? With Alice?"

Ax leveled me with a cool stare. "I figured it was wise to give her a choice."

"You disobeyed direct orders." I pulled out my gun and pointed it at his head. "I told you exactly what to do."

"That's just the thing." Ax didn't even flinch. "You told me what to do, you told her what to do, you were doing so much telling that I figured you needed time to pull your head out of your ass and think about it. You're not gonna shoot me, because you know, deep down, in the darkest loneliest crevice of your body is a tiny little heart that's beating a bit too cheerfully right now."

"I will cheerfully end your life," I roared. "How's that?"

Ax opened his mouth.

But Nixon silenced him. "I can't save you from this one, Ax. He's the new Sinacore boss, tread carefully."

Alice jerked her head in Nixon's direction then glanced back at me, tears in her eyes.

I'd chosen her.

But she was looking at me like I had betrayed her.

Like I'd pulled the trigger.

Like I was the reason for her pain when I was the reason she wouldn't have to experience any.

"Well." Ax sighed. "Didn't see that coming."

"No shit," Dante said from his spot near the bar.

Chase moved to stand next to me. "Ax go stand guard, we have De Lange associates on their way. I'm sure Andrei will deal with you when he stops breathing fire."

A few men chuckled.

The Sinacore men watched with rapt fascination like we were some sort of sick crime drama.

"Alice…" Chase stepped forward. "I have a… quandary…"

Fuck.

I moved but Phoenix was suddenly at my side, pulling me back while I helplessly watched Chase circle her like he was going to devour her whole and then use her as target practice.

Nikolai stepped away.

She was alone.

Completely alone.

I locked eyes with her. I tried to tell her to run.

But she just fucking stood there and looked at me like the hero I wasn't. Didn't she get it? Didn't she see? Monsters didn't save the day.

No, monsters started the war.

Monsters finished it.

She'd officially tied my hands behind my back.

"Oh?" Her voice was strong. "What would you like to know?"

"Your name was wiped from all of Andrei's records, and since we all know that you were supposedly one of the girls sold to him, then later apparently married to him, I just found it… interesting."

She exhaled and lifted her chin. "Ask."

"Ask what?" His smile was cruel.

The bitter part of Chase was making an appearance.

"Ask me what my name is."

I jerked away from Phoenix and grabbed Alice by the arm. "Stop. Speaking."

"Protecting her." Chase inclined his head. "Interesting."

"I protect what's mine," I said through clenched teeth.

"Sergio," Chase barked. "How you doing on that marriage certificate search? Anything?"

"No." Sergio's voice was heavy like he was sad he couldn't find anything. "No record of any marriage between Andrei Petrov and Alice…" He shrugged. "Though it would be extremely helpful if we had a real last name."

"Mmm." Chase nodded. "Try De Lange."

"Son of a bitch," I muttered under my breath, then pulled Alice against my chest, whispering in her ear. "Why? Why would you do this? Why?"

I was panicking.

My throat all but closed up as I clung to her, my right arm wrapped around her body, my gun trained on her back.

I squeezed the trigger.

I couldn't pull it.

I waited for her answer.

And then she whispered softly, "Kill me."

It was Chase's turn to curse, like he was surprised that she would ask me that when it was the deal all along, wasn't it?

She didn't run.

She didn't listen.

I tortured myself with the feel of her skin for a few more

minutes and then pulled away just as gun shots rang outside.

Ax ran in the club and dove behind a couch shouting. "Twelve! I got two, they have—"

More gunshots rang out.

And then silence.

"We know you have her!" A man yelled. "Just give us Alice and we'll leave."

My heart stuttered to a stop in my chest as I stared down at the woman I'd shoved to the floor to protect. Not a chance in hell.

"She's my cousin," a deep voice echoed from outside. "Let us take her and we'll leave."

"You're like cockroaches," Tex yelled. "You'll just multiply."

"So? We are no longer a threat. Give us our cousin."

Alice started shaking beneath me, like the idea of going back to her own family was so terrifying that she'd rather die in gunfire.

"Let's talk," I yelled back holding both hands up, gun still in my right, my finger off the trigger.

Six men walked through the doors in similar fashion. Each of them looked like they'd drunk way too much over the past week and were in need of a shower.

The De Langes had never impressed me.

Even less so now.

I pulled Alice to her feet. "Is this what you want?"

The men's eyes roamed over her body, my body, the body I'd kissed, loved, touched.

"Alice…" One of them licked his lips. "You're looking good."

She glared. "Go to hell."

"Aw." He put a hand on his heart. "They've turned you

against us."

She let out a humorless laugh. "No, my brother turned me against my own family every time he touched me, my father every time he let my brother into my room, my family name when I was forced to hide for a full year wondering if the monsters were going to come. Sorry, but I'm taking my chance with them, I'd rather die than go with you."

"Funny." He sneered. "Because the way I see it, they can't let you live. Regardless of who you've been whoring yourself out to."

Logical thought crashed through the window of my brain as I shoved her back against Chase and aimed for the guy who'd called her a whore.

I opened fire.

I didn't stop.

I shot every single one of them in the head.

And then tossed my gun on the table as I let out a rough exhale. "Rot in Hell."

My chest was heaving, my blood boiling as I stared at their dead bodies.

It was out of character.

I knew that.

The Italians knew that.

I didn't just shoot.

I tortured.

I toyed.

I played.

And then I struck.

Not today. Not with them.

I'd shot without thinking.

In all my life, I'd taken special care in playing indifferent, not showing my tells, appearing unaffected by everyone and everything.

And when it mattered most.

I laid all my cards out on the table and pointed to my only weakness.

A De Lange.

Alice De Lange.

Six thirty-two.

My heart.

My soul.

I'd just damned her to Hell.

CHAPTER FIFTY-ONE

Alice

I'd never seen him so angry.

So ruthless.

Cold-blooded.

That was the same man who'd whispered my name, who'd held me close, the same man who'd shed a tear for me.

That man had just massacred six of my family members.

Because they insulted him.

And tried to take me.

It hit me then, why he was so convinced there was no way out, but death. My own family would have used me against him. They would have done whatever it took to stay alive.

The De Langes were desperate enough.

And a De Lange alive was a dangerous thing.

It threatened everyone.

I hung my head and then put a hand on Andrei's tense shoulder. "*Ubei menya*."

"No," he clipped.

"Yes."

"Alice…" His voice shook.

I leaned up on my tiptoes and brushed a kiss across his cheek. "I don't want it to hurt too long."

He squeezed his eyes shut.

And then someone was grabbing me from behind. My body trembled as I looked over my shoulder.

Chase.

His face was set in stone as he pulled my hands behind my back and shoved me to my knees.

"Not here!" Andrei barked. "Not in the club."

Oh God, he didn't mean it right? He didn't mean to take me to that place? Where nightmares were born? Where dreams died?

Chase pulled me to my feet.

Andrei's eyes flashed as he grabbed his gun and led the way, the only funeral procession I would get would be before my death as the most powerful men in the Italian mafia, and the monster I loved, led me to the cement room.

I swallowed bile as the huge door clicked open. Chase shoved me down the cement stairs and then I was standing in front of all the windows. I imagined all the women who had died there, who had had their throats slit in front of men who paid to see it.

Who were so aroused by it that they went and paid for a girl and a room.

I was going to be sick.

This was real life.

This wasn't a fantasy.

He'd warned me.

He'd given me a number, not a name.

I was Alice De Lange. Six-thirty-two. And I was going to be sacrificed because people can't choose their blood.

And mine was damned.

All of the men, including the older ones I didn't recognize, stood before me as Chase once again shoved me to my knees.

Andrei pressed his gun to my forehead.

I expected it to be hot from all the shooting.

It felt cold.

Lifeless.

"You're so warm…" he'd whispered.

Tears stung my eyes and fell down my cheeks.

"Don't move." Chase shoved me a bit. Footsteps echoed as he walked away and then returned and handed a long black whip to Andrei.

Andrei glared at him. "I don't really have time to teach you how to use this, Chase."

"I don't need a lesson since I'm not going to be the one using it. Blood must be spilled…" He looked over at me. "So fucking spill it."

I hated him.

I hated all of them.

I hated that Andrei was going to do this, I hated that I needed him to.

Most of all, I hated that the Andrei I knew and loved would not come back from this.

What was left of his innocence, I would take with me to the grave.

And in that moment, I hated myself more, for being born a De Lange, for wanting him as much as I did.

For loving him despite the warnings not to.

He raised the whip.

I saw the hesitation.

And then Chase spit out a curse and pulled me to my feet, only to throw me down against the concrete as he pulled out a knife and held the tip beneath my chin. "Should I bleed you dry while he watches? Is that preferable, Andrei?"

I could feel Andrei's anger pulsing around us as Chase very delicately pressed the tip of the knife into my chin.

I was afraid to move as tears streamed down my face.

It stung and then it burned as he pulled it away. "I could carve her a new face, Drei. Now raise the whip."

Chase picked me up with both of his hands, my feet dangled. He was a strong man; it wasn't lost on me that he could break me in half if he wanted.

He could have scarred my entire face, could have broken my jaw. Instead, he gave warnings and drew small amounts of blood. If that's how they would torture me, I'd rather die.

His eyes flashed as he stared down at me. Andrei couldn't see our faces at this angle. Chase didn't blink. "You always like to play with fire?"

"You always stab women?"

His lips twitched and then he was hauling me back to my feet and shoving me in front of Andrei. "Do it, or one of us will."

The guys' faces were all masks of indifference, like they were thinking about their next meal, or the last soccer game they watched.

Did anybody even care?

And then I remembered.

Blood.

The mafia was blood.

Spilling it was as natural as breathing.
I spread my arms wide and locked eyes with Andrei. "Do it."
He raised the whip.
And I was no longer Alice.
I was six thirty-two.
And it was my sacrifice to make.

Blood and dirt caked her face.

Chase had done that.

One day I would murder him for it.

I would smile.

I still grabbed the whip, I imagined the usual audience watching, waiting as I clenched it between my hands.

It came down hard on her snowy white skin. It ripped into her flesh and pulled it from her body — and I could almost smell their arousal even though nobody was in the rooms, nobody would bid on a corpse. A corpse I created.

Hell was waiting for me.

But I still saw heaven in her eyes.

In her beautiful blue eyes.

I didn't deserve her trust.

Or her sacrifice.

Her arms were shaking as blood streaked down them.

Her eyes begged me for life.

Even when she knew, even when I told her again and again — all I had to offer was death.

She'd committed the ultimate sin.

Trusting me. Loving me.

And I'd embraced that same sin and called it my own as I made her mine. Her only mistake was coming back, was thinking that my heart would choose her over blood, over loyalty.

I slammed the whip down on her right thigh.

I hated myself with each hit.

Her blood was too precious to spill.

I was spilling it.

When would it be enough?

She cried out my name.

And I remembered.

I remembered then.

There was once a time where my name fell from her lips in ecstasy in wonder — in love.

But she didn't know — I wasn't capable of it.

This was my legacy.

This was my destiny.

A tear slid down her cheek, falling onto the rivers of blood streaming down the concrete.

Soon the blood would be gone.

The concrete clean.

And her life would be sacrificed.

Not by my hand.

But hers.

Because that was the deal wasn't it?

"Kill me," she'd whispered between kisses.

"Yes," I agreed as I tasted her sweet sin for the last time. "I will kill you."

Her thank you fell on deaf ears.

So, I raised the whip again while she smiled.

It was the smile that shocked me to my core.

The way she directed it at me like I was deserving when I was her killer, her monster, her captor.

Flashes of our time together filled my mind until I was shaking with fury at my own predicament.

I dropped the whip to the ground and grabbed my gun. Only this time I pointed it at my own temple.

The guys all took a step forward. "What the hell are you doing?" Chase said in a lethal tone.

"You want blood?" I pounded my chest with my left hand. "Then take mine! Sinacore and Petrov, the last of the line, is that fucking royal blood good enough for you to let her go?"

Chase held out his hand to me. "Andrei, think about this—"

"IS IT ENOUGH BLOOD!" I spat.

"Don't do this," Alice whispered, her words were laced with pain, "Andrei, don't, please… please!"

I squeezed my eyes shut. "Capo." I opened them and locked eyes with Tex. "Is it enough blood?"

Tex didn't answer right away.

Dante and Nixon pulled out their guns like they were going to shoot me in order to stop me.

"It's going to happen anyway," I confessed to no one in particular. "It's been happening every birthday, I point the gun right about here." I rubbed it against my temple and laughed bitterly. "And I pull the trigger. It never goes off, but it will now. I know it will now, because for the first time in my pathetic life, I have someone, something I want to live for. Poetic, that I would die for her instead."

I let out a roar and pulled the trigger just as searing pain hit me in the thigh. My gun went off, I felt a sting across my right shoulder as I fell to the ground.

Suddenly Alice was by my side, our blood creating a river of sin between us.

"Andrei!" Her tears streaked down her face, landing on my chest. With a groan, I got to my feet and charged toward Chase.

"Son of a bitch." Chase shoved me away. I was losing blood fast. "You're welcome for not letting you kill yourself!"

"You. Can't. Have. Her!" I charged him again, landing a few blows to his jaw before strong arms pulled me off him.

Blood poured from his nose. "I motion for Andrei to take her punishment. If he lives through the night," he eyed Nikolai, "without assistance from Doctor Death over there… then he can have her."

"I second." Dante raised his hand.

"Third." Nixon nodded.

Slowly, the entire room agreed.

I hung my head as the room spun.

Chase looked down at the blood on the cement. "It was never about enough blood being spilled, Andrei. It's about being willing to spill it all for someone you love. She's willing to die for you, and you nearly died trying to save her. I think, after tonight, you'll understand."

"Besides…" Phoenix finally spoke up. Ah good, he was the one holding me in place. That's why my body hurt; he didn't have to stretch my arms behind my back so hard. "Chase really doesn't have a leg to stand on since he's with Luc."

"Fuck you." Chase shook his head.

"I call an official commission," Tex piped up. "Andrei better live, because the Sinacores are in this now. It's not just De Lange blood that has been spilled."

Louis moved to my side and then he pressed his hand to my bloody shoulder. "It is said that a drop of blood from a Sinacore has enough good luck to last you a lifetime."

I shuddered as more blood exited my body. "I'm shocked it didn't work."

Louis smiled. "On the contrary. You tried to shoot yourself for how many years? And the bullet never pierced skin. I would say it worked quite well." He sighed. "We'll talk later."

I met Alice's tear-filled gaze.

She took a step toward me.

Chase held her back.

Still murdering him later.

I winced. It felt like the bullet in my thigh had met bone.

"Lock him in here," Tex barked and then glanced over at Alice. "No visitors."

She gave him one nod and then both Nixon and Chase were taking her away from me.

It wasn't until she was out of the room that I noticed Tex, Phoenix, Sergio, and Dante had stayed.

"Shit," I muttered.

"You lied to the family," Tex said plainly. "So, each of us will deal you with a death blow. It might be best to just let me go first so you pass out."

"Where's the fun in hitting a limp body?" Dante cracked his knuckles.

I snorted. "Been waiting to hit me where I don't hit you back, hmm?"

"Been waiting at least a year to knock your teeth out." Dante grinned. "Then maybe after that, we can be friends."

"Cool, I'll put you down for hair braiding at four," Tex mocked.

Phoenix stepped up first. "I'm glad you did the right thing."

"Yes, that's exactly what I'm thinking right now as you pull out a dagger that looks like it has souls still attached to it."

He winked and then stabbed it directly into my other thigh. "I think I hit bone."

I wheezed out a curse. "Yup."

Phoenix jerked it free as I tumbled to the ground just in time to look up and see Tex looming over me.

His fist connected with my jaw.

Something cracked in my mouth.

I spit out a bloody tooth and moaned.

Sergio was next.

He pulled me to my feet and then managed to dislocate my left arm as it dangled at my side.

And finally, Dante.

We had bad blood between us.

We hadn't discussed it.

There was no need for apologies then.

No need for apologies now.

"You gonna chop of my dick?"

He grinned. "Not when you just learned how to use it, that's not playing fair."

"Hilarious."

He pulled out two knives and shoved one directly into the shoulder with the bullet "El says hi by the way."

I screamed in pain.

El was his wife.

El, I liked.

It was Dante I was having a hard time with.

He twisted the knife at the same time he ran the tip of the blade along my right arm, digging up flesh as he carved. "I was Picasso in another life."

Blood drenched my shirt.

Pain swallowed me whole as dark dots started to fill my vision.

And then.

The nightmares came.

They came full force.

And there was nothing I could do to stop them.

CHAPTER FIFTY-THREE

Alice

My clothes were soaked with blood.

My teeth where chattering from shock.

And all I wanted to do was run back into the room of nightmares and hold him close.

Chase pulled off his shirt and handed it to me. "Put this on, yours looks like you survived an animal sacrifice only to get lost at a vampire fair."

How could he joke at a time like this?

"I prefer my shirt to yours," I spat.

He grinned. "You know I could have broken your jaw."

It's like he read my mind. I shifted on my feet. "Regretting that you didn't?"

He very gently reached forward and cupped my face. "Andrei is a proud man, he's also an idiot when it comes to punishing himself, and since I know exactly what that's like, I did him a favor the way he did me a favor."

I frowned. "What do you mean?"

"He warned her away from me. He did exactly what I would have done in his position. She didn't listen. And his presence alone made me want to act. It takes an act of God for most of us to accept love — and Andrei needed exactly that."

Next to me, Nixon cleared his throat. "He's not comparing himself to God, because that would be idiotic. What he's saying is we could have been harder on him."

"He could die." I said it slowly so they would understand.

Nixon winked. "He won't die. He'll be pissed, and he'll probably need a lot of blood but we have Nikolai here. He'll stay the night."

"If he's staying, I'm staying too." Without thinking, I relented, and peeled off my shirt and put on Chase's.

Chase jerked his attention to the wall while Nixon looked down, grinning, Nikolai turned completely around while Ax examined his nails.

"Sorry," I muttered. "But Chase was right, I was gross."

"At least it's lucky blood," Chase said loud enough for the other family to laugh and shake their heads, just as Nikolai walked over and started assessing the damage to my skin. Before I knew what was happening I was bandaged up and watching as the guys continued to act like nothing was wrong.

How was this normal?

It wasn't.

And yet… it was.

"Can we watch him through one of the private rooms?" I asked no one in general as the door once again opened.

I heard nothing.

No screaming.

Just silence.

I preferred his screaming and cursing.

"Little slugger just tuckered right out." Tex laughed while Dante was wiping his knives on his shirt like it was the best day of his life.

Phoenix just rolled his eyes while Sergio crooked his finger to me.

I walked over.

"Security card for the place." He put a black card in my hands. "I figured you'd want to stay, shower, get some rest. Then you can watch him sleep. But know that if you go in that room without permission you will die."

Great.

"Okay." I took the card as all the guys watched me, maybe waiting to see if I was going to burst into tears or start yelling.

With a sigh, I confessed. "I was locked in a room for one year without going outside, my brother was an asshole, and Andrei literally referred to me as a number for three straight days and chopped off my brother's tongue and gave it to me like you would give a girl flowers. I'm not going to have a breakdown."

"Well…" Nixon chuckled. "When she puts it that way."

"A tongue." Dante nodded. "Huh, no wonder he never got any action."

I could see a few of the men glance up at him with knowing smirks.

And it was Phoenix's turn to shrug and say, "Figured you guys probably already knew he wasn't a manwhore like he made himself out to be."

"Not a manwhore and also not a virgin anymore," I snapped and then wanted to crawl underneath a dark surface and put my hands over my eyes.

My face was hot as each of the guys grinned at me like they had some ammo they could use against him.

And then the strangest thing happened.

The Capo, the man I'd been told to fear more than God, lifted his hand for a high five.

I hit it.

Just as he whispered, "Way ta get your man, tiger."

The moment firmly sealed my place among the monsters.

As bodies of the men were collected, the floor cleaned.

"Come on," Nikolai jerked his head to the door as we both made our way into one of the private viewing rooms. "I'll sit with you."

I sat down in one of the cushy chairs and pressed the button that opened the curtains.

I gasped in horror at what I saw.

Dangling from the ceiling in an array of chains, with blood dripping from his body.

Was Andrei.

And all I could utter was one word. "Why?"

"Some things are worse than death," Nikolai mumbled. "He does this so you don't have to, he hangs there with purpose, with pride. As long as I've known Andrei and his father, I've never seen him willing to die in order to save another human life. I didn't even think him capable of love. Most days he tolerates people. Today he showed all of us that there's more, that it's deeper, that his father didn't steal everything from him."

Tears welled in my eyes. "I deserve to be out there."

"Andrei would of course argue that point." Nikolai leaned forward in his chair and watched; his cold dark eyes were hard to read. In all actuality, everything about him seemed dark, just like Andrei, like he had something in him that fed off the light or would if he let it. “He’s losing a lot of blood, but I imagine they’ll put a stop to that soon.”

“What? How?”

Nikolai crossed his arms and leaned right back in his chair. “I’ll tell them to cauterize the wounds.”

My eyes widened. “With what?”

“Fire.”

I started shivering.

He didn’t look at me, just said, “You should go shower, get comfortable clothes on and then grab wine or whiskey, and enough food to last you the night. And if you’re a praying sort, I’d maybe start doing that too.”

“Praying?”

“It’s best he’s blacked out. I would pray he stays that way. Because you won’t be able to handle the screams if he wakes up.”

“I’ll be fine.”

“I highly doubt that.” He jerked his head to the door. “Go. He’ll still be here when you get back.”

CHAPTER FIFTY-FOUR

Andrei

"Mama!" I ran in circles around her legs until she finally noticed me and picked me up.

She was the prettiest woman I'd ever seen.

"Pretty." I touched her cheeks and giggled. "You love me, Mama?"

Her eyes filled with tears as she nodded and whispered so nobody would hear. "I love you so much, Drei, more than my own life."

A door slammed. "Get away from my son!"

Mama slowly dropped me to my feet.

I clung to her leg as my dad stomped into the room.

He was always angry.

He didn't hug me.

And he hated it when my mom did.

He said it was weak.

I was weak.

"Andrei…" He jabbed his finger at me. "…go get your brother and sister."

"Okay."

I had just had my fifth birthday.

I didn't realize that in two years my mom would ask me to kill her.

I didn't realize that my life was about to change.

I didn't realize it wasn't normal. My life.

I would know on my first day of school that I was different.

I would know shame.

I quickly ran into the nursery. They were twins. Three years old and silly, and they cried a lot when Mama couldn't hold them, so I tried to hold them too.

But it wasn't the same.

I knew that.

It didn't feel the same as a hug from her.

"Come on, we gotta go see Dad."

"Dad?" Katya repeated. "He's home." She didn't sound excited as she slowly rose to her feet and grabbed her doll. I hung onto her hand and squeezed it.

"Pace, come on."

Pace's hair was bright blond.

He clutched a truck to his chest.

And slowly we walked back to the kitchen where my mom was sitting at the table, her tears dripping on top of it.

"Katya, Pace," Dad barked. "Get in the car."

Pace began crying. "Where?" He wanted to know where they were going.

My dad grabbed his toy truck and threw it against the wall.

"Listen to me for once and go wait at the door!"

Pace nodded, his expression hurt as he went to the door.

Katya slowly lifted her gaze to Dad's. "We go on trip?"

Dad didn't answer.

He grabbed her doll.

She couldn't sleep without it.

"Dad, Katya needs her doll if she's going—"

His slap cracked my cheek so hard that I fell to the ground. My mom didn't come get me.

I could hear her cry harder.

"Say goodbye to your children," he hissed.

Mama rose to her feet and reached for Katya first just as Pace came running.

They hugged for maybe three seconds.

I didn't count.

And then Mama said, "What about Andrei?"

"He's the oldest. He stays."

It was on the tip of my tongue to beg him to let me leave.

But my cheek still hurt.

He gathered my brother and sister with another man, and they left the house.

The doll was at my feet.

The truck was in pieces near the wall.

"Mama?" I felt sick to my stomach. "They're coming back right?"

She didn't answer, but she went to the pantry and opened a bottle of something that smelled sweet and strong. She chugged and then set it down on the counter. "No, Drei."

"Where are they going?"

Her eyes flashed and then she fell into fitful sobs. "To heaven, baby, they're going to heaven."

And I knew, she'd lied.

She'd lied.

I grabbed Katya's doll and cried with my mama while my other older siblings turned on the TV as loud as they could.

"*Prosti*!" I screamed as I came back from the nightmare. "*PROSTI*!" Forgive me, forgive me, forgive me.

My lungs burned as blood wet my face slipping down my chin onto my battered body.

"*Prosti*!" Tears mixed with blood.

He'd sold them.

Sold his own kids to the highest bidder.

Used them as collateral.

And kept me as his protégé.

Katya.

Pace.

I never said their names.

Never.

It hurt.

I let out another scream of pain.

The sound of a door opening didn't bring me from the darkness, from the pressure in my lungs as more memories surfaced.

"Kill her." Dad shrugged. "She's of no use anymore." He gave me his gun.

"She's twelve," I snapped at him, ready to point the gun in an entirely different direction now that I was sixteen.

"She's costing us money," he spat. "Kill her or I may just let her kill you."

He was bluffing.

I picked up the gun and pointed it at her.

I didn't look in her eyes.

I made it quick.

And I could have sworn her soul said thank you when she crashed against the cold hard ground.

Later that night, with shaking hands, I took a nail and etched another mark in my bed post understanding that most guys my age did that for an entirely different reason.

To remember the women they'd slept with.

I did it, to remember the ones I had killed.

Thirty-two.

"*Prosti.*" I clenched my teeth tasting blood as I threw my head back and roared until my voice was hoarse.

Something touched me.

The fires of hell were coming.

Licking at my heels.

Burning themselves against my flesh.

I deserved it.

I deserved it all.

And then I was moving, maybe my body was leaving this plane, going into a darker one, if that even existed.

Hell couldn't be any worse than living life as a Petrov.

Something wet touched me next. It was warm.

And then it smelled like rose water.

Lips pressed against my temple.

The same temple I always held the gun against.

"Sleep… Andrei… Sleep."

"Mom?" I rasped. "Mom?"

Arms hugged me.

Held me close.

"I'm sorry." My body shook so violently it was hard to get the words out. "So fucking sorry."

"Don't ever be sorry for sacrificing yourself, don't ever be sorry for living," the familiar voice said. "Now rest."

"The things I did…" My body pulsed with pain so intense that I felt like I was convulsing. My eyes couldn't focus on anything other than the ceiling.

It was dark.

Nighttime?

I couldn't tell.

The lips pressed against my face again.

And then my hand somehow found another hand.

I almost pulled away.

Gloves, I needed gloves.

Her hand was too hot.

My skin wasn't worthy.

And yet, I couldn't find it within myself to let go.

CHAPTER FIFTY-FIVE

Alice

I stayed up all night.

Nikolai had put him under once he was back in the apartment, the bullet in his shoulder had lodged itself really close to the bone, but Nik was able to pull it out.

The knife wounds were all stitched up by both Nikolai and Sergio who informed me that he had studied to become a doctor but never finished school.

And one by one, the guys visited.

With their wives.

It was a strange thing, seeing all of them pull together after everything that had transpired in the last twenty-four hours.

The girls brought food and hung out in the living room like we hadn't just been involved in a bloodbath, and the men stayed to make sure Andrei was alive.

Even Louis Sinacore, who I learned early in the night loved to play checkers, stayed to check up on his grandson.

Their new boss.

It was a lot to take in.

More than a lot.

My mind was reeling by breakfast.

A beautiful girl with cropped brown hair and pretty eyes showed up right when everyone was starting to eat. One of the guys I recognized from Nixon's house was with her.

He was massive.

And looked like he was going to eat humans for breakfast instead of bacon.

She clung to his hand and then burst into tears when she saw Louis. He pulled her in for a hug and whispered something in Italian against her hair.

"He's apologizing." Chase took a bite of bacon and then another while Luc, his wife, came around him and laid her head on his shoulder.

Odd to imagine that twenty-four hours ago he'd punched me in the jaw.

"What's he apologizing for?"

"I'll introduce you," Luc said with a wide smile. "Long story short, she's a Sinacore as well. She was promised to one of his gross arrogant grandsons, and Andrei basically screwed them all over by making them believe that she was killed in the club when really Vic just wanted to marry her."

"Vic." I tried the name on my tongue. "Is Vic the scary one?"

She let out a snort. "Imagine him guarding Chase."

"Guarding," I repeated. "You?" I had a hard time believing that. "How does that work?"

Chase smirked. "Not well."

"I imagine not."

"So, one big happy family," Chase muttered. "At least now

the Sinacores can't be pissed at Andrei. Wonder if Phoenix knew that all along?"

"Heard that," Phoenix said from behind us. "And I only tell you what you need to know, so what do you think?"

"I think you're Satan in sheep's clothing," Chase said cheerfully.

"It's sheep, or a sheep," I corrected.

Luciana burst out laughing. "She's not scared of you; this is my favorite day."

Chase glared daggers at his wife then pulled her across his chest and pressed a kiss to her mouth. "Don't make me punish you later."

"I'd welcome it."

"And that's our exit…" Phoenix grabbed my arm and led me away from them. "Andrei's awake."

I let out a sigh of relief. "Can I see him?"

Phoenix's blue eyes narrowed briefly before he nodded. "He was asking for you, said he had to apologize."

"For what?"

"He threw something at me after that, so I didn't get the last part." He grinned. He was less menacing when he smiled. "But he's very… raw."

"What aren't you telling me?" I wondered out loud.

"He has to ask."

"Ask?"

"You," Phoenix said, not at all clarifying things. "Marriage means your blood becomes his, and vice versa, he needs to ask you. If he doesn't ask you, if you guys don't get married, then I'm going to have to send you away. At least then you won't be looking over your shoulder waiting for someone to get you. You'll have the seal of the families protecting you. You can do whatever you want, be whatever you want, we will obviously make sure you have money and—"

I gawked. He wasn't serious… couldn't be. But his expression said he was.

"No," I whispered. "I won't, I can't… I'm not leaving him."

Phoenix bit out a curse and leaned in. "Then make sure he asks."

"You can't make him?"

Phoenix burst out laughing. "Yeah you'll need a sense of humor if you stick around. That's funny, forcing Andrei, both Petrov and Sinacore to do anything right…"

I swallowed the lump of misery in my throat.

Misery that he would send me away to protect me.

Only this time his conscience would be clean because he'd saved the day.

Because sometimes, the monster won.

I knocked on his bedroom door and then quietly pushed it open, clicking it shut behind me.

He was sitting up in bed. Gauze was wrapped around his right shoulder, his skin was tight across his abs, muscle after muscle peeked through. I inhaled sharply because it was a natural reaction to his masculine beauty.

It kind of left a person in awe.

His beauty was so distracting that I couldn't seem to take him in all at once, like the way his messy hair looked like he'd been tugging it, or the nose ring that oozed sexiness.

His full mouth pulled back into a small smile.

I barely kept myself from running toward him, my own body was sore from getting whipped. Was I insane for not being angry that he was the one that dealt those blows to my skin?

"Are you just going to stare at me or are you going to come

over here and kiss me?" His voice was hoarse like he'd been screaming all night.

I wondered if anyone told him that he did.

That he screamed over and over again until I finally covered my ears and rocked in the corner of the viewing room, weeping on his behalf, wishing I could take his pain.

"I'm going to kiss you, just tell me if I hurt you." I crawled up on the bed and rested my head against his chest first. I needed to hear it, needed to make sure.

"What are you doing, *dorogaya*?"

"Listening." My voice cracked.

His fingertips dug into my hair. "For what?"

"Your heartbeat." Hot tears stung my eyes. "I just wanted to make sure this was real and you're alive."

He tilted my chin up toward him. "What did I tell you about wasting tears?"

They slid down my cheeks.

He rubbed them away with his thumbs. "Don't cry."

"I'll cry if I want to cry." I grit my teeth at his amused smile. "You could have died; you pointed a gun at your own head in order to save me. I have a lot to cry about. And I've been hydrating." I don't know why I was upset. Maybe because I knew what was coming and I was so tired of fighting him, so tired of him telling me what was best for me.

When what was best would snap my heart in half like a pretzel.

He swallowed, his own eyes getting glassy as he cupped my face with his hands. "It was the only way."

"I would have never forgiven you."

"And I would have never forgiven myself, for taking your life. I think it would have killed me."

I pressed my cheek into his left hand. "You're stronger than that."

"No." His eyes darted to my mouth. "I think I'm lacking all strength and self-control when it comes to you, because all I want to do is get you out of this club and send you to a nunnery."

I gaped. "You wouldn't."

His lips curled into an amused grin. "You clearly don't realize how fucking selfish I am."

"Is that a good thing?"

"It means you don't need to go grab your rosary."

"Because I have one of those… in my go bag." I leveled him with a glare.

His chuckle was low, sexy.

I wrapped my arms around his neck and lay against him. "Am I hurting you?"

"Immensely."

I jerked away, but he held me against him so tight I could barely move. "I don't want to lay here and let my stitches heal, I don't want to touch you and not taste you, so yes this is hurting me. It may be more painful than last night, and I woke up with such a hoarse voice you'd think that I'd been at a rock concert."

"Close, real close, more like your own torturing." I shuddered. "Phoenix said something…"

He stilled. "What did Phoenix say?"

I was almost embarrassed. "That depends."

"Don't lose your nerve now, *dorogaya*."

I smiled at his name for me, pulled away enough to look up into his crystal blue eyes. "I'm going to need you to keep me."

He pressed his lips together and then our foreheads touched as he drew a finger down my jaw. "Is that what this is about?

You think I'm the sort of man to see heaven in your arms and then just… toss you out?"

"Yes." My voice broke. "Because you'll want to keep me safe, and I know you don't — I know that… I know it's asking a lot, before it wasn't real it was just to keep me safe and you don't have to do that anymore."

"You're right. I don't have to." He was breaking my heart as he kissed my mouth softly. "I fucking want to."

His mouth was hot.

He kissed me harder, his tongue struck slow and precise as his mouth molded against mine so effortlessly, I melted against him.

And then he said something in Russian. It sounded like he was speaking in tongues, it was the same thing he'd said to me our night together.

Only this time, when he was done, he held up something between us.

It was a ring with three bands interconnected and wrapped together like ivy, on each band was a small diamond. It looked like rose gold. I was too stunned to stay anything.

"In Russia, the tradition…" He grabbed my right hand. "…is to put it on this hand. I would buy you something bigger, something that would scar Chase's face if you decided to punch him, but it wasn't you. It wasn't us." He slid the ring onto my right third finger as tears splashed from my face onto our joined hands. "I'm keeping you, *dorogaya*, and I am never letting you go. Please say yes, please say you'll choose me even though I don't deserve it."

"That's the thing, Andrei. You deserve everything. You just feel too guilty to take it. I came in here willing to seduce you to the best of my ability and use everything in my arsenal so you wouldn't send me away." I wiped my tears. "Because the thing is, I want to keep you too. Even though you called me a number, even though I think we may fight as much as we make love. I want to keep you because your darkness is what makes your light so incredible. I just want this." I touched his chest. "So bad."

"And I…" He pressed a kissed to my mouth again. "Want this." His hands grazed the front of my shirt.

And then suddenly the shirt was off my body and his left hand was roaming across my skin.

I laughed. "You're injured."

"I'm Russian, I'll be fine."

"Italian too," I pointed out.

He stiffened, and then we both looked down at his hand, where the tattoo was cut, where his past connected to his future. "I didn't even want to be boss to one family."

"And now you have two," I pointed out. "It's like having twins."

His head jerked up, his eyes wide. "Twins."

"Andrei?"

"Twins," he repeated again as if I'd just announced I was pregnant.

And then he crushed his mouth against mine like the word twin was his new code word for get naked.

"Andrei."

He kissed me harder so I couldn't talk, had to breathe his air as one-handed he tugged my jeans open and slid his fingertips inside.

"Okay… as impressive, mmph…" He deepened the kiss. "That is…" Damn the man knew how to work his fingers. "Maybe just a few more… seconds…"

"Open for me." He licked my lower lip, and then I was straddling his hurt body like the most selfish person on the planet as he teased me. "This is mine, all of this."

I bucked against his hand. "Y-yes."

"All of you." He spoke in Russian again. I whimpered my release as my mouth crashed against his in a kiss that felt just as good as what he'd just done.

"Marry me, *dorogaya*... marry me tomorrow."

"I'll marry you right now." I moaned digging my hands into his hair, careful not to hit any bandaged or stitched part of him.

"Yes." He moaned my name. "Yes."

A knock sounded on the door.

We both froze.

Andrei's eyes narrowed as the door knob turned. "I'm killing whoever's on the other side of that door."

Naturally, it was Phoenix.

"Typically you wait for the person to respond after you knock." Andrei bit back a curse and kept me close to him. "What do you need?"

"You're injured, take it easy." Phoenix sighed. "And I thought I'd give you an early wedding present."

He dropped two black folders down on the mattress.

"Wait?" I glared at Phoenix. "You said—"

Phoenix burst out laughing. "I was the one who brought the ring to him. I just thought he deserved to be seduced a bit after last night."

Andrei started to shake.

"What?" I was ready to check every bandage. "What's wrong?"

"You found them," he whispered. "They're alive?"

"Who?" I looked between them.

"The twins. My brother and sister. They're… alive."

Alive.

They were alive.

The raw guilt that I'd done nothing while they were taken away had come back when I was getting tortured, delirious from bleeding. I remembered things I'd forcefully kept under lock and key and now I couldn't stop remembering, her bright blond hair and chocolate eyes or the way he always had a smile for me.

I felt heavy.

Exhausted.

And every nerve ending was on fire each time Alice fussed over a bandage or touched a scar or pressed her palm to my skin.

I was ready to lose my fucking mind and risk broken bones and stitches just so I could have her naked beneath me.

I told her that.

She laughed and then abandoned me to sleep.

Like I could actually sleep when I could still smell her.

I clutched the folders in my hand and slowly rose out of bed. My jeans hung low on my hips as I made my way out of the bedroom and down the hall into the noisy living room.

"We having a party that I lived or a party planning my death?" I grumbled, leaning against the wall.

"You're supposed to be in bed." Alice charged toward me.

I smirked at her strength. "You really think you could make me?"

She rose up on her tiptoes and pressed a heated kiss to my mouth in front of everyone, one that had my body burning for more, and then she pulled back as I leaned in seeking just that.

"Nice." Tex chuckled.

"Shhh," Chase whispered. "She's training him."

I gave them a middle finger behind Alice's back and dragged another kiss from her mouth. "Five minutes then I'm locking you in my room."

"Five minutes and you're taking a nap," she said, gritting her teeth.

I choked out a laugh. "Sure." I winked and made air quotes with my fingers. "I'll… nap."

She scowled as a blush lit up her cheeks like fire.

The guys all chuckled while the girls seemed to simultaneously roll their eyes at me.

"You're hurt." Alice reached for my hand and squeezed.

I tensed when I saw the bloodied whip mark across her forearm. I'd put it there, I'd done that.

"I'm sorry." I traced the angry red skin with my fingertip. "I'm so sorry."

Alice just shrugged and whispered. "Worth it."

I had no words.

I wanted to devour her next sentence and throw her against the wall. I wanted all of her right then. In that moment.

"We're getting married," I decided to announce awkwardly, and then she beamed up at me. I was smiling way too much with her in my presence.

"Dibs!" Mo shot to her feet. "As Tex's wife, I get to plan, right?"

Alice scrunched up her nose. "We were thinking something really small, and soon."

"You pregnant?" Tex said with a completely straight face.

Mo smacked him on the back of his head. "What the hell is wrong with you?"

He burst out laughing. "Look how pale Drei got. Shit, that may be my favorite moment."

"Bastard," I said under my breath. "I actually like kids, unlike some people."

We all turned to Dante.

He glared. "I love kids, I'm still young, El's still young, plus we have enough nieces and nephews as it is. Imagine if all of us popped out kids at once."

Nixon groaned out, "Chaos."

Phoenix eyed the folders in my hands. "So, what do you want to do?"

"About this?" I tossed the folders onto the counter. "I want to get married. I want to lock Alice in a room for at least thirty days."

"Damn." This from Chase. "Better set out protein bars and Gatorade."

I ignored him. "And then I want to find them, bring them here, well not here, not the club… I want them in Chicago."

"Surprise," Phoenix said in a tone that didn't seem surprised at all. "They already are."

"Let me guess, need to know?" I crossed my arms.

He just shrugged and then looked down at the two folders. "They won't come into the fold willingly."

I was afraid to ask, but I asked regardless. "Why?"

"That..." Phoenix tapped his fingers against the folders. "...is a story for another time. Let's get you married."

He didn't want to say in front of everyone.

Which meant it was bad.

I didn't have time to ask because the guys were suddenly surrounding me with congratulations and shots of vodka while the wives took Alice and started talking about wedding dresses and tiaras? Really? Then again, if I was technically royalty... I shook my head. It was too much to think about.

"So, I was researching..." Sergio said. "You know, just in case."

"Nerd." Dante coughed.

Sergio smacked him first, Chase was next.

"As I said..." Sergio locked eyes with me. "I found some intriguing little wedding traditions in my search. Is it true we get to kidnap her?"

Tex's eyes snapped to mine. "No shit? What else?"

"Hell," I muttered. "I have to pay to get her back, yes, that's true but if you haven't noticed we're in Chicago, not Russia."

They ignored me while Sergio kept talking. "We get to set up an obstacle course, typically they have to get the bride from her place of residence and the wedding party sets up obstacles until he makes it to her apartment floor since we don't live in giant apartment buildings I was going to set up a paintball field."

I glared.

Willed him to stop talking.

But he didn't.

And since they wanted the full Russian experience, I was told I had one week to semi-heal before I was put through hell again.

I looked across the room.

At least this time I knew the ending.

And exactly where my heaven would be standing: at the altar.

And I, the sacrifice, would finally be welcomed into heaven's arms.

CHAPTER FIFTY-SEVEN

Alice

In my wildest dreams — I couldn't have conjured up what my wedding day would be like. Most days I thought it was out of my reach.

"It's time." Mo and Trace fixed my floor-length dress. It had a small train. I didn't need anything special, but they wouldn't let me argue. It was strapless, and because Andrei had a thing for red.

It was as red as blood.

As red as the blood we'd joined all those days ago.

Now we were making it legal on the outside the way it was on the inside.

I held the white roses in my hands and waited while the rest of the guys, all dressed in black and white tuxes, moved around the mine field of obstacles.

They went from a Ninja course to a strong man competition, then back to Ninja with paintball guns, but finally settled on more of an obstacle course that wouldn't be too hard for Andrei to get through. He had a log he had to walk across, a net to climb, then bars that formed a high A where he had to swing onto a trampoline and try to grab a rope and yet again swing to the final mat where Tex was waiting with one of those gladiator sticks that's used to throw someone off.

The rest of the guys were at different parts in the course, ready to boo his efforts.

"Is this really necessary?" I breathed out as I saw Nixon put his hands on Andrei's shoulders and point him in my direction. He could have been miles away.

He was still healing, and now he had to go through more?

It didn't seem fair.

"Tradition," Trace said kindly from next to me. "It's about tradition, and this is Andrei we're talking about. He'll thank us later."

"Maybe." Bee laughed and shook her head. "It's not like the rest of us had to go through this." She winced when she locked eyes with Luc, Chase's wife.

She'd been tortured, not as bad as Andrei but bad enough. The fact that she had De Lange blood made me feel better about Chase's place in all our lives, though I still felt on edge when he was around, especially since he was still hell-bent on cleansing the entire line.

For good reason.

But still.

El and Val were on the other side of Mo waiting while Renee made her way over to us, her expression amused. "Andrei's restless. Vic had to give him two shots of vodka and even then he started yelling about how unfair it was to make him go through this after hanging from chains bleeding all over the place."

"He's yelling," I pointed out. "In Andrei speak that means he's happy."

The girls all burst out laughing while I clung to my roses and waited for him. It was like I was waiting at the end of the aisle, only a really intense aisle.

If Andrei could make it past Tex, then Tex agreed to marry us right there on the course, if not, well we hadn't really gotten beyond that, but I'm sure Andrei was prepared.

I gulped when Tex made his way over to the gladiator part.

The guy looked ready to rip Andrei's head off.

Great. Would nothing be normal with these people?

I just wanted to marry him, rush into Nixon's huge house, and celebrate with everyone, mainly with Andrei.

Andrei locked eyes with me from the other side of the field. Even far away, he was beautiful, angry, lethal.

Mine.

I smiled brightly.

He blew me a kiss.

And I nearly died.

"Girl…" Mo elbowed me. "Anyone else proud of this one for taming the Russian beast?"

"Monster," I corrected. "Each and every one of them are monsters in their own right. But I'd rather sleep with the monster, hold his heart close and keep it safe, than take my chances with the man."

"Amen," Trace agreed while the rest of the girls wiped away tears. "It's not an easy life, but it's so much more worth living when you realize how precious it really is." She bent over and picked up her little girl Serena. She was our flower girl while Junior, Phoenix and Bee's child, was our ring bearer.

Trace set Serena back down. She stuck out her tongue at Junior, whose eyes widened as he reached for one of her curls and tugged.

"Junior." Bee pressed a kiss to his forehead. "Say sorry."

"I not sorry!" Junior stomped his foot. "She mean!"

Trace exhaled. "Serena, don't stick out your tongue and be nice to Junior, you're stuck with him."

I'd never seen a toddler's eyes widen with so much horror in my entire life. And I wondered in that moment, if there would one day be a story there… between the two of them.

One could only hope.

"He's starting!" Mo clapped her hands. "Man, the guy's like a predator. Look at him run across that log."

I sighed dreamily as he made his way across two obstacles.

Nixon and Chase heckled right along with Sergio and Phoenix. Dante stayed at the beginning with Vic. Tex raised his gladiator stick high.

Great, just great.

"He'll be fine." Mo winked. "Andrei and I have a plan."

CHAPTER FIFTY-EIGHT

Andrei

I was going to murder all of them for putting me through this. My wounds were barely healing as I jumped onto the rope and swung. That was going to hurt later.

Sharp stinging zinged my shoulder as a stitch popped.

Son of a bitch.

I finally made it to the last part with Nixon and Chase both booing their support.

Tex was standing on the last obstacle, a stupid looking gladiator stick twisting in his hands. "You ready for me, Russia?"

I rolled my eyes. "That depends…"

He hesitated; it was brief.

I flashed him a cocky smile. "Didn't know your wife was pregnant with triplets!" I widened my eyes. "Look!"

Nixon and Chase both looked and gaped.

Then Tex turned just enough for me to slam my hands

against him and throw him into the foam pit they'd constructed.

I hopped off in victory as Mo gave me a high five.

Her sign said, "Triplets! YAY US!" Then she flipped it over. "Gotcha."

Tex was on his knees. "Shit, I nearly had a stroke. Three? Three at once?"

"I'm praying you have ten." I patted him on the back. "Never underestimate manipulation or the fact that your wife wants this to happen because she planned the reception."

Tex grumbled. "Touché."

I looked up.

There she was.

My heaven.

Dripping in red.

Blood red.

My body tightened as I took purposeful steps toward her, pulled her into my arms, and stole kiss after kiss, ignoring the throat clearing around me.

"You did it." She stood up on her tiptoes and wrapped her arms around me. "I like you in a tux."

"I like you in red." Our foreheads touched, she was so warm, so pretty and delicate, her hair was down past her shoulders, and a small silver crown rested on top.

The diamonds were real.

I would know.

Louis had them flown in earlier that week.

They were from my family line, the one that I thought had abandoned my mom, abandoned me. The one I never knew.

I was birthed into darkness.

Not knowing, I was truly a child of the light.

"I love you." Alice clung to me tears glistening in her eyes.

"Dearly beloved..." Tex started and then snickered. "Seriously, though, is everyone ready for this?"

A throat cleared.

I glanced up as Luca made his way toward us with Frank, both of the men who had "retired" from the families yet watched us from afar like the perfect puppet masters in disguise.

They were both in black suits, fedoras, and wouldn't you know, Frank had a red scarf wrapped around his neck.

Luca carried a bottle of wine, and Frank held the glasses.

"Hope we aren't late." Luca winked at me. "I couldn't miss my protégé getting married."

"He also couldn't miss his tee time," Frank added.

Luca just rolled his eyes. "It's important to stay busy."

"Andrei killed seven people in under ten seconds a few days ago," Dante just had to point out. "Does that count?"

Luca snorted. "Boy, talk to me when you get it down to six."

"Chase did just last year." I jerked my head to Chase.

"Yes, let's talk about body counts," Mo said through clenched teeth. "Not just on your wedding day but literally minutes before you say your vows."

"Mafia," Alice blurted with a grin. "It's the mafia."

"Blood in." Frank lifted his glass. "No out."

"Thank. God." I kissed her again this time ignoring everyone's protests.

It took another few minutes to settle down Serena and Junior, apparently she'd gone from sticking out her tongue to kicking him.

And he learned how to fake a fall so it looked like he was severely injured. Little faker even closed his eyes.

The ceremony was quick as most Russian ceremonies are; technically you just sign papers and call it good unless you want something big.

And I just wanted her.

"I'm happy to announce Mr. and Mrs. Andrei Petrov-Sinacore," Tex grinned. "You can kiss your bride… again."

And I did.

I kissed her with every part of my soul.

With every ounce of blood I had.

I kissed her.

And I knew she was mine, mine without the ceremony, mine without the tux. She'd been mine the minute she walked into my club.

And now she had my name.

A name that used to cause me shame.

That now held scars I refused to forget, and a name that held my future, one where the darkness didn't stay forever, one where light always came, in the morning and in her arms.

"And NOW!" Chase interrupted us with his loud voice. "We eat."

I grinned at the memory, my eyes locking with Alice. "You hungry?"

"I'm starved." She bit down on her bottom lip, her eyes darting from my mouth back up to my face like she couldn't decide.

"Then I say we feast." I leaned in and brushed a kiss across her neck. "On each other."

Her knees weakened as she leaned against me.

"You guys coming?" Tex hit me on the back.

I winked over at Alice. "Yup."

Her face flashed as red as her dress.

Mo looped her arm with Tex's.

One by one, the couples went into the house. We were last to go in. It was loud, like it always was with the Italians, like they didn't understand the meaning of silence and the person who was the loudest won for the day.

We bypassed the kitchen.

And then I was running pulling her along with me as we made our way down the hall and slammed the door to the bathroom behind us.

Our mouths fused together with a ferocity that I felt in my soul as I shrugged out of my jacket, not wanting my lips to leave hers.

Alice let out a moan as I tossed the jacket to the ceramic tile and lifted her up onto the sink, my fingers digging into the silk dress that seemed too pretty to ruin.

She hooked a heel around my hips pulling me close as she smiled against my mouth. "Thirty days locked in a room isn't going to be enough."

"No." I couldn't control myself, didn't want to, as I jerked her skirt up to her hips, her head banged the mirror as she leaned back giving me access to her thighs, opening them wide for me, welcoming me, making it impossible for me to focus on anything and everything all at once.

"I'll be gentle," she whispered, her fingers touching a few of the scars roaming my shoulders as she untucked my shirt.

"Don't be." I clenched my teeth. "I want you rough, I want you raw, I want you walking back into the reception funny, so they all know where I just spent the last few minutes… making you mine, in the bathroom, with your legs spread like a fucking feast."

Her mouth found mine again while she pulled my pants

open, I tugged a flimsy piece of lace down her legs and tossed it. I'd memorize every part of her lingerie later. Right now, it was all about need.

Essential.

Primal.

I almost let out a roar when she gripped me in her hand.

How I went through my entire life not experiencing this finally made sense, she was the only one whose touch was life.

Who I wasn't scared to share my soul with.

Who made me feel everything.

She moved down the counter. I gripped her hips and pulled her close, as she impaled herself on me sinking down, taking me inch by inch. I couldn't stop my movements, I was hurried as I pumped into her, kissing her with each slick movement. Sensations hit me everywhere as she tugged my hair and moaned against my mouth.

I was so close.

And the only thing keeping me from being pissed about that was the fact that I had her, not just for twenty-four hours, but for every day.

Forever.

"Andrei." She whimpered my name. "I'm so happy to be yours…"

Waves of happiness rushed over me until I was dizzy with the feeling. I bruised my lips against hers, I slid my tongue across her bottom lip then bit, tasting her, sucking her, as she clenched, her body going so tight that I knew she couldn't hold on any longer.

I didn't want her to.

I watched her face then watched the ecstasy slide across her perfect features. I was doing that. No, not just me, us together.

I let go, soaring high with her, gripping her dress, crinkling it in all the wrong places, making a mess of her perfection.

She rested her head against mine. "How long?"

"How long?" I was high on her; I couldn't even remember how old I was. "What?"

"How long until we can get back here and do that again?"

I barked out a laugh. "Give me thirty minutes."

She pouted.

"You realize that it's only because I'm young, right? Tex would probably need five days."

I heard a throat clear.

We both froze.

A knock sounded at the door. "The walls, real thin, just ask Vic. At any rate, I just feel the need to clear my name. It's not days, it's like an hour, you little shit. Now I'm going to give you guys five minutes before we come barging in there. Time to enjoy your wedding feast that my wife worked her ass off doing up for you."

"Be right there," Alice yelled.

"Uh-huh." Tex's footsteps lessened the farther he got away.

I quickly helped Alice get dressed and put the crown back on her mussed hair. Her face wasn't any better, pink cheeks, swollen lips. Not to mention Tex had a big mouth.

We got as presentable as we could and made our way back to the kitchen only to find every single person in there grinning at us like fools.

"Not a word," I said through clenched teeth, then reached for one of the steak knives.

Mo cursed. "Will nothing ever be normal?"

Tex grabbed the other knife.

"I wanna play too!" Junior yelled.

"Son of a bitch." Phoenix reached for the wine while Nixon sat Serena down and started explaining that bitches were, in fact, dogs.

"That was maybe two minutes if you're lucky," Tex teased.

I lunged. "Just how many girls did you sleep with in college? I lost track…"

Mo grabbed a knife.

Tex ran in the opposite direction while Chase did a slow clap and eyed me and Alice. "So, you ready for blood and war De Lange?"

Alice smiled at him. "I think if I can handle you, I can handle anything."

"She's not wrong." Luc nodded handing him a glass of wine.

Chase sighed and then lifted his glass into the air. "A toast, to the new arm of the five families. Andrei Petrov-Sinacore, may you and your wife have many children, a house of love, and peace in between the war. Most of all, may you never have to face betrayal or loss. Each day is precious. Live life to the fullest and love hard. Cheers."

Alice had tears in her eyes as she took a glass of wine and clinked it with his and then stood up on her tiptoes and kissed him on the cheek. The man who killed an entire family line in cold blood, her line. It wasn't lost on anyone in the room the power behind what she did next as she whispered to the other monster, "Thank you."

If you or someone you know has been affected by sexual violence, please know you are not alone.
The National Sexual Assault Hotline is available 24/7
Telephone: 800.656.HOPE (4673)
Online chat: online.rainn.org
Español: rainn.org/es

WANT MORE RVD?

Did you enjoy Debase?
Then check out these other Mafia Romances

The Eagle Elite World encompasses three separate series that can each be read on its own: Eagle Elite (Italian Mafia), Elite Bratva Brotherhood (Russian Mafia), and Mafia Royals (the next generation). Pick a couple you want to know more about and enjoy!

Eagle Elite

Elite (Nixon & Trace's story)
Elect (Nixon & Trace's story)
Entice (Chase & Mil's story)
Elicit (Tex & Mo's story)
Bang Bang (Axel & Amy's story)
Enforce (Elite + from the boys POV)
Ember (Phoenix & Bee's story)
Elude (Sergio & Andi's story)
Empire (Sergio & Val's story)

Enrage (Dante & El's story)
Eulogy (Chase & Luciana's story)
Exposed (Dom & Tanit's story)
Envy (Vic & Renee's story)

Elite Bratva Brotherhood

RIP (Nikolai & Maya's story)
Debase (Andrei & Alice's story)

Mafia Royals Romances

Royal Bully (Asher & Claire's story)
Ruthless Princess (Serena & Junior's story
Scandalous Prince (Breaker & Violet)
Destructive King (Asher & Annie)
Mafia King (TBA)
Fallen Dynasty (TBA)

ACKNOWLEDGEMENTS

This has been such an incredible adventure, I'm so thankful to God that I can do what I do. My family is so supportive, and I truly LOVE writing stories, especially the mafia ones. We've been in this world for a decade (Eagle Elite) and I don't think I can ever end it. So, readers, don't worry, we have so much more mafia coming your way!

Thank you so much to my beta readers for helping out with this one, Yana you are AMAZING with your Russian translations, Krista, Georgia, Tracey, Jill, Candace — I couldn't do this without you guys! Angie, Heather, Dannae, thank you for always being there for me! Jill yet again you killed it with the formatting and editing, along with Kay (who I make content edit EVERY book lol). I so appreciate you guys and all your hard work! Nina, my amazing publicist I truly don't know what I would do without you, you make releasing a book not just a fun experience but different and unique each time! Becca, apologies for all the crazy emails haha and thank you for keeping me organized! To all of my author friends I constantly bother, Lauren Layne (Wife), Audrey Carlan, Corinne Michaels, Jen Van Wyk; I'm only sort of sorry and also thank you for your constant advice and support! To the bloggers who are so on TOP of everything and do such thankless jobs, I will be forever in your debt for not just the reviews, but the promotion you guys do, there are so many to name, just know each and every one of you are important! Readers, authors have jobs because you guys have the same addiction to words we do, thank you for being so supportive and talking books. I love you all so much and if you aren't a part of my fan group, one of the friendliest groups on facebook, what are you waiting for? Join Rachels New Rockin Readers and see what all the fuss is about.

As always you can find me on insta posting about my toddler and Viking husband @RachVD.

Love you guys, hugs, RVD

ABOUT THE AUTHOR

Rachel Van Dyken is the #1 *New York Times*, *Wall Street Journal*, and *USA Today* bestselling author of over 90 books ranging from contemporary romance to paranormal. With over four million copies sold, she's been featured in *Forbes*, *US Weekly*, and *USA Today*. Her books have been translated in more than 15 countries. She was one of the first romance authors to have a Kindle in Motion book through Amazon publishing and continues to strive to be on the cutting edge of the reader experience. She keeps her home in the Pacific Northwest with her husband, adorable sons, naked cat, and two dogs. For more information about her books and upcoming events, visit www.RachelVanDykenauthor.com.

ALSO BY RACHEL VAN DYKEN

Eagle Elite

Elite (Nixon & Trace's story)
Elect (Nixon & Trace's story)
Entice (Chase & Mil's story)
Elicit (Tex & Mo's story)
Bang Bang (Axel & Amy's story)
Enforce (Elite + from the boys POV)
Ember (Phoenix & Bee's story)
Elude (Sergio & Andi's story)
Empire (Sergio & Val's story)
Enrage (Dante & El's story)
Eulogy (Chase & Luciana's story)
Exposed (Dom & Tanit's story)
Envy (Vic & Renee's story)

Elite Bratva Brotherhood

RIP (Nikolai & Maya's story)
Debase (Andrei & Alice's story)

Mafia Royals Romances

Royal Bully (Asher & Claire's story)
Ruthless Princess (Serena & Junior's story)
Scandalous Prince (Breaker & Violet)
Destructive King (Asher & Annie)
Mafia King (TBA)
Fallen Dynasty (TBA)

Rachel Van Dyken & M. Robinson

Mafia Casanova (Romeo & Eden's story)
Falling for the Villain (Juliet Sinacore's story)

Kathy Ireland & Rachel Van Dyken

Fashion Jungle

Wingmen Inc.

The Matchmaker's Playbook (Ian & Blake's story)
The Matchmaker's Replacement (Lex & Gabi's story)

Liars, Inc

Dirty Exes (Colin, Jessie & Blaire's story)
Dangerous Exes (Jessie & Isla's story)

Bro Code

Co-Ed (Knox & Shawn's story)
Seducing Mrs. Robinson (Leo & Kora's story)
Avoiding Temptation (Slater & Tatum's story)
The Setup (Finn & Jillian's story)

Cruel Summer Trilogy

Summer Heat (Marlon & Ray's story)
Summer Seduction (Marlon & Ray's story)
Summer Nights (Marlon & Ray's story)

Covet

Stealing Her (Bridge & Isobel's story)
Finding Him (Julian & Keaton's story)

Ruin Series

Ruin (Wes Michels & Kiersten's story)
Toxic (Gabe Hyde & Saylor's story)
Fearless (Wes Michels & Kiersten's story)
Shame (Tristan & Lisa's story)

Seaside Series

Tear (Alec, Demetri & Natalee's story)
Pull (Demetri & Alyssa's story)
Shatter (Alec & Natalee's story)
Forever (Alex & Natalee's story)
Fall (Jamie Jaymeson & Pricilla's story)
Strung (Tear + from the boys POV)
Eternal (Demetri & Alyssa's story)

Seaside Pictures

Capture (Lincoln & Dani's story)
Keep (Zane & Fallon's story)
Steal (Will & Angelica's story)
All Stars Fall (Trevor & Penelope's story)
Abandon (Ty & Abigail's story)
Provoke (Braden & Piper's story)
Surrender (Andrew & Bronte's story)

The Consequence Series

The Consequence of Loving Colton (Colton & Milo's story)
The Consequence of Revenge (Max & Becca's story)
The Consequence of Seduction (Reid & Jordan's story)
The Consequence of Rejection (Jason & Maddy's story)

The Dark Ones Series

The Dark Ones (Ethan & Genesis's story)
Untouchable Darkness (Cassius & Stephanie's story)
Dark Surrender (Alex & Hope's story)
Darkest Temptation (Mason & Serenity's story)
Darkest Sinner (Timber & Kyra's story)

Curious Liaisons

Cheater (Lucas & Avery's story)
Cheater's Regret (Thatch & Austin's story)

Players Game

Fraternize (Miller, Grant and Emerson's story)
Infraction (Miller & Kinsey's story)
M.V.P. (Jax & Harley's story)

Red Card

Risky Play (Slade & Mackenzie's story)
Kickin' It (Matt & Parker's story)

The Bet Series

The Bet (Travis & Kacey's story)
The Wager (Jake & Char Lynn's story)
The Dare (Jace & Beth Lynn's story)

The Bachelors of Arizona

The Bachelor Auction (Brock & Jane's story)
The Playboy Bachelor (Bentley & Margot's story)
The Bachelor Contract (Brant & Nikki's story)

Waltzing With The Wallflower — written with Leah Sanders

Waltzing with the Wallflower (Ambrose & Cordelia)
Beguiling Bridget (Anthony & Bridget's story)
Taming Wilde (Colin & Gemma's story)

London Fairy Tales

Upon a Midnight Dream (Stefan & Rosalind's story)
Whispered Music (Dominique & Isabelle's story)
The Wolf's Pursuit (Hunter & Gwendolyn's story)
When Ash Falls (Ashton & Sofia's story)

Renwick House

The Ugly Duckling Debutante (Nicholas & Sara's story)
The Seduction of Sebastian St. James (Sebastian & Emma's story)
The Redemption of Lord Rawlings (Phillip & Abigail's story)
An Unlikely Alliance (Royce & Evelyn's story)
The Devil Duke Takes a Bride (Benedict & Katherine's story)

Other Titles

A Crown for Christmas (Fitz & Phillipa's story)
Every Girl Does It (Preston & Amanda's story)
Compromising Kessen (Christian & Kessen's story)
Divine Uprising (Athena & Adonis's story)
The Parting Gift — written with Leah Sanders (Blaine and Mara's story)

rvd
RACHEL VAN DYKEN
www.rachelvandykenauthor.com

Made in the USA
Las Vegas, NV
16 April 2021

21391375R00277